Fr

Grady Stamps took Kate's arm and led her toward the front door. "Been hearing so much about you," Brandi Burns's former manager said. "Your little daughter's outside with Bobbie, naming the constellations, and I promised I'd bring you right out to let her show off. Let's not get them upset, thinking it's my fault. I'm already in hot water for lettin' my business make me late and miss the best dinner in all of Tennessee."

On the porch, door closed, he continued to hold her elbow. "Before you go down to talk to your daughter, I have a word for you," he said. "You know, Nashville's not so big as some folks think. It's a small town, and word gets around on who's doing what. Music Row is particularly close. Word's out, in fact, that somebody from Boston's real interested in the circumstances of Brandi's terrible accident. I just want you to know that some folks are talking. Nobody wants any more harm to come to anybody, especially a newcomer. Some Nashville streets, you got to be real careful crossing. Some streets, you just take your life in your hands."

ALSO BY CECELIA TISHY

High Lonesome: The American Culture of Country Music

Jealous Heart

Cecelia Tishy

A SIGNET BOOK

SIGNET
Published by the Penguin Group
Penguin Putnam Inc., 375 Hudson Street,
New York, New York 10014, U.S.A.
Penguin Books Ltd, 27 Wrights Lane,
London W8 5TZ, England
Penguin Books Australia Ltd, Ringwood,
Victoria, Australia
Penguin Books Canada Ltd, 10 Alcorn Avenue,
Toronto, Ontario, Canada M4V 3B2
Penguin Books (N.Z.) Ltd, 182–190 Wairau Road,
Auckland 10, New Zealand

Penguin Books Ltd, Registered Offices:
Harmondsworth, Middlesex, England

Published by Signet, an imprint of Dutton NAL, a member of Penguin Putnam Inc.
This is an authorized reprint of a hardcover edition published by Dowling Press, Inc.
For information address Dowling Press, Inc., 1110 Seventeenth Avenue South,
Number 4, Nashville, TN 37212.

First Signet Printing, March, 1999
10 9 8 7 6 5 4 3 2 1

For Bill

the first reader

ACKNOWLEDGEMENTS

Starting in Boston, good friends supported my habit and became Kate Banning's staunch supporters, especially Joan Levine and Amy Lang. In Nashville, Holly Tashian read Kate's adventures chapter-by-chapter and offered excellent advice editorially and musically, while Valerie Traub cast a mystery reader's gaze on the manuscript and advised accordingly. Barbara Bennett did double duty as reader and lawyer, and Marilyn Murphy magically volunteered to do the cover art. I am thrilled that Maryglenn McCombs and Susan Sachs of Dowling Press believed in Kate and hereby launch her. Susan's editorial eyesight has been 20/20. Support from the Middle Tennessee chapter of Sisters-in-Crime has been a big bonus.

Claire and Julia have grown up within earshot of the keyboard clickings that brought Kate Banning into existence. The homefront echoes in *Jealous Heart* will sound familiar, and I hope will be keepsakes.

The accident seemed both routine and bizarre: a short local drive, no airbag, no seatbelt. The twenty-two-year-old died almost instantly when her car slid off the rain-slick pavement of the suburban Nashville street on a late summer afternoon. Thrust forward against the windshield, she bruised her forehead, cut her left cheek and broke her neck. Crumpled in the front seat of the Taurus, she looked like a gorgeous rag doll. Rushed by ambulance to Vanderbilt University Hospital, she was pronounced dead on arrival.

Brandi Burns might have been a homecoming queen or pageant finalist. Instead, she was a hot country music star known for blunt, heart-wrenching songs of yearning and desire.

Her blue eyes were wide open when she died, surprised by the ditch, surprised by death.

Chapter One

Where were the cowboy hats and boots, guitars, sequins, beads, the whole nine yards of fringe? Where were the overheard conversations sounding like song lyrics about cheatin' or bein' lonesome or pickups or Jesus?

Nowhere in sight or earshot. So far, no twang, no fringe. Kate checked her watch. It was past 6:00 P.M. and the after-work event was already more than half an hour late starting. The record company staff was in place to meet and greet. Several stood at the hospitality table where a moment ago Kate scanned the alphabetical Who's Who of guest nametags—Mary-Chapin Carpenter, Rodney Crowell, Vince Gill, Alan Jackson, Dolly Parton, George Strait, Wynonna, Randy Travis, Trisha Yearwood.

The tags lay in perfect rows. The waiting Virgo staffers kept straightening them. As host sponsors, the Virgo people had been here a while. A few workday guests mingled too. Very few.

But the stars? Maybe the stars arrived in a convoy of black limos to make an entrance in the hotel lobby together, a country cast of mourners. Kate looked around the Hermitage Hotel lobby. Just over a month in Nashville, and she would rub elbows at this insiders' country music event. Despite herself, the occasion was exciting.

But where was the woman she was scheduled to meet? Kate scanned the room expectantly. If Bobbie Burnside was in this room, she did not stand out in the swarm of record company greeters wearing oversized nametags with the Virgo/Nashville logo. There was no conspicuous figure in mourning in this crowd. Maybe she would arrive with the stars.

What a shame it was death that brought her here.

What a shame about her clothes too. Surrounded by men in suits and music-business women in early autumn caramels and ambers and beaujolais pink-reds, Kate knew she miscalculated. She was hyper-aware of her New England work "uniform"— khaki skirt, white silk shirt, and the navy blazer that was downright stupid in the late September Nashville nineties heat. She couldn't even take it off because the sweat marks would show.

Not to mention the hair contrast—theirs looked molded and cast, like sculpture. Her own, which was a thick dark blond, was worn back and over one ear, and distinctly shaggy because she still didn't know where to have it cut in town. Trying to play safe and blend in, Kate could be taken for somebody on the hotel security staff. Give her a two-way radio and she could blend. It wasn't true what they said about underdressing; you could be too low key.

And now there was evidently a little matter of the invitations. The Virgo/Nashville staff was discreetly screening, although nothing had been said to her about invitations mailed or checked at the door. Moving behind a tufted sofa, Kate found herself faced down by a plum suit in a nametag, spike heels and heavy makeup around a pair of eyes that had a hawkish glint. "So good to have you with us this afternoon. Let me get your nametag for you. Are you on the industry guest list, or the press list?"

Kate paused, somewhat taken aback. She wasn't crashing this party; after all, she was invited, sort of.

"This is a private party by invitation only." Hair to hemline, she looked Kate up and down. "Oh, perhaps you're on the hotel staff?"

"I'm with Fleetwood Publications." Kate's voice turned a little shrill. The corporate *with*, and she wasn't thinking fast enough. Ms. Plum had two clear categories, guest or crasher, and her smile was sliding to a sneer when Kate said, "I'm a special guest of Bobbie Burnside. In fact, if you see her in the room, would you please introduce us?"

Kate leaned forward in a confidential way. "Surely her late

sister would want Ms. Burnside to have things go smoothly, don't you think, especially considering the tragic circumstance? Perhaps you'd care to help me?"

The woman's mouth opened, tried to form a phrase. Kate saw her swallow hard. "Fleetwood Publications, I'm not sure we . . . yes, Bobbie and all the Burnside family . . . I'll have to see . . . so nice having you."

She fled, leaving Kate to feel unreal, like a cyber guest. Yet one fact stood out. Those with invitations, i.e. maps, at least knew what kind of an event this was. Neither a reception nor a cocktail party as far as Kate could see, at least not the New England variety. She would simply have to wait and watch.

But as minutes passed, the atmosphere in this lobby changed like a barometer falling fast. Behind the bright official smiles, the Virgo/Nashville staff all had the same look, stress. Function-room ritual was turning into damage control. The guests were few, the country music stars still nowhere in evidence, and the Virgo people seemed like a flight crew desperate for passengers.

Huddling for a moment—she saw Ms. Plum in their midst—they broke and did a complete turnaround, funneling everyone in sight into the grand ballroom. Free drinks, they promised, and live music, complimentary cassette tapes, CDs.

In the ballroom, the problem was plain to see in the rows of empty chairs. The guest list dwindled down to a precious few. No limos, no grand entrances. Disappointment hung in the air like decay.

With an eye on the lobby entrance, Kate sat down to wait, growing concerned about her own schedule. The old hotel ballroom smelled faintly of cigars, camphor, vintage fabrics, fur, mildew. A stage was set up at one end with microphones, a keyboard, and a drum set, and a young man in jeans was checking brushes and sticks. Another hauled something forward. An instrument? No, it was a cardboard cutout, one of those life-size stand-ups, like the President or the Pope.

Except this was a woman. About five-two, in a fringed turquoise suede bolero jacket and fawn tights. Cleavage. Her raven blueblack hair tumbled in waves over a high forehead. Her full lips parted in a come-on smile.

Mounted onstage, she looked like a giant paper doll. Someone had draped an actual black feather boa across the cardboard shoulders. The crew guy stood it up between the mikes, trying for dignity, as if laying a wreath at the Tomb of the Unknown Soldier. Stepping aside, he moved to the apron of the stage and hung a cloth banner that was draped over one arm, like he was lowering a flag at sundown while "Taps" played.

BRANDI BURNS, the banner read in loopy pink script on black velvet, and the year of birth—and of death.

Kate calculated. Twenty-two years old. A brand new country music starlet whose entrance proved to be her exit. One of those freak fatal accidents. Car skidded off the road into a ditch, broken neck, no seatbelt.

"It's three weeks to the day."

Kate started. Young woman in her twenties, glossy chestnut hair in big dippy waves. The mouth and forehead bore an uncanny resemblance.

"You must be Kate Banning. I'm Bobbie Burnside." The woman slid into the seat beside Kate.

What to say? At the end of the room the cardboard effigy stood in striking resemblance to this woman. Bobbie looked like the cutout come to life, every bit as flamboyant in her hair and makeup.

The difference was in the contrasting facial expressions, which looked like comedy/tragedy masks—no, like sexy versus despair. Kate peered toward the stage. Not exactly an open casket, but close.

Beside her, Bobbie tilted her head back and counted drops from a Murine bottle while trying not to mess up her hair. Under the eyeliner, the rims were red, her nostrils pink from the chafing of tissues. Smoothing her khaki skirt over one knee, Kate registered the fact that the distraught Bobbie had enough presence of mind to recognize her on sight. Dishwater blond, Kate's own description of herself went, about five-six, in her late thirties with light makeup favoring natural tones, and of course the New England uniform.

But what to say now? A brief phone call set this up, a phone call from a well-meaning real estate agent who saw something useful for Kate Banning, the newcomer to Nashville, and something of healing value for the bereaved Bobbie Burnside. Kate thought it amazing that a realtor would go out of her way to arrange an appointment directly related to a client's new job. It seemed so home-townish. Here you got a condo plus networking, a modern form of Southern hospitality.

The realtor, however, did not say the business at hand was to be done practically over this . . . this open casket. In country music culture, was the funeral portrait a cardboard standup? Was mourning mixed with show biz? No, she doubted this was the custom twelve hundred miles down the interstate. Something was wrong.

Softly Kate said, "I really appreciate you taking time to talk to me. I can imagine . . ."

She stopped. Too stiff. And in fact she really could not imagine a sister's sudden death. It would be ludicrous even to pretend. She had no sister, no parents, no family except her daughter. Her parents died in a plane crash in Kate's infancy, and the grandmother who raised her was sixteen years in the grave. One ex-husband now in Oregon no longer counted as a loss.

But this very scene surrounding her was also baffling. Virgo was an important record company. Why had so few invited guests shown up? If only she could look at one of those printed invitations.

What's more, this was a tough site for an interview. She had held them in subway stations, at hospital bedsides, once in a helicopter over the Boston Harbor. Journalists go where the people are.

But this—? Could she propose a coffee shop time-out for ten, twenty minutes to get the needed information from Bobbie, then get home to her daughter and let Bobbie settle back in this room for the . . . the country music whatever-it-was?

The eye drops were back in her purse, and she had just reached for a stick of Juicy Fruit when a man's voice came from behind.

"Bobbie, honey, how you doing?"

"Grady. Oh, Grady." Bobbie took his hand, turning head and shoulders with unexpected natural grace, as if from a life of easy freedoms that preceded this womanhood of the Grande hair. Bobbie's eyes seemed to flutter at him, a thin-faced, slender man with bobbed hair and pitted skin the color of clay. She said, "It's just real hard right now."

" 'Course it is. Terrible. None of us can get used to her being gone. Just lying in that car like she fell and bumped her head." He leaned down. "How's your mama holdin' up?"

"About like you'd expect."

"She's not here?"

Bobbie shook her head. "Too much for her. All of us, truth to tell, the whole family. Mama won't even go near the radio for fear 'Fool Moon' might come on. Be honest, none of us can hardly stand to hear it."

He frowned. His voice was soft. "You know they're going to play it in a few minutes. They're playin' her track through the speakers and doin' it live with the band and the girls." He squeezed her hand again. "You goin' to be okay?"

"I'll be okay."

He paused. "Tell you what, I'll stand right there by the stage. Gets to be too much, you just give a sign. I can have one of the boys drive you home. Drive you home myself."

"Grady, that's sweet. So sweet to all of us." She seemed reluctant to let go of his hand, even to let him go down the aisle.

As if at a memorial service, Kate said, "It must be a comfort to have a friend here."

"More like one of the family." Then Bobbie blushed. "Oh, I'm sorry, didn't even think to introduce you. My manners, I just downright forgot." She daubed her face with a tissue. "Grady Stamps is Brandi's manager. I mean, he was. He's in a real bad way too, because he even helped her pick out that car."

"The car she . . . died in?"

"The car that killed her." She said it swiftly, without hesitation. "That's why I'm wanting to talk to you. It's about the car that killed my sister." Bobbie turned to face Kate and look directly into her eyes. Behind the mascara and eyeliner, behind the blur of grief and loss there was another look, something hard.

Kate started to speak but the ballroom lights dimmed. She leaned sideways to whisper a question about the car, about what she had meant, about going to the hotel coffee shop for a short interview, but musicians came on stage. The drummer settled in, two men on guitar, one on keyboard, two women in black cowboy hats to sing. At centerstage, a tall man with curly copper blond hair, salmon jacket and black suede pants took the mike. His hair looked permed, and Kate saw a flash at his wrist, a gold ID bracelet with huge links. " . . . to welcome everybody on behalf of Virgo/Nashville."

Kate missed his name. He introduced himself as vice-president of artists and repertoires, A&R, and referred often to "The Label." Everybody at the label was so deeply saddened by the car wreck, Brandi Burns being one of their brightest young stars, singer and songwriter, untimely loss, tragic, the debut album just reaching stores coast to coast, fans disappointed to learn this spectacular new talent on the "Fool Moon" video would sing no more, write no more country songs.

The A&R guy said the label felt it ought to mark the sad occasion of this album release, to pay respect and tribute the way Brandi Burns herself would have wanted, with her own music and her band and her spirit. More thanks to everybody who made everything possible. Many names. Polite applause.

Kate turned to scan the ballroom. So empty it felt cavernous. The salmon jacket spoke as if to multitudes, but the audience was mostly Virgo staff and knots of tourists happily sipping free sodas and bulk chardonnay while waiting for the music and souvenir CD. Neither mourners nor celebrants. Whoever planned this no doubt had requiem and promotion in mind. What they got instead was a public relations flop, practi-

cally waving people in off the street. Did the stars stay away
out of respect? Boycott?

Kate looked around again, this time for video cameras.
Maybe the real point was to capture this for replay. No cameras.

Kate did see Bobbie's face in profile and thought the eyes
had that hard look as they faced the stage. Grady Stamps kept
looking her way as promised. This was the moment to suggest
they step outside to talk. As if reading her mind, Bobbie turned
and said, "Don't think I've forgotten about you, Kate. You're
really why I'm here. I just want you to hear my sister's song
first. I want you to hear what we lost in that death trap. Death
trap for sure."

As if on cue, the suit announced, "—now Brandi Burns's
'Fool Moon'!"

Cymbal crash and snare drum, and the bass and electric guitars. It was a country sound all right. The soloist's voice entered—Brandi's—high, supple, slightly nasal. Kate listened.
She had a certain breakout wildness, and yet a plaintive, vulnerable side in high yodels—

> *Full moon,*
> *Fool moon*
> *Rock me in your crescent cradle*
> *Break-a my heart*
> *Tricked me from the start*
> *. . . full moon, fool moon*

Kate listened to the phrasing, the voice all swelling sex on
full, then turning to self-pity on *fool*. Despite herself, she felt a
kind of chill at the raw power of it.

But jolted too. This wasn't just a recording, but a voice from
the grave, though you'd never know it in this room. Onstage,
only the clothes hinted at the somber occasion. Everybody was
in black, including the petite women singers, the blonde on the
left in a long crinkly crepe skirt, the redhead on the right in
skin-tight matte black jeans. Silver accessories, chains, hat-

bands, belts of linked conchos. Cowgirl effect. They clapped
and swayed in a dance-step rhythm and stepped up to the mike
with harmonic ooohs. They echoed "break-a my heart" in perfect sync.

In a grisly twist, the black feather boa around the shoulders
of Brandi Burns began rippling in the air currents, as if to ani-
mate the . . . the star or the corpse, depending on how you saw
it. And what was the *it*? Back in Boston, services tended to
feature string quartets or folk guitars. Mozart or Shaker
hymns.

Kate felt like an utter foreigner here. She could hear the
music and scan the room, but could not for the life of her read
the scene.

Onstage all the musicians had performed as if nothing were
out of the ordinary. That, of course, was one definition of professional. Beside her Bobbie's profile looked fixed, like a
head-model displaying a hairdo, though at the neck Kate saw a
certain tension, or maybe wanted to see it. Down front Grady
Stamps stood with one hip against the paneled wall, his own
expression neutral.

When the song ended, the tourists led the applause, happy to
clap for the cardboard cutout and the live performers alike. The
label people, Kate noticed, seemed more hesitant, reserved, uncertain. Somehow they were more appealing. Onstage Mr. A&R
once more took the mike, reminding everyone in the room to
take home a tape and a CD of the *Fool Moon* album available on
the table by the door. "—a gift from all of us at Virgo/Nashville."

Kate checked her watch. Her own time was running short.
Kelly, her daughter, was at home and counting on a dinner favorite that had a forty-minute oven time. Kate planned on a brief
reception here, not a concert—if "concert" were the term when
the soloist was three weeks in her grave. But if Kate slipped out
to call home now, she might forfeit the whole interview.

Plus, it was clear that Bobbie Burnside had some fixed idea
about the car her sister died in. Probably a product liability
issue. A notion that the car had a hazardous defect, some fatal
manufacturing error. If so, Kate must hear this woman out. It

would be too rude to flee after a few personal questions. Budget an extra ten, fifteen minutes. If Bobbie ran on, Kate could politely leave because her daughter was expecting her. Wasn't country music about family values?

But the biggest irony—this interview was not crucial to her work. Ghastly as it was, Brandi Burns was just one more safety statistic, the casualty of a failure to use her seatbelt. This interview was a way to personalize auto safety problems. It was the cap for a certain article.

She leaned and spoke softly to the sister of the accident victim who, somewhat surprisingly, stepped into the aisle with her immediately. Grady's eyes followed them.

"Why don't we just sit here?" Kate agreed. They were at the tufted lobby sofa. In the ballroom, the band moved into an up-tempo number with guitar flights and heavy cymbals. Brandi's voice soared. "You hear how good she was?" Kate nodded. They listened in silence for a moment. She did sound impressive. The voice surged with power. "Her voice gives me chills, Kate, chillbumps up and down my arms—even at this disgusting, tacky tribute."

Tacky? "So this . . . this ceremony isn't customary in country music?"

"Lord no. Gracious no. We've never seen anything like it. I hope never again." Bobbie looked quite distressed. She peered at Kate. "You see how many stayed away, don't you, and that wasn't because of my sister, believe me. We had a beautiful memorial service at Mt. Olive Christian Church, and so many of the artists were there, and they sang some of their signature songs, the most spiritual ones. And a benefit's planned later in the fall. But this—this is revolting."

She gestured around the lobby. "A hotel, and these tourists, perfect strangers, and that tacky cardboard thing on stage. Why, I could hardly stand to sit there."

Her eyes narrowed. "It was all Roy's idea, Roy Benniger at Virgo. One of the big bosses. He's from L.A., and I suppose that says it all. We all liked him till he showed what a jerk he is."

She made a nasal sound of protest. "*Tribute*, he called it. Tribute to bad taste and disrespect, is what I say." She tugged at her sleeve and smoothed her skirt. She looked back at Kate. "At least the sound system was good, because I really wanted you to hear Brandi's voice. I wanted you to experience it. Oh Kate, she was gonna be a big star. They were really backing her. She had tour dates right up to Christmas. I wanted you to hear that."

" 'Fool Moon' was very moving," Kate said, "and I'm not even a country music fan, hardly know anything about it." She reached for her microcassette recorder and small notebook. She wanted to be nice, but also matter-of-fact. This was solely about the seatbelt issue, and Bobbie must know that. She said, "It was thoughtful of Maureen Kinny to suggest we get together."

"She was real helpful locating Brandi a good condo. Must've found you one too."

Kate nodded. As a realtor, Maureen Kinny was nothing if not thorough. She said, "Maureen of course told you about this article—on automotive safety?" Bobbie nodded. "It will go out to nearly two million customers of a certain insurance company based in Texas. It's for the company magazine. I am doing the final rewrite."

She sat back and faced Bobbie and spoke slowly. "You see, there are millions of older cars and trucks with no airbags, just belts. The insurance company wants customers to be sure to use them. Brandi represents the tragic danger, and the loss of important talent."

She stopped. Bobbie Burnside did not need the list of other examples in this article, the Super Bowl halfback thrown to his death from a convertible, the TV comedian rammed at a stop sign and now quadriplegic, the tennis star—no point compounding the horrors.

Beside her, the sister of the dead singer nodded gravely. Kate counted on that, humanitarian feelings to move the surviving sister to go on the record saying that Brandi's death would not be in vain if young people who had everything to live for would fasten their car seatbelts.

Except that the sister was nursing a private theory.

Bobbie Burnside looked calmly and directly into Kate's eyes. "Brandi didn't die by accident. It wasn't any accident."

Kate stared at that dark mass of hair. Here it came, the "death car" theory, nothing to do with Brandi's failure to buckle up, and everything to do with Detroit or the factory in, say, Atlanta. Okay, let this woman vent for a moment. Quietly Kate said, "I understand the car was a Taurus."

"An '89 four-door. Blue."

"Wasn't your sister the second owner?"

Bobbie nodded.

Don't be combative, Kate reminded herself. Speak mildly. Don't show your impatience to get out of here. "Bobbie," she said, "this particular article has led me into some research. The Ford Taurus has an overall good safety record. They're pretty big, solid. They're not eggshells. They don't crumple."

"This one was different."

Different?—the unique assembly line car, a contradiction in terms. Yet the bereaved seized on anything. Kate said, "Some Taurus model years have a history of electrical problems and rust. There have been recalls. Defective motor mounts, seat assemblies, a latch problem in the wagons. But the '89 sedan, I don't think . . ."

"—oh yes, Brandi's car was a death trap."

Denial, then. Perfectly good defense mechanism. And product liability fed survivors' doubts. Take the GM pickup trucks with saddlebag gas tanks that exploded on impact. Take the Pinto, or the notorious Chevy Corvair, made infamous by *Unsafe at Any Speed*, the book that made Ralph Nader's reputation many years ago and started a whole consumer rights movement. In fact, Kate wished that once in her lifetime she could write an important book like that. Be a good mother, write a good book. Two worthy goals. Three, if you add a long-term relationship with a certain man.

Was Bobbie Burnside asking Kate to crusade against Ford? Megabucks lawsuit? Bobbie could be the delegate from the Burnsides now that the family starship was sunk.

Or was Kate succumbing to cynicism, the occupational hazard of the journalist? She said, "Ms. Burnside . . . Bobbie, I understand . . ."

"No you don't." She snapped. "I mean, you couldn't because you didn't know my sister. She was a very good driver. She never speeded, no matter what the newspaper had to say." Kate recalled the account in the *Tennessean* and on TV news. Car skidded off pavement into limestone ditch, driver thrown forward. Speed a possible factor. No seatbelt restraint. Broken neck. The realtor called her attention to it, gave her the clipping. That's how this interview began.

"She was a very good driver. Excellent."

"But she did not wear her seatbelt."

Bobbie's gaze drifted. "Sometimes she did, sometimes." Her voice sounded vague. Then she looked back at Kate and said, "As good a driver as she was, Brandi didn't need a seatbelt all the time. Out on the highway, yes, but not for short hops."

Kate saw the new defiant look in the eyes. Sisterly loyalty. Should she tell Bobbie Burnside that the figures from the National Highway Transportation Board showed most accident casualties came from local "short hops"? That her logic was as full of holes as Swiss cheese?

No, this was not a moment for lessons in straight thinking. Kate said, "The paper said it was drizzling, so the pavement was probably slick. And the ditch was limestone." Already Kate had noticed the ditches in Nashville, serious ditches of solid rock. Again she reminded herself to be patient. "It's the kind of thing that could happen to anybody. And that's the point I'm making." She leaned forward on the lobby sofa. "This is not about your sister's driving skills, Bobbie. It's about using seatbelts all the time. I saw the car and the ditch on TV."

Bobbie picked the polish off one red manicured thumbnail.

She looked Kate in the eye. "Somebody fooled with that car. Tampered with it."

"Tampered?"

"That's it. That's what happened. Somebody rigged that car so my sister would die." She looked at Kate, her eyes big and so dark.

So Bobbie did not see product liability, not a manufacturer's mistake from dangerous cost-cutting or bad design. She did not see stupidity in Detroit, but murder in Nashville.

Sisterly fantasy three weeks old and counting. A survivor's obsession. Probably a syndrome the shrinks have a name for. More than Kate Banning bargained for today.

And what to do but repeat her own words of moments ago, then exit at the first possible instant. Get gone from a crazy scene bound to grow crazier by the minute. Get home to Kelly and the chicken dinner.

That hard stare was back. Bobbie leaned forward. "Maureen Kinny says you're some kind of an investigator. She says you're like a private detective."

"Now wait a minute." Kate drew back. "I'm a journalist, an editor for a publishing company. My new job here in Nashville . . . we supply articles for different magazines."

"Maureen said you were like a detective back where you came from. New York."

"—Boston. I come from Boston." She felt herself flush. Why did she blab to that realtor in her first days in Nashville? Why succumb to the phony instant intimacy in the realtor's car? Kate guessed she was like a lot of newcomers in a state of talk deprivation, offering coffee to installation technicians, chatting with the telephone man because she had hardly spoken to another adult in days. In this case, telling the realtor more of her work history than was wise. Certainly indiscreet.

She said, "Maureen Kinny hears a lot on the road showing properties." She hesitated, then said, "A very long time ago I was a police reporter, but not for long. It was too gruesome, and I had a baby, and I quit." She thought of Kelly at home now, of the new condo. "That baby is now in the eighth grade."

"But you investigate things."

Stubborn. The essence of that hard look? No matter; Kate needed to break this off even though Bobbie was dug in. She could state for the record that she did not owe this woman a biographical account, then leave.

Yet beside her sat a human being who had suddenly lost her sister. She shouldn't be nurturing illusions, but she shouldn't be bruised either. Kate said, "Look, I used to be an investigative journalist, but that's very different from criminal investigations by police or private detectives. Most of my work involved, well, rip-offs—schools that promise training in mechanics or dental hygiene but don't provide it. Contractors selling roofs that leak." She stopped. Add to those zoning frauds, tax dodges, medical scams.

How best to explain this? "The kind of journalism I did, well, lots of it is just tedious. You put in countless hours in courthouse basements piecing together transactions, many interview hours. Our magazine was small, and financially shaky, and I was moonlighting—writing feature articles—and still not making ends meet. My magazine folded, and I've brought my daughter here for a fresh start." She smiled. "And that's about it."

Bobbie's full red mouth drew into a pout. "That's not what Maureen said."

"I can't be responsible for what a realtor might have said." She added in a quiet but firm voice, "Or what you thought she said."

"Maureen told me you solved murders. She said you told her that." Kate blinked. "Maureen says you actually have helped the police solve murders in New York—"

"—Boston!" Kate flushed. Quietly she said, "I'm from Boston. And I'm not a detective. I got involved a few times. I—"

She broke off. Just a few times, she thought, a few killers

and near-misses along the way. As it happened, the rip-offs sometimes came with Jack-the-rippers. "I didn't—"

But she did. There was the case of the dead sculptor and of the dead aerobics instructor. There was a ten-story fall that was really a push, a heart attack caused by a lethal drug dose. The natural causes turned out to be most unnatural. And Kate Banning made her way through the murderous maze each time— and nearly died for her trouble. Would a drowning and hypothermia seem like her natural causes? Tied to a pier with the tide coming in or freezing on a New Hampshire mountain, would those qualify?

She gazed at Bobbie Burnside. To all outward appearances, two women chatted quietly on a lobby sofa. She planned to keep it that way. Keep out of the sluggish, muddy river snaking through Nashville about six blocks from here and keep out of the lakes invented by the Tennessee Valley Authority. Kate Banning planned to stay dry and safe, do her job well, get her daughter through school and teens, resist all siren songs that might lead to trouble. Resist every one of those songs, even if those sirens had a country twang.

Quietly and very deliberately she said, "Bobbie, consider this. Maybe someone will read about your sister in the insurance magazine and fasten a seatbelt and save their own life. And maybe some readers will go into a record store and buy Brandi's album and appreciate her talent and remember her for a very long time. Those are valuable things."

"Not when there was a killer after my sister."

Killer. Kate refused to say the word, to supply vocabulary for this fantasy. She said, "Who would even want to do such a thing?" She immediately regretted the sort of pop-up question that sucked her into things. Abruptly she said, "I'm afraid I must be going."

Bobbie Burnside did not stir. She said, "The music business is hard, let me tell you. The competition. I decided a good while ago I didn't want any part of it. I just wanted a normal life for myself, even when my family hoped I'd go for it like Brandi did. Not me. I saw too much. Everybody wants to be a star. Those singers on that stage, the blonde and redhead; they're good friends of mine. But if a label looked their way, they'd run like dogs to a T-bone and fight down to the gristle. There's some in this business that will cheat you and do anything to get you out of the way. The public never hears about that side."

Kate slid forward on the sofa. How wide this young woman's eyes. Desperation. Bobbie Burnside reached out her hand, and Kate started to extend her own for a parting shake, only to find the woman reach down to tug at the hem of her blazer, in effect pulling her closer. "My mama said this was no use, that we ought to let it be." Her voice was lowered to an intense whisper. "Mama said there's nobody going to take our word, that we have to let Brandi go to her rest and seek our own rest."

She was tugging harder at the jacket, looking into Kate's eyes. "Kate, I take no rest. My little sister is dead. The person I loved and will always love, and shared a bedroom with all my life, and fought and made up, and laid in the dark on my side of the room and told all my secrets and heard hers. I felt her pain while she fought for her music and got slapped down for it time after time. You don't know. You couldn't know how hard this business can be." She swallowed, her voice almost rasping. "My sister was gonna be right up there with Reba. And maybe, who knows, maybe the next Dolly."

She paused, as if for the awesome moment. Kate felt uncertain what Bobbie meant to communicate—country music superstars as a measure of talent, or yearning, or pure ambition?

She kept on. "The police, yes, they're nice. Everybody's just nice and sweet, and they think I'm crazy for thinkin' this way. Let me tell you, in this town they can nice you to death."

She had taken hold of one of Kate's blazer buttons and pulled at it. "We're from the country, our family, and there's advantages and disadvantages. but I thought maybe you being from up North and a big city, bigger than Nashville, and an investigator too . . . I thought maybe this was meant to be, like you were sent here to us. Thing is, there's nobody else for us to go to."

The desperation felt like a mist in this old hotel. "But your family could seek a private investigator."

Her earrings flung back and forth against her neck as Bobbie shook her head no. "Word would get out. Brandi's memory would be hurt. Our own family disgraced."

Kate was baffled. Was this something Southern? Would they try to enlist an outsider, a stranger to do the dirty work? She did not want to think about it, Bobbie's intensity was so awful. The effect was claustrophobic. Kate stood up suddenly.

She felt the blazer button pull loose. In her bright red nails Bobbie Burnside held Kate's dull bronze button and its trailing thread. They both stared, looked mystified, stunned. Suddenly Bobbie ran toward the ballroom and then back, two items extended in her hand. "It's Brandi's CD and the cassette. You can play the tape in your car. I'm real sorry if I bothered you." Then she ran back into the ballroom, intentionally or not, taking Kate's blazer button with her.

Chapter Two

"First, Mom, that girl beside me in math class asked me to say 'park the car' so her friend from Memphis could hear a Boston accent. And I did, Mom, just to be nice, but then they teased me all morning. They kept saying 'pahk the cah' and laughing. It's not fair. I don't tease them when 'you' sounds like 'yew'."

Kate made a sympathetic hum. In the South, it was true, she and her daughter were suddenly the ones with the accents.

"Then in the French dictation quiz, I couldn't tell if it was a 't' or a 'd.' *Writer* or *rider*. 'The *rah-duh* wore a blue shirt and black belt.' That's how it sounded, Mom. She just stood up there by the blackboard and wouldn't write it down. I got the *chemise bleu* and the *cincture noir*, but if you miss any important words, you fail the whole translation. I pictured a horse, so I went for r-i-d-e-r. 'The rider wore a blue shirt and black belt.' They don't even know how to talk in Tennessee."

Kate was cutting up chicken at the sink. Double stainless sink with a disposal, everything new, gleaming faucets. Kelly was supposed to rinse the chicken pieces, but there was no stopping her now. In fact, Kate must not even try, for Kelly hadn't a soul to talk to in Nashville either, not yet.

Standing against the refrigerator, Kelly gave a great shrug. It lifted her upper chest and showed the developing body curving, lengthening. Her hair, once bright blonde, was darker, long and glossy and thick. These days she used an astounding quantity of shampoo. Kate watched her extend one arm dramatically toward the fridge to imitate the French teacher at the board, all the while taking a certain pleasure in her own mimicry and her spunky horse fantasy.

Yet her eyes showed the jeopardy of the wrong guess, the fearful tyranny of the gradebook. And then the chin-out defiance became something closer to pain as her arms dropped to her sides.

"Today, Mom, in the cafeteria I sat by myself the way I always do eating my sandwich. And I looked around at all the tables—and there was no one for me. No one to be friends with in that whole cafeteria."

"Kelly—" Kate put down the knife, the chicken thigh. She wiped her hand on a paper towel and tried to give her daughter a reassuring forearm touch. Imagine this child, her lively great kid all alone in the school cafeteria day after day, still eating by herself at the end of September after nearly a month in the new school. And this moment was not about French translation or vowel accents. Nor about teachers, fair or unfair. This was about the one theme in Kelly's life these days. All roads led to it.

Kelly looked at Kate. "I hate it here. Why did we have to move here?"

"Kel—" Kate tried not to sound weary or exasperated. "Sweetie, we've been over and over this. This isn't the time to talk about it. Let's try to get dinner on. Here, help me with these drumsticks."

She added, "We've got to give this move some time," realizing immediately she had just opened the door for more "move" talk.

"I don't want to give it time."

Kate said, "What about that other new girl, the one from New Jersey?"

"She doesn't talk to me. She's trying to get in with the popular crowd."

The popular crowd. That awful perennial, both scorned and envied. Insiders and outsiders. And what could she do? When kids were little, you could fluff them up, take them to McDonald's or a movie or make something decorated with apple slice smiles and raisin eyes. No more.

Dutifully Kelly got a brown paper bag and poured Italian bread crumbs into it. Chicken-in-a-bag, her favorite recipe. Put the rinsed cut-up chicken pieces in a brown paper bag with bread crumbs. Shake bag vigorously to coat chicken. Bake in lightly greased oven dish for forty minutes. For years, Kelly loved the bag, the noise, the very comfort of continuity.

But tonight it seemed more like drill than pleasure. Maybe Kate shouldn't have tried it twice in one week. Surefire way to turn a dinner favorite into the same old thing. She said, "At least tonight we won't be so rushed, we'll be eating on time. Not like Tuesday."

"Oh yeah, the night you were at that hotel music party. By the way, Mom, a woman called about your button."

Kate cringed. Bobbie Burnside? Actually phoning her at home? Kelly said, "Wow, does she sound Southern, she's worse than Mademoiselle McMinn. I could hardly make out 'time,' it sounded like 'tahm'—can I have both wings tonight? Anyway, she wants to bring you your button. She asked if you played the CD she gave you. She wants you to listen to a certain song—"

"I know, 'Fool Moon.' "

"No. It's called 'Envy Green.' She thinks it has a hidden message, like a signal, but she didn't explain what she meant. She left her phone number, it's on a Post-it—careful, you're spilling. Mom, are you okay?"

"Fine. I'm fine." Kate tipped the bag back up and kept her voice even. "What did you tell her?"

Kelly shrugged. "I told her she could phone you later. I said the same thing I always say, that you couldn't come to the phone." Kelly's sigh was nearing exasperation. "—since I was six years old, and you went around the corner to buy milk. Do I have to say that forever?" She spread a spoonful of corn oil around the bottom of a glass baking dish and began arranging chicken. They put the baking dish into the oven, and Kate reached for a head of red leaf lettuce. Water splashed. She told Kelly to get out the salad spinner.

"She only wants to give it back, Mom. She wants to stop by with it. And she just wants to know if you listened to the album and recommends that one song. I wrote it down, 'Envy Green.' She thinks it's important." Kelly added, "No big deal."

Kate paused. In case Bobbie called again, Kelly Banning had to be filled in. "Actually, Kel, it is sort of a big deal. Bobbie Burnside is using the album and the button to try to get me involved in her . . . her life." Kate pulled apart the lettuce while Kelly helped. "It's really about her sister. She thinks her sister's car accident wasn't really accidental."

"You mean like somebody killed her?" Kelly stared, first in cop-show thrill, then in horror.

Kate looked directly at her daughter's face and spoke slowly. "Kelly, listen to me. The sister did not use her seatbelt, and she lost control of her car and broke her neck and died. The family is having a very hard time accepting that. Bobbie imagines that somebody tampered with her sister's car to make it crash."

She watched to see that Kelly was still with her, not closing down out of anxiety. "It's a kind of myth-making, Kel. It's the way surviving family members sometimes cope when they can't accept what actually happened.

"It's a kind of cushion too, so they don't feel even worse. I think the Burnside family is imagining things. Sweetie, tell me . . . on the phone, Bobbie didn't go into all that with you, did she? She just talked about the album and the button, right?"

Kelly nodded. "She wants to return it and get it sewed back on. She's sorry she pulled it off." Kelly paused, fingered the lettuce, tugged as if in conflict. "Actually, Mom, she did talk to me for a little while. You know, the thing is, she seemed kind of nice."

Katie tried to nod calmly. The nerve of that woman, keeping her daughter on the phone.

Kelly slowly shook the bottle of Italian dressing as if reluctant to give up something private. Then she said, "We talked mostly about school, being in a new school where nobody knows you." Kelly unscrewed the cap. "Bobbie told me her family moved to Nashville from the country during high school, and how hard it was for her, just like it is for me. She's even from Tennessee, and the kids still wouldn't talk to her for a long time. They made fun of her accent and said she came from a holler—that's like a little valley, Mom, but deep in the woods. She wanted to go back to the country like I want to go home to Boston. Bobbie said it felt like forever before she made friends, but she finally did make them and I shouldn't give up."

Kate paused again in order to be careful. Kelly was at the age when authority moved outside the household. And the advice itself was supportive, a little boost. She must not seem to discredit the message itself.

Though there was another lesson here, about manipulation, about using a child to get to the parent.

She imagined this woman entwining herself like some kind of vine. What was that southern plant that took over everything?—kudzu. She opened the fridge and reached for a cucumber, a pepper.

"Kel, tear some of those leaves a little smaller, more like bites."

Kelly looked distracted. "I don't understand you, Mom. Those Greenpeace people with the clipboards came to the door in Boston, and you always talked to them. So why couldn't she bring your button?"

"Because it's a foot in the door. I just . . . look, there are social workers and volunteer groups to help people like the Burnsides. And ministers. You've seen the churches all over Nashville. There's practically one on every block."

Kelly paused. "But you used to help some people in Boston. When I was in third grade, you found that missing girl. The one hiding with her dad in the mountains in New Hampshire. Remember?"

"Of course I remember." The night Kate could have died from hypothermia or the dad's shotgun, take your pick. Spare Kelly that minor detail.

Her daughter was nodding in a worldly wise way. "I get it, you just don't want to help anymore now that we're in Tennessee."

Kate felt scrutinized and found wanting. "Of course I am. I'm going to help us. Going to earn a salary to save for your college. Going to help us keep this luxurious new home—" With one arm she swept the space, a generous L-shaped downstairs with new thermal windows that fit snugly, central air and heat, appliances, conveniences. A dishwasher. And a new sofa the color of summer wheat with plump, comfortable cushions. And landscaping outside. Magnolia trees with their big glossy leaves. "Just look, we have our own condo."

"We had our own townhouse."

Very softly Kate said, "Kel, we rented the ground floor."

"But it was ours. It was."

Kate paused. The century-old, charming, very shabby South End Boston townhouse, the only home Kelly Banning ever knew. Sold out from under Kate, who had no money to buy a condo even a fraction of the one they left behind. The new people came in Allied Van Lines, United Van Lines, Mayflower. People like Kate left in U-Hauls.

This was the paradox—in Tennessee they had a brand new home and yet felt homeless. She wanted to feel grateful and blessed. Instead, she felt displaced and bewildered.

Kate said, "Anyway, Bobbie's sister was in country music. I don't know anything about country music."

Kelly said, "You're always playing that country music song Maggie gave you. The one about New England."

Yes, the goodbye gift from her closest friend, *Reba McEntire's Greatest Hits*. Kate played one particular song, "Whoever's in New England," because of the place names—New England, Boston, and Massachusetts. Reba McEntire sang them with great feeling.

Kelly said, "You like that song because it's got snow in it and says Boston. I bet you listen 'cause you're homesick too. I bet you want to go home as much as I do."

"Kelly—" Should she admit the truth of it? Let them both

sink into more tears for the home that was not there anymore. Talk about tearjerkers. They could turn into some sob story. Fit right into country music.

Kelly leaned back against the kitchen counter. "Mom, have you thought that not having friends in Nashville is getting to you too? You said Bobbie pulled your button off just so she could call you about it. You think she was nice to me on the phone just so she could get on your good side. Pretty suspicious thinking, Mom. I'll bet Sam will agree with me." A look of sadness crossed her face. "I miss him. When's he coming back to see us?"

Sam, Sam Powers—probably piloting a half-dozen corporate vice-presidents from one city to another at this very moment. Sam flying the executives and their briefcases full of deals. Sam, the person in her life who saw things clearly and actually, miraculously, cared about her and about Kelly too. He was needed here right now. Kate missed him too. "He can't get back here for two more weeks."

"That's a really long time." They nodded together. Kelly looked downcast, her poise becoming fragile. "Anyway, I think you could be nicer, Mom. You say when I should do better—like when we had the food drive and I wanted to take the sauerkraut and beets, and you made me give the white tuna . . . albino."

"Albacore."

"Yeah, well, you said we should do better. And I hope you can do better too. Maybe you can show Bobbie how her sister really did have an accident. Maybe she'd believe you."

Kate paused. What was at stake here? A daughter afraid that her mother had lost her bearings and her decency somewhere over the Appalachian Mountains? A daughter with no father to appeal to, no aunts and uncles to round out the idea of home. Nothing from the outside world but the child support checks that dribbled in from Oregon. A daughter who needed as much continuity as possible right now for her own well being.

No question about it, a gesture was in order, a sign that mother Kate was intact and the world right-side-up. She had to do something strictly for Kelly. No hesitation. "Okay, Kel, tell you what, I'll phone Bobbie Burnside from work tomorrow, and maybe she can come by the office if she doesn't want to mail me my button."

Hr daughter stared, waiting for something more. "And I'll talk with her to see whether she has any more info . . . anything concrete to go on. Evidence."

"And then what?"

Kate shrugged. "You tell me."

"Listen to the album, too."

" 'Green Envy'?"

" 'Envy Green,' Mom. You've got it backwards. Bobbie warned me to get it right."

Kate got it right on the car tape deck the next morning on her way to work. Two stereo plays with Kelly before bed seemed plenty, but test the lyrics and melody a third time for anything ominous. So played the *Fool Moon* album at 7:30 A.M. while driving along a network of tree-lined, two-lane asphalts leading to Magnolia Boulevard. Fast forward to "Envy Green" while on Sixteenth Avenue, the celebrated Music Row itself. Kate heard the late Brandi Burns's husky mezzo cry out against a guitar and keyboard background as her own Buick wagon held the left lane along this country music Gold Coast, a one-time residential street erupting with corporate buildings with tinted glass—Sony, Buddy Lee Productions, Warner Brothers.

Then onto Broadway, the concrete band undulating into the city, a corridor between car dealerships, churches, bars and stores—all the while Brandi Burns vocalized rhymes on green things, on money and trees and emeralds and eyes.

> *Seafoam and summer fields*
> *Green willows on the bank . . .*
> *Emeralds and money and time gone to waste . . .*

She turned up the volume. There was wordplay on leaves and leaving. Then:

His money is paper, her jewels cold as ice.

Finally, the refrain with all stops out:

Envy green, envy green, the color of pain, the color she's seeeen . . .

Everything but shamrocks. It was a satisfying enough song—no, make that a powerful song, a straightforward ballad about true and false values. Who could argue against that? By now Kate had listened at least four times. But if there was a special coded message about Brandi Burns's jeopardy, it escaped her completely. Brandi's voice pleaded for the natural versus the artificial, for love against greed and materialism. A universal message.

Of course, somebody in Bobbie's state was ripe for paranoia from any tune, from Mary and her little lamb for that matter. Rabid lamb bites Mary, butts Mary, tramples, stomps. Mary suffocated by fleece. Endless.

Kate chuckled, enjoying her own joke for a full moment. Then she dropped the cassette into her purse as she parked in the garage at the corner of Union Street and started walking to the Fleetwood Publications building on Second Avenue. In all of Nashville, she worked in the very best spot, The District, several riverside blocks of rehabbed, century-old, four-story brick warehouses whose fronts, the guidebooks boasted, were Italian Renaissance.

To Kate's eye, they were festive and historic and real. Here on The District's Second Avenue, the Music City tourists and the careerists in law, PR, accounting and advertising rubbed shoulders on brick sidewalks. It was the realm of the tasteful Ryman Auditorium, the elegant Gruhn Guitars, the artful Hatch Show Print, the festive Wildhorse Saloon. On Second, you were blocks away from the standard high-rise profile of anonymous glass and steel refrigerators that passed for architecture in every American city including Nashville.

The Fleetwood Building, in midblock, had been renovated inside and out by real architectural talent. There were subtle tile and underlighted creamy glass blocks, brass rails and old cast iron columns painted burgundy and forest green. And a receptionist with large hair and nails to match her lipstick. Plus the daily greeting ritual.

"Morning, Delia."

"Morning, Miz Banning. How're you today?"

"Fine, thanks." Kate knew she was also supposed to say, "How-are-you-today?" in reply. In was a Southern form of greeting, an extended "hi." So far, she resisted. It wasn't her native language.

She walked the four flights of stairs to her office, which was bright and airy with exposed brick walls, slate-gray chairs and the red loveseat Kate had yet to use for meetings or her own comfort. She went to her desk and computer screen and scanned the phone messages to be sure they all were about business, not Bobbie Burnside. Relief.

She took a moment to fill a coffee mug, "World's Best Mom," and look out at the sluggish, pale brown Cumberland River, the Shelby Street Bridge, the barge and cement works on the opposite shore. A tugboat was pushing three barges filled with sand and coal and scrap metal, and she could hear the engines throb. The *General Jackson* steamboat that ferried tourists from Opryland into town would not dock for another hour, and the *Belle Carol* was just preparing for the first excursion run of the day. Eight A.M. and all was well.

Visual patrol done, Kate turned to voice mail and to e-mail from two writers, also several FedEx envelopes, phone messages—piled-up work that meant a job to do. She recited a secular prayer of thanks for the work and this job. And for corporation headhunters and contacts and gainful employment. And pension plans, signing bonuses, health benefits. Ton of work to do? Bring it on. Did your company lay off its trade magazine staff but want to keep publishing? Call Fleetwood.

Trade magazines customized for you, the business client. Plenty of satisfied contractors, as the Fleetwood rep will tell you—airlines, insurance companies, pharmaceuticals.

And now, with a nice title on the door, Kate was the official bundler, using her contact network of freelancers to assign articles, arrange entire issues. Kate Banning as the middleman—middle-woman—with the Rolodex. Kate the clearing house, the nerve center. She had certain flexibility—to edit, do some writing, shmooze as needed.

Today felt just a little less pressured for the first time in six weeks on the new job. She finished up her editorial advice for a travel industry piece on wine tasting at California vineyards. Buck up the adjectives, advised coordinating editor Kate, and the writer faxed her rewrite on a cabernet sauvignon, seducing the palate with overtones of darkest chocolate.

Chocolate wine? Gag. But it would play to younger readers, and the piece was scheduled for February, so echo the Valentine's candy tie-in. Suggest, however, cutting the description of the pinot noir aromatic as kiwi. Fruit and shoe polish together not so good. So on and on, nips and tucks.

Some more FedEx materials came in, disks and hard copy. In fact, the automobile safety belt article was going out today, edited, dispatched. Ironically, for all the fuss, Bobbie had made no useful contribution to the article at all.

Kate checked her watch. It was pushing eleven, and she wanted to get a project off her desk before calling Bobbie. She double checked the hard copy for December's *ActivAge*, a trade magazine for the recreation industry. One piece on spas missed deadline, and she must try to figure out where else she might slot it in. No point stirring ill will from the writer. Cultivating a solid stable of freelancers was part of her job, and this particular writer had a good track record, but was going through a bitter divorce. Cut him some slack.

Kate signed off on the issue and sent the batch and the disk down to layout. It was lunch time. Hot as jaws of hell outside. The eateries full of tourists, state government workers, lawyers. Too hot to eat? Order takeout?

She looked at the framed photo of Kelly on her desk. Kelly at seven with front teeth out, Kelly last summer on the beach at Cape Cod, Kelly the conscience to whom she must report. Kate reached in her purse for the Post-it with Bobbie Burnside's number. The sooner she contacted that disturbed woman, the better. Get it over with.

But then she stopped. Maybe just a little background work on this, nothing time consuming or complicated, but useful. Ignorance might be bliss, but a little country music knowledge could serve as an ounce of prevention. Satisfy Kelly, but nip this in the bud.

Was there a music fan she knew at Fleetwood? The top floor seemed to be all symphony people. Her young assistant?—out sick this morning. Delia, the receptionist? Too many Southern courtesy back-and-forths. But she remembered Jerry, Jerry Lombardi, the bouncy sales rep from Denver. Jerry was supposed to be a big record collector. And, he'd lived in Nashville for a while, so maybe he knew country music. Kate walked down a flight to the sales office to find him just back from lunch. His pale gray suit coat was off and he flicked a toothpick into the trash as he waved her in.

"Kate, so they finally let you out of the fourth-floor ivory tower. Welcome to action central. Sales at your service." He bowed, then loosened his tie and unbuttoned his shirt collar. "Just back from lunch," he said. "Jack's Barbecue on lower Broadway. Ribs, slaw, ranch beans, Texas toast. Good for the soul, forget the waistline." He stifled a belch. He was short and dark, and his clothes looked a size too small from his buckle to his oxfords. "I bet you're not here for tips on good lunch spots."

"Jerry, could I ask you a few questions about country music?"

He grinned. "Hey, you can try, but I'm a niche collector, Kate. Only certain artists. And, I'm an LP nut, which makes me an antique these days. You want to sit down?"

She shook her head and leaned against his door frame. "It's not about artists, Jerry, it's about—oh, very broadly speaking, crime. Can you tell me, in country music, are there certain kinds of crimes?"

"Crime? Sure. Let's see, there's the outlaws, like Waylon Jennings. And Billy-the-Kid songs. Marty Stuart has one. And different artists have cut 'Poncho and Lefty.' And prison songs too. Merle Haggard and Johnny Cash—"

"No, I don't mean the songs. I mean, in the business itself. In the way that . . . say, embezzlement happens in banks, and illegal gambling pops up around pro sports. Is there any crime pattern that fits country music?"

He paused, considering. "Well, probably theft. Trucks full of equipment and instruments. There's a story about Albert Lee— you know who he is?" Kate shook her head. "Fantastic electric guitarist. I've got an LP of his. Just amazing. Anyhow, his guitar was stolen and sold, and the guy that bought it turned out to be a big Albert Lee fan. He bought the stolen guitar just so he could return it to Albert. Act of pure devotion. Great story, but there's no trend, if that's what you mean. Kidnapping instruments for ransom, I've never heard of anything like that." He shook his head.

Kate stayed in his doorway. She folded her arms. She said, "How about crime that's specific to the nature of the business?"

He shrugged. "Well, it's late-night work, and there's muggings and shootings from time to time. Musicians at recording sessions along Music Row, occasionally somebody's shot at about 2 A.M. coming from the studio to their car. Or a rape. But the industry has raised hell about safety, and it's lit up like a Christmas tree and heavily patrolled." He paused. "I wouldn't exactly call that country music crime. More like being vulnerable after night shift."

Kate nodded, remembering the distant past when, married to Kelly's father, she feared for his safety in a hospital parking lot in the middle of the night. That was ancient history, back when the two of them still thought they had a life together, the crime reporter and the medical resident. Medical residents, convenience store clerks, or country musicians—wee hours bait.

Jerry Lombardi unbuttoned his right shirt cuff and rolled it back. "—'course, Kate, there's fraud that makes the newspapers and TV from time to time. You'll see it in the *Tennessean* as the months go by. Lawsuits alleging that a manager or an agent stole a lot of money from an artist. And then, if you're talking about the music clubs, probably the usual skimming and kickbacks that go on in any business dealing in cash." He shook his head. "Nothing that stands out."

She said, "—and nothing that particularly makes a woman vulnerable in the business? I'm not talking about rape now."

He shook his head. "From what I gather, it's very tough for women in country music, but crimes like fraud—I think fraud's an equal opportunity crime."

Kate nodded, still leaning against his doorway. "Okay, last couple of questions if you'll bear with me. Suppose, just suppose, an artist died suddenly. Promising career, one album out, big promotion budget. The artist dies. Who benefits?"

"Hey, Kate, what is this? You sound like some kind of detective." His eyebrow raised, the good humor suddenly had a wary edge.

She laughed to break the tension and reminded herself that she was talking to an acquaintance of a mere six weeks. Creating impressions was still a part of daily life here. New kid on the block. In the Fleetwood Building anyway.

She deliberately smiled warmly and said, "Jerry, I've probably been watching too much TV. Just humor me a minute, will you, because I've promised my thirteen-year-old daughter I'd follow up on something she cares about. I won't bore you with it, but it's a little bizarre, and I want to be extra ready with my facts. So suppose, for instance, there's a big insurance policy on a recording artist. Does the record company usually buy such a policy?"

He gave an exaggerated shrug. "Not the faintest idea. It'd make sense, though, wouldn't it? Sort of the Lloyds of London idea. But think about it, Kate, why kill the golden goose? Or the platinum goose." He chuckled, pleased at his own word play. She joined in very heartily to ease the moment. "Any-way," he said, "they'd be cutting their own throats."

She nodded. "Agreed. Final question, then. Have you heard of a young singer named Brandi Burns?"

"Nope." He shook his head. "Remember, I'm the guy in the LP time warp, Kate. If she's not on vinyl, I probably never heard of her. Patsy Cline, sí, but Brandi . . . Burns, is it? Nah. You know what, though? You should take your lunch hour on lower Broadway and check out the country record shops. Ernest Tubb, Lawrence Brothers, Slim Carruthers, they're around the corner and up Broadway. Just look at the display and talk to a clerk. You'll get a quick take on the whole scene if that's what you're after."

"A thirty-minute country music crash course?"

"The music's bigger than that, Kate. Better start by giving it the whole hour."

So in the heat and glare she walked left down Second and then right at the corner of Broadway. She passed a couple of bars, including Tootsie's Orchid Lounge, a furniture store, Service Merchandise, a pawn shop window full of guitars. One banjo looked especially menacing, the pressure of those steel wire strings against your fingertips—torture.

She felt perspiration down her back by the time she reached the block of record shops along lower Broadway. Lawrence Records and the Ernest Tubb Record Shop were ahead, but Slim Carruthers Records was first and so she ducked in out of the heat. Slim—it was doubtless some old country music name like Hank and Tex and Buck, all that cowboy stuff.

But there was a pleasant, old-fashioned feel to the long, shotgun store with a high tin ceiling, Patsy Cline posters and signed publicity photos from the 1940s to the 90s along the walls, racks of CDs, a pyramid of videos, Willie Nelson and Merle Haggard, Pam Tillis and Lorrie Morgan. Magazines and songbooks stood against the back in rows, while the front counter featured souvenirs from guitar-shaped ashtrays to the country music calendars, which, with three months remaining in the year, were on sale for one dollar. Several customers were browsing, an older man in powder blue buying tapes, a woman in striped green shorts picking out souvenir key chains with enameled guitars in gold plate.

"May I help you?"

A difference noticeable in the South. Clerks actually did try to help. "I'm just . . . I was wondering about a certain CD, a young singer who died recently. Brandi Burns."

"Oh, *Fool Moon*, it's over there in special displays, beside the new Trisha Yearwood and Mary-Chapin Carpenter." He pointed, then walked over with her to make certain Kate found the album. He was a round-faced man, late twenties, with a thin, neat moustache and hair short in front, long in back, like the musicians in Brandi Burns's band. He wore jeans and a Garth Brooks T-shirt, and he stood before a rack of the *Fool Moon* CDs and pointed in silence.

Kate said, "I guess a young singer like Brandi Burns was just getting launched." He nodded, still silent as another, forties-ish clerk with an oily pompadour bagged a customer's CDs and chatted freely. Kate's luck to get the quiet one.

Give it another try. She said, "I guess a person in your line of work can really appreciate what it all means, a career cut short like that."

He was looking grave. "Terrible thing. Just terrible. Real good songwriter too."

Kate heard a special tone, like reverence. She said, "Is that unusual? I mean, for the singer to write songs?"

"Yes, ma'am, that's a little unusual. Not all artists can write, you see, not by a long shot. It's a whole lot harder than it might seem."

"Sounds like you know what you're talking about. Maybe you write songs yourself?"

He nodded with a hint of a smile, seeming pleased to have that secret guessed. He relaxed a bit and stood taller, as if his stature increased with his identity as songwriter. Maybe Kate could keep this going, careful not to make him wary. Jerry Lombardi's raised eyebrow stuck in her mind as a warning. She said, "I'm new in town and don't know much about

Brandi Burns except the album and the accident. I was looking at the autographed photos of music stars on your store walls—did she ever come in the store?"

"Funny you mention it." He shook his head. "She was scheduled for an in-store next month. That's when the artist comes in for an hour or so to autograph their album. Real good for business. We were looking forward to it, but then the accident . . ." His hand reached automatically to straighten the CD display and he got quiet again.

Kate said, "I had the opportunity to meet her sister."

It primed the pump. "Yes, I heard about her singing with a sister when they were kids." He put a hand on one hip. Garth Brooks smiled across his chest.

Kate said, "You probably know the ins and outs of all the careers."

Kate could measure the flattery when he hooked both thumbs in his jeans pockets and rolled forward from the hips. "I know a little," he said. "This and that. One thing, Brandi Burns paid her dues. Mostly they all do, working the writers' nights at the small clubs and singing around town."

He ran a thumbnail across the painted portrait on his shirt. "This guy too; he paid his dues. Used to sing in a bar out in Madison."

He expanded his chest, and Kate guessed the image of the country music superstar was supposed to send a message about the clerk's own identity. He saw himself not as a fan, but a buddy. It was Garth as a regular guy, the clerk as a potential star himself. "Country music artists," he said, stepping closer to Kate, "they've got to get that experience. The overnight successes take years—that's a Nashville saying. Lots of stars say so, and it's pretty true."

Kate nodded. She picked up a *Fool Moon* CD from the rack.

"Do you happen to know the song 'Envy Green'?"

"Yeah, I sure do." He brightened more. "You like that one too? It's my personal favorite." In a soft baritone he sang, " '. . . emeralds in the summer grass/velvet in the mossy bank.' " He broke off. "Awful good song. In my opinion, they ought to picked it for the single."

"For the radio?"

"—better than 'Fool Moon.' No doubt in my mind. Picture 'Envy Green' on WSM or WSIX or any country station in the USA—it's the one to get fans into the stores for the album. It's a woman's song for a woman singer, and you ladies buy an awful lot of albums, even if the record execs don't believe it." He smiled at her and ran his palm across a row of CDs. 'Fool Moon,', it's still doing fine, got up to number three on the charts before it started to slip. It's twelve on this week's chart." He looked her in the eye. "But I bet the single'd be up in the single numbers if they'd picked 'Envy Green' instead."

Kate said, "—just one song to promote for the radio, that must be a tough decision. Like, hit or miss. I bet that's a source of conflict sometimes."

"Oh, you bet. Picking the first album track to pitch to the stations—feelings can run real high. The artist wants one song, the producer maybe wants another. But when all's said and done, it's the label that picks."

The label again, the almighty label. Kate nodded as he rolled his other sleeve up very neatly and checked for symmetry. She said, "The display looks good."

"Album's selling pretty fair. We reordered already. 'Course, last June's when we could've *really* sold it. She showcased with her band at Fan Fair. You know, twenty-five thousand people come into town that week, the biggest country music fans on the earth, and the ones that heard Brandi Burns, they came in the store just itching to get her album. People were crazy about her. We could've sold plenty if we had 'em. Bad timing at the label for sure."

"At Virgo/Nashville?"

He seemed to hesitate, as if on the edge of trade secrets. Then he tucked his T-shirt a little tighter, took another half step closer and said, "Virgo should've released that album last June like they were supposed to."

"So it was behind schedule?" He nodded with emphasis.

Kate said, "I work in magazine publishing, you see, so schedules are always on my mind. Nothing more important that meeting deadlines. Everything's at stake, customers, advertisers. I'd think a big record company like Virgo would have it running like a clock."

"You'd think so, wouldn't you?" He looked her in the eye like an ally. "But they're human; they can mess up." He added, "But it's not the first mistake they've made lately."

Kate fingered the album. Idle chat. Useful? She said, "Sounds like you keep a finger on the pulse of the record companies."

"In retail we have to. Plus there's always rumors. Who's hot, who's not. Who's in trouble. In the store, now, we take heat for the mistakes. If there's problems with the albums, customers blame us, think we've screwed up."

He almost whispered. "Virgo, they need to get their act together. They lost a lot of good people over the last year. It's even in the newspaper and TV, so I'm not telling any secrets. Some folks are wonderin' what's going on over there." He paused. "Nothin' good. A lot of big disagreements is what I hear. And firings. New people from California. Real nasty."

He shrugged. Did he have any firsthand knowledge, Kate wondered, or was this mere clerk talk? He hooked his thumbs in his jeans pockets again and moved his hips and lowered his voice. "Be frank with you, I think Brandi Burns got some bad advice. They say RCA wanted her, and Mercury was interested. But Virgo wined and dined her first, and she probably got a little impatient, you know how it is. Real eager."

He shook his head. "Timing's bad at Virgo. Anybody could've told her." He leaned even closer. "Should've told her."

Kate recalled the clay-faced man at the hotel. "—like her manager?"

"Manager, producer, anybody." He shifted his weight. "Guess it's all hindsight now."

Kate looked him in the eye and nodded slowly, and was about to ask a question when a metallic voice called, "Rob to the register."

As if a midnight hour had struck, he stepped back and exhaled and slumped a little. Garth Brooks in retreat. "You can bring the album up," he said softly. "We'll ring it up."

Kate held the CD. How could she fail to buy it, having bought his time? She smiled her thanks, said it was nice to talk, walked the linoleum floor alongside him, and without another word, purchased her second copy of *Fool Moon*.

Back down Broadway, she stopped into AmeriLunch for a salad. Salad greens and "Envy Green." She carried the takeout box back up First Avenue. The back stairwell at Fleetwood was blessedly empty, and she shoved the CD into an empty desk drawer in her office and reached for her plastic fork and salad and Bobbie Burnside's phone number.

Her desk phone rang.

"Miz Banning? This is Delia downstairs. There's a Bobbie Burnside hoping to see you. She's waited the better part of an hour here in the front lobby. Are you available this afternoon?"

Kate braced and took a deep breath. "I'm available, Delia. Tell Ms. Burnside I'll be right down."

Before stepping out, she decided to listen to her voicemail and found herself hearing a familiar voice. " . . . 'tahm,' Kate. This 'tahm' I have something real to go on, and I'm coming over to your office building. I just want to get your button back, and it makes my blood run cold to say this, but I got it on good authority about the car now. I hope you'll take an interest because this time I have the proof. This is not hysterics and grief talking, but cold hard facts. Please get in touch with me as soon as you get the first chance. This really is life or death."

Chapter Three

"That sun is fierce. Don't you just hate driving out Charlotte this time of day."

Glossy red manicured nails reached for the passenger sun visor of Kate's Century. Kate reached to pull down her own, squinting against the late afternoon glare. Bobbie Burnside was beside her.

"Bayne Street's way up, we got another couple miles."

Kate nodded, checked the rearview mirror so she could change lanes, get around a UPS van. Along the avenue, the Red Cross, Royal Crown Bottling, a couple of lumberyards, a transmission center. Also pawn shops, the Salvation Army and Goodwill. She noticed a beige pickup behind her.

"You might want to just stay in the right lane. On the whole, I find it's faster."

Kate felt her jaw tighten. A front seat version of a backseat driver. Bobbie offered to take her car, but Kate insisted on driving for territorial reasons. Her car, her terms. She might have known better. Bobbie's large purse felt like a passenger between them, and her scent filled the car. Gardenias. Every intake of air as thick as those air fresheners. Bobbie was wearing jeans and sandals, a white tank top and a sheer lemon overblouse.

In the pumps and tailored green print dress she wore at work, Kate felt like a suburbanite bringing bags of clothes to the needy. This was the first time she had driven Nashville's Charlotte Avenue, which had a back-alley feel. Not the side of town to impress prospective newcomers, though it had its own

gritty vitality. She liked it. She also wished the beige truck
would ease back. Tailgaters made her nervous.

At the moment, however, Kate focused on how best to get
Bobbie to repeat her so-called story. And not just repeat it, but
hear how thin it was, how light and inconclusive despite the
high drama of the voicemail and the plea in the Fleetwood
lobby right in front of Delia. Riding literally into the sinking
sun, Bobbie ought to face the fact of her own myth-making.
Probable myth-making, Kate asked quietly, "Would you tell
me once again what the voice said?"

"Kate, I told you so many times I feel like I'm yodeling in a
canyon. There's no more; I said it all." Bobbie leaned to look
at Kate's face. "You're not having any memory problems are
you Kate?"

It was said with a sympathetic touch. Warmth and kindness.
It was almost unnerving, Kate said, "No, no problems, Bobbie.
I just want . . . sometimes a person remembers new details
when they repeat a story."

"Well, in this part of the country, stories tend to grow a little
bit every time. Now I've told you everything I know, but here
goes again." She held up one hand from the waist, as if to
itemize on her fingers. "First, I was working the early shift,
started at six, right after the night clerk gets off. We had the
early checkouts, the ones that want to hit the road at the crack
of dawn.

"Then I reviewed the occupancy like we always do, and in-
ventoried the continental breakfast bar, which is one of my du-
ties. I was right at the front desk checking somebody out, a
business man from the look of him. Must've been about eight.
The phone rang, and this voice asked if it was me. I said yes,
and the voice said, 'Check the fluids.' And that was it, just
'check the fluids.' And they hung up."

"And the voice did not say *what* fluids?"

"They didn't have to. What other fluids could it be?"

Kate paused. Couldn't Bobbie put two and two together,
given her job? "Motels use so many liquid cleaning prepara-
tions," she said. "Couldn't the reference be about supplies?"

Her voice verged on snippy, and she reminded herself this woman just lost her sister. No clear thinking, grasping at straws. Be merciful.

"—not to the front desk, Kate. Housekeeping deals with all that. Besides, what other fluids are there?"

"Okay," Kate said, "then what about the river in 'Envy Green'? '—winding through the summer hills back home' That's fluid all right."

"I thought of that, and I wanna talk about that song because there's a lot going on in it, and I have my suspicions, like I told your little daughter Kelly. But I don't think 'Envy Green' fits this particular. First things first." Bobbie shifted in her seat. "I know what I know. It was brake fluid. That's what they meant. I'm positive we're gonna find the brake fluid gone from Brandi's car."

Kate nodded, eased up on the gas, turned slightly to see Bobbie's face. What was that schoolroom jargon for reality sinking in?—teachable moments. Let Bobbie have a teachable moment here on Charlotte Avenue. She said, "You told me your sister did not complain about the brakes on her car."

"No, she didn't complain, but—"

"—and she was particularly careful about any kind of malfunction, noises or warning lights."

"—always watching the engine temperature, yes. Because one time when our daddy's Plymouth overheated—"

"—which suggests, Bobbie, that Brandi's car was okay, that she skidded because—"

"—because the police never checked the brake fluid, just called the ambulance and the wrecker. Nobody thought about it."

Kate sighed. Deaf. Why go on? This had the feel of a third-rate opera. Bobbie straightened her shoulders against the seat, energized, but also ready to be indignant at the stubborn Kate Banning.

"This is about Brandi's car, Kate. That's what they meant."

They again. She said, "You identified the caller as *they*."

Bobbie shrugged. "He, she, they—I mean whoever it was. I'm not bein' technical on this, Kate. I mean whoever. He or she. I picked up my phone, and this voice was real muffled. Tell you what—it was like on TV when they don't want to show the face because of privacy or they're snitching on somebody. They turn the faces into little squares so they look like Picasso. That's how the voice was. Sounded like a sock over the phone."

Kate nodded. She would not suggest the caller might have a cold, that the connection might not be clear. She did not want to play skeptic-of-the-day. Besides, this was for Kelly, though she did not want to tell Bobbie this trek was for a merit badge to restore her to her daughter's good graces. The blazer button was secure in her wallet change purse, deposited over protests about who should sew it on. Kate had both hands on the wheel. Literally going the extra mile—along Charlotte Avenue, an extra four or five.

But she needed to avoid more misunderstanding. She said, "Bobbie, I'm glad to make time to run out here with you. Just this once. Based on experience, though, I wouldn't pin high hopes on . . ." An anonymous tip? A wrong number? A misheard few words? "On this lead."

Bobbie's hair seemed to nod by itself. "Kate, you probably don't go fishin' where you come from? Didn't think so. Well, around the lakes and rivers here in Tennessee lots of folks fish. And the line they use, the fishin' line, let me tell you— monofilament line's just as thin as can be, but it holds a lot of weight. You can pull in a big bass from a mighty thin line, and that's the way I feel about this call. It's like there's a fish on the line. It's just the break we need."

Kate sighed. Folksy homilies everywhere. Another minute and it would be home remedies. They passed McDonald's, Burger King, Krystal, home of the steamed hamburger. In the car was a certain tension which Bobbie quickly broke.

"Whole bunch of wrecker yards up this way," she said. "Out in the country, you know, you've got a wrecker yard right on your place. Great thing for little kids, they can play like they're driving, which all kids love to do. It gets to be a collection, a regular parts supply—" Kate was silent. The image of rural poverty, rusted hulks, and Bobbie chatting away as if a front yard full of abandoned vehicles was a combined playground and Western Auto.

Then it struck her that Bobbie Burnside might be nervous and ill at ease, worried about what they would find at Hillgate Wreck and Tow when they looked at Brandi Burns's wrecked Taurus. They were passing a yellow school, a red Pentecostal church with white trim. "This is the back side of Richland," Bobbie said. "Look, there's the library back there. One time me and Brandi sang there. We were little kids, and coming to the big city to sing—we thought we were something; I can tell you."

Kate looked sideways at the red brick building set far back from Charlotte across a grassy park. In profile, Bobbie had looked wistful. "It was for a bunch of old ladies, least they seemed old to us. We sang some hymns, 'Abide with Me' and 'Precious Memories.' And we sang 'Cabin on the Hill' and 'Blueberry Hill.' We slipped in that one rock oldie, the Fats Domino. Boy, did we work on the harmony on *thrill*. It came out thri-hi-hill."

Then she actually sang it. Suddenly, without hesitation or an intro, Bobbie was singing. She filled the car with song. Kate was taken aback at how much Bobbie sounded like her sister. It was a voice that could envelop a listener. Stunning, out of nowhere. For the moment the perfume and the gaudiness vanished, became something else, pure vocal passion. That record shop clerk had sung a passable couple of lines, but Bobbie's voice carried song from the soul.

"Kate, you got the green. Say, Kate, the cars behind are wantin' you to go."

She nudged the gas. The voice for a moment canceled everything out, literally stopped her. And this from the sister who quit music. Kate wanted to say something, but a version of my-what-a-nice-voice-you-have would sound so trite. Bobbie was looking through the windshield as if nothing were unusual.

"Few blocks yet. It's just up from the White Bridge intersection. It'll be on the left."

Kate said, "You've got some voice."

Bobbie smiled and shrugged. "Ever'body in my family sings. It's nothin' special to us; we just do it." She looked at Kate's face and managed a short laugh. "It's just front porch music, Kate, like folks do in the country to pass the time and to give praise and sometimes grieve too." She grew quiet, then said, "But if you're gonna do it like Brandi did, now that's a whole nother thing. It's real different if you're working down on Music Row with the pros."

"Like at Virgo?"

"Like at Virgo, for sure."

Kate was listening closely. No irony. No undercurrent suggesting that Virgo was anything less than a towering music giant in Bobbie's estimation. No hint that the label had made any mistakes with her sister's career or album. Not even a crack about that executive from L.A., the one who arranged that hotel thing with the cardboard standup—Benniger. Clearly, the signals from the record store clerk were not Bobbie's signals.

She was now pointing ahead. "Okay, get in the left lane and watch the cross traffic. Drivers really like goin' fast down this hill." Kate put on her turning signal. The beige pickup was still behind her, almost bumper to bumper. Sunlight glared on the windshield, so she could not see the driver.

It was a relief to turn left at the bent sign reading Bayne Street, the name barely legible in the backlight of the savage sun. The corner was a weedy lot with a realtor's sign: "Your Business Here, Sale or Lease," and further in, a few rundown dingy white cottages with ruined porch furniture from which they saw the cyclone fencing and the bashed vehicles of Hillgate Wreck and Tow. The pavement ended, the surface now packed-down clay, ruts, holes. Kate saw suspended dust in the rearview mirror.

The office was a windowless, cinderblock cube with a metal door and the predictable signs—"Beware of Dog," "Security,"

"Trespassers Prosecuted." The gate into the yard was closed and wound with heavy chain. Kate noted two big padlocks.

She parked alongside the building, a good fifteen feet from a red Firebird with a foil sun protector across the windshield and a very shiny blue tow truck with "Hillgate Wreck and Tow" stenciled on the doors. With Bobbie beside her, Kate opened the office door and stepped in. Inside, it was dark as a tavern.

It took a moment to make out the front desk and the thick-set, heavy-lidded man with a remote and a phone at hand. "Ladies, afternoon. What can I do for you?"

He was outlined against dark grooved paneling and green wall-to-wall shag. A trash can overflowed with Wendy's wrappers and cups. Light came from two fluorescent tubes, a TV, and an enormous aquarium where two fat goldfish with bulging eyes nosed in a bed of purple gravel. Algae engulfed the tiny diver, pirate, and treasure chest. Aquarium kudzu. The Formica desktop was strewn with papers, and the plastic nameplate read Dennis A. Corl in blocky letters. Bobbie said, "How're you today?"

"Jus' fine, thanks. So what can I do for you ladies?" He waved the remote and notched down the volume on *Oprah*. He was red-faced and his short blond hair a mass of cowlicks. Maybe this was his cushy job, cool in the long punishing summers, warm in winter.

Bobbie cleared her throat and said, "We're wantin' to take a look at a certain wrecked car you got. It's an '89 Ford Taurus, and it belonged to my sister. She— It—" Suddenly she broke off with a snort and began fumbling in the huge purse. For an instant Kate thought this staged for effect, but no, Bobbie was choking up. A moment passed. She could not continue.

Kate stepped up. "It's a car on your lot," she said, "recently involved in an accident. It's a car a woman died in about three weeks ago. I believe it was registered to Brandi Burns. The police would have brought it in."

"No ma'am, the police did not tow that or any car. The police call us, and we're the ones do the towing. That job was

dispatched from here." *Dis*patched. The Southern pronuncia-
tion. Slight defensive tone. "I'm just about closing up for the
day here, but I can say about the ownership of that vehicle—
Let me just look it up." A self-important swing around to a file
case. No computerized records here but the old manila folders
with pastel, tissue paper copies, pink, green, yellow.

He leafed through. "Here. 1989 Ford Taurus sedan. Registered to Brandi Burns, title held by DeLauney Banking and
Mortgage, Memphis. Insurance papers on it and a bill of sale
from National Continental Insurance." He looked up from the
folder. "That car's declared totaled, ma'am. The adjuster was
out last week and gone over it with us. Axle got bent. We own
the car as of five, six working days ago. Signatures are right
here. You'd have to talk to the insurance company." He folded
his arms across his chest. "I can't just let you go on out there
to the yard, if that's what you're thinking. It's restricted. It's
for your own safety."

Bobbie continued to rummage in the huge purse, produced a
tissue, blew loudly. Her shoulders slumped in the tank top. Her
very sexiness might work with a man like this, but not in such
misery. There would be no point returning after hours either,
not with those padlocks, the chain, the inevitable dog.

But Bobbie was not likely to give up, not with the fixation
on brake fluid. Picture another call from Delia saying Miz
Burnside was waiting in the Fleetwood lobby. If possible, get
this over with now. Kate must try to take the lead. Speak
slowly, she told herself. Yankee fast talk would put him off.

She said, "Mr. Corl, this is Ms. Bobbie Burnside, and it's
her sister who died accidentally in that car." She leaned toward
the desk and lowered her voice to a tone she hoped was reverence itself. "I know it's nearly closing time, Mr. Corl, but I
think you can see Ms. Burnside is trying to set her mind at rest
about her late sister."

Kate gave him a concerned, almost confidential look. "She
never saw the car after her sister's accident, you see. I believe
if she could actually see it, her suffering might ease and she
could begin trying to get on with her own life. We were hoping

that she might be able to just look at the actual car. That's the reason we're here today."

Kate paused again and gave him a look of sincerity. "You understand, Mr. Corl, this is totally about the personal side. This is not about insurance or the book value of the car or damage to the axle. Nothing like that. It's about a loss. It's . . . well, if you take my point, almost like a graveyard visit. Maybe you could let us go on out there for a few minutes? Maybe you would just walk out with us—?"

He wasn't eager to say yes. That was obvious in the way he clapped the folder shut, stuffed it in the file drawer, stood and hitched his pants and looked at his rubber wrist watch even as the closing segment of *Oprah* told him the local time in his cave. There was reluctance in the way he looked aside and scratched his chest, but he fetched keys from the ring in his belt loop. "I'll go on out with you."

They went outside into the slamming heat, the glaring sun on a downward arc. He opened the padlocks, unwound the chain, slid the cyclone gate back on wheels that raised dust and gravel. Kate saw reluctance in the way he moved his very arms. From his viewpoint, what did he see but two mourning women, the sexy one just a pitiful sight, and then the nineties heat, and the dust? And who needed that when you could stay in the cool office and wrap up the day, catch the last few minutes of *Oprah*, work the phone and maybe start up the Firebird to cool it down before leaving.

He took a few steps with them, then said, "Tell you what, you ladies go ahead, just yourselves. Take a couple minutes, whatever you want. And don't worry about it. Just be private. Nobody's out there to bother you." He pointed. "Third row back behind that white Olds Cutlass. See it?"

"I see it." Bobbie squinted forward. "I couldn't miss it."

Kate said, "What about the dog? The sign out front—?"

"Don't worry." He rubbed his head. "Dog's dog-gone." He did not wait for a laugh. Too hot for wit.

So Kate walked with Bobbie in silence, past destroyed cars and trucks, garden variety, a Blazer, Malibu, Peugeot, Hondas.

Two Crown Victorias. On-the-ground facts of the careless, the incompetent, the victims of impossible weather, the drunk, stoned, the mistaken intentions—all in the crashed and bashed. Democracy of sudden violence, Corollas to Cadillacs, spanning twenty years. The Stonehenge of twentieth-century America.

The blue Taurus was already coated with dust. The driver's front side showed the impact, bumper and fender stoved in, the hood buckled. Ford meets limestone at X miles per hour. Kate looked at the windows. The car was locked. Bobbie stood back, arms at her sides, silent and staring as if at a memorial stone. Her profile looked somewhere between awe and horror.

Maybe for the surviving sister this was a macabre cemetery visit after all. Maybe it would have the effect Kate described in her impromptu pitch to Mr. Dennis A. Corl of Hillgate Wreck and Tow. Maybe this was the shock therapy Bobbie needed. Maybe, after all, the spell would break and they would not have to look under the hood for screwcaps and dipsticks.

At that moment, however, Bobbie reached into her jeans pocket and said, "I have a key." But the hood was already ajar. It raised with a creak. Then the usual look of an engine compartment, a maze of coated wires, snaking hoses, cast metal. The impact in the ditch had shoved up the battery and the air filter.

"This car doesn't look totaled to me."

"You can't always tell," Kate said. "Sometimes the worst damage isn't visible." She scanned the maintenance access points. A cap showed an outline of a dripping oil lamp. "There's the oil."

"I see it." Bobbie peered in. "Reminds me of oil cans in the country," she said. "They never had tops. We'd shove a potato over the spout. Worked fine."

Kate kept quiet, in no mood to hear about make-do country ways. Or was this nostalgia for a time when the Burnside family life was simpler? She reached over and pulled the oil dipstick. Clear amber. She said, "This oil was changed very recently, look at it. Clean and full to the mark."

Bobbie nodded. "Let's get to the brake fluid. That's what we're after, Kate. Now where is that?" They stared. No more cute cap diagrams.

Kate said, "Manuals are usually in the glove compartment. Take a look." Bobbie used her key, leaned in, opened the glove compartment. *Ford Taurus Owner's Guide*, 1989. "Let's see, seat controls, window controls, if you have a flat tire. Don't know about you, Kate, but if I have a flat tire, I just wait for the first Good Samaritan."

"Bobbie—"

"—here it is, engine compartment. Look here."

They stared at the diagram and tried to match it with the car. It was like those high school biology texts when the specimen did not quite match. Carotid artery and spleen, PVC valve and grommet. "There, brake master cylinder." Kate pointed. In the engine compartment the cylinder looked large and intact.

She walked to the driver's side and reached toward it. "Okay, this is the brake cylinder, and the fluid goes in here." She reached to unscrew the cap. Then she paused and looked back at the office. "That guy, Dennis, is he watching us?"

"Lord, Kate, why would he want to watch us?"

"Can you see the office from your side?"

Bobbie craned her neck. "Kate, the man's inside where it's cool. Probably looking in that trash for a few french fries."

"Try to keep an eye on the office. We're supposed to be looking at the car, not poking around. No point disturbing him." She unscrewed the brake fluid cap. Again a clear fluid. "Bobbie, I want you to see this. Come around to my side and look at this. Here, look at this drop on my finger. It's brake fluid, and there's plenty of it." Savage heat. She reached for her handbag, wiping the fluid on a tissue. The car was very hot to the touch.

Then she wiped her arm across her forehead. "Now let's look up something else in the manual." She took the booklet from Bobbie, flipped to the table of contents. "Page seventeen. Okay, look at this. 'Brake system and parking brake warning light.' Look on with me, I want you to see this." She made a space at her side. Seen from the office, she thought, they would resemble two choir women over the music.

Kate read aloud: "This light will glow red . . . if the light stays on or if it comes on while driving, the hydraulic brake system requires immediate servicing." Kate pointed to the words to make certain Bobbie was reading along. "You follow this?" At her side, nodding.

Kate went on. Lesson time. "Bobbie, the point is, if the brake fluid drained out, there'd be a warning. A dashboard light would flash on." She paused briefly. "Now, you told me Brandi watched out for problems of that kind. And you said she did not complain about any such light, and we verified there's plenty of brake fluid in the car."

"Maybe somebody filled it up again."

Kate sighed. "Bobbie, I want you to kneel down with me and look underneath this car—no, I mean down in the dirt." She bent, dress hitched up. Sacrifice one pair of drugstore nylons. She was on her knees in the yellow dust and gravel. "Come on."

Bobbie obeyed. The hem of the lemon overblouse brushed the dust as she met Kate on all fours. Even here in the open, the *Jungle Gardenia* perfume was overpowering. Kate said, "Go ahead, look underneath. Tell me, do you see any spills, any fluids that might have leaked out?"

It was reluctant and a long time coming. "No."

"It looks dry, doesn't it?"

"I guess." Another long pause. "I guess it does."

"So we know there's plenty of brake fluid in the reservoir. Nothing to indicate a leak. And there's no indication that the insurance adjuster found anything amiss except for the accident damage. Because if he had, the police would be notified and involved by now."

Kate rose, brushed at her knees, her dress. One shoe had a stone in it, and she steadied herself on the bumper and dumped it out. Bobbie had also stood and now looked morose.

Kate reached to lower the hood, one last look at the engine

compartment. Everything dark except for the damaged area, the scratches and gouges exposing bright metal.

She was about to close the hood when she noticed another bright spot off to the side, something silvery. "What's this?"

"What?"

"Probably nothing. Looks like . . . just a new clamp over a hose." She scanned the other hoses, all of them fastened with dull grimy clamps. "It's the only new clamp I can see. Here, let me check the diagram." She followed the arrow, the name. "It's the power steering reservoir. There's a dipstick." Kate pulled it. Then pulled it again. Both times, it came up dry. Except for the barest drop of clear liquid at the end, dry.

"What are you doing? What is that?"

"It's the power steering fluid. There doesn't seem to be any." She dipped it again. Same result. Then she reached down, feeling the hose with her fingers. Like an accordion, both bumpy and smooth. But then a rough spot. She ran her thumb back and forth, then picked at it with her nail. Definitely rough. "You don't have a flashlight, do you?"

Bobbie shook her head. "What is it? What do you see?"

"A certain spot I can feel. How about a match? Got a match?" From the cavernous purse, a book of matches. "Rodeo Ranch, dine and dance nightly—Be a Cowboy or a Sweetheart of the Rodeo!" Some sweetheart.

And what were the odds of gas fumes catching fire? Minimal. Negligible. She struck a match; held it low.

She saw the puncture in the orange match light.

"What do you see, Kate?"

"A little hole, looks like . . . ouch!"

"Here, let me light up another one." This time Bobbie held the match.

"Lower here. See it?"

"I see it. What's it mean?"

Kate frowned. Dust on her dress, a hole in the left knee of her nylons, thumbnail black, hands black. "There's a hole in the hose of the power steering fluid reservoir. It's at the top. I'm not sure exactly what it means." She rubbed a tissue on her fingers, a futile gesture. Bobbie's manicure was perfection itself as she blew out the match, dropped it, dusted the knees of her jeans.

But she leaned toward Kate as she shouldered the purse. "It means my sister couldn't steer her car, that's what it means, and you know it, Kate. Whoever tampered, they did it with the steering fluid. I was a little off, thinking brakes, but it's fluid for sure. That phone call was right on." She brushed a wave back from her forehead. "Just don't go tellin' me to look up *fluid* in the encyclopedia, Kate. Don't tell me to check the mouthwash or act like I'm soft in the head. Not anymore."

I-told-you-so. It left Kate to rub the Kleenex against her blackened, greasy fingers. They stood silent, each in private thought. Bobbie bit her lip, and Kate looked away from her at some distant trees. Her mind seemed to float.

And then in the dry heat of landlocked Tennessee, Kate suddenly thought—of all things—about sailing. In a boat with Sam Powers, her Sam, day sailing offshore in New England—and tacking to change course, the helm brought firmly to the starboard or port side. The boom would swing, sails snap. You did it consciously, made a decision to change course.

But at times, running downward, a shift in wind direction brought you very suddenly about. Involuntarily. The boom swung, you ducked, nothing to do but cope. Jibing, it was called. Mostly unwelcome, at times a sign of incompetence.

That's what she thought about now, in the heat and dust of a car junkyard so very far from the salt shore of the Atlantic. Here in Tennessee she jibed, her head doing a one-eighty. Check the fluids. Forget the Windex or the bathroom scrub of the Quality Seven motel where Bobbie worked at the front desk. Set aside neat terms like hysteria and myth. Jibe. Focus instead on a car recently serviced, at least an oil change, and a hose newly clamped for no apparent reason. And punctured. Jibe, whether you want to or not. Change course when it's the last thing on your mind, the last thing you need or want.

Wordlessly, she and Bobbie walked back, sandals and pumps the only sound in the silent yard. Somewhere in the distance a horn sounded. Through the gate, they instinctively tried to walk well clear of the cinderblock office, though the door opened and Dennis Corl came out to stare.

He nodded. "Y'all take good care." Better than have-a-nice-day. She called thanks, then saw his stare fixed on her hands. Black, greasy, more like a mechanic's. A sure signal that she did not simply hold the hand of her grieving companion but took some hands-on action of her own.

Dumb, but she couldn't dwell on it. Get back in the car; get going. She was braced for more backtalk from Bobbie, grief compounded with gloating.

It didn't happen. They both were quiet. "You might want to take I-40 back into town. Pick it up off White Bridge. Be faster this time of day." Rush hour, she meant, and at White Bridge Road Kate waited through two changes of lights and then made a left toward 40 East.

It had seemed so simple. Get the blazer button, take Bobbie on a field trip, say bye-bye, watch her own daughter's approval rating soar.

Instead, the wrongful death of Brandi Burns? Had the car been tampered with?

Was this, after all, homicide?

Beside her, Bobbie was still silent. Down the ramp onto I-40, Kate thought the woman seemed smaller as if drawn into herself in mourning and grief. Despite herself, Bobbie might not find satisfaction in the discovery that her theory was perhaps valid. In truth, maybe she would rather not find disturbing signs that her sister's car was sabotaged.

In her side vision, Kate saw her shoulders beginning to shake. There were droplets on Bobbie's lemon yellow blouse, tears down the face of cosmetic and nature's own perfection.

Tear droplets, in fact, as clear as the power steering fluid. A few tears' worth, the amount left in the reservoir. So let her cry. Let her bravado fade to grief.

Though once past this, what would she ask Kate to do? What could Kate give? There were grease marks on her steering wheel.

Distracted by the traffic, she was glad not to think as she tracked the cars bursting from this lane to that. Green signs for I-265, I-440, and names she was not used to, Clarksville, Knoxville, Louisville. And on either side, the limestone from which these interstates had virtually been quarried. She edged into the right lane, headed for downtown Nashville. Get Bobbie back to her own car and go home.

Kate didn't see the truck at first, not in any particular way, not with so many tractor-trailers here, rolling, roaring, vans and four-wheel drives, a Bronco, a Grand Cherokee. And the sun behind her, the sudden shade of the limestone bluffs. There were flashes of glare and dark, and she was thinking about sunglasses when the beige pickup started coming up fast behind her, getting close, way too close for her comfort.

Hateful tailgaters. She accelerated just to get some space. Her highway pet peeve was riding the rear bumper.

But the pickup immediately closed the gap. From in the right lane, Kate was relieved to see the truck pull out left. Fast lanes in rush hour traffic—welcome to them. Instant of relief.

But only an instant. It was a beige truck—beige again—driver in a ballcap. It slid closer. Ford Ranger. Kate swerved right to the edge of her own lane. But the pickup still pressed, kept exactly parallel and then, seconds later, moved to force her steadily off the side to the right.

She blew her horn. No response. Blew it again.

She tried to see the driver, meet the eyes, send a distress signal. Impossible. The face was hidden by the cap visor. Was he—or she—drunk or stoned? Crazy?

The truck moved closer yet, just inches now between them.

The passenger door, she noticed, looked bumpy, dimpled. A detail, one dimpled door. Stupid, useless. And the limestone wall was coming closer; the drill marks visible where it was dynamited out.

Her eyes darted left. Through the truck side window, big knuckles on a steering wheel, and the cap visor curved like a knife. She floored her gas pedal, edged right by degrees. The Ford matched her speed, forcing her further to the right.

Trapped between the beige truck, the beige rock. Into the curve toward the city, 45 mph yellow blinker, she was going sixty when her right wheels struck the shoulder, then her left as well. Rock hit the underpan like hail. A spray, a storm.

In the curve, she was losing control, skidding on loose gravel while the pickup now sped off, disappearing ahead in the traffic stream. Kate gripped the wheel as if the wheel itself might save her.

"Kate—"

The figure beside her already alert. "Steer with it! Brake steady . . ."

For Kate, the next moment was the voice of Bobbie Burnside telling her step-by-step how to regain control of a car gone wild on shoulder gravel.

Kate flashed on memories of winter ice in Boston, glare ice, sheet ice. But she followed the advice of the passenger with plenty of driving time on graveled country roads.

At last she brought the Buick to a stop, just inches from a metal light pole. The sound in the car was two women panting.

Kate put her flashers on. Her hands shook, teeth chattered. Cars and trucks whizzed by. Bobbie spoke, and her voice sounded different now, no longer the cool navigator-instructor or the told-you-so surviving sister. She now sounded shrill and frightened, and she was looking right at Kate. "They tried to run us into that rock. That was deliberate, Kate. Somebody in that truck was trying to kill us."

Chapter Four

The American Airlines TV monitors listed flight 2007 at gate 26C, on time. Passengers came and went. As of ten minutes ago, there was not one beige Ford Ranger in the airport short-term parking lot. Kate had cruised the rows to make sure. There was a dark blue model in row three and a brown one in row five. She even got out of her car and felt their passenger doors for dimpled bumps. Nothing. Clean sweep.

Now it felt good to be in a pedestrian area, no fast or slow lanes, no rock cuts. The terminal was modern, the atmosphere spacious, unhurried, the predictable scenarios playing out on the carpeted stage as she strolled. A stocky grandmother with apricot-colored hair rushed to embrace her toddler grandson, who burst into tears and hid his face in a teddy bear while his young parents looked on, dismayed.

Behind them, three couples in tropical, flowered aloha shirts with straw hats askew moved rubber-legged with fatigue. Vacation over, they wearily toted souvenir pineapples-to-go, identical to those in the local grocery produce section. There were soldiers too, a private and two corporals in blinding black patent shoes, eyeing a henna-haired woman in a tight leopard patterned T-shirt. Typical evening moment at the Nashville airport.

Kate checked her watch again and lingered in the souvenir shop. Or malingered. Another twenty-five minutes with the Music City sweatshirts and shot glasses with cowboy hats and guitars. She drifted to the books, the romances, thrillers, a special selection on country music stars, Barbara Mandrell, Randy Travis.

She paged through *Nashville's Grand Ole Opry*, a coffee table gift book with splashy photos featuring straw hats, bandannas, Roy Acuff, Dolly Parton's wigs. No black-bordered pages, no tributes to murdered singers. She closed the book, trying to push away gothic thoughts. A death dance with a pickup truck. She put it in a wayback mental file.

She twitched when a wiry man in a long-visored ball cap moved up close alongside her on the left. She moved away. Try to get reoriented. Try to think positive. About the Opry, for instance. Maybe she should go to the Grand Ole Opry sometime, tourist curiosity, see what it's like. Maybe with Sam.

Speaking of Sam, finally it was almost time. She headed to concourse C, went through security, noticed the flight schedules on the monitors. Flights to Chicago, New York. And to Boston. Boston. She looked away, unexpectedly blinking back little tears. The onscreen name caught her off guard, so near yet so far. Home, not home. Constantly being brave for Kelly's sake.

She daubed her eyes with a tissue, determined to be intact for Sam, to be poised when she told him that life in Nashville had strange new complications. Very briskly she walked the length of the gray tile corridor as passengers came in waves, heading in and heading out. Kate looked straight ahead, resolved to make the best of his one-hour layover, this unexpected gift.

She was so focused she did not see the figure in the brown jacket until he blocked her way. "Hey, good lookin', whatcha got?"

"Sam!" He embraced her, had her hands in his, Kate both laughing and startled. "—didn't see you. When? Where. . . ? "

"Few minutes early. Grabbed a seat up front so I could get out of that 727 the instant the door opened. More time with you. Every minute I can get. I saw you from way back, and you looked hell-bent." He leaned toward her and brushed her mouth against his and whispered, "—even for one hour, even here at this, uh, airport Club Med." They looked around. She said, "Let's go to the lounge."

Hand in hand, they walked back toward the main lobby, to the terrace area with rattan chairs and plants. Passengers with briefcases and carry-ons nursed drinks and eyed the clock. Sam pointed to a table for two by a stand of philodendron. They sat and he signaled. "The usual, Kate?—cranberry and soda with a lime slice for the lady, and one Michelob Dark."

They locked hands across the table. His dark hair was thick, just barely wavy with flecks of gray. His square jaw, brown eyes. The look he gave her, the look that brought the world into this shape, just the two of them. She lingered in that world. Back in New England, they would go from here, go to his place on the Boston waterfront, have their own private time-out.

But this evening in the Nashville airport, instead of touching, it was merely touching base. Public, even awkward. Funny notion, pilot Sam Powers as passenger. No shoulder boards or braid for now, no cap raked at that certain angle. Instead, khakis and a shadow plaid sportshirt, and the light-weight suede jacket she gave him for his last birthday. Sam between flights. She held off talking about herself, wanting first to hear about him. Kate said, "And how was it?" Her eyes were locked on his. "How was Washington?"

"Too much marble and too many suits."

She laughed. It set a mood they could live by for an hour. "You didn't wear a uniform?"

"At the hearings? Oh, you bet I did. Newest one, right from the cleaners."

"And you gave the Senators the word."

"I gave them a message from the corporate and business pilots. Gave it to the FAA people and the alleged lawmakers. And their staffs."

"Big hearing room? Microphones?"

"Affirmative."

"And what did you say?"

"And what did I say?—that the FAA is diverting their limited resources from real safety concerns to nit-picking. That suspending pilots' licenses for minor infractions, like wandering three hundred feet from an assigned altitude, is asinine."

"—but you didn't say *asinine*."

He squeezed her hands. "No, my dear Kate, I said *dangerous*. I said that many private pilots are afraid to express an in-air problem for fear that they might be busted and incur a record of violations. These pilots often hope to fly commercially, and a record of minor violations would diminish their career and employment opportunities."

Sam's voice, tinged at first with mockery, now took on the tone of steady seriousness from the memory of the hearing room.

"Because I also said, that it has come to our attention that some small craft pilots flying near restricted areas are turning off their radar beacons to avoid detection. Since the beacons help controllers locate a plane and keep it away from others, the corporate pilots are concerned about a dangerous situation." Sam looked into her eyes. "Like that."

"Sounds scary."

"Well, the agency is overreacting to one fatal incident. We're supporting the idea of requiring remedial training. If you just suspend somebody's license and take them out of the air for sixty days, how can they come back a better pilot?"

He drummed his fingers on the table. "Everything taken under advisement. This is Washington, remember. Nothing actually happens, just reports." He shook his head. "I've never seen so much paper. Those guys should have their burial mounds made out of paper."

He put her hand to his face and kissed her palm. "Sorry, Kate, I'm a little fed up. I've said these same things a hundred times over the last three days. Makes me unfit company. Saying hello and goodbye to you at the same time doesn't help. I'm a creature of habit. I like homecoming. I like our own private customized greeting. Don't like this at all—except if it's the only way to see you now, I'll take it. Oh, by the way, I picked up something for Kelly. For her collection."

He felt in his jacket pocket, produced a bright plastic snowflake dome. He shook it, and the Washington Monument swirled with white glitter. "So now she's got the Golden Gate Bridge and the Sears Tower and the Statue of Liberty. How about Nashville?"

Kate squeezed his hand. "I'm not sure she wants Nashville, Sam."

"—still having it hard?" Kate nodded. Their drinks arrived, and she squeezed the lime wedge. They touched glasses. "Kelly just needs a little time," he said. "She'll be fine. You'll see. I'm not worried about Kelly, she's one solid citizen. She'll make her place." He leaned closer. "But how about her mother?"

"Fine. Great. Busy at work. Very busy."

He nodded. His gaze was steady. "Glad to hear it, but I know your face, Kate. I wouldn't say you've been crying, but I'm not looking at any portrait of peace and serenity." She looked down. "No, look at me. Is it the job?"

She looked directly into his eyes. "Sam, I'm damned grateful for this job. So far, it's working really well, and it's interesting, and my office is—well, you saw it."

"Cumberland River keeps you entertained?"

"Barges and riverboats, you bet. All it needs is a little salt air, a few seagulls—" She looked away, blinking, vision blurring again. He was reaching in his pocket, handing her a white handkerchief. It smelled like Sam.

She tried to smile. "Kelly gets a toy, and I get a hanky. Or is it a blankie?" He touched her cheek with his fingertips. She folded the cotton square and tried to smile. "Mostly I'm fine, Sam. Busy at the office, upbeat for Kelly. The new condo's great, everything works. Lots of room. Even the alcove for that damned exercise machine, which I use religiously."

She winked. "In fact, on my new, improved salary, I can consider joining a health club or buying a real NordicTrack instead of that ratty off-brand. I mean, a whole world of upscale products and services awaits me." She looked at his face. "Just once in a while it catches up with me, the newness, the . . . dislocation. Like I got all teary at the Motor Vehicles Test Center when they made me turn in my Massachusetts driver's license. I felt like a castaway."

She wanted to start telling him about the other rupture, the one from a lane of traffic on I-40 East, the one essentially navigated by Bobbie Burnside.

But Sam squeezed her hand, raised it to his lips. "We both knew this would be hard, Kate. Hard on you and Kelly, and hard on me too."

He looked steadily at her. "But I look at the plus side. I like knowing you're safe and sound here in Nashville. You're out of that townhouse firetrap in a dangerous city neighborhood. You're in a nice condo, and your new job won't get you shot at or damn near drowned. And no more of that detective stuff you used to get caught up in. No more of those near misses. Like the time that diet doctor tried to slice you in two with his boat propeller." He drank. "I'm looking at the benefit. There's peace of mind about your safety."

She bit her lip. His peace of mind, ignorant bliss. But her own essential peace depended on his knowledge, his guidance. If she couldn't tell Sam, then who?

Besides, wasn't honesty their thing? Frankness a rule? She could swap worries about him, Sam in the Lear dodging Cessnas and Beechcrafts around airports all over the U.S. Each of them feeling the other's peril.

He reached across for her hand. "Kate, I know Boston still feels like home, but Nashville's got a lot going for it. You're gonna love country music someday. You're going to be glad I've got those old Chet Atkins and Buck Owens records you never would listen to." He smiled. "You still playing that Reba McEntire song about New England?"

"Music therapy, sure thing. Play it twice a day." Kate managed a smile. " 'Whoever's in New England.' " She paused, wet her lips, poked the straw in her ice. She said, "I listen to it, but these days I'm listening to some other country music, Sam. I'm listening to a singer named Brandi Burns. Spelled with an *i*."

"Brandi Burns? Is that a real name?"

"Actually, it's the late Brandi." She paused, poised for the talk that would necessarily dismay him. For an instant she weighed the decision to go ahead. Worse if she didn't, a lie by omission. She said, "Brandi Burns died in an auto accident, Sam. At first it seemed straightforward, uncomplicated. But indications are, it wasn't an accident. I've been talking with her sister."

He was already on alert, his mouth tightening. She could have predicted it. "Kate, don't tell me you're getting involved."

"Involved—that's too big a term. I'm just helping out a little."

"I've heard that before."

"But it's true. I know what you're thinking, but believe me, I'm only on the sidelines of this." She looked at his face. "Just for a few moments, let me talk about it. Please. We've got such a short time, and I need your best advice." She paused, sipped the sweet bitter cranberry juice, closed her eyes to see that rock wall on 40 East into the city, the dimpled door of the Ford Ranger pressing closer, closer.

Eyes suddenly open, blinking, she told him, sketched the story, told it all in cool terms, almost like a technical report, the kind he was used to reading. She made it the Kate Banning advisory on Bobbie, on the Taurus, the hose clamp, the puncture, the anonymous call. And of course, the beige pickup. But she could not avoid the dismay on his face. "I know what you're thinking," she said at last. "You're going to tell me this family ought to go to the police."

"Of course that's what I'm thinking. Hell, Kate, you're here a damn month, and already risking your neck."

"No, I'm not. I'm not committed to anything. I'm just—"

Just what? He waited for some statement which, she realized, she could not make. She looked at his face. "Sam, there's one special fact in all this—Bobbie Burnside saved my life. She kept her head in that crazy curve and guided me to a stop. True, I got into the situation because of her. But she got me out of it."

His beer bottle clicked on the tabletop. "Kate, that's a version of the old joke about hitting your head against a wall because it feels so good when you stop."

She sighed. That very irony had not escaped her. He went on. "And what do you owe this woman, Kate? More time? More risks, and all because you're grateful you weren't forced off the highway into a stone embankment?"

"Sam, I get your point. Believe me, I've gone over this stuff so much it feels like a tape playing in my brain. But if you'll just help me think for a minute, think theoretically. I need some feedback. Maybe you'd say I need a flight plan, need to punch in my coordinates."

He laughed. "Don't you woo me with airplane talk, Kate. I can see right through it." Then she laughed too. He said, "Even prisoners get a conjugal visit, and what do I get for an hour between our nation's capital and the Learjet waiting for me at the Dallas/Fort Worth airport?—one beer and a Kate Banning game of *Clue*, country music style. Difference being, this isn't a board game. Is it?"

She looked intently into his face. "Never a board game, Sam. Not with me. And not with you."

He paused, sipping his beer, thoughtful. He held her hand in both of his for a full moment before letting go. "Okay," he said, "consider my options. I could declare this an impasse. I could refuse to play and make a speech and go off in a big huff." He shrugged. "But that would only postpone the next round, wouldn't it? We'd be on the phone in the middle of the night trying to work things out, and we've had too many phone marathons already." She nodded. "So my dear, since I happen to love you and have lost all ability to deny you any damn thing you want, what choice do I have? It's unlawful to kidnap you."

His face took on an earnest look. "So I'll play the game and hope it stays just that, Kate—a game, an intellectual exercise. Maybe you can put it in that category yourself. Maybe you can draw the line, skip the adventuring with Brandi's sister, Cognac or Kahlua . . ."

"Bobbie."

"Bobbie." Sam nodded, rubbed his palms together, and then folded his arms across his chest. "So what's the draw? What's the appeal?"

Kate jiggled the ice in her glass. "She's a country girl from the Tennessee hills. She strikes me as naive and shrewd and stubborn all combined. She's pretty and talks nonstop in down-home sayings that sound like reruns from *Hee-Haw*. 'Colder than a well digger's tail'—that's how she described last winter in Nashville. She said persuading me to take her seriously was like 'lickin' dew off a rose bush.' She said a tough workday made her feel like the 'hind wheels of hard luck.' "

"I get the picture."

Kate swirled her deep crimson juice. "She's charming and irritating both at once. She seems fiercely loyal to her sister, so much that she can't think straight. It's the innocence and the danger, that's what worries me—she's like a child wandering around in a mine field."

She swirled the juice till it eddied. "But as of yesterday, Sam, I was in that minefield too. So I need your help to go forward."

He did not hesitate. He took a deep breath. "Okay," he said, "let's go on to the sister's death. First off, I don't buy the tampering theory. At least not this particular version. Take the power steering. If the steering fluid reservoir was drained, you'd know it the minute you started driving. You'd be struggling with the wheel immediately. Even if it leaked out more slowly, you'd feel the steering stiffen in your hands."

He spread his own hands. "You get several seconds' warning, time enough to pull over. Your own engine died that time on Cape Cod on Route 3, so you know what it's like." He shifted in his chair. "Tell me, at Brandi Burns's accident scene, is there a pullout or a breakdown lane? What's it look like?"

She shrugged. "I don't know. I haven't seen it myself. I'm told it's a suburban intersection."

"Kate Banning hasn't been on the actual scene? I'm shocked."

"Sam—" She leaned forward. "Contrary to what you think,

I have a job to do. I had to get that seatbelt article for the insurance company magazine to the production department today. I am also a mother. I do not spend my days playing Nancy Drew in Nashville." She tried not to be annoyed.

The lines at his mouth eased a little. "You told me everything about the circumstances?"

She nodded. "Nothing remarkable, as far as I know. Brandi Burns went shopping with two friends one afternoon at the Green Hills Mall—it's a mall west of town, upscale specialty shops and boutiques. You could never get a broom or a package of hooks, nothing so useful. Her sister says she went for makeup. It was on the way back home that she died."

Kate shrugged again. She pushed the lime wedge deep into her glass, leaned forward, sipped, sat back. "It seemed at first like a freak accident. The seatbelt that would have saved her, the drizzle that was unusual for this time of year. Oil-slick pavement, the skid. . . ."

"Oh yes, what about the tires? How was the tread when you saw the car?"

Then she felt embarrassed. Not to check out the tires, capital-D dumb. "Okay, it's obvious but I missed it." Yet the thought of returning to that wrecker yard— And to ask Bobbie about the tires and be subjected to more down-home sayings from the hayloft or the fishing hole? Useless.

She said, "I just don't know. Maybe the police report says something, corroborates the accident. I could probably get the sister to look into it." She shook her head. "Even if the tires were bald, Sam, we're back to the phone call on the fluids."

He sipped his beer. "True enough. How do you read that?"

"Two ways. Three, actually. It's totally irrelevant and random, that's one. That's the one I started with. But after seeing that new clamp and feeling the hole in the hose, I had to believe the call was targeted. If it was a well-meant message, the caller probably has some actual information, but for some reason can't act on it."

"Or won't."

"Or won't." She nodded. "In which case, the caller makes Bobbie the active agent."

"And Kate Banning."

She ignored that, looked at him. The waitress approached, and Sam waved her away. Kate said, "On the other hand, suppose the call was a setup. Bobbie has probably told anybody willing to listen that her sister was murdered. This young woman is a talker, and I'd bet she's broadcast her death theory far and wide. Won't shut up about it."

She shook her head. "If Brandi *was* murdered, then whoever killed her must be afraid sooner or later somebody's going to take Bobbie seriously enough to help get an investigation going. So before that happens, silence the loudmouth sister. Arrange another accident. Follow her onto the highway and run her off. A second sister killed."

Sam drank. "A tragic coincidence. And milked for all its worth on *Eyewitness News* at six." Kate was nodding. Sam poured out the last of his beer. "Where does that put you?"

She shrugged. "Personally? Maybe just a bystander, kind of an extra. But if somebody thought Bobbie was going to push for an investigation of her sister's death, then it wouldn't hurt to also dispose of the . . ." The what? Not detective, not the PI. But not the friend either. "The helper. Make it a two-for. Get rid of them both."

Kate looked at her own hand around the icy glass, the thumbnail still darkened from picking at the hose of the Taurus. She remembered the moment when Dennis Corl stared at her blackened hands, the possibility that he could have gone back inside and made a phone call. To a cell phone in a beige pickup? Was that a stretch? Should she try it out on Sam?

He was finishing his beer. A nearby table of businessmen broke up, and she heard them say Birmingham and Baton Rouge. Deep, deeper South. Sam pushed back his bottle and glass. "Kate, there's another angle too. You're assuming the sister is a little scattered but basically honest and innocent. But in fact you don't know this woman, her family, her circumstances. Maybe Bobbie got involved in something likely to make her a target too. Maybe she and her sister were both mixed up in something. Aren't you taking things at face value?"

"Rock face value." Poor humor.

He began whistling a little tune. "There's a song, 'Rocky Top,' fits the Tennessee limestone. Even the Nashville airport here, BNA. It's a good airport, but one runway's a little close to a quarry. Everybody knows about it. Never pull left, or you're in that rock pit; that's the word. Every pilot knows." He looked at her face. "Okay, what this pilot knows is, if the second sister was driven off the road too, there might be a specialist at work—"

"Somebody skilled at making sure that motor vehicles and Tennessee limestone meet up in a very fatal demolition derby." Kate shuddered in the air-conditioning. A moment passed, and she said, quietly, "One thing I do know—Bobbie saved us from a horrific accident."

"And maybe it was just that, Kate—an accident. Bring this back full circle. You started with a bunch of coincidental events, including your run-in with that truck. You know the crazy drivers out there. New England, Tennessee, Anyplace, U.S.A. Nuts, psychopaths, you-name-it. Could have been purely random." He swirled the last of his beer. "You didn't get a look at the driver?"

She shook her head. "Not his face. He wore a baseball cap pulled low. Except that a beige truck was behind me all along Charlotte Avenue."

"Following?"

"Can't say. Tailgater. You know how crazy that makes me. I was glad to turn off."

He nodded and looked at his watch. So did she. That sinking feeling that time was nearly up. He opened his wallet; put down a ten. "Kate, you know my view. You know what I think. If I could, I'd ask you to back off this. But I can't give you orders, and I respect your independence too much to try." He pushed back his chair. "And I have too much pride to beg you."

He paused, shook his head. "Maybe it's like flying is for me, in the blood. I'd be miserable grounded, and maybe you need these . . . these damn crime puzzles like I need flying."

She was standing too. She wanted to protest, deny any such truth. And yet she could not.

He paused, leaned toward her, spoke low in her ear. "You know what I think about this Nashville move, that it's a good idea in lots of ways. But my offer stands, Kate." She walked in lockstep beside him back down the concourse. Sam was headed for the gate to Dallas to pick up a corporate plane. He would be back in Boston after midnight.

Now he leaned close and whispered in her ear, just the way he knew to do, and she tingled and found herself flushing. He said, "Marriage proposal in an airport corridor, it shows how desperate I am. Pitiful. But it's not every day a man has a chance to propose between gates at BNA."

"Sam—"

"Propose for the twenty-ninth time. Maybe thirtieth."

"Sam, I . . . we'll work this out." She found herself blinking back tears again. To work what out? Her need for independence? Her fears that marriage would somehow spoil what they had together? Her sense that she, herself, wasn't ready. Certain of their love but uncertain of marriage, of how life would be day in, day out with Sam Powers and Kelly.

She started to say these things but his look stopped her. "No, it's okay, I'm holding. I'm good at staying in a stack pattern when I have to, when it's necessary. I'm doing my damnedest to re-route my own schedule too, to bring me into Nashville as much as possible. Meantime, I'll be back for the weekend of the fourteenth. Start counting the days."

"Hours, Sam."

He looked directly in her eyes. "I need you, Kate. You know that."

She said, "Call me that name again?"

"What?"

"When you got here—"

"I said, 'Hey, Good lookin'. It's a song title. It's Hank Williams."

"I like it. Makes me feel good."

"Someday you'll like the song too. I want to make sure you're right here to hear it. Healthy and strong. And sexy." At his gate he stopped, bent close in a sweet, strong kiss that brought past, present and future into one moment before he broke away and disappeared through the jetway door.

Two days later, it was October, new page on the calendar. The Sierra Club had picked a western desert scene. Good. Kate did not want to spend the month weeping over a four-color calendar spread of the gold and fiery maples of Vermont or New Hampshire each time she passed her Nashville kitchen bulletin board. Nor cope with Kelly's lament that they could not do their "leaf peeper" day-trip into New England's White Mountains. Let October be represented by desert and succulents in Arizona, at least in the kitchen. Though they shouldn't hide from the season. She ought to ask around about autumn drives. Fall in Tennessee. Get into it with Kelly.

The light, meanwhile, was changing, the days noticeably shortening and Kelly in need of a desk lamp for her room. The last thing she said before school, "Don't forget I do my homework in the dark." On the way home from work, Kate promised to stop at the lamp shop she found in the Yellow Pages.

On this first day of the new month, however, she got stuck on the phone with a writer in Tucson. His assigned piece on hotel and motel swimming pools had come in, but the emphasis was all wrong, and Kate had to break the news that Fleetwood could not publish it in any of its magazines.

The article was supposed to be a how-to guideline for indoor and outdoor pool management, but the hard copy in hand was the paranoid's approach to motel aquatics. Bacteria lurking in kickboards, fungus on poolside furniture, pool chemicals carcinogens, dire warnings about diving boards. The writer practically wanted a skull and crossbones along with *no running, no alcoholic beverages*. And maybe what he wrote was true, the figures looked reliable. But such gloom and doom for a trade magazine? In America?

Would he rewrite? Absolutely not. The exclamation point was audible.

And Kate was sympathetic to a point. This kind of thing happened once in a while, even to her. You got wrapped up in a subject and it took you over. You wanted to start a movement. You found your purpose in life. A national agenda loomed on the horizon of your vision, anything from banning nukes to eradicating head lice. Usually the reformist zeal subsided with the next freelance assignment.

This writer, however, was at the apocalyptic stage. If he wanted to do an exposé, Kate suggested, maybe *Mother Jones* would be interested. He needn't take this problem personally, a matter of matching up the audience to the piece itself. Fits and misfits.

Besides, he was paid, according to Fleetwood policy on work commissioned but not published. Kate had a certain budget for that. A budget, but not a license to print money, and she was too new at this to be inclined to authorize big checks. Good will had a limit. She was accountable to the offices one flight up.

Now the writer charged Kate with a cover-up, suggested she go work for a tobacco company newsletter. The air felt sour when they hung up. Tempted to call it a day, she stayed to write him a civil note. "—and hope we might work together in the future whenever a suitable opportunity arises. Yours sincerely." Better not fax this, nor e-mail it. Allow a cooling off period. Nothing cooler than U.S. mail. She signed the letter, folded it, licked the envelope.

She dropped it in the outgoing bin, taking note of a certain discomfort of her own. This Tucson guy was on the edge, but also a reminder of Kate's liability. Three months ago she was this man's peer, both of them members of a beleaguered and misunderstood fellowship of writers trying to get the truth out and earn a living too. Three months ago she might have been on the receiving end of a call like this.

Now it was very different. In her new riverfront office with a title on the door, she worked for the company. She had the company's interests to advance and protect. So far, it was easy to do because no magazine piece trapped her between conscience and profit. But it could happen. This nasty exchange was a kind of reminder that she had crossed to the other side of the desk. She had the keys, if not the kingdom, to the readers. She was a gatekeeper.

The gate, however, finally opened for the evening. There was just enough time to get to that lamp store on . . . Woodsomething. She reached for the address in her purse. Just about every street in Nashville seemed to have "wood" in it, Westwood, Hillwood, Woodmont, Woodmere, Woodbine. And Bandywood, that was it. The lamp store was on Bandywood. She figured the route to get there, guessing twenty, twenty-five minutes. She found the store, but the lamps were so plentiful Kelly would have to pick her own. Novelties, student lamps, soft light, focused beams, halogens and incandescents. Staggering assortment. She and Kelly could come here on Saturday, mother and daughter; make it an outing.

Back in the car, Kate got her Nashville map to figure out her route home, tracing it with her finger. But as she did, she noticed a certain cluster of streets within a small area. Hillsboro Pike, Glen Echo, Runcroft—

There it was, off Glen Echo, the very street where Brandi Burns died. It was Runcroft. A short street, maybe a short cut for Brandi. The ultimate short cut. Sam's chiding came to mind, his surprise that Kate hadn't been to the actual scene. Well, maybe she ought to have a look. It was close enough, a short distance from here, a very few blocks out of her way. Five minutes total for the round trip. Better to see it firsthand than filtered through Bobbie's description.

And so she turned right on Bandywood and took another right at Abbott-Martin. Then left onto Hillsboro, the traffic inching past the mall and Hillsboro High School on the right, white and rectilinear, something of the Bauhaus idea. A marquee announced a football game Friday. Then the light changed ahead, and she was moving again, watching for Glen Echo, where she turned right again, passed the corner shops and post office and made a left onto Runcroft.

It was a nice residential street of brick ranches, capes, and Tudors. The houses were set back on sizable lots and fronted by the ditches, block-long moats. The driveways over them had huge drainage pipes, each driveway a little bridge. She slowed, looking at the numbers and the street signs. The crash site ought to be just down from the corner.

And there it was, the very place, the house numbers according to Bobbie's information. In her rearview mirror Kate saw one car, a green Pontiac Ventura with a bad muffler. It passed, disappearing into a driveway ahead. Somebody coming home for the evening. She waited until the car and house doors had opened and closed. Then she pulled to the side. There were two boys playing in the street, one with a bike, the other a skateboard. About ten years old.

Should she stop? There was no particular reason, except to stand at the actual spot and see whether the pavement itself showed anything. Once in Boston she saw a shooting, two carfuls of men firing handguns at each other before they sped away, tires peeling rubber while nearby pedestrians stood like statues. The black rubber getaway streaks stayed on the pavement for months and months. Might still be there.

As for this spot, if Brandi Burns had been forced off the road, then the other vehicle might have raced away and left tread marks on the street.

Kate put her car in park, set the emergency brake and got out. As usual in Nashville, there were no sidewalks, her own personal test for a real neighborhood. The asphalt paving had a chalky cast to it, which was good. It would show marks. She walked down the street. Dogs started to bark.

Close to the corner Kate stood over the ditch and looked in. It was bone-dry, but bits of glass twinkled from crevices in the limestone, doubtless headlight shards from the Taurus. There were bunches of dried stems tied with faded yellow and blue ribbons, doubtless the remains of bouquets brought by fans to the site. She took a step down, feeling the rock bite into her leather heel. She identified a point of impact, the stone a powdery white in two places, and a blackened spot where rubber from the bumper stuck, and even an iridescent blue paint streak, also from the bumper and the fender.

From the look of it, some facts seemed unquestionable. The car either took a turn too fast and skidded or fishtailed, or else was forced out of control.

And if the power steering fluid was a problem? She imagined Brandi struggling with the steering and at the same time coping with the menace of another vehicle forcing her to the side, to the edge and beyond. Another driver maybe knowing her route, knowing what turn she would take, exactly where she would accelerate and be vulnerable to a squeeze.

How about a beige pickup?

And had anybody on the street seen it happen? On the east side of Runcroft, Kate noticed, the draperies were dropped and the blinds shut tight against the late afternoon sunlight. Whatever happened on this street from about three to six P.M. this time of the year, the event could go unobserved by half the street.

All the houses, in fact, were set so far back that only the sounds of the impact or of sirens would summon neighbors to witness after the fact. Children out playing after school might have seen something, but it was entirely possible that no one saw Brandi Burns crash into this ditch.

Kate looked at the street pavement. Oil spots, plastic chips from some child's toy, Big Wheels. But no telltale rubber streak from a car or truck in full getaway. Nothing but the glitter of the glass bits in the rocky ditch.

She walked back to her car, the late afternoon stillness broken only by the birds and dogs barking. A month ago a woman had died here. An ambulance had come screaming, and police cruisers, and the tow truck. Neighbors had doubtless come out to watch the rituals of a fatality.

Now, except for the sparkle in the ditch, there was no marker of any kind, only the pastoral green and quiet of a suburban street. Kate opened her car door, slid in, started the engine, drove with the radio off. No *All Things Considered*, no Reba McEntire. For twenty minutes she made her way in silence, solemn, a private memorial drive that brought her to the tucked away condo she now called home, just four units so that everybody felt secluded, each unit divided by the great magnolia trees. Her car crunched on the pea gravel drive.

But in the visitors' spot, she saw a police cruiser and another car too, the dark red Malibu she remembered from days ago downtown. And she heard the voice before she saw the Nashville Metro policeman, his spiffy creased navy uniform, his badge and gun. And the woman beside him with the hair, the voice.

"Bobbie."

"Kate, this here's Officer Kemble. Bein' so nice to help me out."

He nodded. "Off duty, Miz Banning. Just doing Miz Burnside here a favor at this time. This is not in the line of duty."

Kate stared. Why here at her own home? And her daughter, where was Kelly?

As if Bobbie read her mind. "We just got here, Kate. I knocked to see if you'd got home yet. I said howdy to your Kelly and told her we'd just wait out here a minute. Officer Kemble was about to go. We'd've missed you."

Kate looked from one to the other. The policeman cleared his throat. "Ma'am, Miz Burnside came into the station this afternoon. She came with the possible intent to file a complaint pursuant to the death of her sister. Miz Burnside is considering making a formal complaint."

"—so we went out there again, Kate. Officer Kemble went with me to the wrecker yard. Hillgate. We were gonna see. I was gonna show him. That was the proof."

"Miz Burnside—"

"—and it's gone. Just gone."

Kate stared. "The car?"

"Disappeared."

"Sold, ma'am—" The policeman stepped forward, mirror-finish regulation shoes crunching in the gravel. "Ma'am, the vehicle in question, it's been sold."

"For parts. Do you believe that, Kate?"

She looked back and forth from one to the other.

"Miz Burnside is a little upset. This is the kind of sale that takes place. The wrecker yard got an offer, the car was sold for parts, and the buyer had it hauled off."

"Just got rid of it."

"A customary kind of sale, like I was trying to tell Miz Burnside. I'm not real sure she understands."

"Rid of it. All the evidence. Bought and sold it, and it's gone. The proof my sister was killed."

Kate still looked from one to the other. The cop so neat, like an older brother. And Bobbie nearly hopping on the pea gravel in her sandals. Kate managed to say, "Who bought it? Who bought the car?"

"Private party, ma'am."

"—private party. What do you think about that?" Bobbie cried out, "The police just have to find it. They have to investigate." Her voice squeaked. The gravel crunched.

Officer Kemble shifted his weight, stepped back. "I just wanted to leave Miz Burnside in good hands. She insisted on coming here. I offered to follow her home. This is not in the official line of duty, understand."

Officer Kemble gave a little half-salute and got into his cruiser, inched to the street. They stood and watched him go. In the deepening shadows Kelly opened the front door and started their way. The sound of the cruiser driving off. A random thought passed through Kate's mind, that it wasn't quite as hot, and Bobbie had painted her toenails.

"Kate? They could get away with murder. What are we gonna do?"

Kate found herself listening to the *we*.

Chapter Five

The Cumberland smelled like mud. The riverfront brick and cement at First Avenue radiated midday heat. Crossing First, Kate looked left toward the stockade fencing of Fort Nashboro, the site of the founding of the city. To commemorate that occasion, two huge bronze buckskinned frontiersmen named Robertson and Donelson faced one another in a legendary handclasp. A flock of grade schoolers in shorts and backpacks were crossing First Avenue on a field trip to see them.

Kate sat down on a wood and iron bench that overlooked the river. She scanned the scene once again—the fourth graders with teachers and parent chaperones, a teen couple, retirees. It was Friday. Nobody watching. No beige truck. She smoothed the skirt of last year's deep blue challis that would carry into winter.

This was her meeting, her call. And she wanted this moment for mental planning, though three men in greasy twills loitered, and one broke away to make the approach. Did she have a cigarette? Sorry, she didn't smoke. Match? No. Dollar to spare? She handed over the dollar.

"Kate." She turned. "Why Kate Banning, you *are* a soft touch."

A few minutes late, Bobbie sat down too. Kate wished she hadn't seen that little exchange. She had conditions to impose, a few laws to lay down. A stern image would work better. Bobbie was still in her work uniform, the gray skirt and burgundy jacket with the Quality Seven crest. Her bracelets jingled, and the gardenia perfume marked her turf.

"So Kate—got here quick as I could. We had a sales seminar, and I just couldn't leave until I checked off the coffee service for the meetin' rooms."

"That's fine, I just got here myself." Kate was deliberately matter-of-fact.

"I did what you said, went out there to the wrecker yard yesterday. My cousin Floyd Akers went too, like you said not to go alone. Floyd's real handy with machines, fixes anything from a broken heart to the crack of dawn."

"And?"

"It's their policy not to say who buys parts or whole totaled cars. But I was real sweet to him and Floyd talked cars like guys do, and we got out of him that the buyer's over in Cheatham County."

Cheatham? Counties were huge in Tennessee, territories big as Rhode Island or Connecticut.

"The buyer's name's Clyde Bunrat. But Kate, there's no Bunrat in the phone book. I looked. Spelled it every way I could. Two *n*'s, two *t*'s, and one of each. Floyd tried too, and my mama, and we near wore out the phone book, but there's no name like that."

"What about the check, Bobbie? Did Hillgate have a record of the check?"

"It was cash. Whoever bought it paid cash."

Kate sighed. Dead end already. Odds were, if Brandi's car was a murder weapon, it was through a chop shop or crushed into a cube by now. She said, "Did you make the pitch about hoping to buy back the car?"

"Family was hopin' to acquire it. I told him so."

"And—?"

"Just nodded his head and said how sorry we didn't make an offer the day we came out. He wouldn't say a word more about this buyer, where I could get in touch with him."

Kate nodded. Then, "Bobbie, you didn't wear this to the wrecker yard, did you?"

She looked down. "Awful uniform, isn't it? We all hate it. Quality Seven ought to get us a designer." She pushed back her hair. "Kate, what's the matter. You upset?"

Kate wet her lips. Dennis Corl now knew exactly where Bobbie Burnside worked and thus could be found. You planned everything out, and a variable escaped you. Life as usual.

"So Kate, I came down here to meet you like you asked. Maybe you have some idea about Brandi's car?"

Kate had only one—if the police formally investigated, then Hillgate Wreck and Tow would be required to release all information on the sale. She decided not to tell this fact now, however, because she had a statement to make.

But so did Bobbie. "I know you hated me coming to your house Tuesday evening, Kate. I could tell that upset you, my bringing a policeman."

"It wasn't the policeman as such. It was crossing a boundary into my private life. My home, my daughter."

"—sweet as she could be. I can tell you bring her up not to open the door or let strangers in. She kept the chain lock on. She knew what to do."

Kate said, "Living in the city, we . . ." She stopped. A pickup was moving up First Avenue—beige—heading toward them. It slowed.

"Bobbie, that truck."

It slowed to a crawl. It inched forward in the lane closest to their bench. Almost at idle now.

"Kate, should we run?"

The windshield was tinted very dark. Shape of a man behind the wheel. The engine gunned, gears gnashed.

"Kate—"

It was almost stopped. The driver leaned toward them. Kate saw the baseball cap turned backwards.

"Kate, look at that passenger door, it's all stoved in. The passenger door."

Her neck prickled, stung. The gears mashed again, steel teeth. The exhaust felt like hot breath. Then a roar, explosion.

Blue fumes, clouds from the rear. She looked at the hood, saw the silver curling horns.

"Bobbie, it's a Dodge truck. Dodge Ram."

It was moving off, gears engaged. "It's the clutch, engine trouble. It's somebody different. We only thought—"

The truck moved past them. They were left panting in the thick exhaust, relieved, weak. Bobbie coughed. Their heads turned in sync, watching the Dodge Ram being pickup limp up the hill to their right and disappear. They heard sounds like faint firecrackers. Backfiring.

The prickling stopped at Kate's neck. She felt limp. Engine trouble, clutch problems. Nothing to do with Kate Banning or Bobbie Burnside.

But how to take charge in a minute like this, when mutual terror leveled everything?

Bobbie said, "—like one of those *déja vu*s. Anything beige, any guy in a ball cap, I just freak out."

Kate started to agree, but refrained. No more kinship of fear. She had an agenda and must take the lead. "Bobbie," she said, "let's try to get back on track. We need to understand something." She paused to take a deep breath. "First, my private life is just that—private. My home is not a drop-in center. And my daughter is off-limits. I don't involve her in my work. Besides—"

She cleared her throat, gasoline fumes lingering. She needed to make a point. "I don't know how much help I can be. I have a job here, and claims on my time, and—"

"And you're not a real official detective. I know all that." Bobbie looked down at the bricks. "You don't have to repeat it again, Kate." She sighed. "If Officer Kemble'd just taken me serious. He was real nice, but you know, in some way he didn't take me serious."

"You mean he didn't believe you?"

Bobbie stared out toward the river. "I think he thinks I'm a little touched in the head. Mental."

Kate bit her lip. Acting impulsively, this woman already squandered an important opportunity to gain a police ally. "It's always good to know the cops," she said, and paused to let it sink in. In Boston, she had her police contacts, a couple of detectives' cards in her wallet to this day. More than useful, they were often essential. "Nobody in your family knows an officer with the Nashville police? You've asked? Your relatives?"

"—Floyd and all the rest too. Kate, I told you that day at the Hermitage Hotel; we already did try. Back home, we knew the sheriff and some of the deputies too. First-name basis. But that was in the country, and Nashville's too big, 'specially these days. Officer Kemble says there's nothing much to go on."

She wet her lips. "I asked Officer Kemble, you know. I pressed him real hard. He looked up the files and said the record showed one of the neighbors on Runcroft Street heard the crash and looked out and called 911, and so the uniform division got the first call, and the beat car went out. Then they got the ambulance, and Brandi got taken to the hospital, and the police on the scene wrote out their reports. He said Sergeant Klingman was in charge, and he's one of the best on the force."

Bobbie sat straight on the bench, as if at military attention in order to get through these facts without crying. "He told me the reports are complete down to the details—like the neighbor that called is a man named Eck, and temperature in Nashville at three-thirty P.M. on September fourth was ninety degrees. There was no sign of a criminal act, that's what Officer Kemble said. The pavement was slick from oil and drizzle, that's what the reports say. It's all so detailed, there was no reason for a criminal investigation."

She shooed a yellowjacket that buzzed her hair. "And the pathologist's report showed no drugs or alcohol in Brandi's blood and no sign of bodily injury except the broken neck from the impact of the crash. They didn't even ask a detective to come out. It was open and closed."

Kate nodded. Maybe somebody else on the force could be brought in some way or other. "I'll try to work on it," she said, "figure something out." Then Kate deliberately lowered her voice and spoke more slowly. "Bobbie, tell me, who would want to kill your sister?"

"Well now, as to that . . ." Her eyes glazed in some faraway vision. She said nothing.

"Who wanted her dead? Who wants you dead? Even both of us?" Kate shifted on the bench, sat straighter. "This is no time to keep quiet, Bobbie. Not to me. If you really want help, you've got to do two things—open up to me and keep quiet every place else. We need an agreement. I have conditions. First, the gag order on you." Bobbie flinched. Her bangle bracelets dinged and her hands fluttered.

Kate said, "That's very blunt, but it's for your own good and mine. If somebody killed Brandi, they went to a lot of trouble making it look accidental. Right now nobody's raising questions about the accident but you. The more you talk, the more you endanger yourself and make it harder to get information. Killers get nervous. You expose them, and they get desperate and try to kill again."

She turned toward Bobbie and crossed her legs. "You're loyal to your sister, and I respect that. You're protective of her memory. But it looks like Brandi had a mortal enemy. Simple as that. As close as you were, that enemy could be somebody you know. So my help comes with your silence. That sounds bossy, but that's the deal—because the police won't work on this until they see evidence of criminal wrongdoing. Getting the evidence is crucial. All they've got right now is a simple accident case and a grieving sister they think is hysterical."

"—but I am. That's how I feel lots of the time."

She said it in a plaintive, pleading way. Looking up at Kate, she seemed at the moment helpless in sorrow. And Kate backed off, paused, moved down on the bench. It was a fine line between firm and cruel. Very lightly she touched Bobbie's shoulder, her fingertips against the rigid cloth of the motel uniform. The cloth itself felt harsh. This young woman ought to be in soft and comforting fabrics, silk or a fine cotton. Yet Kate could not yield to sympathy. This bench had to be a grille. If necessary, Bobbie had to be shocked into cooperation. "Have you driven I-40 in the last few days?"

"Scared to."

"Good. That's healthy. Scared and cautious, that's what you need to be." Skip over scared-to-death. "Do we have a deal? You talk to me and keep quiet everywhere else. Deal?"

The murmured "okay" was almost inaudible.

Kate slipped a small notebook from her purse. She checked her watch. "I've got about twenty more minutes, Bobbie, so let's start with the car. Do you know where Brandi had it serviced last? And when?"

"At the Ford dealer, English Ford out on Eighth. She was real good about that, following the manual. Oil changes and lubes. Took it in last July, I believe. No . . . August, it was August."

"You have the service records?"

"They were in the glove compartment."

Kate bit her lip. Another mistake at the wrecker yard. Another *should have*.

"Okay, let me check that out at the service center. You okay?"

She had folded her hands, possibly to still them. "Throat's kind of dry. Feels like the third degree, Kate. You're makin' me squirm like a worm in hot ashes."

Kate blinked. These sayings seemed like a second language. She said, "I can't help you unless I ask questions."

"Do my best. Fire away."

"Brandi's love life. Did she have a boyfriend?"

Bobbie paused, wet her lips as if to prepare her statement. "Not lately. She dated Roy Benniger for a short little while."

"The Virgo executive?"

She nodded. "Got dazzled for about ten minutes, then figured out what a jerk he is. French cuff shirts and gold bracelets—all flash. Fact is, that man's got a roving eye, and my sister wouldn't lower herself to get in cat fights over him. Her career was launched; she didn't need him. She let him go." Bobbie shrugged. "It comes down to, lots of guys wanted to date Brandi, but this last year she got real busy with her career."

"And before that?"

"For a good long time she went with Wade Rucker. They were together two, three years off and on. Brandi broke it off."

"Why?"

"Because that boy's got his feet planted in quicksand, and my sister finally saw it.

"To be frank, Kate, most of us couldn't understand what Brandi saw in him, except his looks. He's got no gumption. Sort of thinks the world owes him a livin'. Chip on his shoulder. There was some friction in the family over it. My family's big on work."

"What's he do for a living?"

"Music—sort of."

"Did Brandi's success make him jealous?"

"I wouldn't say it that way." She paused, considering. "Her song writin' with other people, that got him real upset. Wade couldn't stand it. See, when they first got together, she was just a country girl with a lot of dreams, and he was coming on like a big songwriter and musician. He plays bass in a band and fools around on guitar.

"Anyway, he bragged how he knew all the big bosses on Music Row. He was gonna help out little Brandi Burnside, let her sing a few tunes with his band. First time Wade Rucker heard her songs, he stuck to my sister like glue. They'd write a song together, Brandi and him, and I couldn't find nothing of him in it, not the words, not the music.

"Brandi said he was her inspiration. Fact is, he wanted to cash in on her music, and she finally figured that out. You ought to talk to Judy Swan about that. She could tell you a couple things about Wade. Judy's over at Trystar Music, right on Music Row. That's Brandi's publisher."

"You mean like ASCAP?"

"No, Trystar's the publisher, where they copyright songs and demo them and try to get 'em recorded." Kate handed over her notebook and pen, and Bobbie scrawled a number. "Judy'll remember real well. She knows Wade's all vine and no taters."

"How did they break up?"

"My sister came to her senses. Told him it wasn't working out, and she needed her own space. He begged to be her manager, crew, whatever. He was drinkin' quite a bit, and I think she saw the trouble comin'. She stayed firm. Sure wasn't gonna let him drive that bus."

"The tour bus?"

"Luxury liner, like the song says. It's a Silver Eagle. Gorgeous. Got a kitchen and a grand salon, queen size bed and wood inlays like you wouldn't believe. Rosewood and mahogany. They leased it for Brandi's touring."

"And how did Wade react to all that?"

She paused, and Kate saw her blink. "He's a sulker." Bobbie said it a little too fast, as if that term had come in handy before.

"What's that mean, exactly?"

She wet her lips slowly. "He'd sort of hang around. Come out to our place. Brandi wouldn't let him in, so he'd sit out front in his car and drink and play tapes real loud with the windows down and speakers up full volume. Tapes they made together, living room stuff. After awhile he'd leave, kickin' up dust, tires squealin'." Bobbie paused. She blinked several times again and looked at Kate. "All wrapped up in himself, but he makes a small package. Mostly put him down as a sulker."

Mostly—but not always? Kate said, "What does *mostly* mean?"

Bobbie was blinking again. She opened her mouth and then closed it, and her face again looked remote. She said, "Means just what it says." She looked at Kate as if to see whether she was satisfied or if something more were required. Then she cleared her throat. "Means most of the time that boy pouts and frets when things don't go his way. Makes a typical nuisance of himself. I expect most every woman meets up with at least one like that." She shrugged.

Kate paused, looking closely at Bobbie's face. The expression was bland. No, it was vacant, like photos of models. It seemed aggressively opaque. It made her uneasy. Kate said, "He plays in a band?"

"Bass for Yucca Flat. That's their name. Plays a little guitar too, and sings, or thinks he does. That band doesn't play too many dates. Fraternity gigs over at Vanderbilt and off-hours at the beer joints on lower Broadway. Like Mac's Hitchin' Post. You could ask Judy Swan about that too. She booked them for a while. They think they're funky. I think they sound terrible."

Kate nodded. "Just to deal with the obvious, Bobbie—I assume Wade Rucker does not drive a beige pickup? Or any of his friends?" Her head shake was vigorous. "One more question, then. What about 'Envy Green'? That line about pain— 'the color of pain, the color she's seen.' Is that about Wade?"

"I don't know. I've sure thought about it, but I just don't know. He had plenty to envy. I was trying to remember anything green between the two of them. Two years ago Wade gave Brandi a gold pendant for her birthday, some kind of green stone she thought was an emerald but was worthless as glass. And the fuel tank of his old motorcycle, it's painted green too. Other than that, I don't know."

Bobbie reached for her purse and took out a handkerchief she held to her nose, her eyes. Monogrammed. "BB" in tiny red scrollwork embroidery. Bobbie's voice was audible but metallic. " 'Bout a month before she died, my sister told me she was scared. Said it was all too much, too big. And too fast. Too many decisions. Said somebody was so worked up over her good luck they might try to hurt her bad. She told me, if anything happens to me, the reason's in 'Envy Green.' It's in my notebook, she said. Look for 'Envy Green' in my notebook."

"And did you?"

She shook her head. "Didn't need to, Kate. The song was released by the time she died, so anybody could just listen to it. You, me, or anybody. CDs, cassettes, every place you look." She shook her head. "I must've listened to that song a hundred times, Kate, and I can't make it out. It's a secret Brandi took with her."

"—or a secret waiting to be told."

Bobbie shrugged as if to shake off the burden. "Kate, my sister's life was mostly blessed. People loved Brandi. The troubles she had . . . why, who doesn't have a no-'count boyfriend, at least one? Who doesn't have somebody come into their life and turn out to be some kind of leech? Who doesn't have trouble with stress and a boss that's a jerk? I mean, this is life."

"It's life, Bobbie, but it's not usually death." The bench was very quiet. A water taxi engine throttled down at the landing, and a yellowjacket hovered by her knee and buzzed Bobbie's face as she waved it away again. The fourth graders were trooping back to their bus. TGIF.

"Kate, you couldn't know my sister and not think the world of her. Everybody loved Brandi."

"Not everybody, Bobbie. At least one person hated her enough to want her dead. We won't get anywhere unless you face that fact."

But Bobbie Burnside said nothing.

Kate sighed. To know her was to love her, that was the sister's party line. Was it for public consumption or did Bobbie know something she could not bear to say? Did she need to believe the killer came from outside the warm circle of loved ones, the friends and acquaintances? In country music, didn't they call each other friends and neighbors? How much cozier to have the homicide be an outside job, and the investigator too. All outsiders, even if statistics showed seventy-five percent of all murder victims killed by somebody known to them.

A moment passed. Bobbie said, "You ought to talk to my mama, Kate. She has certain views. She'd like to visit with you. Have you out to the house. Bring your little girl, my mama loves kids. Love to feed you all."

"That's nice, Bobbie, but I never mix my daughter into my—" What? Her work? Her hobby? Charity?

"It's not to mix things up, Kate. It's to be friendly. That's what my mama would say. Just friendly folks. I can't say it better."

Kate stood. She put the notebook back into her purse.

"That's nice, Bobbie. I appreciate the invitation. It's time to get back to work. Let's stay in touch. Remember our deal."

"You sound like my mama. She's got a sign in the kitchen that says 'you can learn more from listenin' than talkin'.'" Kate left her swatting the yellowjackets that mistook her for a gardenia bush.

Back upstairs she opened the notebook to the scrawled phone numbers and called Grady Stamps's office. A woman's voice answered. "—calling at the suggestion of Bobbie Burnside," Kate said. "Just wanted to speak with Grady for a few minutes."

"Kate, you just missed him; he's in a meeting. Leave your number, and we'll try to get back to you."

Try? How hard could it be? A manager's job was to hang around a client, be the official pilotfish. Certainly respond to queries. Though with Brandi's death, Grady might not think it necessary to return calls any longer, not even from a newfound family helper. Figure the manager was now an ex-manager in exit mode. Kate left her number anyhow and went to her desk.

The world might be electronic, but at the moment Kate was an old-fashioned editor facing a copyediting question in an article on low stress recreation, namely, bird-watching. She read the same sentence over and over: "Nesting cardinals are found in pairs, and some enthusiasts camcorder them year round."

Camcorder as a verb? Lots of nouns become verbs in a culture that sits all day in meetings, cars, trucks, even cockpits. Action centered in the language, not the body. Managers use zippered planning books called Day Runners, and the only running was the zipper. Channel surfers never even get wet.

So, to camcorder? Kate Banning as the grammar police. Between rigid and sloppy, where was the line? She reread the paragraph, the sentence. And was this really worth the minutes she was spending on it? Would Rome fall either way? Okay, let it through. If readers and/or the fifth floor howled, she'd tighten up.

Another try at Grady Stamps's office. Another meeting. Maybe this afternoon he'd be free to return her call. She was pondering the "maybe" and the "free" when her phone rang. Fleetwood fifth floor calling. If Kate had a moment, Mr. Amberson would like a word with her. It was the most courteous of Southern summonses, a modest request that she kindly spare a moment for her boss.

Vowing to find a salon for a haircut by week's end, she brushed her hair back, ran the tube of *Bronze Leaf* across her mouth, centered the dress belt buckle that always inched sideways. Then she climbed the stairs two at a time, the slight clench in her stomach, the dread that something might be amiss in her office. Some mistake already come to the chief's attention? "Mister Amberson is expecting you, Kate. Go right in."

He was tall, early fifties, light blue suit, thinning blond hair, long face, and he spoke in a deep drawl of the kind you heard from Southern senators and generals on TV. They stood in his front-to-back loft space, and he shook her hand warmly. "Good to see you, Kate."

Kate said, "Such a wonderful view." It was both true and neutral. The opening gambit was his.

He said, "I worry over it. Sometimes I think views of the Cumberland help everybody work better here at Fleetwood, but at other times I think we're all too distracted for our own good." He smiled a courtly smile. "Maybe you can help us figure out which it is."

Then he gestured toward a seating group, mocha leather sofa and chairs. He offered coffee; she declined. "Kate, I just wanted to tell you how pleased we are to have you with us. We already can see the benefits, and I'm tickled pink with the last quarter's figures. We've had two more inquiries over the past week, companies interested in Fleetwood taking on their magazines. One is a regional airline, though I better not say the name."

He watched her face, gauging response. "That would mean some additional staff, of course, and we'll need to talk in detail if they get serious. I just wanted to sound you out on the possibility."

"Mr. Amberson—Hughes—my office will have another production cycle complete by mid-November, and we can talk specifics about capacity then. But it's exciting to think of expansion, and I'm confident the first-rate writers are out there to back up any new Fleetwood proposals. We can offer a quality product in an expanding market. I'm confident of that."

"Good, good." Kate hoped her language was tinged enough with business-speak. Hughes Amberson toyed with his black Mont Blanc pen. "That's what I need to know, that the writers are out there. That's the well we draw from. That's the signal we need to move ahead." He capped the pen, chunky as a cigar. "We'll take it from there. But I do mean it when I say I hope you're as happy as Fleetwood is. And your daughter too. We like the Fleetwood family to be content. Is there anything more we can do? You finding everything else you need on the personal side? Services?"

Kate thought of Hughes Amberson's gleaming Jaguar, of service reps who probably spoke with a straight face of "coachwork" and the "glove box." She had found the local Minit-Lube. She said, "We're working things out step by step." She wanted to seem at ease. "Personally, my daughter and I are settling in. It takes a while in a new school, and I'll be looking for a music teacher next. She played flute in the school band."

"Ah, flute. Lovely. A classical instrument. We need more of the classics in our city these days, I dare say. Sometimes I think the guitars and fiddles are taking over."

"You don't like country music?"

He smiled indulgently. "Well, everybody in Nashville has to like country music, don't they? It's economic lifeblood. Even if it sounds whiny and the words to those songs, well, good gracious—" He leaned back in his chair and smiled. "We have a little family story. A cousin of ours married a fellow from San Francisco, a graduate of Stanford University, and he wanted to write country music songs. He came down here and stayed a few weeks with us. We made some calls and got him together with some local songwriters. But he went back to San

Francisco because it turned out his lyrics weren't simple enough.

"Imagine—he couldn't write that far down. Like the school textbooks they complain get dumbed down, well, this fellow couldn't dumb down the songs low enough." He chuckled. "He's a tax lawyer now, very successful."

Kate tried to seem pleasant. She was thinking of "Fool Moon" and "Envy Green." And Reba McEntire's voice in "Whoever's in New England." And Bobbie singing at the intersection on the way to the junkyard. The words were simple, but not dumb. And the twang was not a whine.

She wanted to say something back to him, an on-the-other-hand kind of statement. But what? Guitar strings and heart-strings would sound trite. Her country music database of four songs hardly entitled her to an informed opinion. She said, "There's a certain folksong, 'It's a Gift to Be Simple'; it's an old Shaker hymn. I used to joke about it, until I finally understood that 'simple' means essential. Maybe some country music is like that."

He smiled. "Give it the benefit of every doubt, Kate, but when those guitars start to sound like howling cats, just remember we've got some fine classical music here in Nashville."

She smiled and nodded. Hughes Amberson was rising, so this exchange was at an end. It would become one of those talks she rewrote in her head, wishing she hadn't folded even if he was her boss.

Another handshake and she was back one floor down, dispatching magazine manuscripts and wondering what airline seat pockets Fleetwood might be stuffing in another year or so. By three-thirty, however, when the odds of Grady Stamps calling back seemed dimmer by the minute, Kate packed up her black canvas briefcase tote. Grady's office was an unlisted number without a published address, but Trystar Music was in the phone book. Best to drop in. If Judy Swan was in a meeting, Kate could wait a while, maybe chat with whoever's at the front desk.

So at three forty-five she checked her voice mail, left word for her assistant, then shouldered her purse and picked up the briefcase of evening homework. She walked up Second to Union to the parking garage and tossed the case in the back of the Century. Air-conditioner on blast, she drove out Broadway and fifteen minutes later cut over to Seventeenth, Music Row. A few tourists straggled from the one attraction located on Seventeenth, RCA Studio B, a one-story gray cinderblock where Elvis once recorded. No sightings today.

Kate eased off the gas and slowed to twenty-five, tracked the street numbers that got higher block by block—music management, lawyers, real estate, booking agencies, Music City Coiffures. What kind of haircut would they give her— waves shaped like a G-clef? Forget that. She noted the music publishing names. Copper Kettle Music, Sure-Fire Music, Seven Seas Music.

Trystar Music was out toward the end of the street in a small clapboard cottage between a brick four square and a duplex. The four square had become a dental practice, and the duplex shared a Christian music agency and an insurance office.

She parked around the block and followed the cement walk to the wood porch, which felt soft underfoot. The paint on the clapboards, she noticed, was freshened only in spots, which gave the building a blotched look. One shutter had broken and was nailed up to the wall. The heavy front door was mission oak with glass panes, one of which showed fresh putty. The door operated from an electronic lock, and Kate was buzzed in when she pressed the button.

"I'm looking for Judy Swan."

The sharp-featured woman at the desk wore a batik blouse with a scoop neck and a gold cross on a chain. She had straight-cut bangs and hair that probably kinked in damp weather. Right now she bent over the desk shuffling a messy pile of papers and folders, some of which slipped to the floor with a splash.

"That's me. I'm Judy." She had a soft but firm voice, a good phone voice. "Excuse our appearance. We're moving next week, and if that's not enough, somebody broke in last night."

"A robbery?"

"Kids, probably. When they're after drugs, they hit the dentists next door. Maybe we're just extra. Looks like whoever did this just made a mess and trashed the file cabinet. Nothing missing that I can see. Not even my boom box. Don't think they stayed long enough to wreck the place. Probably got scared and ran off."

She stooped to pick up papers from a brown tweed carpet that was worn and stained. "What can I do for you?"

"My name's Kate Banning. I'm trying to help out Bobbie Burnside, and she suggested I talk to you. She says you know something about Wade Rucker."

"Wade? And the Burnside family—oh, God, those two names shouldn't even be in the same breath. That poor family, your heart just goes out to them. Brandi . . . such a horrible thing. Terrible." She shook her head. "And that Wade. He's nothing but trouble. Real bad penny."

She stopped. "Hey, wait a minute, bad penny. You know that saying, 'a bad penny always turns up'? 'Scuse me a minute, maybe that's a hook. Let me write it down. You never know when a song idea might pop up." She jotted on the flipped-over side of a daily date calendar page.

Kate said, "My first grade teacher loved that saying. I haven't heard it since."

Judy Swan sighed. "Maybe you're right. It's a bygone; nobody says it anymore. Well, so much for that great platinum idea." She crumpled the calendar sheet.

Though, Kate noticed, she didn't throw it into the trash can. She said, "You're a songwriter?"

"Try to be. Wanna be. Like three quarters of the people in this town. I came here from Indianapolis six years ago to try it. The first guy I ran into in the music business was Wade Rucker. My luck. He comes on like he's just biding time till his ship comes in. Big ship, see, ocean liner. It's docking any day. Meanwhile, he's gonna be a big-hearted guy and let me help out with his bookings, which mostly turn out to be fraternity parties like Gamma Nu and morning gigs in bars on lower

Broadway. Country music for the winos. The bonus is, I also get to write a few songs with him."

"As a co-writer, you mean?"

She nodded. "Like that old line about come-up-and-see-my-etchings. It's 'let's write together,' so you do and you show him your stuff. He says you've got very raw talent, but he'll help you out of the kindness of his heart. He'll be your song doctor. Of course, he'll need co-write credit, meaning if the song gets anywhere, he gets half the royalties."

"So you're saying he's a con man."

"Leech is more like it. His big brilliant idea was a take-off on 'D-I-V-O-R-C-E.' Only he wanted to make it D-E-V-O-R-S-E. The hook was, the woman singing it was so upset by her divorce that she couldn't spell. I told him Tammy Wynette and Billy Sherrill would have their lawyers all over him. He backed off that one."

Kate nodded. A goofy example, but the exploitive side of Wade Rucker was checking out. If Judy Swan also saw the sulking side, she wasn't eager to say so. She busied herself for the moment in another rifled batch of file papers. Kate couldn't have picked a less opportune moment to drop in.

She looked around. If Judy Swan had spent much of the day restoring order, why wasn't the place a little neater? For instance, wouldn't she straighten the pencils and pictures and water the dry plant? Instead, it seemed as though the robbery had mainly bypassed the work space and centered instead in the one rust-red file cabinet, which was gouged at the lock and bashed on top from repeated blows, maybe a crowbar. Each point of impact looked like a half-moon, or maybe a cloven hoof.

Judy Swan was shaking her head. " 'Course, there's nothing much left in the building because of the move. No recording equipment, no audio components. Made it lots easier when the police came. The glass guy too. They dusted for fingerprints, and then he put in a little glass pane and some putty. When I get these folders put back, it'll be just like before."

She straightened a few of the folders as if to demonstrate. Kate noticed a certain pallor under her eyes. Despite the claims of normality, Judy Swan was probably shaken by the break-in. People in her state often needed to talk, to recite their story several times. Answering questions for the police wouldn't be enough. Kate said, "It's got to be a shock, coming into work to find the broken glass and not knowing whether the robber is still inside."

"Oh, for sure." Judy Swan gave a nervous grin and shook her head. "I was a wreck. Took a couple Valium." She tugged the cross on its chain. "It was weird, though. Whoever it was came onto the porch and broke out the little glass door panel with a rock and just reached in and turned our deadbolt and walked in. Easy as pie. Too easy. We should have put a steel grillwork over that door glass a long time ago, as the police told me loud and clear."

She paused, forehead furrowing. "Thing is, we have a security system, but it was turned off. See over there?" Kate looked. There was a wall-mounted keypad with a light glowing green. "It's like most of them," Judy Swan said. "You punch in the numbers to arm it, punch in the same code to disarm. The light goes from green to red when you do. I could have sworn I set it last night when I left. I mean, barring Alzheimer's, I'd swear to it."

Kate tried for nonchalance in her shrug. "But the police must have asked who else has the code?"

"Sure, Cliff Harnes does. He's Trystar's president, but he's in Europe right now. Cliff and me, that's it. It's a small shop here, and the part-timers don't have the combination. Of course, with the move, there's been a lot of in and out, different people. But not even our writers have the combination. When they come to use the rooms, Cliff or I have to be here—"

"Use the rooms? You mean like bedrooms?"

Judy Swan laughed out loud. "Oh, you're not in the music business, are you?" She laughed again. "Bedrooms, that's a good one."

She dabbed the tissue at her nose. "No, Trystar's not a motel. I'm talking about song writing rooms, like little offices or studies." She pointed to an archway. "Back down that hall are four different rooms the songwriters can work in, all specially soundproofed. You know 'Lonesome Slant of Light'? It went to six on the charts. 'The Hills of Tomorrow'? How 'bout 'Denver Lover'?"

Kate shook her head, feeling somewhat embarrassed.

"Well, they've all been hits, and they all came out of those four rooms."

At that moment footsteps came from that hall, and a voice said, "Okay, Judy, I've done 'bout all I can—oh, hey, hello there!" A petite redhead stopped in front of Kate. "Didn't know Judy had company. Startled me for a minute."

"Becky, this is Kate Banning. Kate, Becky Yowell."

Close up, she was young and vibrant, tiny and yet in command. She wore black leggings, thong sandals and an oversized light blue T-shirt knotted at the waist. Her features were sharp, with high cheekbones and wide-set hazel eyes. She carried a guitar case in her left hand and a big woven macramé bag over the right shoulder. She shook hands firmly. There was something familiar about her.

"Pleased to meet you, Kate." She dusted her palms together. "Been giving Judy a hand with cleanup. Good thing I stopped by, Judy would be workin' all by herself, wouldn't you, Jude?" She winked at Judy Swan and shook her head disapprovingly. "Too stressful to do this all alone. Creepy. Good thing I showed up." She looked at Kate. "Just so happens I came over this afternoon to use one of the writin' rooms, second one on the left, my lucky room—you a writer?"

Kate shook her head no.

Becky went right on. "Wanted to see if I could get somewhere with this one particular half-a-song spinning around in my head for the past two months. My uncle dropped me off. He's visiting his old Army buddy at the VA hospital. I walk in, and lo and behold, here's Trystar looking like a hurricane hit. Got to pitch in and give a hand." She ran a hand through her shimmering red hair.

Judy Swan said, "Not a cashbox in the place, not a piece of equipment you could pawn. If it's kids, they have no upbringing. I say, how low can you get?" then she added, "I was just telling Kate about Wade Rucker."

Becky Yowell grimaced. "That's how low—low as Wade. The man is swine." Then she cocked her head. "Hey, you think Wade did this?"

Judy shrugged.

Kate looked at them both. The earnest Judy Swan, the fiery Becky Yowell. Would either one have a motive to harm Brandi? Could the robbery here be staged for some reason? Were these two women in it together?

Becky put down the guitar case and stretched her arms.

Then Kate remembered. "Now I recognize you. You're in Brandi's band, aren't you? You sang at the Hermitage Hotel at the, uh, memorial concert?"

"That weird gig? With that cardboard paper doll onstage? Talk about stress. Bless her heart, Brandi barely laid to rest and the family naturally all upset, and the band—frankly, we didn't think we could get through it. Our bass, he got behind the beat." She shuddered. "But you bet, that was me on backup. Beca Yowell, rhymes with Noel. Judy here likes to call me Becky. Becky, Beca, take your pick."

"You harmonized with another singer."

"That's Dawn, Dawn Mulligan, my roommate. She's not a writer, though, and my chord changes bug her, so I come over here. Hey, I better start lookin' out for the truck."

"Truck? Did you say truck?"

"My uncle's pickup. He's comin by—"

"What kind of pickup truck? What make is it?" She spoke in a rush.

"Big black Sierra, Kate." Then Becky's eyes narrowed as if to reassess Kate. She said, "Hon, you okay? You from around here?"

"Boston."

She nodded. "Well let me tell you, lots of Tennessee folks drive a pickup. We got a U.S. Senator that campaigned state-wide in a bright red one, and he won real big. You got me?"

"I didn't mean—"

"That's okay, we're cool." She turned. "Hey, Judy, how many more days I got here?"

"Till next Wednesday."

She rolled her eyes. "Movin' us out on the street, that's what it feels like. Nobody gives a hoot about all the hits out of this cozy little Trystar house." She looked at Kate.

"Brandi's songs too."

"I didn't know that."

She flashed a big smile. "For sure. 'Fool Moon' was written right down the hall, first room on the left. Many an afternoon Brandi worked in there, and Dawn and me too, working out the harmonies, especially when we went into the studio to record her album. Heck, we went from here out to the Green Hills Mall the last day of Brandi's life."

Kate shook her head. Judy Swan looked sad.

"We were buying makeup at Dillard's, and we all got in our cars to go home. That's the last we ever saw her alive, when we waved and beeped at each other leaving the parking lot." Becky shook her head. "One minute we're picking out eyeliner together, the next minute she's gone for good. I still can't believe it."

"Terrible." Judy blinked back tears.

Kate shook her head and said, "I knew Brandi was shopping with friends. The news report said so."

"That was us, Dawn and me. We were buying makeup for the *Fool Moon* tour. Play the boonies, there's no makeup artist. You do your own. Estee Lauder makes a light-diffusing base. Works good under the stage lights, so you don't look orange or pasty. That's our last memory of Brandi, radiant in the makeover mirrors at the Estee Lauder counter."

Judy Swan slid her gold cross back and forth on its neck chain. "Her manuscript notebook's been right there too."

"Manuscript notebook?" Kate looked around the room again. "What notebook? Where?"

Judy scooped up some pencils and put them in a crock. "Here. I mean, here at Trystar. She was supposed to come back later that day when she . . . had her accident. She was going to work on a song here toward evening, five or six o'clock. We've had her notebook ever since. I've been meaning to take it to her mother as soon as I can get out there. Maybe tomorrow, Saturday's my best shot. So busy with this move. I put the notebook in the trunk of my car just a couple days ago, but up until then it'd been in the file under lock and key. Secure."

Under lock and key in that rust-red file cabinet.

Together the three stared at the bashed steel cabinet. Judy Swan said, "I've been checking the files all day. Everything's accounted for. I keep a log."

Kate stared at the cabinet, which at the moment started to tell another story. It told of a break-in and a popped lock and a search. It suggested a pencil flashlight held in one hand while the other methodically walked the fingers from file to file. It suggested somebody who knew exactly what he or she was looking for.

Like a certain notebook.

But the file cabinet told even more. The three, no, four whacks of cold forged steel against rust-red sheet steel were a diary of rage. Probably the noise of that impact suggested a new notion, to scatter the files and flee without delay when the object of the search was not found.

Kate asked, "What's in that notebook? Is it songs? Songs in progress?" The two women nodded. "Just let me ask one more question. Can you remember what color it is?"

Judy Swan managed a short, tight smile. "No problem. I used to kid Brandi about it. I told her she was printing money with that notebook. I told her lots of people would covet it. I said it was her own U.S. mint, and in fact it was greenback green."

Chapter Six

At exactly 4:15 P.M., Saturday, Kate started for the Burnside household with Bobbie's directions on the back of an envelope on her lap and Kelly beside her. The traffic on I-24 was moving at about 45 mph in the light weekend rush hour, though it was difficult to settle into the flow.

Bobbie wasn't the only one edgy out on the highway. Kate flashed on the near-miss each time she passed a limestone cut. Constantly she scanned the other lanes, checking her rearview and side mirrors for every beige vehicle. On one curve, she was sure she saw the very truck, its driver in a ballcap. It veered across two lanes in her direction, and her chest pounded before it vanished down an exit ramp.

Kate, meanwhile, slid out of her own lane until a blast from a big rig horn brought her up short—that and Kelly's "Mom!" —before she managed to settle behind a brown Voyager with a tinted back window.

Kelly took that moment to break a strained silence. Forced to wear a skirt, she provoked a nasty back-and-forth at the closet door and kept it up here in the car. "I still don't know why I have to wear this skirt."

"I told you, to show respect."

"I didn't have to wear skirts to show respect in Boston."

Kate eased off the accelerator. "We knew the dress code in Boston. I don't want to insult people, especially not tonight. It seems like a Southern thing. Bobbie's mother is cooking us dinner."

"Probably grits. I don't want it. Them. I don't see why we have to go there just so you can look at a stupid notebook."

"Kel, this can't wait. I'm in a race here. Somebody else is trying to find this notebook too. Probably the same person who arranged to get rid of Brandi Burns's car. We were too slow on that one."

"The killer?"

Kate heard the cop-show tone in her child's voice. No fear, no dread. Good. No ice up Kelly's spine. No thoughts of the human cranium subject to the same half-moon blows printed on Judy Swan's file cabinet painted the color of dried blood.

"So is it a secret killer notebook?"

Kate said, "It might tell us who wanted to hurt Bobbie's sister. And Brandi's former manager will be at the Burnsides' too. He doesn't return phone calls. This is my chance to ask him a few things."

Kelly tightened her seatbelt. "Then it's one of those boring adult dinner parties."

"Not exactly. It's just sort of one family to another. The Bannings and the Burnsides."

"I thought you never wanted me in your work stuff."

"This is an exception."

She sighed. "I see. I have to eat grits every time you work on a murder in Tennessee."

Kate let it go by. Give a child the last word, and the atmosphere sometimes improves. She turned on the radio—classic oldies—and they sang about beautiful balloons and yellow submarines to the I-24 West exit at Springfield/Joelton. Then she made a left on White's Creek Pike and looked for the school on the old Clarksville Highway and the fire house on Eatons Creek Pike.

Then it was left at the Amoco, past the cinderblock Assembly of God Church, and finally down Lawler Road, a ripply two-lane blacktop with post-and-wire fences marking the property lines of modest houses on lots carved from farm acreage. Creeks and stands of trees seemed to mark boundary lines, and the houses, probably built in the 1940s, definitely predated the era of the subdivision developer.

Kate spotted the Burnside mailbox just as the red ball of a sun sank over a ridge, and she turned down a packed-dirt, 400-foot driveway at the end of which she saw Bobbie's dark red Malibu and a dusty white Sentra, probably Mrs. Burnside's, possibly Judy Swan's. It was 5:08. Judy promised the note-book delivery sometime before 4:00. The margin of an hour should be plenty.

Kate pulled in beside the Sentra and heard a dog bark from inside the gray shingle, low-line bungalow with a sloping roof on wood porch pillars. Close up, the house looked ready for gutter and roof work and new screens. The concrete stairs were cracked. Before Kate and Kelly got to the porch, the door burst open.

"Why Kate Banning? And Kelly? So pleased to meet you, so glad you're here." Kate found her hand gripped in a damp half-clasp, half-handshake. "I'm Leona Burnside, but every-body calls me Dukie. You just come right on in. I feel like we've been expectin' you since the day we laid my Brandi in God's green earth."

Braced for a grief-stricken figure layered in black and mute with her sorrow, Kate instead faced an older version of Bobbie and the cardboard image of Brandi. Dukie Burnside had the same big-dip wave over the forehead and wore her chestnut hair in a stiff bouffant popular about fifteen years ago.

She wore black all right, black stirrups and an oversize loose-weave pistachio sweater cinched at the waist with a tas-seled belt in flamingo pink. Little flamingos danced from her earlobes, and her stirrup slings disappeared into gold leather flats in a tiny floor-sample size. "You come right on in," she said again. "Pardon my hollering—Bobbie! Bobbie, they're here!"

She pointed Kate and Kelly to the immediate right, a living room with a roll-arm sofa and matching chairs in a huge tea rose print with matching throw pillows bordered in eyelet lace. A curio cabinet glittered with rhinestone crowns on the top shelves and novelty salt and pepper shakers jammed together on the bottom. The fireplace mantel nearly disappeared in overflowing pink and blue silk flowers centered by an ornamental—guitar?

No one else was in the living room, no Judy Swan and no green notebook either. In a gilt frame over the sofa, a poster-size, sultry Brandi Burns smiled down in white fur bathed in moonlight pouring over her left shoulder—doubtless a *Fool Moon* publicity shot. The end tables held enough framed family photos for entire albums.

Tempted to look at them, Kate instead looked back at Bobbie's mother. In the lamplight she saw a face whose forehead was higher and nose sharper than her daughters', as though it took another generation for these very features to be realized as magazine-cover pretty. It was in Dukie Burnside's dark eyes, however, that Kate saw the hollows of grief.

So she was thankful for the distraction of the dog, a brown and white beagle ushered in by Bobbie, who was wearing jeans and a plaid shirt. The dog rushed to Kelly, eager to play, and Kate tried to make eye contact with Bobbie—thumbs up or down on Judy Swan and the notebook—but no go. Bobbie was busy with Kelly and the dog. "Now Chop, don't you jump on that sweet girl, show her you have some manners. Kelly, honey, he won't hurt you. Loves everybody. Down, Chop."

"Is that his name? Chop?"

Dukie Burnside nodded. "Dog loves pork chops. I used to fry up extras, he'd get his two. These days we're not eatin' as much. Fat grams got ever'body worried. I'm readin' the label on Cool Whip, and we got angel food cake coming out our ears. Nothin' but egg whites, tastes like dust. Cottage cheese, I grew up thinkin' it was for the sick and elderly. Tonight, though, we're having a real supper. Fact, y'all come on back to the kitchen. Everybody ends up in the kitchen anyway."

"Oh, Mama, no—"

"Now Bobbie, don't you fuss at me."

"Sorry, Mama."

Immediate retreat. *Fuss*, Kate noticed, seemed a Southern

word of particular power. Obediently they walked down the hall. Bobbie took Kate's wrist in a signal to stay back while her mother and Kelly entered the kitchen. "Judy Swan was here," she said softly. "Got here real late. You prob'ly passed her on the road just now. Don't worry; she brought the note-book. Mama put it upstairs in a chest of drawers under a bunch of old quilts. You'll have to coax her some for it, though, Kate. She's thinkin' it's just Brandi's songs. I didn't say nothin' to her about that notebook bein' like a smoking gun."

Kate nodded. Typical Bobbie to turn the task over to some-body else, even when it involved her own mother. Couldn't she just slip the notebook into Kate's car?

They entered a kitchen filled with the aromas of roasting turkey, and they sat at a rock maple table with matching chairs and places set for six. "Grady's comin', and Floyd and Lu-cille," Dukie said. "Their boys play Pop Warner, so they'll have to eat and run." Kate recalled Floyd's name. He was the cousin who went to Hillgate Wreck and Tow with Bobbie, the one skilled in mechanics. Maybe as a family member he knew Brandi's history with the car. How much of this, however, could Kate expect to ask him in the presence of the bereaved mother?

It felt clannish here, both a little too tight and a little too loose. She looked outside through windows with white cur-tains edged in the eyelet lace Dukie Burnside clearly liked. In the dusk, there was no sign of approaching cars down the road, no headlights to signal Grady Stamps's arrival.

Inside, pots bubbled on the stove, and the countertop was piled with Tupperware and shiny Corning serving dishes with tiny orange and yellow flowers. Chop settled at Kelly's knees, and Dukie's gold shoes tapped across the no-wax blue Delft floor. The microwave hummed.

Not exactly the country kitchen. Did Kate expect homespun calico? Earthenware bowls? Chickens in the yard? There was a black cat wall clock with a wagging tail pendulum marking seconds by the back and forth movement of the eyes. The

handtowels and potholders had the ubiquitous black-and-white
cow pattern, and on the walls, framed sayings:

You Won't Get Indigestion From Swallowing Your Pride

*You've Reached Middle Age When All You Exercise Is Cau-
tion*

"Y'all sit down and get comfortable. Bobbie, get the folks
some iced tea." Country music was playing low on a portable
CD/tape player by the refrigerator, a female vocalist, not
Brandi. Dukie took a potholder and opened the oven door. The
turkey glowed. "Cookin'," Dukie said, "that's how I spend my
waking hours ever since Brandi . . . I just bake and put up pre-
serves and freeze and roast and freeze some more. Not many
have deep freezers these days. Not many can their own vegetables as far as that's concerned. A whole generation doesn't
know a Ball jar." She basted the turkey, squeezed the rubber
bulb of the plastic tube that looked like a giant eye dropper.

Kate said, "Everything smells wonderful."

"Just a regular down-home supper. Turkey and dressing,
pole beans, okra and tomatoes, tater pie—that's sweet potato
pie—cracklin' bread, cheese grits, cobbler and chess pie for
dessert. You like grits, Kelly?"

Kelly smiled and avoided Kate's gaze. "A little."

"Turn you into a Southern gal."

Kelly kept her smile and scratched the beagle's ears. Bobbie
was warming dishes in the microwave. A new song began, and
Dukie sang a line—" 'Don't come home a-drinkin' with lovin'
on your mind.' You like Loretta Lynn, Kate?" She turned to
Kate. "You see *Coal Miner's Daughter*?" Her "no" drew a
look of amazement. "Didn't they show it in Boston?"

Kate blushed. "I guess. I missed most everything after Kelly
was born. The only music I heard was *Sesame Street*."

"I know what you mean." She turned to look Kate in the
eye. "Myself, though, I couldn't've lived without Loretta's
songs. 'The Pill,' 'When the Tingle Becomes a Chill,' 'You're
Lookin' at Country'—why, she sang our lives and spoke our
thoughts. That's what songs do."

Kate heard Dukie Burnside's depth of feeling, her sincerity.

She remembered the moment on Charlotte Avenue when Bobbie sang a few bars of "Blueberry Hill," how moving it was. She said, "I don't know much about country music."

Kelly said, "But Mom listens to 'Whoever's in New England.' "

Dukie turned to her. "Reba. Well, of course she does. Prob'ly helps your Mom with her homesickness."

Kate felt her mouth open without sound. Kelly said, "Mom's not homesick."

Dukie Burnside lifted a pot lid and stirred and tasted and salted. Then she faced Kelly. "Sugar, when you uproot from your home and your people, you are bound to be sick at heart. B'lieve me, we Burnsides know. We're from way over in East Tennessee, and Tennessee is one big state in this union. Like we say down here, from Nashville back home it's a fur piece. Most of our family, except for Floyd and Lucille and the kids, are back home. We suffer from that distance. You got to be missing your own people."

Kelly scratched the dog's ears. "We don't have any people."

"—no close relatives, that's what Kelly means." Kate sat very straight. How many times had she said this to teachers, camp counselors, school parents? "Kelly's father and I divorced when she was a baby. He's in Oregon, and there isn't much contact. On my side of the family, unfortunately, no one is living." She stopped, unwilling to name names. The fact was, next-of-kin were long dead, Kate's parents gone in the plane crash, the late grandmother who raised her memorialized in three side chairs and a chest of drawers. Kelly never knew her.

Dukie and Bobbie Burnside now stared as if Kate and her daughter had landed from Mars, and it was a relief to hear a car door slam. Maybe Grady Stamps. She hoped. But two voices called, and Bobbie cocked her head. "That would be Floyd and Lucille."

It was. Lucille Akers came in first, a buxom woman of about forty in heavy makeup with champagne hair tied back in a velvet ribbon and a print dress with an empire waist. She held a pie and held herself as if corseted.

Her husband Floyd, on the other hand, walked with supple, double-jointed movements, entirely at home in the world as he tucked his blue striped shirt into ironed jeans under the hand-tooled belt with a buckle the size of a personal pizza. His mesh cap read "CAT" over the visor, and he sat down and immediately pulled up the white tube socks from his loafers and said an easy "How-do" to Kate and Kelly. If any man could get information about a wrecked car at a junkyard, surely it would be Floyd Akers.

There was much talk of early fall weather and of Chop faring better in the fields now the flea and tick season was coming to an end. Conversation veered to something that sounded like bug dance.

"That's buckdance, Kate."

"Clogging?"

Dukie made a sour face. "Clogging, now that's real popular. Cute little matching skirts and lots of competitions. But it's got an ugly look to the kicks; that's my opinion. Besides, everybody in our family's too much an individual to bother with a routine. Buckdance is freestyle, and that's what we like best. Brandi and Bobbie are both real good. They won talent contests, and I hoped Brandi would dance some in her stage show on tour. She—she—"

Then her voice faltered, broke off in a gulping sound. No one said a word. Kate looked down at the surface of the table and imagined the seventh place setting. Dukie Burnside reached for a paper napkin in a holder and blew her nose. Kate could only imagine the effort of will it took to move the evening forward. The woman looked at Kelly. "You'd probably be a real good buckdancer, Sugar. Maybe after supper we can get you to try it?"

Kelly nodded. Kate knew it was from politeness and discomfort and a wish to help.

"Mama, I think everything's ready. Grady'll be here any minute, but he'd want us to go ahead." So they did, with much passing and deciding about white and dark meat, about trying everything and saving room and having second helpings. Midway through, the phone rang, and Bobbie answered and reported that Grady had indeed been delayed but was now on his way.

Kate tried, without success, to think of a way to get Floyd Akers to talk about Brandi's Taurus and the visit to the wrecker yard. As a man in this family, he might well know something about the history of the car. But she could not ask after that buckdance moment. Dukie was too fragile, her grief too powerful.

They settled into the neutrality of small talk and food rituals. At last everybody tried both desserts, and Lucille's chess pie was explained as a Civil War-era recipe of resourceful Southern women coping with shortages of staples like pecans. The pie met a high standard, all agreed, and coffee was served with family jokes as Dukie declared Lucille's percolator made it strong enough to stand up by itself, and Lucille retorted that Dukie's was so weak it had to be helped out of the pot. Floyd said he ate so much he ran aground.

They apologized for having to run off to get their boys from football practice, and told Kate and Kelly it was real nice meeting them both. They urged Dukie and Bobbie to come over after church on Sunday. Then they were gone, and Kate hoped this dinner was at least a raincheck redeemable if necessary for a future chat with Floyd Akers.

Then Bobbie invited Kelly to help take Chop for a walk. The dog was obviously unaccustomed to a leash, and Kate guessed Bobbie was actually clearing space for a private talk with her mother. "We'll keep a lookout for Grady, Mama. He'll want his dinner soon as he gets here. Just leave the kitchen be, and I'll tend to it later. Why don't y'all get comfortable in the living room?"

So they did. Kate, seated on the rose sofa, was aware that she sat directly under the *Fool Moon* poster of Brandi, which her mother faced as they talked. "Bobbie's keepin' an eye on me," Dukie said. "Since we lost Brandi, my heart and blood pressure tend to rabbit around. I don't pay it much mind." Kate nodded. She looked at the mantel with the instrument amid the flowers. A family shrine? Dukie turned to follow her glance. She said, "You're lookin' at Bobbie's mandolin."

"Oh, it's Bobbie's . . . and it's not a little guitar?"

Dukie Burnside chuckled. "Lordy, nothin' like it except they're both wood and strings. You see, I thought my girls would be a family duet. Sort of like the Mandrells. I named Bobbie for Barbara Mandrell—maybe you remember her TV show, *Barbara Mandrell and the Mandrell Sisters*? She was real popular in the seventies and the eighties too, nationally televised on ABC." Kate nodded politely.

" 'Sleeping Single in a Double Bed,' that was hers, and 'I Was Country When Country Wasn't Cool.' " Kate nodded again. " 'Course, the Mandrells came from Texas and then California. We're all from East Tennessee, and we just love the McCarters—you know the McCarters? From East Tennessee? Around Sevierville, near where Dolly Parton's from."

Kate shook her head.

"You don't know *The Gift*, their first album?" She spoke as if to jog Kate's memory. "Well, there's three of them, not two, but I thought we favored them around the eyes. So Brandi started on guitar, and Bobbie tried the mandolin. Reese Berry gave them some lessons. You know him?" Kate shook her head again. "Used to play on the Opry. Played with Roy Acuff for a while; he was one of the Smoky Mountain Boys. Plays just 'bout everything—guitar, fiddle, banjo . . ."

She seemed ready to take shelter in the reminiscence. Kate had seen so many of the bereaved do the same thing, ease away from pain. "Anyway, I got Reese Berry to teach them, and he was nice as he could be. I gave Brandi a big old Sears Silvertone our uncle had, and got Bobbie a second-hand mandolin. She liked it bein' small, but she had a real hard time with the strings."

Dukie gave a short sigh. "Most of all, that girl just couldn't stand playing and singing in front of people. Made her so nervous she threw up every time. But Brandi, well, she just thrived on it. Choked by childhood, that one."

She reached up her sweater sleeve and took out another paper napkin, daubing her eyes. "The Burnside Sisters just weren't meant to be, and yet—" She crumpled the napkin. "I have to say, our name, you know they shortened it when Brandi signed with the label. They talked about it being risky—no, risqué, French, I believe it is.

"I thought it was trashy, like she *burns*. But they went ahead. Sex sells. In past times country music wasn't like that. Loretta wears those gingham gowns to this day, but Tanya Tucker does real good bein' sexy. You see her at that Super Bowl half-time show in leather? No? Well, it was like underwear, black leather. Woooeee. Move over, Madonna." She grinned, a little sheepish. "There's always a lot of competition. You got to stand out. That's what the Virgo executives kept sayin'. We had to take their word."

Kate saw her opening. The green notebook was buried in the upstairs quilt drawer, but the strings attached also mattered. And these were not the strings of the ornamental mandolin. If only she could get this talkative woman to say some of the things that mattered.

She said, "Dukie, Bobbie tells me you have certain opinions on Brandi's . . . Brandi's trouble. I'm trying to help out; I think you know that. It would be useful to have your thoughts. For instance, about Wade Rucker—?"

"No." She stamped her small golden foot. "No ma'am. I will not discuss that boy. The Lord will deal with Wade, the Lord and not the Burnside family. If Bobbie wants to talk about him, I can't stop her, but I will not do so. I like to remember the good things. They are salve to my soul."

Kate nodded. "Then I'd appreciate hearing some of those good things."

Dukie flicked the tassels of her belt. "Those folks at Virgo," she said, "like I was saying, they were real nice. They had a limo for us, and some of the caterer food was out of this world. Disappeared like a T-bone steak in a dog pound." She folded her hands. "It's no exaggeration; they treated our family like royalty. They're just the nicest folks."

Kate edged her thumbnail between her front teeth. Nice, nicer, nicest. Seduced by the perks. "Dukie," Kate said, "remember that it could also help to hear any doubts you might have. Telling negative things doesn't make you a negative person. If you have any doubts at all about Virgo— For instance, what about that vice-president Bobbie dislikes, the one from Los Angeles, Benniger?"

"—Roy Benniger. Ladies' man. City man too. He's just too slick for us, Kate. He'd tried slipping things over, things that sounded fine till Grady showed us how they weren't good for Brandi. Like he tried making Brandi pay for the promotion gifts for all the big country disc jockeys. Cutest little radios in moon casings, and they went to DJs from California to Maine. That's nearly ten thousand dollars in costs that Roy Benniger wanted to take out of Brandi's earnings. Grady put his foot down, said the label was responsible. There's a saying, 'He'd pee on your back and tell you it's rainin'. No offense, but that's Roy. I don't think he belongs at Virgo/Nashville. He's not one of their family. He's just too different."

"Was he involved in scheduling the album release? I understand Virgo's having some problems. Firings and low morale."

Dukie twirled her belt tassel in her fingers. She said, "They had a few scheduling problems that tested our patience. Kept changing the dates for releasin' the album. They wanted the single to hit just right at the dance clubs, and there was some talk of a dance called the Fool Moon.

"They brought in a dance instructor from Dallas to work on it for a while. And then it was hard gettin' the tour schedule to fit with the album when they couldn't seem to make up their mind. It sounded like double-talk when they tried explaining. That's why Grady was so good. He came in like an angel from the blue."

She crossed her legs. "It was startin' to feel confusing and messed up till he took charge in this nice quiet way. When Brandi needed to get her band together for her album and road tour, Grady saw to that. He tried out the singers and musicians, and he sat down with Brandi and the people from Virgo and got everything worked out. He put a stop to the dance; it was so complicated nobody but the advanced could catch on, not even the backup singers for the album, Dawn and Beca. They're in the video and they were going on the road with Brandi too. Did you meet them?"

"I met Becky—Beca—at Trystar music. I heard them sing at the Hermitage Hotel too. They wore cowboy hats."

She nodded. "Real good singers. Sweet gals, mighty talented. Brandi was workin' with girls from our church, but Grady said it had to be professional all the way, and he got Dawn and Beca. Even their hair, Dawn's the blonde and Beca's the redhead. Grady said their hair would go good with Brandi's. 'Raven-dark,' he called her hair. You see how he thinks about the details. He's got a saying, 'God's in the details.' "

She frowned, her mouth pursed as if tasting something sour. "But even Grady couldn't keep Roy Benniger off Brandi's album. He's co-producer. Nothing we could do to stop it. I just wish Virgo would send him packin'. He's even messing around in the benefit they're planning for early December. Bobbie's worried if he gets his way it'll be real tacky." She paused. "Problem is, the man knows about publicity, but not respect."

It was a keen distinction, thoughtful and smart. Kate must not underestimate the Burnsides. Yet this was hard because Dukie was unwilling to talk directly about murder. Her mind worked at a tangent. Kate said, "Dukie, if Brandi had danger-ous trouble in her life, then her green notebook could help a great deal."

"You mean her song writin' book." Kate nodded. The mother stared at the wall behind Kate's head. Her eyes were dry. She said, "It's just a regular old notebook like they use in school."

"But what she wrote in it—that's what matters. I would like to see it." Kate's voice was low and gentle. "We could look at it together."

Dukie Burnside did not move a muscle. "I had in mind to show you the tiaras and crowns my girls won in the pageants.

Brandi was Junior Miss Northern Hardwoods. Bobbie won her share too, annual pageants at the Talent Palace Festival."

She pointed to the curio cabinet where the rhinestones glittered. "The notebook, well, I don't know." She looked into Kate's face. "I figure, Brandi's in the Lord's hands. That's our belief. Some of the music legends, the Lord called them in ways we must not pre-judge. Hank Williams passed in the backseat of a Cadillac, and Patsy Cline left us in a plane crash. Dottie West went to the Lord on Briley Parkway on her way to sing at the Opry."

Dukie looked at Kate and lowered her voice. "Where we come from, mamas hold babies on their laps on a starry night and whisper that the lights in the sky are floorlights of heaven. That's just how it is. I lost my daughter, but having your faith shaken is not the same as losing it . . . No matter how dark it is, if I have faith, I have a song in the night."

Kate nodded, knowing that Dukie Burnside was imparting the most profound conviction of her world. Heaven was a destination, not a concept, and her Brandi was in heaven.

But it did not follow that Brandi's killer ought to walk the earth scot-free. Surely her mother could see that. Surely Kate did not have to voice that sentiment. The pause at this moment seemed endless. From the kitchen came the sound of a faucet dripping into a pot put to soak, a water clock measuring the moments.

Then Dukie Burnside rose from her chair and started slowly for the stairwell. Kate heard steps going up and back into the bedrooms. Then a scrape of a drawer and the footfalls back again, her steps very heavy coming down, the weight of the world. She walked slowly to Kate. "I don't know why this notebook. I have in mind to give you her video. It played on CMT and TNN all last August and into September. It was a Hot New Country feature."

She repeated these words as she handed Kate the green spiral notebook with white lined paper. A notebook familiar from high school, junior high, English and social studies. How many of these had Kate bought Kelly? But her hand trembled as she opened the notebook. Envy green. In Bobbie's words, the smoking gun.

Except there was no smoke at all. Judy Swan exaggerated. Or was mistaken. If this was a money machine, it was empty—or emptied out. Kate turned the pages and read.

Stick with me
I'm stuck on you
Love you, love you.

Don't stick it to me
stick with me.
Stuck, stick, ick. Sick, ick.

Off the book without letting him down (her down)
You ran out of my time
She ran out of his youth
She ran off with his youth.

So many diamonds,
like an ice storm
the shining sun on winter's ice . . . and who needs diamonds,
who needs diamonds? Winter ice, winter ice.

So it went, only seven pages long. Nothing green but the cover, nothing incriminating. Nothing worth breaking and entering. Or bashing metal in a rage. Yes, the safe was cracked, the vaults blasted. The big moment, call the media. And what did you find? Jottings. Bits and pieces of songs in the making, songs abandoned and aborted. Crumbs.

Though there were some pages with number codes, lines of numerals, some in boxes, some like fractions. Like something a bookie might keep.

Could Brandi have been into gambling? Was that it?

And how could she ask Dukie Burnside if her late daughter was involved in illegal betting?

"Mama Dukie, how you doing?"

Kate jumped. The voice was soft as a funeral.

"Grady. Grady Stamps, you're a sight for sore eyes. Didn't even hear your car."

"Got a new car that flies under the radar." He laughed.

Kate turned. She would not have recognized him. His hair was shampooed and expensively styled. He wore black slacks and a gray silk shirt with full sleeves and a soft collar. His pitted skin looked ruddy and tan in the evening light. His boots were some kind of exotic hide, and dusty, perhaps from parking his car near the road and walking down the dirt driveway? Though why would Grady Stamps come sneaking in? "Grady, like you to meet Miz Kate Banning."

He shook hands. "Been hearing so much about you from Bobbie," he said.

"And I've been trying to reach you."

"—and looks like you're getting ready to play us some music out of Brandi's songbook."

"You know this book?"

He smiled. "Oh Lordy, do I not? It was like a part of Brandi herself. And look, there's the music for 'Fool Moon.'"

They stared at the bookie numbers. Kate said, "Where?"

"Right there. That's the Nashville number system. That's how our musicians write and read music. You've never seen it?"

"Without notes?"

"Well, they're notes to us."

"So these boxes and lines are really music?"

He laughed easily. "We'll forgive you," he said, "because you're new in town. Somebody needs to give you a lesson, kind of orientation. In fact, your little daughter's outside with Bobbie naming the constellations, and I promised I'd bring you right out to let her show off. Let's not get them upset, thinking it's my fault. I'm already in hot water for lettin' my business make me late and miss the best dinner in all of Tennessee."

Dukie managed a smile, and Kate stood as if commanded.

Grady took her arm and led her toward the front door. On the porch, door closed, he continued to hold her elbow.

"Before you go down to talk to your daughter, I have a word for you," he said. "Maybe more orientation. You know, Nashville's not so big as some folks think. It's a small town, and word gets around on who's doing what. Music Row is particularly close. Word's out, in fact, that somebody from Boston's real interested in the circumstances of Brandi's terrible accident. I just want you to know that some folks are talking. Nobody wants any more harm to come to anybody, especially a newcomer. Some Nashville streets, you got to be real careful crossing. Some streets, you just take your life in your hands."

Chapter Seven

Mac's Hitching Post was on lower Broadway, the seedy and the sleazy catchbasin of broken dreams and busted business. It was the kind of bar the tourists hurry past with breath held and a tight grip on the kids' hands. Most places like it were bygones, boarded up or limping along temporarily as souvenir shops hawking airbrushed T-shirts. Mac's window featured water-stained photos of Barbara Mandrell, The Lone Ranger, Faron Young and His Country Deputies. A ribbon of duct tape mapped a crack in the plate glass.

Inside, it was dark enough to cancel out sunrise and high noon, the whole sundial of light and shadow. Kate took a deep breath and walked in. Ten-thirty, a Monday morning in early October. Light rain in the forecast. The beery darkness provided a certain relief.

From her Fleetwood office, she had walked with care, crossed only at the lights with the *walk* sign, looked both ways twice. Be careful crossing streets, as Grady Stamps advised and warned.

Or was it threatened? The memory of his hand on her arm felt as creepy as an amputee's ghost limb. The Burnsides thought Grady was the greatest thing since sliced bread because he soothed their nerves and smoothed the way. Grady the ingratiating.

She peered into the gloom. No sign of Wade Rucker, the featured A.M. entertainer here at the Hitching Post, a narrow room that shot back maybe thirty feet with the bar running half the length of the left wall. The usual neon signs for Bud and Bud Light cast a gloomy sheen on the black Formica.

Her eyes adjusted. In the window by the entrance sat a drum set, the kick drum head bandaged with more duct tape, and an electric guitar with amplifier on a four-foot stage bordered by a post-and-rail fence with a wagon wheel leaned against it, a gesture to the idea of a hitching post. At this hour of the day the customers included a fifty-something couple in windbreakers trying to see to write their postcards, three men hunched over drafts at the bar, and a guy in a camouflage jacket talking to himself at a table near the back.

On the silent screen of the bar TV a local morning show was doing a makeover. Table service had not been invented here, and Kate stepped to the bar, whose red and blue backlights shone in the scalp of the bartender. She leaned forward. "Wade Rucker plays this morning?"

"Usually starts about eleven." If the bartender had an opinion on the entertainment, he kept it to himself.

Kate ordered an O'Douls, put three ones on the bar, picked a table well away from the dim red and blue lights and set the bottle down. Her eyes were still adjusting. Each step on the linoleum tiles felt slick. She pulled out a chair and sat. Kate Banning's coffee break. Slip out for a little excursion on lower Broadway. Catch the early show, Wade Rucker on display.

And what did she expect to see and hear? A song about breaking into a music publisher, on memorizing the code of a security system? A ballad about plotting murder? At the moment she strained to see her watch. Her assistant had plenty to do for an hour, like phoning the flaky Adirondacks writer who identified himself as a freelance nature instructor.

Some tasks, however, were first-person assignments. Would Wade Rucker's music sound like Brandi's? Would any of the notebook fragments appear in his lyrics? And would some body language other than sulking show up? In short, check him out.

Or was this another wild goose chase like the notebook?

What did that get her but more questions—like whether the music number system meant anything special or whether crucial sheets were torn out and, if so, when? Even a few minutes were time enough to remove many pages. And what might be written on them?—maybe specifics on why Brandi Burns felt her life was taking a very dark turn.

Or maybe songs. Was the thief hoping for a treasure trove of music? For that matter, what about those who handled the notebook since the break-in? Judy Swan, Bobbie, Dukie. The friendly and responsible music publisher, the sister, the mother. For Judy Swan, some torn-out notebook pages would be a goldmine, the bad penny she would turn into pennies from heaven.

And Bobbie might secretly begin to imagine taking on the rhinestone mantle of her dead sister. Some new songs on notebook paper would be a musical launching pad. No question, she had the voice, and nobody would expect her to play the mandolin or even hold a guitar. An actual sister, Bobbie could be a tragic survivor carrying on the tradition of Brandi. Better than an impersonator. They'd probably write her some onstage pathetic lines and work up a big-screen video that could keep *Fool Moon* sales going for another couple years while they launched her.

So get Bobbie into that Silver Eagle tour bus and put her in front of an audience. Do it to honor her sister's memory. Make Brandi a young legend in the tragic tradition built on country music mortality. Grady Stamps might already be at work on it. After all, he was now unemployed, wasn't he, and Bobbie a possible meal ticket?

And then Dukie. A group of songs tucked under the quilts would represent her daughter's very spirit. As Brandi's mother, she could wait for the call to send that spirit forth. Surely a music publisher in the Virgo/Nashville conglomerate would like to be that spiritual gateway—or Warner Brothers or RCA or any of those record labels Dukie Burnside found so awesome.

She took a sip of the non-beer and checked her watch again and hoped Hughes Amberson didn't try to summon her for an impromptu pep talk in his Fleetwood suite for the next forty minutes.

She was too absorbed to feel the sudden shadow of a presence at her side. "Well, li'l lady, a fine Monday mornin' to *you*."

The deep whiskey voice was startling. Beside her, from nowhere, stood a heavyset man in a swirly red and black polyester form fitting western shirt that clung to his pot belly and his chest. He must have come from somewhere in back. His black hair was slicked straight back with oil or gel, and his long face had dark eyes and a flaring upper lip. The thick fingers of his left hand were wrapped around a Miller High Life and displayed a gold horseshoe diamond ring, his filed nails gleaming with clear lacquer.

He was somewhere in his forties, too old to be Wade Rucker. Out of shape, judging from the belly, but probably strong.

He said, "If you're a tourist, where's your postcards? If you stopped in for a beer, where's your beer?" The heavy voice tried to joke but Kate heard a demand for some ID. Maybe he worked here. Maybe he was Mac.

She said, "Just taking a short morning break."

"Is that a fact?"

She looked down quietly to send out a *not-interested* message. Nothing personal but just go away. He said, "Your tourists, they mostly head into Tootsie's this time of day. You know Tootsie's?"

Kate nodded slightly. Across Broadway, Tootsie's Orchid Lounge, its walls painted vivid lilac, was the one semi-official honky-tonk that would probably survive all tasteful renovation and tourist franchises. As newcomers were informed, decades of Grand Ole Opry performers belted back shots and beer at Tootsie's between their numbers at the Ryman Auditorium. Tootsie's was an institution. Which would probably save it. Mac's was an eyesore. Which would probably send it belly-up.

He said, "You know Willie Nelson hung out at Tootsie's, and Waylon Jennings. Kris Kristofferson used to be a janitor there. Got his start mopping the floor. One of the original country music Outlaws, and he started with a bucket and mop."

He was sitting down at the table beside hers. Kate edged away, her arm against the wall, which felt sticky. "We got a boy here plays weekday mornings; he's getting his start. Could be a breakthrough act. Be here in a few minutes. Went to see a man about a dog, if you know what I mean."

Was he drunk or just belligerent? She said, "Just stopped in for a little music."

But he laughed, or maybe snorted. "You can't fool me. You're no tourist. I gotta bet. You're with Gaylord, right?"

She shook her head. "Gaylord? Don't know him."

He slapped his knee. "Think you can kid me. You're scoutin' Wade Rucker for Gaylord or one of them."

Then Kate understood. Of course, he meant Gaylord Entertainment. Anybody in Nashville for ten minutes knew the name of the corporation that owned the Wildhorse Saloon, the Grand Ole Opry, the Opryland theme park, the convention hotel and water taxis and half of Second Avenue. If he wanted to think she was a corporation scout, okay. Harmless enough.

He said, "You don't wanna miss the hometown talent, right? Talent right under your nose."

"Right under your nose."

"Well, you can bet on Wade Rucker. It's high time for another Outlaw bunch. Waylon and Willie, that's how it's done. Those hat guys today, they're pansies that hardly shave. Bunch of queers and babyfaces. Wade, now, he's the real thing. None of this play-acting, he's gonna live his songs. Like Hank, Jr. Just keep him off mountains. You don't want your stars of tomorrow with a steel plate in their skull."

Steel and skulls. She shivered. Was this a sideways hint, or a threat? Maybe just a reference to something she knew nothing about. "Just the steel in their guitar strings," she said, hoping to get by.

"You betcha." Then, "Hey, Wade boy, Wade-e-o."

The feature entertainer was coming through the front door, pivoting right as he swung himself onstage without a glance at the room or a sign he'd heard his name called. Wade Rucker wore tight black jeans and a black, narrow-brimmed cowboy hat, a black T-shirt and a shiny leather vest. The jeans were stuffed into pale reptile boots with steel tips.

The stage spotlight showed a waxy face with a jutting jaw and boyish softness at the cheeks and mouth. His eyes revealed nothing, though his mouth pulled down at the left corner to give him a wan look.

It was the kind of face some women yearn to baby, to pamper and please and forgive and carry a torch no matter what because he looks like a forlorn lost boy.

"Wade Rucker, folks," he said, "and it's the ol' blue Monday lineup."

He picked up the black electric guitar that showed surface smears in the spotlight, and he flicked a fingernail against the microphone until the sound popped loud as he bent to turn the knobs on the amplifier. His arms were sinewy. "Gonna call this electric Monday," he said. "Here's an old song called 'Walking Dead.' " Kate sat back, forced herself to sip from her bottle.

He began to play, high screaming chords. His voice was hard and flat. It had no shadings, only volume, loud and louder, and the guitar riffs tended to drown it in big slides. He sang a prison song she couldn't quite make out and then announced some love songs. "Not your simple boy-meets-girl," he said at the mike. "This is hard-core love when your baby turns bitch and does her Texas two-step on your heart."

He scowled, struck a pose, jacked out his leg. Two of the men at the bar turned, and the couple with the postcards retracted their ball-points, while the camouflage jacket staggered back outside, still mumbling. The man beside Kate fingered his diamond horseshoe ring and stared at the stage as if at prize breeding stock.

Wade Rucker rocked forward and back and sang a song whose key phrase turned on snubbing and knifing. "I cut her good, I cut her dead—dead—dead / Then she turned the other cheek, and the blood ran red—red—red."

Kate saw the shoulder coil and recoil with every word, and he moved immediately into a song about whipping a girl into the dirt when she did him dirty, and bruising and stomping and seeing her beautiful hair in the crosshairs of his mind. Didn't musicians call their guitars axes? His was ax and hatchet and shotgun all in one. Then he turned down his guitar and announced a slow ballad. "You heard of 'Blowin' in the Wind,' " he said.

> *This is—how we blew each other away-ee*
> *You just blew me away, blew me away-ee*
> *But baby, you did me so wrong, so damn wrong*
> *A man's gotta do what a man's gotta do*
> *So I kissed your lips, and I held you tight*
> *The Magnum cold steel in my belt felt right*
> *So babe, I blew you away too.*

He echoed the last lines as if reluctant to let go of the song. Kate saw the muscles of his forearms knot tight on the final line. Unless these songs were pure onstage sado-dreams, the man was no mere sulker. She wondered what the young writer of "Fool Moon" and "Envy Green" thought of all this. Did it scare her?

Did it kill her?

She thought about Grady Stamps's warning. Was it about Wade? Maybe Grady knew enough about Wade Rucker to keep clear of him. Knew so much he'd swallow his own suspicions about Brandi's death and urge Kate to curb hers.

Maybe Bobbie's *sulker* label was meant to placate, and Dukie's trust in Heaven's justice a way to keep everybody safe here on Earth.

It was high time to get out of here, by the back door if possible, before Wade Rucker looked at the faces in front of him and saw Kate. She took another sip and made a deliberate show of searching her purse for a phone quarter and holding it between thumb and forefinger in full view of the diamond ring man in the red marbleized shirt.

She quickly made her way to the back as Wade launched another electric tirade against women who done him wrong. By the restrooms marked Bulls and Heifers was a red exit sign.

The backdoor had a push bar, and she opened it quickly and slipped out into an alleyway of blinding daylight.

It was also an alleyway of parking slots. Against the building were a black Lincoln Continental, a weed green Nova, and a dark gold, old, filthy Dodge Power Wagon with two bumper stickers saying *Life's a Bitch* and *Yucca Flat*—Yucca Flat, Wade Rucker's band. Wade Rucker's truck, probably.

Kate stepped close. The patches of rust looked like scabs. The left tail light was taped, and the tailgate held up with a length of chain. In the truck bed was some soil residue—no, gritty to the touch, sand. And a coil of wire and plywood scraps. She looked inside. Over the rearview mirror hung a shocking pink and black lace woman's garter, the souvenir kind. The black vinyl seats were cracked, and on the floor on the passenger side lay two Rolling Rock empties and a tool box with the lid down.

It was the toolbox that held her, made her hesitate here at the back walls of old brick buildings, kept her from walking briskly through to Fourth Avenue. Just suppose inside that box lay a crowbar with flecks of rust-red paint? Wade Rucker's calling card? The box was snapped shut but apparently not locked. The truck door lock buttons were pushed down, but she tried the doors anyway. Both locked.

The driver's side window, however, was down a crack. About a half inch. Opportunity knocking. Sam had taught her the old coat hanger trick one freezing day in Boston when she locked herself out with the keys dangling in the ignition. All you needed was a length of that wire lying in the back of the truck bed. Wade Rucker furnished the tools to the toolbox. Piece of cake. Kate could hear the throb and wail inside. As long as the music played, she knew the whereabouts of Wade Rucker. She looked both ways once, twice.

Just then a Sysco Foods panel truck turned in, made its way down the alley, passed her at about 15 mph, then stopped at the corner and turned right. Gone. She was alone in this alley that cut between the numbered avenues, Second to Third, Third to Fourth. She would get her plaid dress rusty, but that was okay.

She moved in from the back fender of the Dodge, stepped up, reached over the side to grab a piece of plywood to drag the coil of wire closer until she could reach it and guesstimate a two-foot length. A plywood splinter wedged itself under her right thumbnail. Pain. Nerves. She ignored it and bent the wire back and forth fast until it got hot and snapped.

She shaped a loop and began to thread it down from the window opening and maneuvered it down to the door lock button. The splinter hurt. Ignore it and focus on the wire. The loop slipped off twice, caught the flange the third time. Like a fish tank treasure hunt at an arcade. Easy, easy, steady pressure. The lock button was almost up.

The sudden pain came next, the clamp on her upper arm out of nowhere, and the piercing jab like muscle and fangs. She jumped and gasped. Attack. Snakebite. No, lacquered nails and a red marbly shirtsleeve and beer breath. The diamond horse-shoe ring—and Kate mashed against the truck door. "Why, little lady, where's your manners? That's no way for a talent scout to do."

He had to come from around the alleyway, around from Mac's front door to Third and down the alley against the building back walls to her left. His approach took less than a minute's time, the very minute she was doing handicrafts with the wire. She saw white spittle clot at the left corner of his mouth. His nostrils flared. Hairs, greasy face.

He backed her harder against the truck and tightened the grip on her arm. The splinter hurt like hell. The door handle dug into her back. His voice was low and soft. "I b'lieve Wade's gonna be real interested in somebody trying to get in his truck. Myself, on Wade's behalf, I'm real curious just what it is you think you're doin'?"

Kate opened and closed her mouth. No words. Wade was in his corral, but she did not factor in this loose cannon. "Okay," she said, "I'm no talent scout. I don't work for Gaylord. It's . . . stupid of me. Stupid thing to do."

"You don't say." He stepped closer, bolder. "Now that's a revelation."

Options? To scream? Knee-in-the-groin and make a break? Not a chance, not in pumps on brick pavement. But give it five minutes more and Wade Rucker would join this little alley party. Inside, another song began, maybe three minutes' worth. The grip was like a tourniquet, her arm starting to throb. She twisted away from the door handle but the splinter hurt like crazy. Play this scene wrong, and the splinter would be the very least of it.

She said, "Look, I'll tell you . . . if you could let go my arm." He didn't, and she knew he would not. But his grip eased just a little. His breath came in short huffs and smelled like beer and tobacco and terrible teeth. Kate tried to keep her voice steady. "I shouldn't even be over here. I work on Second Avenue in an office."

She looked him in the eye, tried for sincerity. "My little sister, you see, she's over at Vanderbilt and she's crazy about Yucca Flat. Any fraternity party they play, she goes. And she's a big fan of Wade Rucker. Talks about him all the time, how good looking he is, how she loves his music. I just wanted, you know, to check him out. It's a big sister thing." She looked him in the eye. "Be frank with you, I'd prefer my sister idolize a guy that doesn't sing about hurting women."

He laughed. "Some love it."

"Some don't." She tried for a shrug, and he clamped down harder. Pain. "I got tempted," she managed to say, "by the truck and the Yucca Flat bumper sticker." She bit her lip. "I locked myself out of my own car twice, so I know how to get in with wire. I was heading back to work. Monday mornings are a zoo at the office, and it's a shortcut down the alley." She looked him in the eye. Snake eyes. "When I saw the garter over the mirror, I just lost it. My sister, she'd go bonkers to have that garter."

His grip held. "Real nice story, lady, except it's got a big crack in it. You think Wade's kind of music is bad for your sister, but you're gonna break in his truck and steal his garter for her? Birthday present, maybe? You think we're gonna fall for that?"

So he wasn't drunk. Caught in her own contradiction. "You don't have sisters, do you?" Gamble, but worth a shot.

He wasn't biting. No response either way. "—if you did have sisters, you'd know how it is, girls so close, sometimes too close. We've been on the outs lately. She thinks I'm always checking up on her, telling her what to do. I saw that garter; it was an impulse thing. If I got her that garter, she'd be nice. We could get along better, smooth things over. Like a peace offering. It was stupid, but I didn't mean any harm."

Kate's arm was numb, the splinter pure piercing torture. Her eyes began to water from the pain. She blinked to get actual tears flowing. Any advantage.

He hesitated, on the edge, maybe surprised by his own indecision. "I think we better talk to Wade. Let him decide."

"Oh, please, no." She said, "I'm awful embarrassed, and I'll be so late getting back to work. My boss is already talking cutbacks. If I have to go through another layoff . . ."

She made her chin tremble like it did at the dentist's. "I said I was going over to Kinko's on lower Broad to pick up some copies. Look, I'll give you my name, and you can call me. I'm Brenda Carter. I'm at Bean Associates at 280 Second. It's a management company. You can write down the phone number. It's—" And she made up a number two digits off from Fleetwood. And repeated it. He released her arm, but she didn't move. One step either way, and he'd grab her again. "I learned my lesson, and I'm sorry, and if you want to call the police I don't blame you."

The word "police" made him twitch. Almost flinch. Her best bet yet. "Maybe you'd better call a policeman," she said. Rub it in, this magic word. "—so I can explain. I'll tell the officer what I did and he'll have to deal with it. Maybe I deserve it, the kind of breaks I've had lately. I'll give up, and you can call the police, and I'll admit it. I've never been in trouble with the police, but first time for everything. Just my luck, the police." She kept up the trembling chin, hoping she managed to say "police" half a dozen times.

He rubbed his nose and squinted and licked the white spit.

And now looked worried. Last thing he wanted, the cops. Some history here?—maybe promises about no more trouble. This one he could do without? Did she push the right button, finally?

He said, "Tell you what I'm gonna do. Just this once I'm gonna let you go. This once. But if Wade's truck ever gets touched, one finger on his personal possessions, then, Miss Brenda, we'll see about you. You touch that truck, and we can snap your bones like itty bitty sticks. Here's a taste—"

Hard wrench. Left forearm. Elbow snapped at the joint. It sent her reeling.

Pain. Not to scream. No noise. Her heel caught between the paving bricks and wrecked her balance, and she slammed against the truck door, wrist raked against jagged steel. Off balance, she staggered, murmured, one shoe barely on and scuttled away, walked quickly with shoulders hunched, cradled. She held her arm and stuck her thumbtip in her mouth, tried to suck out the splinter, exited the alley with those snake eyes on her back.

She kept it up all the way down to Second, past Fleetwood and up the hill past Mere Bulles and the Spaghetti Factory to the cream brick building with Bean Associates lettered on the glass. From the lobby she saw a stairwell and took the steel stairs all the way down and left through a door that led to First Avenue, then walked back down the block. She was buzzed in at the unmarked heavy gray door that connected, four flights up, to the Fleetwood offices.

Inside the locked washroom, she leaned against a sink and closed her eyes and allowed herself to tremble. For real. Limp, wrung out. She tried to move her elbow. Sprained, surely sprained.

And she was pissed, Feeling set up and stupid. Sloppy and angry. She released pink liquid soap directly onto her thumb and wrist, soaped up her hands twice, rinsed, cranked the paper towel and patted dry. Then she cranked down another length and wiped at her dress front, her sleeves. Sore arm. Sore thumb. Back alley souvenirs.

Safe in her office she sat for long moments, pulled herself together, and checked messages. It was lunchtime, nobody available for return calls. Lunch recess. Just time, in fact, to make a personal call of her own, the second of this rotten day.

So she left the office, took the stairs to the basement level, and retraced her route back up First, crossed at Church, and, constantly looking both ways on streets and sidewalks, got her car from the garage on Union and stayed on Union to avoid lower Broadway. She headed west to the Interstate 40 on-ramp just as it started to rain. Steering with her right hand, she turned on the wipers for the twenty-minute drive to Briley Parkway north, to the Fessler's Lane exit, where she made two right turns and pulled into the Quality Seven motel.

Bobbie was one of two clerks at the desk, and she looked up and beamed a smile tinged with apprehension.

"Why Kate, you saw the newspaper this mornin'."

"No, Bobbie, I have not been reading the paper. I have been listening to Wade Rucker sing, and I need a few minutes of your time. In private."

Bobbie went a little pale. Her co-worker, a buxom blonde with hair pushed back in a banana clip, glanced sideways from the computer screen and said, "I'll cover, Bobbie, if you need a little time."

Bobbie looked glum, as though some time was the last thing she wanted. Very slowly she moved from behind her desk while the Muzak speakers piped "No Other Love" and the phones warbled. "This a private talk between us, Kate?—I thought so. Why don't we go in the Chestnut Room. All our meetin' rooms are named for trees."

She unlocked it and they stepped into a stuffy dark space. Bobbie flicked on the lights and gestured toward padded blue chairs around a conference table under a vinyl wall mural of a green and brown shade tree. Ventilation was not a priority at Quality Seven, and every breath felt like a molecule stew from the Stainmaster to the Herculon. Bobbie leaned to brush at Kate's sleeve as they sat. Pain zinged to the elbow. "Kate, you got something on your nice plaid dress. Looks like you rubbed up against those bricks where you work."

Kate's voice became taut with anger. "This is rust from Wade Rucker's truck."

"Oh."

"—because I had a kind of close call with a friend of Wade's in the back alley behind Mac's Hitching Post. A big man with greasy black hair and a horseshoe ring. Maybe you know who that is—because I had a hunch there might be more to Wade than you told me, Bobbie. And you know what? I was right."

She made another soft "Oh."

"So I'm here to verify a few things, and this time I need the straight story. I don't want to come back here with my arms in plaster. Or on crutches." Bobbie seemed to go paler in the fluorescent light. "Wade Rucker sulks, but's not just a sulker, is he?" Bobbie shook her head. "First tell me about the man with the horseshoe ring."

"I imagine that'd be Chuck Munde." She twisted her rings. "He doesn't own Mac's, I don't think, but he's some kind of partner. He tries to be a promoter. Brandi and Wade sang down there a couple times. He wanted to make her and Wade into an act, like the Ike and Tina Turner of country music. Wanted them to work up their act on that stage at the Hitchin' Post. Brandi said no—just refused. She couldn't stand it down there. Called it the black hole of music. Couldn't stand Chuck Munde either. She said he brings out Wade's bad side."

"Tell me about Wade's bad side, Bobbie."

She looked away. Kate's arm settled into an aching throb. She could imagine both of them on these blue chairs a good while as the woman held out and her co-worker soloed at the front desk. Why the hesitation? Was it family loyalty? Southern customs? Somewhere deep down Bobbie had to know her sister's killer was someone close at hand. Had to be. Why deny it? Why go to such lengths dodging the truth?

Kate leaned toward her. "Bobbie, you kept important information to yourself, and I had a very nasty scrape because of it.

Now I need some answers from you. Did you lie about Wade to protect Brandi? What's the story?"

The young woman ran her cuticle against the lapel edge and then adjusted her jewelry, two gold rings with aquamarine clusters. She pushed at her chain and bangle bracelets and pulled at her cuff. "It's just—there's another side to Wade Rucker. A mean streak."

"How mean?"

She looked at Kate. "Mean like venom. He just gets out of control. I saw it once and it was real ugly. Grady saw it too. You could ask him."

Kate spoke softly. "Was he ever violent with your sister? Did he hit her?"

Her nod was barely perceptible. "Brandi always said she could handle him."

"But you knew better?" Bobbie paused again, twisted one of her rings. Kate said, "Tell me about Brandi 'handling' Wade?"

She dropped to a little-girl voice and spoke to the fluorescent wall fixture. "I thought she was goin' up fool's hill on the slippery side." She paused and uncrossed her legs. "One time last spring, May it was, Brandi came in from a weekend gig in Paducah. Must have been two, three in the morning. Sounded like stones rattling on the kitchen floor. Woke me up. It was Brandi cracking ice to put on her face."

Bobbie touched her cheekbone. "—right here. Said she got banged up from helping load equipment back in the van after the show. She was shakin', tremblin' all over. Me, I never did believe that equipment story, and it wasn't the first time Wade had her lookin' like death warmed over. She put a load of base and powder over her cheekbone, but it didn't cover up the swelling."

Bobbie stared at the mural wallpaper. "Her cheek was plum color under the makeup. Sometimes I was scared for Brandi." She paused, clasping and unclasping her hands. "You don't see that side of Wade too often. It just breaks out now and again, like he's storing it up in the heat and sun and then explodes like a storm over the ridge. When he's like that, you don't want to get near him."

Kate nodded. So one family secret was out. Brandi Burns stayed too long in an abusive relationship, and Wade Rucker was periodically violent. He brooded. He lashed out.

Did he go even further, to plot the death of his former lover? Was he a calculating killer making Brandi Burns the ultimate victim?

"Kate, it's hard to think Wade would kill my sister. He could knock her into next week, but that's different from killin'. You couldn't know Brandi and want to kill her."

"You're wrong, Bobbie. Somebody wanted to kill her and succeeded." She pressed close. "And it was probably somebody she knew. Maybe somebody you know, Bobbie, an acquaintance, a friend—"

"No."

"—a relative, or someone in the music business."

"Kate, stop it."

"—or maybe a conspiracy. Two or more persons combining for unlawful purposes. Maybe Wade Rucker and Judy Swan."

"Kate, you're actin' crazy."

"I'm trying to bust that rosy bubble you live in, Bobbie. You dragged me into this, and I'm trying to help. But your viewpoint is dangerous. You're being an ostrich."

"Big ugly bird."

"Hiding from the facts." Kate bent even closer, felt the table edge press at her diaphragm. "You are not honoring Brandi's memory by pretending she was a beloved saint adored by the whole wide world." She took a breath, staring hard at this woman. "If you really want to honor her memory, you'll help me get to the truth. You're the one who dragged me into this."

Kate stopped, her voice tight. For a moment, the only sound was of breathing. Across the table, Bobbie's face ran the gamut from injured pride to pitifulness and distress. Eyes downcast, she put her pinky to her mouth and sucked the tip.

When at last she spoke, her voice sounded very small. "In my family," she said, "we speak no evil. Mama insists. It's like our golden rule. Partly it's the Lord's way, and trying to do right."

She glanced up at Kate, shyness in her face. "But partly it's about Brandi's music career. When we came to Nashville, just us, none of our close kin, except Floyd and Lucille, well, Mama got 'specially strict about it. She was worried we'd offend somebody and hurt Brandi's chances in music. That was always her worry, that me or Brandi might mouth off and hurt Brandi's career.

"It's like a way of life in our family, like second nature, though Mama's loosened up lately. She'll talk real frank about Roy Benniger. But she's strict, like my granddaddy. He was a sailor during the war, and they had a saying, 'Loose lips sink ships.' Mama drilled that into us." She briefly met Kate's eyes. "But you're right, Kate," she said, "I didn't speak up." She dried her pinkie on her skirt. "I'm sorry Chuck Munde scared you. I hope you didn't get hurt bad."

"No bones broken, if that's what you mean."

Kate stopped. No point in sarcasm. She waited a minute, worked to calm down. Bobbie's face was a portrait of remorse. Maybe this was a turning point, a signal of change. She needed to think so. She rose, and so did Bobbie, who fingered her ring of Quality Seven keys.

"Kate, just to get a head start on speakin' up, I should mention the announcement in the paper this morning."

"I didn't see today's paper."

"Usually I don't either, but Grady knew the story was coming out today, and I got a *Tennessean* out of the newspaper box out front. Grady stayed, you see, and talked to us about it after you and Kelly left Saturday night. He wanted me and Mama to understand and feel right about it. It seems like a real good opportunity for him."

"What opportunity?"

"About his new management job." They stood in the tiled foyer as Bobbie turned off the lights and shut the door marked Chestnut Room and double locked it. "Grady's going to manage Jon Hartly Owens—the one they're calling the Texas

Lightning." The key crunched. "It's in the business section. Jon Hartly Owens is supposed to be the next Garth Brooks and Billy Ray Cyrus combined. That's why Grady wanted to talk to us out at the house, make sure we understood why he'd need to leave off workin' for Brandi this fall. With two artists, he couldn't've handled the work load. But of course our tragedy canceled out the conflict, like he said." She sighed. "All the contract stuff was hush-hush. He wanted us to know."

Kate stared at those wide eyes of the true believer. "Bobbie, you're telling me Grady Stamps was planning to break his contract with your sister?"

"Got approached by Jon Hartly's people last spring; that's what he told us."

"So a big new management contract was in the works before Brandi's death? And Grady Stamps planned to break his contract with Brandi?"

They stood in the lobby. "Kate, bless your heart, sometimes I think you could go on the stage yourself. Why, you even make it sound like our Grady could be connected with my sister's death. You Yankees have more suspicions than a hound has fleas."

Chapter Eight

She was trying to get home, but her legs would barely move on the brick sidewalk. Stumbling, grasping Kelly's hand, Kate pulled mittens on her shivering and sweating little girl who begged and pleaded and seemed both thirteen and three years old. Around them roared an ocean storm piling snow in drifts that blocked the way. And somewhere in the weird sky Sam was flying. Sam Powers. She heard his voice. If only he could land his plane in the storm and help guide her and Kelly back home.

But the snow whirled them to an icy bridge over a muddy river and a salt marsh. There was fog, townhouse brick, the harbor. And cabins, some rustic place smelling of kelp and pond scum. And a banshee wail, a keening sound, eerie at the center of her brain. An alarm cry of violins, no, these were fiddles.

A stage became a barn, a limestone cliff where seagulls screamed. Gasping, Kate rolled onto her back and felt like a diver surfacing for air. She found herself staring, not seeing. No water, no storm. It was dark as a bruise in the room, whatever room. Boston in summer. No, Nashville. Autumn. In her bed in the new condo, Kelly in her own room. The banshee cry turned into the telephone. It was ringing.

She reached across to the night table, groped at the Kleenex box, knocked the Chapstick and the empty glass and got hold of the receiver. "Kate Banning." Her at-work greeting, voice thick from the dream. The nightmare.

"Kate, it's Dukie." The voice pitched strangely high. "Dukie Burnside, Kate."

"Time is it?"

"After four."

Four A.M. Middle of the night. Country morning?

"Kate, the fire trucks just left. Bobbie's on her way. She told me, 'Mama, call Kate . . . Get Kate . . . Tell her to come out to the house.' I beg you, Kate, come out here. They nearly burned us out."

Kate leaned on one elbow. "What burned?"

"My house. My home. My kitchen." She coughed, her voice choked.

"Dukie, what are you saying?"

"—gasoline and rags, and just lucky I smelled it. Oh Kate, like Bobbie says, could you just come out to see? We wouldn't ask, but I don't know how else to do."

Kate turned on the table lamp. 4:27 on the clock radio. She swung her legs off the bed. "You had a house fire?" Still groggy, still processing.

"Firebug. Captain says so. They left the empty gas can laying in the yard." She coughed again. "If you'd just come out for a little bit. Bobbie will be here."

As if Bobbie Burnside were the draw. "I have to get dressed." As if putting on clothes were a major consideration.

As if talking about dressing were anything less than a promise to come. "I have to get Kelly up. I'll be there by—" The clock radio read 4:29. "—as soon as I can."

The high-pitched thanks dissolved in another cough and then the line went dead. Kate put down the receiver. Her arm still ached. Her yawn was like a tremor. Did she dream all that too? Arson at the Burnsides'?

She went into the bathroom, flicked on the light and stared in the mirror at the reflection of a groggy woman in an XL T-shirt/nightgown that said Legal Sea Foods and had a fish printed on it. Boston cod. On her front a fish, and in her thoughts Dukie Burnside, Dukie of Dixie. Could you straddle both sides of that line surveyed by Messrs. Mason and Dixon?

Or did the very attempt put you in a third place, a zone where your mind and heart tallied up the price of uprooting and gave it to you in screaming black virtual reality? Boston and Nashville in some scary neural synthesizer—the disorient express, and Kate Banning was riding it all the way.

She reached toward the toothbrushes stuck in an amber plastic water glass, just like in Boston. Tonight Sam Powers would be here to use his. Just like in Boston. She needed him right now, but, just like in Boston, she would have to wait. What else was new? What wasn't new? She looked around the bathroom. Nice new tiles. Just like a motel.

But Kelly—Kate went barefoot down the hall to her daughter's door, turned the knob silently and peered in. The room smelled like apples and sneakers, cologne and crayons, and she walked to the bed and rested her hand on Kelly's shoulder and pulled up the light cotton blanket and straightened the stuffed animals, Edgar the hippo and Beary the potbellied bear, and felt comforted herself by the steady soft breathing of her dear child.

But now the practical considerations. Kelly was up till after ten last night—or was it this night?—planning her plant growth school project. Grow lights and a beaker with metric markings. Very scientific. To wake her for a predawn drive to the Burnsides' for a firsthand view of a house fire, a fire at a home where people were real and the dog so cute. Terrible idea.

Kelly's Mickey Mouse alarm read 4:58. Kate added up the travel time. She alone could get out to Joelton by 5:45 and back here in time to get Kelly up and off for school. She could write a note in big letters with green marker and tape it to the inside of Kelly's bedroom doorframe. Barely doable. She went back to her room, pulled on jeans and a black jersey, and ran a brush through her hair.

But if her daughter awoke to find Kate gone, she could panic. Life in Nashville was too new. Scrap the predawn field trip. New logistics—wake her daughter early and get her to school when the building opened. Early-bird special. Then go to the Burnsides' before work. Skip the note.

Kate rubbed her sore elbow, went into the kitchen and put

the coffee on, half caf, half decaf. She showered and shampooed and vowed to get her hair cut as she ran the blow dryer that wouldn't work on high, then applied base, light powder, blush, the penciling. All those Clinique greens. Then on to the closet. What to wear to the scene of a fire in the country in the South. Fire scene chic?

She reached for a skirt with a deep kick pleat, the better to walk in, my dear. And a cotton shirt, washable and okay for the workday. Belt. Light jacket. Brown pumps, but throw a pair of moccasins into the car. Her arm showed the bruise from the alley faceoff with Mr. Chuck Munde. Her stiff elbow and shoulder kept the memory fresh.

She said nothing to Kelly about the fire when she woke her at 5:45 to drag her out. Complaints rolled off as she poured the orange juice and the Cheerios, spread the peanut butter and apricot jam on the wheat bread, cut the sandwich and wrapped it in Cut-Rite and washed the apple and then counted three ginger snaps and wrapped them in wax paper too. The pleasures of the mundane. The daily rituals of stability. The school lunch as fortification against arson, against murder. Nice occupational therapy.

She kept the fire in the back of her mind driving Kelly to school at 6:30. She kept an eye on the surrounding vehicles as her daughter, fully awake, her grievances exhausted, now spoke eagerly of Sam's arrival this evening. An easy conversation as Kate scanned for signs of anybody in pursuit. Where was Sam flying in from, Kelly wanted to know. It was a self-interested query. He brought her mementos from wherever.

"The upper Midwest," Kate said. "Michigan."

"What do they have there?"

Have? The consumer outlook of the modern child. "Cars. Motown music."

"Oldies."

"Golden oldies to you, kid." Diana Ross as history. Don't tell Kelly that her mother danced to Supremes records with Sam Powers. At age thirteen, what could Kelly imagine but the gyrations of the old with the oldies. "I'm sure Sam will find

something just right to bring you, Kel. He always does." They
pulled into the circular drive at the opposite end from the
school bus entrance. In the turn-around behind them was a
beige Ford 150—occupied by parents and kids.

In the rearview mirror Kate watched the passenger door
open, swing out. Smooth paint, no dimples. At the drop-off
line she let Kelly out and looked sideways at the old red brick
building, stairs scooped from decades of kids' feet, today's
Nikes to history's Buster Browns. The school reminded them
both of buildings in Boston, even though the kids' voices said
South with every syllable. Kate watched Kelly say hi to two
girls, fall into step with them. Her "Bye, Mom" was dismis-
sive, and Kate was relieved. Was her daughter beginning to
take hold, make friends at last, six weeks into the move? The
girls looked nice.

The beige truck moved off.

Then to the Interstate 440. Almost a full tank of gas. The envelope with directions to the Burnsides was in the glove compartment, and she reached for it as she accelerated into the
center lane. The ride was fast and uneventful, outbound
against the rush hour stall. Lots of trucks had running lights
on, and everybody behaved. The car clock said 7:03 as Kate
turned down the dirt driveway in front of the bungalow where
Bobbie's Malibu was parked. No sign of the white Sentra. Or
the fire, for that matter, though an acrid odor hung in the air.
Leaving her own car, Kate laid a hand on the hood of the Malibu. Warm to the touch. So Bobbie had been someplace else.

She started up the front steps, thought better of it, decided to
walk around back. There were big tire prints on the grass. Fire
trucks, from the look of it, two of them. At the foot of the
porch steps was a lumpy cloth bag which she passed by for
now. Along the side of the house, the burnt smell hit her. And
there at the back stood Dukie Burnside in bare feet and a big
pink satin quilted robe.

She looked like a huge lawn ornament. Bobbie stood beside
her with one arm around her mother's shoulders, the other
cradling an agitated Chop, his front paws working against her

arm. Bobbie wore jeans and tan boots, and a blouse with a striped vest. Not the clothes you throw on in a middle-of-the-night emergency. Wherever she was this past night, odds were Bobbie never got to bed. Mother and daughter were staring together at the blackened, burned-out corner of their house. The beagle yelped.

"Kate! Here's Kate!"

The two women lurched forward with cries and open arms, and Bobbie drew Kate to them and clutched her hand as Kate, too, stared at the scene of the fire.

A full corner of the house, the kitchen corner, was eaten away, the standing timbers now columns of ash. Dukie's eyelet lace curtains were entirely consumed, the rods buckled and black. The wood backdoor stairs were all but gone, the whole section blackened like campfire marshmallows. The plaster and insulation were melted and sodden from the firemen's work, and it felt steamy and marshy underfoot from so much hosed water.

Kate looked up. Soot streaks surged up the gray shingles to the window and beyond. Darkened and broken from the heat, the glass shards in the window frames stuck out like black daggers. Wire coatings had melted too, and you could see through the burned opening into the kitchen, the table, the framed mottoes on the wall. In a bowl, a bunch of bananas. It was a ghastly version of those sugar Easter eggs with a peep hole view.

"We were lucky. That's what the firemen said, lucky the whole house didn't go up." Dukie clasped her neck with one hand. "It's confined to the kitchen. They said if it got to the stairs, there'd probably have been no stopping it."

Kate said, "Fortunate nobody was hurt."

"I blame myself, Mama facing this all alone." Bobbie shifted the dog's paws from her forearm. "Not even Chop here with her."

"So you weren't at home?"

"—over at Dawn and Beca's, and they both just love this dog, so I took him with me." Bobbie scratched the beagle's head. "We were packin' stuff. Gonna be just Dawn's place now. Beca's moving out. I was helpin' her pack up."

Kate took a step back from the puddle of plaster mush. "Where's she moving?"

"Out of Dawn's hair. They're real close but livin' together didn't work out because they're such opposites. Anyway, I was glad to help. We all got to be friends when . . . when Brandi was gettin' ready to go into the studio for *Fool Moon.* Dawn always had great makeup ideas, like with Brandi's eye-shadow—" She swallowed as if to avoid a pitfall of deep feeling for her sister. "Anyway, I was over at their place, and it got late, and I decided to stay over. I thought Mama was spending the night on Lucille's foldout."

"Then you weren't planning to be at home overnight, Dukie?"

She shook her head no. "I was keeping Benny and Glenn while Lucille and Floyd went up to the V.F.W. But Floyd's off Tuesdays and could change my oil, so he brought me back and went on home in my Sentra."

"—so it was just coincidence Mama was even here to smell it."

"Like lighter fluid. Woke me up. Like cellophane cracklin'. I thought I heard a motor start up too."

Kate was scrambling. Two women talking in family short-hand. Put this together. She said to Dukie, "You mean, you were here in the house, but no car was parked outside?" They both nodded their heads. "From the outside, then, the house looked empty. No lights, no cars. Middle of the night." Kate was halfway thinking out loud.

Dukie nodded.

"No vehicles in view. That's what the fire captain remarked on. And the detective too."

"The police have started their investigation?"

"Comin' back later this morning. They took some rag pieces and the gas can for evidence. The rag pieces—" She shrugged.

"—they were some kind of flannel, looked like a checkered shirt. It was hard to see in the dark. The gas can they found

was ordinary, the cheap kind you get at Dollar General."
Dukie's voice dropped to a monologue. "The police and firemen shined their big lights on it. Carl Ruff from State Farm,
he's our insurance man, Bobbie called him."

Kate nodded and stared back at the fire scene. She could see
where fire axes gashed the door sill. She stepped closer and
felt the retained heat. "So somebody soaked rags in gas and
lighted them here at the back steps."

"Far as we know. Just burned up my kitchen. My new floor
Floyd put in." Bobbie tried to keep a comforting arm across
her mother's shoulder. Dukie clenched and unclenched her
hands, nervous and angry. "I shudder to think if the backstairs
door wasn't closed at the landing upstairs, or if I slept on . . .
see, I keep a window open, and the smell and cracklin' woke
me. I went down the front stairs and came through the hall and
saw it and couldn't believe my own eyes. I ran back upstairs to
the phone in my bedroom. The 911 operator told me, go outside, the fire department will be right there. At first I did. But
I'm not one to wait."

Kate heard defiance in her tone. She looked at Dukie's face.
The woman seemed poised to make a statement. Let her. "So
what did you do?"

"I went back in and grabbed me a pillow case and started
rescuing things. The tiaras from the curio case, my girls won
every one in pageants. They're a promise of destiny. Talent
and beauty a girl needs for success. Put 'em in the pillowcase.
And Bobbie's mandolin, I pulled it off the mantel. Let the artificial flowers burn up, but you never know if that mandolin's
in my daughter's future. This life isn't going up in flames if I
have anything to say about it."

She stood with feet planted wide apart on the grass. Like a
pink monument. Like the captain defiant on a burning deck.
No fire safety week slogans for Dukie Burnside.

Maybe this was a test—what did you rush to save when
your place was burning? No eyelet lace for sentimental value
for Dukie. No dolls, no little ribboned dresses. That pillowcase

of tiaras was not a keepsake of the Burnside daughters' childhood, but a milestone in their careers.

Dukie's stance on the grass had not changed, though Kate saw her literally in the new light of day. This mama was not the handmaid of Brandi's ambition, but the iron will that drove them all, glowing hotter than flames. Bobbie might or might not harbor secret desires to take up where her sister left off. But, you could bet this surviving daughter would be decked in fringe and spangles by next spring if her mother had anything to say. Goodbye Quality Seven.

Kate's eyes smarted. Ash particles and too early in the morning. And, the inevitable question— Who did this?

Dukie clutched the pink quilted robe around her. "I get along with all my neighbors. I pay my bills. I don't have an enemy that would dare to show their face and say I did them wrong. Some are jealous, some driven to evil ways when they do not prevail."

Her right hand swept her brow, then turned into a fist and anchored itself on her hip. "Materialistically speaking, Kate, there's nothing worth burning up. The living room furniture's our only splurge. That and the new upstairs bathroom. But if breaking our spirit's the point of this, or scaring us like a bunch of rabbits, then somebody made a worse mistake than they know. I have lost one daughter, but her spirit is with us forever. We honor her by moving forward."

Kate nodded. She walked in silence around the side of the house toward the front. Bobbie trudged behind, also silent. Chop whimpered. But Dukie was on the march, steps in cadence as she picked up the cloth bag, the pillowcase stuffed with trophies.

In the daylight Kate stopped to pick up a piece of something. Trash? No, a strip of orange colored cloth lying in the grass.

"That's it, Kate. You're holdin' the evidence." Kate smoothed it and saw the pattern of orange and cream checks. "That's a little bitty piece like the firemen found. That's the rags."

Kate held it to her nose. No gas odor. "And you've never seen this cloth before? Nobody's shirt?"

Both women shook their heads emphatically. Chop wiggled, and Bobbie switched arms to support her. Kate stared at this scrap of fabric, some three-by-six inches and torn on three sides, finished off on the fourth. Too small to bother igniting as a gas rag, too big to leave carelessly behind.

If it were left carelessly.

So what did this amount to? Kate handed Dukie the fabric scrap, which she pocketed. The rags and the gas can pointed to an amateur.

Or maybe a professional's blind lead, deliberately littering the site with misleading evidence that would point to a novice. Either way, this was a crime of destruction, not theft.

She stood at the front of the house. As Grady Stamps showed, you could park up on Lawler Road and walk down the driveway unseen and silent in the darkness. Neighbors' dogs might bark, but the house was screened on both sides by trees. The dogs would settle down.

And how much gas could the arsonist carry—at most three or four gallons held tight against the body? A light plastic bag of rags looped over one arm? Anybody in a passing vehicle would spot a fire set at the front, so it made sense to go around back. It was practical.

She stared at the porch pillars, the sagging gutters, the patched screens. Shafts of golden sunlight broke through the trees on the east side and bathed the house in a mockery of its dilapidation. Such a sorry-looking target. Why burn it? And if the objective was total incineration, wouldn't a skilled arsonist encircle the house with an accelerant to really torch it?

But suppose, on the other hand, that the goal was not total destruction. Suppose a selective target, in which case there was perhaps a reason to set a fire at the backdoor to the kitchen. The ruined kitchen would be a strike at Dukie Burnside's life center, at the cooking that was her comfort in the wake of her daughter's death. Did somebody hate Dukie enough to destroy her kitchen for spite? A hate crime? An old grudge?

And the obvious question—did Brandi's killer do this? Was it a murderous saboteur at work? And was the beige truck part of the pattern? Kate kept on walking around the house to the other side. A window on the second floor toward the back was open a few inches. All other windows were shut, so this must be Dukie's bedroom.

Dukie said, "I didn't see headlights in the driveway. I thought I heard a car."

"Not a truck?"

She paused. "I couldn't say. Car or truck, it was an engine. It could've been anybody. People around here, some work nights."

Kate nodded. Right now she was thinking of the arsonist as somebody familiar with the house, somebody knowing about updrafts and downdrafts as they knew about automobile fluids. "Dukie, if you hadn't closed the upstairs landing door, the kitchen fire would have been sucked up the back stairs."

"That's what the firemen said."

"Tell me, what's at the top of the backstairs?"

"Empty bedroom. Spare room."

"Not your room, Bobbie?"

Hugging the vest, Bobbie stepped up. "No, mine and Brandi's to the front, and off it is the new bathroom. We're the windows that face the road. The back ones are Mama's on one side and the spare on the other. Guestroom, sort of. Lucille and Floyd's boys stay in there when they sleep over. Anybody that visits, really."

"And what's in that room?"

Dukie cleared her throat. "Just an old double bed and a rocking chair that never rocked smoothly."

"And that's all?"

"And a chest."

"—with some old quilts." Bobbie chimed in.

"Quilts?"

"From Mama's Aunt Mae. From over in East Tennessee."

"You mean the quilts where Brandi's notebook was stored?"

Dukie did not blink. "I thought about that, Kate. I do not believe it's connected."

Kate saw her expression. In an instant it went blank, as though Kate had ventured out of bounds. Stone wall. Shut down. The kitchen in ashes, her daughter dead, and the very notion that an insider who knew the house might try to destroy evidence by burning it to the ground—this was a taboo thought. The notebook could be a firebomb target, but that very notion was not acceptable, so Dukie quite simply would not hear of it in her forward march. Not in my backyard.

Kate turned to face her. "Dukie, you called me to come out here. Got me up in the dark, and I drove up as soon as possible. This isn't a social visit. I'm horrified by what happened, and believe me, I sympathize. But for me this is work. I think you know that. Floyd and Lucille can comfort and guide you, but my part in this is different. I want you to tell me how many people knew where you put Brandi's notebook."

Dukie Burnside pulled the pink quilted robe closer and seemed to hug herself. Her tone was reluctant, as if disloyal. Or as if a plan were foiled? Finally she said, "Kate, you could figure that out on the fingers of one hand. You know where it's kept, and Bobbie and I do, and I mentioned it to Lucille. I believe I told Judy Swan where I planned on puttin' it. So that's five. And Grady, of course, being he was here when we all looked at the notebook Saturday night. I told him."

"How about Wade Rucker?"

Dukie shuddered. "He couldn't know a thing about it. Truly he couldn't."

Kate turned. Bobbie was pulling the striped vest closer as if for warmth. Kate said, "Have you told anyone—anyone at all—who might tell Wade? Have you spoken to Chuck Munde?"

"Not on your life. And I wouldn't tell Wade the time of day. You know that. Besides, I promised you, Kate. I take promises serious." She stuck her thumbs in her vest pocket. "—maybe Judy Swan, though, accidentally. Sometimes she blurts stuff."

Kate nodded. "And now how about Grady Stamps? Did you call him this morning?"

"Grady?" Dukie's voice was nearly shrill. "Wake up Grady when he hardly sleeps as it is? That boy does so much for us, I spare him when I can. Not that he wouldn't come. He'd be here in a minute if I called. Any of us."

Kate paused, puzzled. Wake up Kate Banning at four A.M. but let Grady Stamps slumber on? Saint Grady again, the canonized manager. Ex-manager who was planning his exit even as this family clasped him to its bosom. His help would be sought for Bobbie's debut in country music, of course, at least as a consultant. So give him plenty of rest now at the front end.

Kate looked at her watch. Dukie turned. She was padding back into the house, the steps now tender on her bare feet. Bobbie squatted to put Chop down, and the dog scrambled and scratched and barked, frenzied by alien scents on home turf. Maybe the dog was the sanest of them all.

"I have to get going," she said, "get to work." She turned to Bobbie, squinting in the early light. "I want you to do something."

"—for sure, Kate. Tons of stuff to do. I called in already at the motel. Floyd's coming out, and Carl Ruff from State Farm, and he'll . . ."

"Bobbie, listen to me. Brandi had a contract with Grady Stamps, didn't she? A formal management contract?"

Bobbie blinked. "The contract the lawyers did up? That's the formal one. Reality was real different, more like family. Why—"

"Where is the management contract, Bobbie? Do you have a copy in the house?"

"The accountant's got it." She bit her lower lip. "But maybe in Brandi's special accordion file. With all her paperwork, we started keepin' records. I'd have to look. What do you want with it, Kate? What's it got to do with the fire? You don't think Grady was a part of this fire?"

"I want to know what penalty Grady Stamps would pay if he broke his contract with your sister. Contracts often have penalty clauses." Kate kept her tone matter-of-fact. No explanations, no hedging. "Let me see the contract. Then we'll talk. You can phone me at work or home. You can fax it to me. It could be very important. Do not discuss it, not even with your mother."

"Here she comes back."

Still padding on bare feet, hugging the quilted robe, Dukie looked determined. Kate moved toward her car, opened the door, got in. Enough of Dukie Burnside for now. She started the engine as Bobbie moved to the side of the house and called for the bewildered Chop who was running in circles and eights like a windup toy.

Kate rolled down the window to wave goodbye, only to see Dukie hold up a finger to signal her to wait. She moved to the car window as if walking on hot coals she refused to feel. Kate could smell the smoke in her robe, her hair.

She was leaning in and fumbling at the quilted robe. "Kate, I don't know why the notion took me. 'Learn or be taught' the sayin' goes." She opened the robe and swiftly thrust something into Kate's lap. The notebook. "I want you to have it. For safekeeping, just in case. I can't think anything in that book's worth burning up my house, but I want you to take it for the time being. I'm not even telling Bobbie. You just hang on to it for us, hear? Keep it safe. Be seein' you." And she turned and started back to her daughter and the crazed beagle.

Kate's first move was to shove the green notebook under the seat. Her second was to push the gas pedal a little too hard and spin her wheels in a cloud of smoky clay.

Her third was to open her car windows and turn on the fan blower en route back to the city. Clear the air. Back in the city, Music City, she opened the car windows wider. The notebook was still under the seat. Spiral bound, lined pages of lyric bits and those peculiar Nashville number-notes like some kind of contraband smuggled in by a country music illiterate in an old Buick. Irony.

And danger too? The bottomline question—was this notebook an incendiary device? If the Burnside house was torched to destroy it, what did the culprit think it contained? Pages imagined? Pages torn out? If so, by whom? Judy Swan? Bobbie? All that trouble to haul the gas and set the fire. All that jeopardy. All that viciousness. What for?

The questions circled and looped, and when she pulled into her slot at the parking garage, Kate made a decision. She put the notebook inside her canvas work tote, walked down to lower Broadway, giving Mac's Hitching Post a very wide berth, and entered Kinko's where she picked up a Vendacard at the counter and went to the photocopy machine farthest from anybody. The night customers were long gone, the morning bustle yet to come. Perfect timing, just a few eager beavers making copies before work, the blonde fledgling lawyer in a new Brooks Brothers double-breasted, the two women in caramel and wine tweeds with mid-thigh skirts. Interior designers? Travel agents? Kate smiled pleasantly and looked around once again. Outside the front window, passersby were crossing, but nobody in particular.

Nobody sitting in a curbside car either. And no car or truck—beige truck—visibly circling the block repeatedly, even though she waited through three changes of lights. In her dark separates, was she memorable? If asked to recall, would anybody at the counter remember a woman dressed for the workday Xeroxing a green spiral notebook?—perhaps a working mother copying a school notebook for her daughter or son?

At the moment a tall black man with dreadlocks and gray leather pants came in and approached the counter with a portfolio. A complex project—blueprints. All the staffers gathered to confer. Good.

Kate inserted the card and promptly began working fast. Two copies of each page. The Xeroxed sheets were a little crooked. No matter. It took less than a minute. Fourteen pages altogether. She sorted and stapled them and put them in the tote and snapped the fasteners. Then she took the card back to the desk and paid the dollar, three dimes, one penny.

Outside she walked fast, taking a circular route from Broadway up Fifth, then along the red brick walkway by the Ryman

Auditorium and past the bronze Captain Thomas Ryman at the wheel of his perpetual riverboat. Then down the brick terrace steps and left up Fourth to Commerce Street, where she turned right again and then left on to Second.

Then up mid-block to the parking garage. With a scanning glance she walked swiftly and deliberately to a black Oldsmobile Cutlass sedan five cars away from her own.

She paused as if to unlock it and simply stood a moment. Nobody following. At least nobody she could see. A silvery Lexus came through, then a red Jeep Cherokee, both spiraling to the second level, drivers not even glancing in her direction. Tight quarters, all concentration needed to steer.

A garage worker walked through to the front booth, his two-toned shirt with the badge, TransCom Parking Systems. She recognized his face. They waved. Another fifteen seconds and Kate proceeded to her car, opened the driver's door and set her tote on the seat, unfastened the snaps and took out the notebook. Which she stuck back under the seat, refastened the tote, locked the car and walked down the block to Fleetwood.

"Morning, Miz Banning. How are you today?"

"Morning, Delia. Fine, thanks." Then Kate said, "—and you?" And she watched Delia blink, register this new sign of civility on the part of the barbarous Yankee, then say she was just fine too, thanks.

Kate was moving toward the stairs when the receptionist called her back to say a service technician would be in to check her phone today.

"But there's nothing wrong with my phone."

She smiled. "Just making sure, Miz Banning."

"How come?"

Delia seemed hesitant. "Not to bother you, busy as you are. But several of your calls the last few days, they disconnected when I tried to transfer them."

"I haven't noticed."

"It goes dead if you don't pick up on the first ring or two." Delia's smile stayed fixed. "Frankly, it sounds like the same gentleman. Just a little gruff."

"What gentleman?"

"Never leaves his name. It's happened quite a few times these last few days. He asks for Kate Banning. It rings once and then there's a click."

"Does he call right back?"

"Usually not. But then I'm handling all the Fleetwood phone traffic, I really couldn't say." She smoothed her snowy collar. "We just want to be sure the voicemail and forwarding systems are operating correctly."

Kate felt her armpits prickle. "Delia, if it happens again, please let me know. Appreciate you keeping track."

"Glad to help out." The receptionist turned to take a call, and the moment felt frozen until Kate took the stairs two at a time to her office, shut the door, stared at the white telephone. She picked up the receiver. Benign, dial tone normal.

What "gentleman" with a gruff voice? Was Delia intercepting trouble meant for Kate?

And what about hang-ups on the home answering machine? At day's end at home, she was always thankful to be spared the day's credit card offers, investment deals, rug cleaning.

What if the hang-ups were something else? What if she was targeted? Should she get Caller ID?

Immediately she opened the tote and took out one copy of the notebook pages, which she buried in a file already marked *Leisure—Golf.* The remaining copy she left in the tote. Final resting place undecided.

Resting place, burial site. She shivered a little. She felt thankful to see her desk piled with work. Plunge in and do the day and try not to think about the damn phone or the evening, except for the pleasure of Sam Powers and the gratitude for Kelly's life on this earth.

But in the moment before digging in, Kate paused to give a second's thought to this private security drill. Kinko's, the Ryman, the garage and car. Now the phone. What for?—protection of a stripped, once-upon-a-time song writing notebook? Such effort for a clueless clue? Was she that neurotic?

She picked at a hangnail. Of course it was good to stay in training. Security aerobics.

But she could not quite fool herself; this was not a mere drill. Brandi was dead, her sister and Kate nearly run off the highway, her mother's house badly damaged in an arson fire. All in two and a half weeks. If somebody was desperate enough to try arson to destroy the notebook last night, it was possible that the contents were dangerous. The contents as is. The seven pages Kate had disparaged and dismissed and copied and hidden.

So that was the possibility she acted on this morning. *That* was why she behaved like an A.M. paranoid. It was on the chance that this notebook was trying to speak. And if it was, could she hear it before the Burnsides or she herself fell victim to what the media loved to call an incident?

Chapter Nine

The mussels came in a net bag at Kroger. Three pounds. To which add garlic, linguine, virgin olive oil, the last real tomatoes of the season. Kate slit the net. Beard the mussels, as every recipe began. But also turn the phone ringer to high and listen for Sam's call. Listen for any strange noise.

It felt like three years since Dukie Burnside woke her from a bad dream this very morning—and pulled her into a nightmare. She wished Kelly would get home. The after school science review seemed late. At the sink she yanked at seaweed and shell bits. She tossed out two dead rank specimens and hoped the lot wasn't somehow contaminated, as if mussels in Tennessee were an unnatural act.

As if Kate Banning in Tennessee were an unnatural act.

At 4:32 it was the doorbell, not the phone. Kelly? She checked the front door fisheye lens, a reflex from Boston, and the figure she saw through the door was pure surprise. She turned the bolt and—

"Sam!"

"Got a ride in. Guy at the maintenance hangar—"

"Don't explain just—get in here."

Inside, his flight bag, himself. She fell against him, stood back to see him, collapsed against his chest once again. Here he was in familiar sportswear, the light suede bomber jacket, gray slacks, and black shirt she bought him at a sale. Friend and lover and her, what, witness? Next-of—? Better than kin. Someone to vouch for her, for her daughter too. She said, "Kelly should be here any minute. She'll be so glad to see you."

The line so dopey, they both laughed. Glad wasn't good enough. They kissed long and deep. They went toward the kitchen, arms entwined. She said, "How was—was it Grand Rapids?"

"—mostly Traverse City. Interesting. More interesting if you were there. We'd shack up." He moved his hand to her breast, down her hip.

"Sam, we can't. Any minute Kelly—"

He groaned, laughed and groaned again. "I'm gonna have to rent us a little place here in Nashville. I love Kelly, but this condo doesn't have a west wing. Our west wing." He kissed her once again, drew back, took her hand and squeezed it. He dropped his jacket over the back of a chair and stretched and hugged her again, closer, then reluctantly parted. "Okay, let's behave, set an example. Here's—" He looked her in the eye with a playful expression. "Here's a *National Geographic* report."

"Traverse City?"

"On the shores of Lake Michigan. From the boom days of shipping, according to Geography 101. Iron ore, lumber, wheat. Now it's a water hole for the affluent of the upper Midwest. Cabin cruisers, sailing, lovely autumn weekends. I flew company brass in for golf and deals with bankers."

"Sounds . . . inland."

"You'd like it. They have seagulls."

"And what's the local history?" She smiled. It was their ritual. When his work took him to new places, he reported back. Standard opener between them. Ice breaker. "I picked up a couple books on storms and settlement of the Great Lakes. Read 'em at dinner in a nice restaurant at sundown yesterday. I figure, you ought to know the price somebody paid a hundred years ago in blood, sweat, and tears so you can dine on whitefish with cherry sauce in a Lake Michigan resort town at the close of the twentieth century."

"And you found out."

"Storms, wrecks, floods, ice. Miserable log cabins. The usual havoc of pioneering. Very interesting. Raises the question of what we're going to hand down, besides gridlock and plutonium. Oh, and sports utilities. The whole country feels so damn nervous and worried, they're driving around in armored cars." She heard the wry tone. This was Sam. His need to know, the way he never took things for granted. His thoughtfulness, his calm. His edge. "Hey, I brought you something." He went to his flight bag, opened it, took something out. "Traverse City is the cherry capital of the U.S." He put down a jar.

Kate picked it up. "Cherry butter?" Her "yum" tried for enthusiasm.

"A regional specialty, my dear Kate. Well-rounded persons need to know. Can't spend their life yearning for Boston baked beans."

She paused, looked directly into his deep-set brown eyes. "Sam, believe me, I yearn—but not for beans." She moved close, kissed him again. Enveloped in his arms, welcomed to his body.

They drew apart. Kelly any minute. The self-consciousness of that. "Brought you something else." From his flight bag, he took out a small square. A CD.

She took it. "*Country Classics*?"

"Dolly Parton, George Jones, Patsy Cline. Picked it up in Boston. Country music doesn't get much better than this."

"Country music flown all the way from Boston to Nashville?"

"—by way of Michigan. 'Coals to Newcastle,' isn't that the saying? I'm taking charge of your education. You need to expand beyond three country songs."

"Four, Sam." Slight edge, but playful. "Sure, I'll listen to it. Steamed mussels à la Dolly Parton."

"Thought you might fry up some country ham." His eye twinkled.

She said, "I've already had too many smoked things today." She put down the knife, opened a kitchen drawer and pulled out a plastic grocery bag. Sam pulled out a chair to sit down. By reflex Kate scanned the windows—kitchen, living room. Magnolias, hackberry trees, the rear end of a neighbor's Honda visible from a corner window. She must not be lulled into normality, even if Sam exorcised the menace from her world. She scanned the windows again. All signs normal. She reached into the plastic bag and said, "Exhibit A, the notebook."

He took it, felt it, put it to his nose. His face changed from curious to somber. "Been in a fire?"

She nodded. "Open it." She watched his expression as he did, turning pages forward, backward, forward again as if in search of real substance. Kate went to the refrigerator, opened a bottle of Amstel, put it in front of him. She poured herself a cranberry juice and soda and stood sideways at the sink to resume the mussels and tell him about the fire, the Burnside women, this notebook, the day at work, including her lunchtime and coffee break scrutiny of the Xeroxed version. "—which got me nowhere. Gibberish lyrics. As you see."

"And all these numbers."

"They're chords. That is, they correspond to notes. It's a local Nashville notation system for musicians who don't read music." She moved beside him and turned two pages. "See this? I'm told it's 'Fool Moon.' "

"Looks like fractions and suits of cards, at least diamonds. Interesting."

"I checked every page of the notebook with a magnifier the minute I got home. And held each one up to the light. Nothing. *Nada.* Unless rhyming 'sick' and 'ick' is a big clue. If this notebook is important, I can't figure it. So if you want to play me a country music album, that's fine. Patsy Cline, George Smith—"

"Jones."

"Jones. Just don't announce a quiz, because I'm up to my ears in questions I can't answer." She sighed. "What we need at this point is the anonymous caller."

"With the tip on the fluids? An update?"

She nodded. "Somebody out there knows something, Sam. If ever there were a time to pipe up, it's now. At least about the car. Or its history."

"—speaking of which, what about the tires?"

"I don't know yet. Too busy chasing around to ask about service records. At this point, the tires seem like a moot point—no, don't give me that look, I'll get to it. Meanwhile, there's plenty of suspicion to go around."

"The boyfriend?"

"Wade Rucker. Prime candidate. Met his goon promoter in a dark alley—been there, done that. But Wade and his buddy Chuck both seem, to put it kindly, crude."

Sam frowned. "—and that young woman's death wasn't crude enough?"

"It's not the death as such, Sam. What I mean is, if Wade Rucker killed Brandi, he seems like the type to personally strike the fatal blow. Pull the trigger, plunge in the knife, crush a throat with his bare hands. The break-in at Trystar fits him perfectly. Crude bashing, that's his style. If I'd just got a look in that toolbox."

She reached into the sink. Another six mussels. "—but that's exactly what bothers me," she said, "the style. Wade Rucker seems like a hands-on guy. He'd hide in the back seat of the Taurus and lunge out at Brandi. He might shove her headfirst into a rocky embankment or over a cliff. All one-on-one. Would he plot a death from such a distance? Is he subtle enough to drain most of the steering fluid and sit back out of sight to wait for the fatal result?"

"Or hope for it?"

"Hope? What do you mean?"

"I mean I've been thinking about all this too, Kate—the way I always do. If I can't stop you, it's better to help. The sooner it's done, the sooner you're safe again."

He paused to drink. This was the junction of their mutual worry—of her flights of crime, of his flights at thirty thousand feet. He leaned back, unbuttoned and rolled his left cuff, then his right. He rested an elbow against the kitchen table and stared off for a moment. "I'm thinking the obvious—an empty steering fluid reservoir is not a car bomb. Now, if Brandi had a steering failure—"

"—no *if* about it. I saw the car firsthand at that junkyard with Bobbie. The fluid was drained, and there was a hole in the hose. And the new clamp—" Her voice rose.

"Wait a minute, Kate, I'm not questioning those facts. I'm saying that to kill somebody with their own car, the steering fluid seems pretty much of a longshot."

"So what would you do? Cut the steering cables?"

He poured more beer and drank. "No. Stay with the fluids. Come back to the question of why steering fluid. Why not brake fluid? If you can't hit your brakes and stop your vehicle, that's the big test. That's a worst case scenario. It's what the highway downhill sand runouts for the eighteen-wheeler big rigs are all about, failed brakes. If I plotted an 'accident,' I'd go for the brakes."

Kate shook her head. "—but the panel warning light would flash. If Brandi was the safe driver Bobbie says she was, then she'd notice the red warning light on the panel. I went over all this with Bobbie." She looked at his face. "—unless the light was disabled, is that what you're thinking."

"Bypassed." He nodded. "And it's not that hard. There's a wire that attaches to the master cylinder. To disable the panel brake light, you unplug the wire. Any mechanic could show you how. If you knew about cars, you could do it yourself. And if you decided to trigger a fatal accident by draining fluid, the brake fluid's your best bet."

She paused. "—if you wanted to kill." She said it again, and her sentence hung suspended like the blade of the paring knife. "If . . ."

Sam rubbed his palms together. "What do you mean, if? Brandi Burns died. Cause and effect, action and reaction."

"No, I mean . . . of course she died. But maybe that's the problem, that she died."

"Kate, are you talking to yourself? Help me out. What am I missing?"

She put down the paring knife, rinsed her hands, dried them, and went to her purse and got the long folded sheet of thin paper. She said, "This is what you're missing."

"A fax?"

"From Bobbie. Came in late this afternoon, a little after four. It's a page from a contract between Grady Allan Stamps,

Management, and Brandi Lyn Burnside, dated eight November of last year. Wiedmeyer and Folkins, PC, Attorneys at Law. Plenty of herewiths and thereunto pertainings. But look at this language. Look at this section—'Termination for Cause.' "

She leaned closer and read, " 'Manager has the right within thirty days advance written notice to terminate the contract upon occurrence or any events of default by Artist.' And here's the default list. See, '—Artist's incapacity to perform for a period of fifteen days.' So if Brandi is out of the picture for a couple weeks, Grady Stamps is released from the contract. Says so right here, 'Manager shall have no further obligation to Artist.' "

Sam nodded. "So Grady Stamps just walks away and looks for another job."

"—in this case, a job already waiting for him. I saved last Monday's business section of the *Tennessean*. Bobbie told me about it. Tiny write-up announcing Grady Stamps a partner in the management of a new young country music singer named Jon Hartly Owens."

"Another new young star? Does this Grady guy collect 'em?"

Kate pushed back a lock of hair. "Arista Records has Jon Hartly Owens's face on a huge new billboard off Interstate 40. Four point two million is the figure for his new deal, according to the paper. They think he'll appeal to pop and soft rock fans too. So he's a bigger market than Brandi. Probably a bigger star. My guess is Jon Hartly's manager would have to be on the job full-time. No splitting the week between him and Brandi. Grady would be obligated to cut ties with her. But look here, Sam, the contract gets even more interesting. Read this part."

He traced his index finger further down. " 'Termination Without Cause'?" She nodded. His voice was slow and steady, pausing at the commas. "Manager may terminate this Agreement without cause upon thirty days advance written notice, at which time Manager must pay Artist sixty thousand dollars in cash as a termination fee.' So—a sixty-thousand-dollar penalty."

"—that's if Grady Stamps broke his management contract with Brandi Lyn Burnside, a.k.a. 'Artist.' "

Sam shrugged. "But that alone does not make Grady Stamps

a suspect in her death. And frankly, I can't imagine an ambitious manager being stupid enough to kill off a client for sixty thousand. If he's heading into a fat new contract, he could probably raise the money somehow."

He paused, drank some beer, then abruptly snapped the bottle down. "—oh, I see. Okay, Kate, dumb of me. I see your point. If Brandi is incapacitated, right? If she can't perform, she agrees to release Grady Stamps Management from all financial liability. Cancel the sixty grand. You're thinking about an accident that would injure not kill. An accident where Grady Stamps could arrange the kind of short-term injury to let him out of the contract free of charge."

"—the kind of accident likely to happen if the steering fluid were drained. And to happen just when her record promotion tour was ready. All Grady'd have to do is get her offstage for fifteen working days. So maybe a few broken ribs that would hurt too much to sing. Voilà, the contract dissolves."

He nodded. "He wouldn't want to kill her, only to get her away from the microphone for a couple of weeks. But the plan blows up. Instead of cracked ribs, Brandi dies. He's up for—?"

"Negligent homicide. And when Bobbie starts making noise about her sister's killer, Grady arranges to buy the Taurus from the wrecker yard and get it disposed of."

Sam grinned. He took her hand. "Great theory. Makes sense." Then he paused. "—unless sixty grand is peanuts."

"Peanuts? Did you say peanuts?"

"Small change."

Suddenly she felt an anger from a source she could not have named. It rose from her chest to her throat. It filled her with a flash of red rage.

"Peanuts? Sam Powers, if I had a bag of those peanuts, I could make a condo payment in Boston. And start a trust fund for Kelly's college and a little retirement nest egg, and—and have my regular life at home in Boston. And not pack up and move where I don't know a soul. And feel like it's a desert island while I wait for you. And crazy mussels in the middle of Tennessee." Her eyes smarted from sudden tears.

"Kate, Kate—" He stood and reached to hug her. "Oh Kate, this move is still weighing you down. I didn't mean to be a jerk. I'm . . . I'm talking about money out there in big bucks business terms. Not the dollars you're scraping together or working your buns off for. Terrific buns, by the way. I mean the money sloshing around in the business world. This sixty thousand is nothing compared to the bucks I hear those money jockeys talking about in the back of the cabin in the Lear."

He kept his arm around her. "You're right to call me on it. I'm getting warped from listening to those guys. But it's a whole different economy of scale, and music business money's bound to be in it. Sixty thousand bucks can be small change."

He took her hand. "The question is, wouldn't Jon Hartly Heartthrob's people just buy out Grady's contract with Brandi Burns? Contract buyouts happen all the time."

"I don't know. I can try to find out. I'm betting Grady Stamps wants to hitch his wagon to the brightest star he can find."

"I want you to stay out of back alleys."

She flushed. "No alleys. Going uptown from now on. Going to check on Wade Rucker at Vanderbilt. Yucca Flat plays fraternities. Nice safe college campus."

"I like the *safe* part." He sipped. "So just one more question for the moment. Tell me how this notebook fits."

She sighed, suddenly grounded. "That's what I can't figure, because it doesn't fit. Except for the fire at the Burnsides', I'd say that anything important in that notebook was long gone. Unless I'm wrong about that too." Square one, she thought. Or zero. Or nowhere.

The phone broke the moment. Kelly needed a ride home. Somebody's mother couldn't take her but was standing by. Kate promised to be there in fifteen minutes, but Sam volunteered, Sam for whom getting from here to there in a new place was a point of pride.

He took Kate's car keys and was gone, sending Kate back to the last of the mussels, the garlic, the steamer set up on the stove. Plus a pot of water for the pasta. And then the bottle of

Alsatian wine that floated cork bits from her tug-o-war with the corkscrew. Uncorking wine was one job where she believed in gender.

She opened a jar of Ragu, since Kelly would go "yuck" to mussels. Then she turned to salad greens, the Kirby cucumbers and the peppers. She was crumbling feta on the two adult salads when at last she heard the tires on the pea gravel, followed by doors and the voices closest to her in this world. She opened the front door.

"Mom."

"Hi Kel. Gimme a hug—and don't wrinkle your nose, because you've having Ragu. You two sure took a while."

"Sam wanted to stop at a bookstore. I took him to Bookstar because I know where it is. Only took a minute."

"You went shopping?"

Sam laughed. He dropped her car keys into her purse. "Just a little cryptography project." He held out the book for Kate to see.

The Nashville Number System.

"—by Chas Williams. It decodes all those music numbers. Thought we could check it out after dinner. With Kelly's help."

"My help? Hey, what do you mean?" Kelly was setting the table.

Sam said, "You're the in-house musician, aren't you? Got your flute oiled up?"

"Yeah, but I haven't played since June. I can't fit band into my schedule, and Mom hasn't found me a teacher yet."

"How about that Casio keyboard I gave you?"

"I guess that would work if the batteries are okay. I haven't played since we moved."

Sam nodded. "Batteries are no problem. And you'll remember enough. We're counting on you."

Then he gave Kelly her souvenir gift from Traverse City, a throw pillow with needlepoint cherries. Politeness and dismay skirmished in her face. Sam said she and Kate were clearly a mother-daughter duo. He'd give them both a rain check on a cherry substitute. So they sat through the dinner. Kate and Sam exchanged glances while Kelly wound her linguine and tried not to slurp.

It felt nice, familiar, like old times—as though old times were all of six months ago. Was the present moment to be nothing more than an exercise in nostalgia? Awful thought. She mentally backed away from it.

Finished, the dishes cleared and cleaned up, Kelly got out her little Casio keyboard and tested the batteries. She played a scale and a few chords. Kate made another mental note to find a flute teacher. Sam opened *The Nashville Number System* and read for a few minutes. All this felt like a family game of Pictionary or Monopoly, except for the clench in her stomach. Interactive Clue for real life, real death?

Did Sam feel this way too? He gave no sign. Kate went around closing all the blinds. The night outside looked quiet. It was a new moon and very dark.

At last Sam looked up. He said, "From what I gather, the Nashville system seems like a version of that easy code that kids make up when A translates as 1, B as 2, C as 3 and so on. You pick your key, and that's always number one. In the key of A, A is 1, key of B, B is 1. All the numbers go up the scale from there. You ready to try it?"

"Let's get Brandi's notebook." She opened it on the table. Sam asked which song was "Fool Moon," and Kate showed him the page Grady had fingered in the darkness at the Burnsides'.

"Okay, Kelly, you know how 'Fool Moon' goes, right?"

Kelly nodded. "Played it a million times on the stereo. Almost as many as Reba McEntire."

"Good. So let's play these on your Casio. Kate, you've listened to it. Why don't you sing the melody and see if it fits with these chords."

Kate pulled up a chair. " 'Key of D' is penciled at the upper left. That means D is the first note?"

"Right. So let's see if the song turns out to be 'Fool Moon.' "

"Kelly, this isn't Carnegie Hall. Just play what's there. See if the chords sound like 'Fool Moon.' "

They focused as if working a puzzle.

The sequence came forth in the absolute stillness. Then Kate sang, " 'Full moon, fool moon, rock me in your crescent cradle.' That's it. We did it. That's it." Then the rush was gone and the next question flashed. "—what, though? What did we do? I mean, we got the chords, but so what? What are we learning here, besides what we already know?" She pointed to the three other pages of coded numbers. "You think we ought to play these too?"

"Why not?"

Kate shrugged. "It seems like null-and-void exercise. Why would somebody cause damage and mayhem to destroy a few chords?"

Kelly said, "Mom, I have some homework to do. I'm supposed to read two chapters of *To Kill a Mockingbird*. Any more chords you want me to play?"

She and Sam looked back at the notebook. Kate said, "How about one more, this one? It's circled. It seems to be emphasized." They looked at the notebook page. There were the numbers, but a heavy penciled line encircled the song, if it was an actual song.

Kate said, "Let's try it. Key of E, so let's figure it out. Here's where it says chorus." So they counted on their fingers again. "Numbers 5 1 6 4. That would be B, then E. The next would be D, no, C-minor, and then A. Kelly, come try this one."

Again she played her Casio, stood poised, raised the instrument, played the sequence. Kate paused, and Kelly too. It sounded familiar, or almost familiar. "Mom, you know what it is, it's 'Envy Green.' I mean, it almost is. The third chord's a little different. Let me try something." Kelly thought for a moment and played, "Yeah, that's it—it's 'Envy Green' except for the third chord. Here it's a C, and on the album it's a B. Maybe you and Sam made a mistake."

She played the chords again. And Kate sang, "Seafoam and summer fields, green willows on the bank . . . emeralds and money and time gone to waste." Then the chorus to "Envy Green." That mournful feeling, the distinct melody. "—'envy green, envy green, the color of pain' . . ."

"Yes, that's it. Now Mom, you can play the CD for Sam. That one chord's different, and you'll hear it. Can I go do my homework now? I've got a lot to do. I'm really tired."

"Sure, sweetie." Kate felt a twinge of guilt. Child labor. "Go on up, Kel. I'll bring you a cup of Sleepytime tea."

"In my blue mug."

"In your blue mug."

Kelly came forward to give Sam a hug. Kate watched. Closest man in her life, a combination uncle, pal, father. Together they watched her mount the stairs, almost lanky in these early teen years.

Sam said, "Great kid." Kate nodded. "And fun too. Neat collaboration tonight, the three of us. And how 'bout that, our own codes project—?"

But Kate's smile was rueful. She said, "Yes, it was fun. I'm just skeptical, Sam. Call it the so-what factor. Give or take one chord, we've got the manuscript for two songs that are copyrighted, recorded, legally out there in record stores and on the radio. They can't be stolen or destroyed even if this notebook turns to ashes. So we're reinventing the wheel, unless these other two pages are new songs—or useful fragments."

"Useful as kindling in the funeral pyre of the Burnside house?"

She hesitated. "Maybe somebody's so hell-bent on claiming ownership of the fragments they'd plot to destroy the original. God, Sam, it was a ferocious fire. If you'd seen it— And I didn't tell Kelly. She'll be upset . . ."

She paused. At that moment the image of Brandi Burns flashed across her mental screen. The cardboard standup, the publicity portrait in white fur on Dukie's living room wall. The look on Brandi's face. A daughter, a sister. Stakes so high and deadly, but whose stakes?

She stopped, stood, went to the stove and pulled off the kettle. She filled it partway at the sink, set it on a burner and turned the gas to high. They should have a cup of herbal tea and calm down.

She flipped the notebook pages back to the fragments of

lyrics. Image of an ice storm diamond, plus the wordplay on running out of youth, running off with youth. The lyric fragments seemed so feeble, so stunted.

Yet an experienced songwriter might see possibilities. Somehow the image of Judy Swan floated up.

"Sam, try this—you listening?" He nodded. Kate said, "I'm back to the notebook lyrics. Maybe that's the lead. Let's say whoever's interested in this notebook has already stripped it, but wanted to pass it off as intact. So they left some garbage lyrics and the number charts for 'Fool Moon' and 'Envy Green' and some fragments of melodies.

"But let's say they also copied those garbage lyric fragments and to their surprise found some of them useful in songwriting. Maybe one or more of these fragments became crucial. Okay so far?" Sam nodded.

"So suppose they've already used them in a song, or songs. I read something about the process while standing in line at the supermarket the other day, some country music magazine piece on how an idea eventually becomes a recorded song. The article talked about writing and publishing and going into the studio to make the demo and how the song shops work and about pitching the song to artists. You know, how the song comes to Garth Brooks's attention." He nodded again.

She lifted the kettle again to make sure it had enough water, then turned back to Sam. "So suppose a demo containing Brandi Burns's lyric fragment is already making the rounds, maybe this line here—'you ran out of my time.' " He cupped his chin in his hand, listening.

She said, "Brandi's been dead for over a month, so if somebody worked fast, there's enough time. Now imagine a country music star is interested in recording the song, somebody you hear on the radio and see on TV, like Wynonna or Hal Ketchum, somebody big.

"Maybe the plagiarist never thought it would come to that, not in their wildest dreams. Suddenly they've got a big hit song looming, and the dirty little secret is almost out of control. It's going to come out in public. Because if song X gets released on an album that makes it to the charts, and Bobbie and her mother hear it, then this notebook is proof positive that the song is stolen property."

He nodded. "—and wham, big lawsuit, and the songwriter's name smeared all over Nashville. The music industry's big on policing. There'd be heavy-hitter criminal lawyers and their pals specializing in intellectual property." Sam peered at the number fragments with new interest. "In which case this notebook really does become exhibit A."

Kate reached into the cabinet. Tea. Orange Zinger, Peppermint—Sleepytime. She pulled down the box, picked a bag, dropped it in Kelly's favorite mug with the seashore scene painted on the side. Another New England reminder. She poured in the boiling water.

Sam stood, stretched, arms out. "Kate, we've got great theories here. The only problem is, there's one for Brandi Burns's murder and a very different one for the arson fire. So far, they fork off in different directions. One road goes to Grady Stamps and the contract, and the other leads to somebody you think is maybe stealing Brandi's lyrics. This Grady, he's not a songwriter, is he?"

She shook her head. "Not that I know." Sam shrugged. Then Kate shrugged. And sighed. Exasperation. Two crimes, two criminals? For the moment, tea time. Mother time. She took the mug upstairs and approached Kelly's room.

She stopped at the threshold, seeing Kelly propped up on pillows on her bed. Asleep. Kate tiptoed close, slipped the paperback novel from her hands, pulled up the cotton blanket, turned off the light and backed out on tiptoe and silently shut her daughter's door. Back downstairs.

She went to Sam and reached around him to close Brandi's notebook and slip it into the plastic bag. She put her finger across her lips to signal quiet. In a very low voice she said, "Sam, Kelly's fallen sound asleep. And believe it or not, even I have reached my quota of speculation on murders and motives on this the ninth day of October, year of our Lord."

She traced her finger lightly at his neck, his mouth. "I think

Kelly Banning is doing us the great favor of falling into a very deep sleep from sheer exhaustion. I see a message in this. I suggest we stop talking and take advantage." She stood on tip-toe and whispered low, "What do you think?"

He said not a word. His arms were around her, his mouth closing on hers as both felt suddenly for the other's body. Every nerve alive, they fumbled with clothing, buttons, zippers, silent and listening, urgent and needy and yearning. Furtive and grasping, they reached the sofa, the floor, their bodies driving and riding, and shifting, and clenching throats and jaws to silence at climax.

The whole of it was lightning. Desire and thrill and necessity kept at bay until now. And the feeling of willing collapse as, afterward, they held one another, gave the caresses impossible moments ago in their intensity. He touched her face and said, "I love you," and she whispered these same words back to Sam, then signaled they must dress in case Kelly—

But in a pantomime Sam said he understood, and they had to silence giggles as they collected clothing and then misbuttoned and caught and freed zippers and hooks. They stayed up much later, lying side by side on the couch on which Sam finally slept the night. What was left of the night.

Deep in the morning, nearly hallucinating from a second night with so little sleep, Kate drifted off in a semiconscious mental mix of Sam, of Kelly at a music stand, Bobbie and Dukie Burnside with a smoked ham, and Wade Rucker beckoning from the stage with a promise of a broken arm and big black bruise to match the one already on her left arm.

It was a P.S. Kate had in mind the next day. It was a low-grade loose end she wanted to tie up. So at noon she drove out Eighth Avenue, also called Franklin Road. She passed antique malls at Douglas Corner, and music and comedy clubs, then spotted English Ford in an auto row block with a Saab dealer, a Toyota lot. She parked in the customer area and walked around to the service entrance.

Tools chimed against the stutter of high-pressure wrenches. A steel guitar cried in the background of the sound system. Sweet lubricants caught her nostrils. Service manager would be with her in a minute. She passed on the free coffee and gazed at the framed wall photos of the mechanics of the month. They all had hair like the country musicians at the Hermitage Hotel. Who set the style, the musicians or the mechanics? These guys in the frames could come out from under the cars and take the stage.

"Miz Fanning?"

"Banning. Kate Banning."

"How are you today? What can I do for you?" A thin-faced man a light blue shirt, about forty. Music hair. Steve Stecker, Service Manager read the badge on the pocket, which bulged with reading glasses and ball-points.

"I just came by to ask about a car you serviced last month. An '89 Taurus sedan." Keep the fatality out of this if possible. "The car was totaled in an accident, and the family just wants to know their daughter had the proper work done."

He cocked his head to one side, wary. "You with an insurance company? You a lawyer?"

Kate laughed. "Nothing like that. I'm a magazine editor. This is a favor for a friend. It was Brandi Burns's car. Maybe you remember it? Brandi Burns?" She said it slowly and a little loud and looked closely at his face. The name could register from music or from the media report on the accident. Or not register at all.

So she hoped. His thoughtful frown looked staged, as if called on to remember too many cars. Pricey custom Crown Victorias, he'd need to remember those, the local owners being a who's who of the dealership, part of the job. Or any notorious lemons. But a run of the mill Taurus, forget it, literally.

"Name sounds familiar," he said trying to be polite.

"Brandi's in the music business."

"Miz Banning, half of Nashville's in music."

They laughed. Kate said, "Well, I was out this way and said I'd stop in. They just want to be sure the work got done, you know, in the confusion after the accident when the service records get mislaid. The family's trying to deal with a lot of paperwork. They want to be sure."

"We don't usually provide records."

Kate shrugged. "I just volunteered to stop by, give them a hand on this. The bill is hanging on a credit card, and it's like paying for nothing at this point. You know that feeling."

He shifted from one foot to the other. "You just want to verify a service record?" She nodded. "I guess we could take a look. Come on over to the desk. Ordinarily we don't—" But he went behind the console of an ancient computer, put on his glasses and began typing as Kate spelled the name.

"B-u-r-n-s. '89 Taurus." She tried to sound nonchalant.

"Here it is. Okay, it was in the shop on August eleven. Oil change and lube. New muffler. Replaced the wiper blades."

"Any hoses or clamps?" He looked at her sharply. "That's always on my mind," Kate said. "My radiator hose burst once on the highway. Now I'm a hose-and-clamp fanatic."

He smiled a little, relaxed. "Uh, no ma'am, hoses must have been A-Okay. Checked the usual fluids, all fine. The tires."

"Tires okay?"

He nodded. "Fine. No rotation needed. One thing, though. We recommended new front brake pads. Looked worn to us."

"Oh? How worn?"

He peered toward the screen and shook his head slowly. "Our mechanic thought they ought to be replaced. Recommended it. We phoned the responsible party, which is our standard procedure before going ahead with work. That person authorizes us to go ahead or not. Last August eleven shows no authorization given."

"I see."

Steve Stecker leaned toward the screen. "Here, let me print this out and I'll show you." The machine chattered, and he tore the paper and came from behind the counter with the computer form. "See, service, parts, labor. Oil, lube, tires, fluids, all checked. Then here's the line item miscellaneous: brake pad replacement rec. Customer refused. We make note of all that. Can't be too careful these days. Car was totaled, you said?"

"Just one of those things." Kate shrugged. "Slick pavement," she said, "speed, embankment, ditch. There you have it." Then she added, "—Just wondered, maybe the mechanic who did the work would recall."

"That's Gary; but with our volume, it's a long shot. But wait a sec, I can page him if he's not on lunch." A reach for a telephone. "Gary-at-the-service-desk."

Gary was young, earnest looking, maybe two years out of high school. He wiped his hand on the leg of his blue coverall. "Taurus sedan, you say? Couple months back?" His voice was nasal.

"You recommended new brake pads. Owner wouldn't give us the go-ahead. Woman's car, name of Burns."

He shook his head. "Don't think so. Women mostly take advice on brakes. Men too. Last August? I remember one bald guy with a red Taurus LX; he thought I was giving him the run-around. Gave me a real hard time. He—no, wait, blue Taurus sedan, yeah, one other guy. Guy with bad skin. Looked like he never sees the sun. I remember because summers, you mostly don't see that. You said the owner is a lady?" Kate nodded. "Well, this was a man. I remember the complexion."

Kate shrugged. "Look, I don't want to make a big deal of this, taking up all this time. But I wonder, does the printout have the payment record too?"

"Cashier's office has that," Steve Stecker said. "Just let me poke my head in; Lorene will check it for me. Hey, Lorene, sweetheart . . ." In a minute he was back. "Just for the record," he said, "this particular work was charged to a man."

"Oh?"

"Least it sounds like it. Visa card was signed by somebody . . . let me make it out. Yeah, there it is. First off, the person who brought the car in and signed was a woman, but the name's not Burns. See the name here, looks like Swain—no, Swan. Judy Swan. And here's the authorized party that refused the new brake pads and paid the charges. It's not Burns either. It's here on the Visa card imprint. Looks like Gordy . . . Stumps? No, it's Grady. Excuse me. That's the name, Grady Stamps."

Chapter Ten

Back at the office. Where to go from here? Ask Bobbie whether Grady customarily took care of Brandi's car? Didn't Grady Stamps help choose that car? Bobbie said so that first day at the Hermitage Hotel.

Did an artist's manager normally oversee automotive maintenance? The brakes? The brakes, brakes, brakes. Mr. honorary-member-of-the-Burnside-family refused to authorize new front brake pads less than a month before Brandi's death and his own departure. Was it penny pinching? Negligence? Worse than negligence?

Kate leaned across the desk and looked at her Fleetwood calendar and did a quick calculation. Brandi's Taurus was serviced on a Thursday, August eleven, and she died the next month on a Tuesday, September fourth. Those final twenty-four days were a mortal grace period.

Or maybe Grady Stamps's window of opportunity. Did he think—hope?—her brake pads were worn enough to cause an accident? Did he count on bad brakes putting her out of action long enough to trigger the exit clause in the contract? Did the bad brakes actually give him the idea to disable the car—and then, frustrated as the days passed uneventfully, did Grady finally decide to go ahead and sabotage it?

As for Brandi, did she notice her brakes weren't working well? Was the pedal mushy? Judy Swan took the car in for service, presumably an act of friendship or courtesy. Did she, Judy, notice brake problems when she drove it to English Ford? Suppose Brandi gave Judy Swan an itemized list—oil, lube, check the muffler and the brakes. Maybe Brandi wrote the items down, or else Judy thought she could remember. In any case, Judy omitted the brakes. Mislaid the list. Or, relied on faulty memory and forgot it.

But suppose Judy Swan and Grady had somehow hooked up. Say they arranged for Judy to take the Taurus into the shop and for Grady to pick it up. Suppose they planned to keep Brandi out of the transaction, both of them with motives amounting to criminal conspiracy. She could use unpublished, stolen music—but only if Brandi Burns were permanently out of the picture. He simply needed Brandi offstage for fifteen days so he could get out of the contract. For Grady, it wouldn't matter if the country singer-songwriter were out of commission for fifteen days or fifteen years. He and Judy could make a deal.

And what about the break-in at Trystar? Somebody else wanted that notebook—like Wade Rucker.

Unless the break-in was only staged to look like Wade's work. Anybody could smash a small door glass, turn a dead-bolt, bang a crowbar against a file cabinet and strew some folders around. And Judy Swan had the keypad combination to the security system. As office manager, she used it more than anybody else and probably could punch it in her sleep.

Still, that cabinet was bashed hard. Behind each blow was violent force. Judy Swan was a slender woman, and Kate doubted she could mimic Wade Rucker's sheer brute strength. Rule out Judy Swan on a copycat break-in. Eliminate one probability and get left with the giant combo pack of confusion, doubt, dead end. Dead Brandi. The line between plausible and farfetched was blurry, and somebody's clock out there was ticking.

At her desk, Kate tapped a pencil hard enough to break the point. She turned to her computer screen, stared at an e-mail query, felt annoyance and frustration. A writer based in Minneapolis demanded Kate's reasons for objecting to certain phrases in his piece on bed-and-breakfast hosts. Why did she insist on these editorial changes, he demanded to know.

Why couldn't he call one B&B host a "high-maintenance ultrablonde," another an "Arkansas-bred, nouveau gothic gourmet?"

The why nots went on, and this the third such query from Bart B. in Minneapolis. Writers like him made e-mail an editor's curse. Kate already gave double the usual attention to this piece, slated for the winter issue of a hospitality trade magazine. Bart would not be writing for Fleetwood again. He did not know this yet. She hit the keys for the *reply* mode and typed in her explanation, which finally came down to because-I-say-so-that's-why, the only message Bart could hear.

Then Kate checked the time. 1:59. She was due at 3:15 at a Fleetwood interview with an entry-level job candidate, chunks of whose time would be spent in Kate's office. Meanwhile, she needed to make a quick trip to the Vanderbilt campus. Call it a scouting mission. She had not been inside a fraternity house in adult memory. Come to think of it, she had never been inside one in the daylight, never thought of them as places where people lived. Field trip to partyland.

She grabbed her purse, freshened her lipstick, headed for the curbside meter where she left her car. Reaching for sunglasses, she scanned the street, always on the lookout. Check out the inevitable tourists, the office workers, the loiterers. A sand colored Caravan went by, but no beige pickup. Nothing noteworthy.

And no signs of tampering with her car as she looked it over at the meter with seven minutes left on her six quarters. Good. On Sam's advice, one of the notebook Xeroxes was stuck under the seat. The green spiral itself was in her condo in a kitchen drawer under a million plastic bags. It felt like a shell game with the outcome pending. Or looming. Too much mortality. Another oh-so-casual glance around, and Kate got in, slipped her key into the ignition, eased out.

Out West End, she stayed in the left lane, moved with the traffic, kept a watch on surrounding vehicles and looked for the Vanderbilt campus with its brick-and-stone clock tower that was reminiscent of a ship's mast. Didn't Commodore Cor-

nelius Vanderbilt make his fortune in shipping? In the multiple
choice test on robber barons, didn't you tick off oil and steel
and rail and then come to ships and shipping and blacken the
circle marked Cornelius?

Kate passed the main campus entrance with the bronze commodore on his pedestal standing watch. She slipped into the
turning lane as her Buick paralleled the campus boundary
fence of wrought iron and the brick walls ending at the corner
of 25th. She waited for the green arrow, then turned left and
left again two blocks later at Memorial Gym. She was now on
Kensington Street, Greek Row.

No place to park. Was every campus in America like this?
The private fraternity lots were posted with warnings that the
unauthorized would be towed, pronto. You could be desperate
enough to join up just to be authorized. The brothers and sisters with upscale autos clearly had an edge at Vanderbilt, judging from the models in the restricted lots—Grand Cherokees,
BMWs, Corvettes, here and there a Probe or Celica or a family's surplus sedan. No aging Buicks.

Kate slowly circled Kensington, made a right onto 24th, another right onto Vanderbilt Place. In her rearview mirror she
saw a dark green Camaro right behind her.

And behind it, a beige pickup truck. Her heart thumped.

Beige pickup with a dark tinted windshield.

Did it follow her from downtown? She could easily have
missed it in multilane traffic.

Should she pull over now? Get out? She scanned the curbside. There were no open parking spaces. She could double
park, turn on her flashers and get to the sidewalk. Plenty of
open campus buildings. Where was the Vanderbilt police headquarters?

She decided to circle the block, to keep circling. At the first
intersection, the Camaro peeled left and roared off. The beige
pickup pulled smack up behind her. The hood, the grill—it was
a Ford Ranger, she was almost sure. She made a right, another
right. It stayed on her bumper like glue. She checked her gas

gauge—quarter tank. In her mirrors, the truck windshield was all black shine.

Two more circlings. Would anybody notice two vehicles in a cat-and-mouse game? If they did, would they think it a Greek Row kids' prank? How often did campus cops cruise by here? One thing clear—she needed a plan. Maybe pull over and run for it, find out whether that ski machine kept her legs in decent shape. Circle and think.

Third time around this block, she slowed to let a Maxima pull out, then eased forward.

In her rearview she watched the beige pickup slow up and slide into parallel park position, reverse, wheels cut to seize the open spot and back in. Now it was fifteen yards behind her, now twenty-five. She watched the doors fling open, two students jump out, a young guy from the passenger side, a strawberry blond woman from the driver's seat.

They had only wanted to park.

She let out lungfuls of breath. In the left side mirror, she saw them join hands, saunter down the sidewalk. Just to be sure, Kate circled once more to check out their passenger door. Smooth as glass. She breathed deeper relief. Would she ever again in life see a beige pickup truck without freezing, or was she wired to be spooked forever?

Near the Sarratt Student Center she found a small visitors' lot with a 30-minute limit and one open space. Take it.

She pulled in between a blue Lumina and a mud-spattered Blazer. She locked up and entered the student center to find a campus map. At the desk a sixty-ish woman with iron gray hair in a pixie cut worked the Ticketmaster computer for a student in a persimmon cardigan.

The counter was stacked with flyers for string quartets, Shakespeare, modern dance companies. Kate spotted a worn map taped to the surface. You are here. She found the gym and the street names and translated the tiny Greek symbols printed on the house outlines.

Out the glass doors, she put her dark glasses back on and started down Kensington on foot. The students passed in twos and threes. Sage and heather looked big this year, J. Crew and the Gap and L.L. Bean among the major suppliers. These young people glowed with health, energy, advantageous genes.

What would they see in Wade Rucker?

One address on Kensington and Vanderbilt Place might tell her. The brotherhood of Gamma Nu. She walked quickly and noticed the architectural styles up and down the street, brick colonial, Tudor, ranch. She noticed sorority names too, the TriDelts, the Kappas and Thetas. She imagined the brave jokes of the holdouts and the excluded, something like cuppa cappuccino or wordplay on delta deltoids. The ins and outs of the in and the out.

The Gamma Nu house was a sprawling Californian one-story yellow stucco with a huge wraparound deck stained in redwood tones. Approaching from the side, Kate could see an alley behind these houses and the parking lot around back where Wade Rucker's Dodge would be parked on a Saturday night. It mattered. She had to try again for that toolbox, assuming Wade was dumb enough to leave it there after her encounter with Chuck Munde. Definitely worth a try. With college kids around, it could be easier.

She started up the front walk. Two of the flagstones were cracked, and potted cactuses stood on the deck railings at regular intervals. Cigarettes were stubbed out in the sandy soil, and a black streak at the end of the deck told of a near-miss with fire, probably a cookout, but Kate shivered remembering the Burnside house. How the name fit.

She looked down at a pair of huaraches, about a men's eleven, on the deck by the doormat which said Gamma Nu in a brushy brown. The Mediterranean door had an iron lion head knocker with a ring in its mouth. Kate clanked it twice and waited.

"Hey. Oh . . . I mean, afternoon, ma'am." The door was opened about two feet. " 'Pologize, ma'am. I thought you might be one of the brothers. I'm Dan. May I help you?"

Kate smiled. He was tan and blue-eyed with a crewcut, and wore an oxford shirt and Dockers with penny loafers without socks. Probably a first-year pledge on door duty. "I don't have

an appointment," Kate said. "I'm Kate Banning with the publicity publications office, and I'm doing a little feature write-
up on entertainment and music here on campus."

She smiled very brightly. "I just wanted to include a few of
the fraternities in my feature. You know, a quick sketch of the
kinds of bands you like to have at your parties. Whether
they're jazz or rock or what. Just briefly, you know. Nothing
too deep."

"Yes ma'am, you'd want to see the chair of our Social Com-
mittee on that. That's Lee." He turned, facing inward. "Lee?
Hey, y'all seen Lee? He's not? Well, is he or isn't he?" He
turned back to Kate. "He'll be with you. Would you like to
wait out here?"

Not when she needed to see the interior layout. Not when
she was scouting the logistics for Saturday night. "Would you
mind if I just stepped inside? I try to stay out of the sun as
much as I can. Skin sensitivity. My dermatologist—"

He opened the door wider. Count on good Southern manners. "Have a seat, ma'am, please."

She was ushered into a dark vestibule with two cracked ma-
roon leather couches. She put her purse on an end cushion and
looked to the left at a cafeteria-size dining room with three
rectangular tables and more chairs than she cared to count.

To the right—she looked around the corner—was a grand
hall with furniture in groupings and a cavernous fireplace. Living room, party room. A band could set up in that corner, and
she saw the back door where instruments and equipment could
be brought in on a weekend night. Loud music could be heard
outside in the parking lot. Good cover.

But how much traffic came through that door? Could she
count on access to Wade's truck for the span of a song?—
three-plus minutes and no Chuck Munde on patrol? Her best
bet.

She looked around the room. Here and there were piles of
sweepings that looked like sand. Two men stood talking together in front of the fireplace, one obviously a fraternity
brother, the other older, in workman's greens. They talked and

pointed at the mantel and wall, which looked damaged, as though a bracket gave way and the ledge splintered.

The fraternity crest also looked damaged, plaster and wood banged up. The mantel wall was charred as if a roaring fire got out of control. Some lounge chairs were stacked in one corner, legs missing and cushions burst. Maybe too many Viking parties, a series of Erics with pikestaffs and cudgels and tapped kegs.

Kate waited, sat, stood, checked her watch, cleared her throat. Gamma Nu brothers came and went, all managing a "ma'am" in greeting. Nobody used that back door. Maybe it was only a supply line. Good. At last the fraternity brother by the fireplace broke away from the workman and approached her.

"Yes ma'am?"

"You're Lee?"

"Yes, ma'am." He had Asian features and black hair, and wore cutoffs, a white button-down oxford opened to the navel, unlaced red Converse high-tops. An unlighted Camel dangled from a corner of his mouth, and he flicked a disposable lighter and drew deeply before exhaling. "Dan tells me you have some concerns about the bands we hire for social events?"

"No concerns. Just a few simple questions." He seemed older than the pledge, a little warier, less open to smiles, but also edgy, even uncomfortable. Well, what fraternity brother wanted some Aunt Sally in the foyer of his house? She took her notebook from her purse to look like legitimate media, and she repeated her line on the feature write-up. "—wanted to include the kinds of music the fraternities might feature. For instance, rock?"

He flicked a nonexistent ash to work off nervous energy. "Yeah, sure, if you just want a list. We had Trueblood and Black Forest last month."

"Trueblood . . . Black Forest." She made a show of writing them down. "And they're rock. Okay. How about rhythm-and-blues?"

"Uh . . . The Asphalt Kings. I guess they count. That was last spring at Rites of Spring."

"—last spring, good." Another note. "Rap?" He shook his head. "Okay. Now, how about country?"

"Not from now on."

"No country music here in Nashville?" She kept a smile of surprise and hid the disappointment. Judy Swan said Wade Rucker played Gamma Nu. "No country music at all? Why, shame on you." Try to sound lilting. Try to sound the way a college student thinks a campus PR media hack ought to sound.

But his nervous energy was back. "I mean, not regular country. The brothers aren't that interested. We're in full compliance with university regulations."

University rules and regs? Odd thing to say. She said, "Regulations? Well, this is just a music survey. Did I get my signals mixed?" She flipped pages of the notebook, stopped at a grocery list with tomato paste and juice. "Here it is. Yucca Flat. The young men at Lambda Tau said they were sure Yucca Flat plays here."

The cigarette flicked like mad. "Ma'am, don't worry, they won't be back."

Won't be back? Defensive tone. A child promising not to do it again, whatever *it* was.

He took a quick drag on the Camel. "Gammu Nu is in full compliance with IFC-Panhel."

Kate kept her pleasant look and scoured her memory back to ancient history. The Interfraternity Council and Panhellenic something-or-other. Regulate the Greeks, governing board. She said, "But Yucca Flat did play here?"

He shook his head. "Not anymore. Put down the Virgil Vingel Danceband instead, OK? They played one of our formals. If you'd excuse me, please. I have this appointment." He moved toward the front door, opened it, ushered her out like an obnoxious door-to-door salesperson.

She was on the flagstones, feeling herded, almost tripped on the broken stone, headed down the sidewalk in a stupid state as if something bungled. Kate was nearly back to her car when she heard the "ma'am, oh ma'am" and the feet behind her. Turning, there was the door pledge running along behind and carrying a purse. Her purse.

"Oh, thanks. Dan, isn't it? Thank you so much. I just for-got—"

"On our sofa. That's all right. Lee asked me to chase you."

She took the purse and smiled and slipped it over her shoulder. "Don't think Lee meant any rudeness, ma'am."

"I don't."

"He's got house stuff on his mind, you see. After the weekend."

"Rough weekend?"

"Desert party on Saturday night. Here it's Tuesday already, and we're still cleaning up."

Kate nodded. Desert party? She recalled the potted cactuses on the deck, the huaraches. And the sand sweepings. Probably Mexican beer and tequila. A worm-eating contest. But wait—yucca was a desert plant. Was the house band maybe Yucca Flat? Take a stab. She said, "Wade Rucker and Yucca Flat can be really wild."

He shook his head. "Just tore up the house."

She shook her head in sympathy. "That's a shame, hard as you boys work."

"Tore it up. Believe me, this time it wasn't our fault, the damage. Cost us plenty, too—the chairs and mantel wall. The national seal."

She put her hand to her throat and kept shaking her head in sympathy. "Things just get out of hand sometimes," she said. "And Yucca Flat—well, they're not exactly Muzak."

"Totally out of line. Their lead guy, Wade—you ever hear him?"

"Once."

"Then you know. Heavy electric, great beat. Cool lyrics too. You know, you sit in class all week, you need some release. Wade's songs are all about that, break out, punch it, get out of my way. Blow it off or blow it away."

"Anger songs."

He nodded. "Some of the guys' dates don't like him at all. Saturday, though, that was too much."

"I hear he can get kind of . . . violent?"

"Ma'am, we handled it. We took care of it. But we're not into bar fights. Back home, some of the townies from high school, Saturday night means brawls. But this is a national chapter; there's a level of respect. You don't think the band you've hired is gonna slash the chairs and come at you with a bottle or an iron bar."

"An iron bar?"

"Iron, steel. We're not up for that. And we're not the fire department."

Kate stopped. She repeated. "The fire department—?"

"When he grabbed the tiki torches and made like to run at people. Ran out on the deck. Ran back inside. The tikis, they're just bamboo and wax. Nice light but you have to watch them. Flammable stuff. It was pretty tense."

Kate herself felt suddenly tense. Make the effort not to show it. Nice talkative pledge, keep him going. She said, "So that burn mark on the deck, it's not from a grill?"

He shook his head. "The mantel either. There was some damage; I won't lie to you. We don't want trouble with the IFC. We don't want to call campus cops. We're not looking for any more problems with Dean Cotter. That Wade's a great singer, but there's a limit. The plant operations guy talking to Lee, he's fixing our mantel off-hours. So it's gonna be all right. We, uh, we don't want it broadcast we had some trouble." At that moment he looked at her apprehensively, as if suddenly aware Kate might be a member of a dean's spy network.

She smiled. "Believe me, nobody on campus is going to hear anything from me. But if a band does some damage, don't they pay for it?"

He stared as if she came from another planet. "Ma'am, nobody wants more trouble from Wade Rucker or Yucca Flat. Our furniture, the upholsterer's bringing a truck to pick it up. Hey, we have some chairs left with all four legs. We have windows with glass. Our deck and mantel, they're scorched but nothing really burned up. The brothers want to keep it that way. Wade goes his way; we'll go ours. Bands aren't that hard to find in Nashville. Well, you got your purse. Thanks for thinking of us. Take care."

Sure. Make every effort. Thirty minutes later, she sat with the Fleetwood interview team doing job-talk questions while Wade Rucker flashed in her mind like an FBI poster on a movie screen. The bashing Wade, he was an old story. Wade-the-torch, however, he was new. To grab a garden-and-deck lamplighter torch and make a run at people and things—was he high on some drug mix, uppers and psychedelics? Speed? Or did he only overstep the bounds of the outrageous behavior that his student fans enjoyed vicariously on a Saturday night before buckling down to the books?

Or was Wade Rucker a firebug along with everything else? Bottom line: Did he torch the Burnside house? Last Saturday night, when Kate and Kelly were in Joelton eating turkey and vegetables and pie with Dukie and her family, was Wade Rucker in the fraternity house rehearsing the arson he would commit at the Burnsides' in the wee hours of the following Wednesday morning?

She smiled and asked a polite question in this interview. Courtesy interview, meaning the job candidate was hopeless— brash and boastful, terrible nasal voice. Insecurity might bring out the worst, but this was a job, not rehab. Or hab. She asked about word processing skills and exchanged co-worker glances that said this should wrap up in twenty minutes. Eye contact, teamwork.

And what actions did Wade Rucker's team, the Yucca Flat band, take when he rampaged with the bottle, the metal bar, the torch? Ask young Dan. Find out about the other band members. Ask Bobbie. Ask Judy Swan.

It was ten minutes in, and the interview rounding the turn when Kate's assistant came in to hand her two pink message forms. She unfolded and read. Sam Powers had phoned. He was unexpectedly called to Wichita, hoping to return Friday night or Saturday morning. Will call this evening. That was it.

Kate sighed, allowed that empty feeling to move in. Come and gone, here and already vanished. No Sam at the table tonight, holding hands, holding one another at midnight. His voice, his laugh. Literally no Sam to lean on, to bounce ideas off this evening. But not his fault. She repeated that. Nobody's fault, both of them trying, working it out as best they could. In good faith, Kate and Sam. As for the future, was it up for grabs? Anybody's guess? Could they ever stay in one place long enough to talk it through?

The job candidate was braying about career goals. Kate heard the phrase "all fired up" and the term kicked her thoughts to Wade Rucker and Dukie Burnside's blackened kitchen as she moved to the second pink message slip. Bobbie called, please call immediately. The assistant wrote one word and underlined it: *urgent.*

What wasn't urgent in Bobbie's world? She hyped everything. Yet Kate felt an adrenaline edge. Some dangerous new twist or turn? She looked around for the nearest phone. Could she excuse herself, leave her co-workers and return the call?

No. Short of an emergency, she was stuck. Unwritten rules had power. Job flexibility was not autonomy. Everybody in this room was obligated to sit and row the boat together and do the interview drill. Bobbie would have to wait.

Kate crossed her legs and sat forward and pretended to take an interest until the time was up and everybody rose, shook hands all around. Exit the candidate. Coffee refills, a quick postmortem, Fleetwood folks dispersed to their own offices.

With her door closed, Kate dialed Bobbie's number.

"Kate?"

"Yes."

"Kate."

"Yes, Bobbie, Kate here. Speaking."

The voice moaned and then wailed high. "Dead, he's dead, you got to come out. He's dead, Kate, and horrible. Mama's not here. I'm by myself. I'm alone. Can you come? Please, can you?"

Pounding in her ears, "Who's dead, Bobbie?"

"Blood all over. Blood. Sick, I'm sick." Retching sounds. Two barely audible words, "Come. Please."

The calm that takes over panic. The functional calm that moves you step by step, each act itemized from parting sentences to car keys to gas pedal. The 911 orders to Bobbie. "Just 9-1-1, just punch it in." Then the phone call to Kelly, voice bland, reassurance and promise, food in fridge, gas in tank.

Car to the on-ramp, traffic thick and halted entirely at a construction site. Snail pace. Kate did what she could. Inched and mentally asked the question, Who was *he*? Was it Grady? Beloved Grady Stamps lying in a pool of blood at the Burnside house? Was Grady at the house for some reason, followed and attacked there? Shot? Stabbed? Or was it Floyd? The cousin most likely to be on site doing construction repair, was he caught by surprise and killed? And did Bobbie call the police? Speechless, did she dial 911? If she was beyond speech, the police would trace the call and dispatch a car.

Dispatch an aging Century wagon. From luxury to clunkers, here was the democracy of the interstate, gridlock. Finally she exited White's Creek Pike and the Old Clarksville Highway. Then the fire house, the Amoco, the church. Third time around, she did not need the envelope with directions in the glove compartment.

Bobbie came running the minute Kate started down the dirt drive. The Quality Seven skirt was streaked dark red. Dukie's Sentra was not in sight. Bobbie's Malibu stood with the driver's door open. No police cruiser in view. Kate stopped the car midway down the drive. She threw it into park and cut the engine because Bobbie was already alongside and wrenching the handle.

Before Kate could get out, Bobbie clutched her in a fierce grip. Her eyes were huge, her face blue. Kate tried to hold her as the young woman's teeth chattered. "Bobbie, who is it? Who is dead?"

It came out like a dance. Cha-cha. Cha-cha-cha. Every second mattered, and where were the police. Kate was still holding her. Cha-cha.

Then it clicked. No dance. "Chop? You mean Chop?"

A nod against her shoulder, the sprayed hair scratched her cheek. Kate's own pulse hammered. The dog. Relief and pity both. No corpse, no human being. But make sure. "Bobbie, it's your dog? Somebody killed Chop?"

Another nod. This time she pulled away, face wet, eyes wide and blind. No cop car, and no wonder. Kate trembled herself with relief. No body in the house. No murder. Not this time. "Run over? Was he hit on the road?" She shook her head.

"No . . . no accident." It was a murmur and a cry.

Kate tried to walk them toward the house, Bobbie stiff and limp against her. They approached the back. No sign of the dead dog. New timbers were in place, and plastic sheeting made a temporary wall. A building permit was tacked up and curling. "This way. Here."

Bobbie led them through a curtain-like break in the plastic. They stepped over new lumber. On a plywood ramp Kate saw red droplets that started and stopped. Bright red and dark brown. Two-toned blood, dry and fresh?

Then the dining room, now a makeshift kitchen. The refrigerator stood to the side, the coffeemaker and a toaster oven and the dining room table piled with dishes, pots and pans, cardboard cartons with boxes and canned goods and . . . the pale green dining room rug splashed dark red.

And a bump covered with a towel. A bump the size and shape of one beagle. Paws angled out in tiny tents. Blood was pooled all around and turned the green carpet brown. At one end the terrycloth did not completely cover the tiny white tip of a tail.

"Oh, Bobbie . . . horrible." They held hands. Clenched hands. Kate tried to read the scene. No trail of blood, just this pool. Strange place for an accident, well out of the construction area. Nothing in the room looked disturbed. Earmarks of an improvised life with set routines during construction repairs, but no signs of any major fracas.

She must lift that towel to get a clear reading. "Bobbie, I want you to turn away. I need to see this." The hand clenched tighter, then loosened. She heard Bobbie suck in her breath and hold it. Kate bent down and lifted one corner.

It took a moment to make out the dog's head. No question—bludgeoned to death. Bludgeoned beyond death.

She replaced the towel and heard Bobbie breathe again. And breathed herself. "You covered him with this towel?" Bobbie nodded. "You found him here?" Another nod. "And where did you get the towel?"

Very softly she heard, "upstairs."

"So the blood drops on the plywood ramp from the kitchen, they're not from touching Chop?" Bobbie shrugged. A detail, but she was too distraught to care. "Have you called the police?" Head shake. "Bobbie, where's your mother?"

"Shopping," she said. "Lucille and Mama. At Rivergate. They were going to a movie. I don't know."

"So your mother's been gone a while?" Nod. "And there was no one here? What about construction workers?"

"They leave about two."

"So the house was empty for . . . about an hour, right? Just Chop. And you came home from work and found . . ."

But Bobbie was shaking her head no. "—Tried Floyd's, but he was working. I left a message on the machine. Then tried Dawn, but she's still moving Beca out. I was scared to come back by myself."

"From work?"

"—after the call."

"You mean after you called Floyd and Dawn. And me?"

"No. The other call." She stared straight ahead and put two fingers to her mouth. Sucked them.

Kate took her free hand, squeezed and tugged gently and led her away from the bloody carcass into the living room. She chose the sofa below the huge *Fool Moon* photo of Brandi.

Bobbie must not face her dead sister. Kate sat her down and sat beside her and held her face between her palms as she might hold Kelly. The mandolin was still off the mantle, she noticed, the tiara shelves still bare in the curio case.

Very softly she said, "Bobbie, you need to tell me about that other call. You need to tell me so I can help."

She watched the eyes try to focus, try to come back from some far place, a safe place where the home is intact and your dog is alive. And your sister.

Softly Kate said, "It's okay. I'm here, and I'll stay here until someone in your family comes. In a few minutes we'll call the police because they need to know. First tell me about the call. The call that scared you. Were you at work?"

She nodded. "Working the front desk. He asked for me personally."

"He?"

"—and I came on. 'Quality Seven reservations. This is Bobbie. How may I help you?' That's what I say. I'm trained to say it. And I heard a voice, like spitting something. And kind of gruff."

"Gruff?"

"Kind of."

Kate blinked, thought of Delia and the telephone check. All systems in full working order, though Delia reported more hangups daily.

"And he said we weren't learning the lesson. The fire was a lesson, he said, and we didn't learn. And he had to teach us another one. He said, 'Be ready. You're in for a nice surprise.'" She turned her face to look at Kate. Tears were streaming now. "Like he already did it, Kate. Like he killed Chop and called to tell about it."

Kate took a Kleenex from her skirt pocket. She dried Bobbie's cheeks. "Was the voice the same as the other one, the one about the fluids?"

"No. No, this was just a man. Deep down voice. He sounded like he wasn't even talking."

"But the words were clear?"

"—not at first. But after that spit noise. Like he was reading. He couldn't read good but like he was reading something written down for him to say."

She sat very still. Kate daubed her cheeks and eyes. Then she turned. Her voice trembled but held firm. "Kate, you been so good to us. You tried helping and gave us time. You been a friend, almost like our own." Bobbie hiccuped and swallowed and forced herself on. "Now's enough, Kate. That's what I'm sayin'. No more lookin' where we don't belong. Let's just call it off. Brandi's gone, and you tried. But no more. My heart's not in it anymore. 'We are going down the valley one by one,' that's the hymn we sung when Brandi died. I don't want them singing it for us too, Kate. I want to turn back while we can."

Chapter Eleven

Through the plastic Kate saw the spot. "This was blood," she said.

"Reds are hard." The tone was world-weary. "Tomatoes, lipstick, juices. Hawaiian Punch. Blood, too. Blood's hard."

Kate stared. The cleaner's bag hung from a bar. Inside, her beige gabardine skirt was clean and pressed and spotted. Unwearable, at least to work. She touched the plastic. Juices and lipstick and droplets from a cut finger, from your period. Here in Nashville, from pets and their killers. Blood droplets on plywood. The sight of Chop. How could she stand here and argue about dry cleaning?

"I've never heard of dry cleaning problems with reds."

"You won't be charged. You can file a claim." The clerk produced a tablet and pen. Only a few sheets remained on the tablet. "Put down the estimated value. They'll let you know."

They. The bureaucratic nobody in particular.

The somebody in particular out there. A claim for the skirt, a claim for Brandi. Wrongful death? Negligent homicide? And did the Burnsides complete a form from a tear-off tablet?

"I took the skirt off the bill."

"All right." As though anything were all right. Handing over a twenty, geared up for a fight, she was no-faulted. From death to dry cleaning, all confrontations blunted. She wondered, was Bobbie struggling in a scene just like this at a dry cleaners in Joelton, her Quality Seven uniform skirt forever stained with the blood of her mangled pet? Kate put the change in her purse and started for the car. The breeze riffled the plastic like a shroud. Four dollars to seal spots in your skirt and exit with a smashed dog on your mind.

A dead young singer-songwriter on your mind. And the family scared off. And Kate run off? Thanks for your efforts, but you can go home now. One dead beagle and mission accomplished. The spunky Bobbie with no more stomach for the pursuit of her sister's killer. Kate Banning could close the file.

But should she? Could she? Bobbie thought she could placate the killer. Back off, back out. Make nice. Smile sweetly and keep her mouth shut, and the deadly boogie man would show a civil restraint. Add Dukie's mix from Biblical scripture, and the Burnside household could seal itself in a bubble of magical thinking. Hocus-pocus with the Lord's blessing.

Kate knew better. Out there in the darkness killers were always ready to do it again. Sticks and stones. And a hatchet and game of chicken on the interstate and the sabotage of one steering fluid system. Not to mention these hang-up phone calls. What next?

Cleaner's bag across the back seat, Kate got in and headed out. She turned on the radio. WSM, hot new country. It was Dwight Yoakam. "Try Not to Look So Pretty." That distinct country nasal style. In Yoakam it was especially fluid, those come-on yodels sounding downright double-jointed. If she ever bought country albums, maybe one of his. Big if.

"Try Not to Look So Pretty." Was that Brandi's downfall? Part of it? Too pretty for Wade Rucker? Too successful in the recording studio and on the concert stage while Wade played Mac's Hitching Post and the fraternities canceled him? Or did Brandi's new money make Wade so green with envy that he killed her? Or was the management contract clause too tempting to Grady Stamps? Did the sixty-thousand-dollar penalty become the manager's deadly greens fee? What about Judy Swan?

And Bobbie? The Burnside sisters swapped secrets in the dark in the bedroom they shared. It made sense for Brandi to confide in her younger sister. Before her death, did she or did she not tell her suspicions directly, suspicions which Bobbie might harbor for reasons of her own, like a smoldering ambition?

Did Bobbie perhaps fabricate the story of the phone call urging her to check the fluids of the wrecked Taurus? And if she did, why? But Bobbie didn't seem the type to set her own house on fire. Certainly not the type to bludgeon a dog, her dog.

Kate slowed to a stop at the intersection of Woodmont and Estes. Red light, green light. Green itself, what could it mean but money, that song title? Greed-green was the oldest fashion color going.

She hit the fast forward on the tapedeck. She could do a sing-along on the whole *Fool Moon* album by now. She found "Envy Green" and played it from the beginning. And heard the usual lyric message, nothing more, nothing less. "Emeralds in the summer grass / velvet in the mossy bank . . ." Another line on foliage. "His money is paper, her jewels cold as ice."

Then the refrain, "—envy green, the color of pain, the color she's seeeeen." Kate tried to sing along until her voice screeched.

Could any part of this song map out the route to a killer? By now, Kate listened so many times she felt deaf to it. In terms of its message, "Envy Green" was a country music spin on a very old theme, "the best things in life are free." No mystery. If she lived in fear of harm, why did Brandi Burns bury her clue in a song whose theme was an open book, a song whose very clear message made it opaque? As a treasure map to a killer, a dud.

Off Woodmont, Kate rewound and played it yet again. She picked out the instruments named in the liner notes, lead acoustic guitar, electric guitar, electric bass, harmonica, keyboard, percussion, Brandi Burns on rhythm guitar. Plus harmony vocals by Brandi Burns herself and background vocals by Dawn Mulligan, Beca Yowell.

On the tape she could hear Brandi singing with herself, along with the voices of Dawn and Beca further in the background. The good friends in the background. Their names threaded through Bobbie's conversation. Their apartment sheltered her and Chop the night the arsonist came calling at the Burnside house with gasoline and rags. Fortunate slumber party for Bobbie.

But Dawn and Beca, both of them were Grady Stamps's "find." She should have talked to them before this. Find out to what extent they are Grady's "girls." Find it out soon, before somebody else gets hurt.

Or gets dead.

She pulled onto her street, braked for the driveway, eased into her parking slot. As always, she scanned the scene. The magnolia trees were black-green towers. Potential hiding places. Get them trimmed, thinned. In the urban northeast, criminals hid in dark alleys. In the suburban South, was it magnolias?

She got the mail, let herself in and stood behind the closed door drawing a deep breath. Inside the condo, the air was calm. She dumped the mail on the table, where a half-moon bite in a piece of toast marked the morning scramble to get going. Right now the breakfast remains looked remote as archaeology.

She went to the phone. Four messages, one to say the pictures she left for framing three weeks ago were ready—followed by three hang-ups. Average two to three hang-ups per day for the last week. Slightly more at Fleetwood.

The gruff "gentleman," a phone stalker?

Or the law of averages?

The room felt chilly, and Kate looked at the clock. Kelly was at chorus practice. Pick her up in an hour. Hope she might meet a new friend in the alto section. Boil water for tea and screen all calls and cope with the clothes in the plastic.

She was headed for the bedroom closet when the phone rang. Hope for a rug-cleaning special or another Citibank card at extortionist rates. She shifted the dry cleaning and lifted the receiver and braced when she heard who it was.

"Kate, it's Dukie—"

"I'm here."

"Good, real good. We want you to know we took your advice. We called the police on this, and they're taking it serious. They're investigating. They came out and dusted for fingerprints and took samples."

"Great." She held the hangers high and felt relieved the cops were coming in at last.

"We laid Chop to rest in a back corner of the yard, and they dug him back up for tests. We couldn't hardly watch."

"Dukie, what do the police say?"

"Nothin' about Brandi's Taurus, Kate. It's Chop they take serious. Out in the country here, a dog's more than a dog. There's pets and there's your dog. It's different. I don't know that a city person could understand. The police out here, they know how it is. They asked about neighbors we might be feudin' with. Any bad blood between us and them. Even asked is there anybody at our church would do us harm.

"I said the Lord's house would not be defiled by ill toward the Burnside family. Like I told you, Kate, not one of my neighbors could say I did them wrong. Or my daughters either."

Kate murmured sympathetically. The clothes hangers dug into her hand. She imagined a dog sniffing in the phone background. "How about the blood drops on the plywood? What do the police say about them?"

"—one of the workmen cut hisself, most likely. But they're testing. That's what they have the labs for. And if those little bitty drops lead them to the monster that did this to a little dog—"

"Especially if this is connected to Brandi's death."

"Just what I was tellin' Bobbie. Nothin' in this world happens by chance." There was a pause. Kate again heard a background noise, like a yapping. As if the ghost of Chop echoed on the line.

She said, "Dukie?"

"Kate, I'm right here. But I got to tell you, my Bobbie's not herself. I believe she said things she didn't mean to you. Taste your words before you let 'em pass through your teeth, I always say. Bobbie forgot her tasting."

The hangers still bit her fingers. She eased the dry cleaning over the back of a chair and said, "Bobbie's message was very honest. And direct."

At the other end Dukie cleared her throat. "See, we had a family meeting, Floyd and Lucille and me and Bobbie. Just this last couple hours. And talked to my sisters over in East Tennessee. I'm telling you this, Kate, because we are workers in adversity, our family. We got to look within and find the strength. My girls did not win twirling championships. Their cousins went out for twirling, majorettes every one. Retired at eighteen. My girls' talent's music. Music lasts a lifetime."

Kate heard it, Dukie in for the long haul. Running the family conference with her grief as her leverage. Not her kids at the deadend of twirling trophies. Those tiaras in the curio cabinet were stepping stones, not peaks.

"We count on you, Kate, to be on the side of good. We want you with us in our hour of need. Lucille and Floyd, they couldn't be more appreciative. On the phone, Lucille told Mae and Uncle Larcom and all of them back home. We all marvel that you're bein' such a friend. We're hopeful you'll keep on. We need you."

Need. So this was the point. Dukie was calling to override Bobbie. That was the point of the family conference, to get the votes to persuade Kate to stay the course. Was Dukie frightened? No doubt. Threatened? Yes. But not stopped. Her ambition was not sacrificed to her grief. Her loss did not cancel her ambition but fortified it, focused it.

Kate was staring from a window at the thick dark magnolias and asking herself how much a one-woman safety patrol could do. Over the line she heard a yapping sound again, like a dog, unless she was hallucinating. Kate said, "Dukie, do I hear a dog?"

"Why Kate, if you could see this little fella. Doin' our heart good, I tell you that. Grady, he knows what to do."

"You mean Grady Stamps was at your family meeting too?"

"Lord no, Kate, family's family. Blood's blood. But Grady, he came out here with this baby that's lickin' my face right here and now. Purebred beagle, cutest markings. We'd've said no way if Grady didn't just come on out with him. Bought out the store, that man. Wicker bed with a red flannel cushion, leashes, case of puppy food and one of those rawhide chew-bones. Bought out the pet store to ease our pain. Chop's in our heart forever, but this new baby is one brand new little sweetie."

"Dukie, how did Grady find out about Chop?"

Dukie cleared her throat again. "From our grapevine. Bobbie told Dawn and Beca. Called them down at the studio, Noah's Ark. The girls are doing backup vocals, overdubs, whatever it is, Jon Hartly's new album. Anyway, Bobbie phoned down at Noah's Ark, and the girls told Grady. Didn't take but half a day for him to get out here with this puppy like he was on a healing mission."

So now Grady the healer. Kate felt her eyes close. She heard the whine and bark and licking sounds.

Somehow the new puppy tipped a scale. On Grady's part, it seemed like a pivotal chess move, aggressive and sly. As a tactician, Grady Stamps couldn't do better. He could kill the dog and come on like a benefactor when he brought the replacement puppy. A diversionary tactic to cover his tracks—assuming he and not Wade Rucker torched the Burnside house and smashed Chop to a pulp.

And killed Brandi.

But the backup singers came into a new light too. Maybe Grady brought them to Brandi the way he brought the puppy. Maybe they were his trained poodle act and K-9 corps.

If so, what kind of leash held them—career threats and promises? Was their friendship with Bobbie a ploy?

She said, "Dukie, I won't quit on you. But stay in touch. Work with the police as much as possible, and let me know what they say. You've got my work number. Call anytime." She hung up. And knew she lied. There was no more "any" time. Killers canceled leisure, made the days shorter, sliced and diced the very minutes. She had work to do.

Ten A.M. Saturday. Kate circled the blocks. No signs, no logos, no marquees. No animals two-by-two. Noah's Ark was some-. where on Music Row. But where? No phone book address. Recording studios were anonymous and faceless, a secret from the fans. The plain brown wrappers of country music.

Kate circled again. Noah's Ark? It even felt like rain. Through the windshield, a half-dozen buildings might qualify—a glass high-rise, a half-timbered stucco, a brick four square. Up and down the streets looking. And looking.

Minutes passed. 10:08. Hardly a soul in sight. One man loaded equipment into a Voyager. She passed him twice, circling. Ten minutes more and she'd be forced to call Bobbie and Dukie to get the street address.

And blow her cover. Talk to the Burnside women, and you might as well broadcast. Their grapevine felt like an open mike—or an early warning system. To Judy Swan? To Wade Rucker? To Grady Stamps and Dawn and Beca? A telephone tree to Brandi's killer? Not this time if she could help it.

She pulled up to the Voyager. Give it a shot. "Mister—" He looked up. Mid-thirties, pudgy. "Mister, I'm looking for the Noah's Ark studio, and I lost the street number. Friends of mine are doing overdubs, and I'm supposed to meet them there this morning. I haven't driven in circles like this since my cat ran away."

He paused and rolled his lower lip. Red eyes. Up all night in a studio himself? She said, "Look, I'm not a tourist. I'm supposed to pick up a video from my friends, Dawn Mulligan and Beca Yowell. They're harmony vocalists. Said to meet them at Noah's Ark at ten. I'm trying to spot their cars, but they probably parked someplace around back."

He squinted, put one hand in his pants pocket and jingled change. "Why don't you call the studio? There's pay phones at Hillsboro Village. If you need a quarter—"

"I tried. Rang a zillion times."

He scratched his head. "Saturday morning. Figures." He looked closely at Kate, a woman in jeans and a red plaid shirt, light makeup, Reeboks. Decision time. Hesitation. Then slowly, reluctantly, he pointed. "Two blocks up on the left. Gray brick house with, like, hurricane shutters. There's a wood arch out front like the front of a ship."

"The Ark?"

"Gotta use your imagination. One thing though. They won't open the door to just anybody, so—"

"I know. Tight security. I'll take it from here. Thanks much." In the rearview she saw him watching her drive the two blocks, slow down at the gray brick house she'd passed twice already, then pull in past a pine and wood front-yard structure that did look vaguely like the prow of a homemade boat. There was a space in the asphalt lot around back for maybe ten cars. Four were parked, a slate blue Celica, an ancient Datsun, a Bronco, a Jeep. Add Kate Banning's Buick.

She walked around front to an oak door banded in brass, like a hatch. The hurricane shutters over the windows looked like hatches too. Noah's Ark battened down for the flood. On the door three security system plaques bristled with lightning bolts and swords. No other identification. She rang a silent bell and waited.

Waited to talk herself in. Waited to talk to Dawn and Beca. Play this longshot.

The electric lock snapped. The door opened a crack. A male voice. "Yes?"

Kate stepped back. Door-to-door salesman's tactic, back off one full step when the door opens. She spoke to the crack. "Hi, I'm Kate, and I'm looking for Dawn Mulligan or Beca Yowell."

"Beca's not here."

"Dawn then."

"She's in session. Busy. Sorry."

The door was closing.

"Hold on, it's important. I mean, I could wait till she's free."

"Sorry. Security."

"Oh, security, I know." Kate smiled. She spoke in a rush. "I know how it is. If I wait till afternoon, I can go to their apartment, but it's so important. I need to borrow the 'Fool Moon' video. It's a very, very precious memory. It's the late Brandi Burns. Her family wants me to see the video. Dawn and Beca worked with Brandi, you know. They're on the video with her."

The door opened a crack wider. A sandy-haired, thin young man, about twenty, with bony cheeks looked out. He was wearing jeans and a black T-shirt that said Zildjian Cymbals and glasses with red plastic frames that slipped down on his nose. He looked confused.

"Or I can sit here on the steps and wait if that's okay—except it looks like rain. Looks like it might just pour any minute. I don't think I brought an umbrella."

He hesitated. A closed shop, a high-power studio. Offer to sit on the stoop?—no, keep quiet, give him space. At last, "Guess I can let you in. It'll be a good while." The door opened fully, and Kate stepped in. Behind her, the snap of the electric locks.

He led her through a reception area with mounted plaques of gold and platinum albums—Dolly Parton, Kenny Rogers, Tanya Tucker, Vince Gill, Pam Tillis.

But to the side she spotted a small, black-framed photo of a young woman in white fur with the full moon over her shoulder. It was the photograph over Dukie's sofa. Behind the photographer's slick shot, Brandi's eyes looked eager, shining and brave for the adventure. Most of all it was a portrait of trust—trust in her family, her record label, her manager who was to look out for her, keep the contract, keep her car maintained. Fluids and brakes.

Ensnared and killed.

"You can come on in." She followed.

"Impressive wall," he said. "Kind of a museum."

"And a memorial to Brandi."

"Yes, ma'am."

Another Southern boy with a "ma'am" reflex. She said, "My name's Kate Banning, by the way."

"I'm Eugene." He turned to look her in the eye. "Eugene Gilster." He led her into an informal room with casual furniture, orange corduroy sofas and chairs and a dark yellow area rug. There was a table with an odd lot of playthings, a Teddy bear, a football, a clown nose. To the side a sink with cabinets, fridge, countertop with coffee maker. And a bowl of apples and snack packs of Twinkies, Fig Newtons, granola bars. Telephones as plentiful as ashtrays used to be.

"Ever been in a recording studio?" Kate shook her head. "The actual studio's in there." He pointed behind a closed door at one end. "Soundboard, speakers, mikes. During breaks, people come out here and relax a little bit, have a bite, make calls. Want some coffee? Snack?" She shook her head. His hair, Kate noticed, was matted across the crown. Like winter earmuffs in New England. But of course, studio earphones. She said, "You must be a sound engineer?"

He beamed in bliss, then humility. "I'm learning," he said, "or trying to. I'm a student intern from Belmont University. I practically live here some days. J. T. gives me lessons on the soundboard. That's J. T. Wolfe. He's the best. We worked a couple hours early this morning. He did some mixing and I helped. He's in there right now with Dawn and Dick Hayes. Dick's the producer. I'm just hanging out. Nice on a Saturday, peaceful. That's why a studio should be closed sometimes. In my opinion. Too many people in here; I think it makes problems."

"Noise?"

"Distraction. That's just my opinion." He opened the cellophane.

Kate nodded. She watched Eugene Gilster bite a Fig Newton and jiggle his knee and push back the red glasses. If he knew Grady Stamps or Beca Yowell, Dawn Mulligan or anything useful, she had just minutes to pry it out before he sprang from the chair and vanished into the recording studio. "Maybe I will have a snack," she said. "Haven't had a Fig Newton in ages." He bounced up and brought two packs. They crinkled. "So many recording sessions," she said, "they must just blur together in your mind."

"Not so far. No."

"You actually remember who's who?" Nod.

"Wow." She nibbled. Fig Newton was stuck to the roof of her mouth. "I'll bet lots of people show up here, like publicists and photographers. And managers? For instance, I'd guess Brandi Burns's manager came when she recorded. His name's Grady Stamps. Maybe you remember him?"

"Stamps? No, I don't think so."

"Soft-spoken guy. Slender. And his face . . . like he never sees the sun. Like maybe he had chicken pox or bad acne."

He shook his head. "Could have missed him. Mostly I was here for those sessions, though. Don't remember any Grady Stamps."

"He's managing Jon Hartly Owens now."

"Yeah, Jon Hartly's hot. But I don't remember Grady. Not at Brandi's sessions. Actually, that's not unusual. Artists' managers don't necessarily come to recording sessions."

Now he swallowed, crumpled the wrapper, tossed it, began to stand. "Better get back inside. See how the overdubs are coming."

She stood up too. Gone in seconds. "Eugene, I really would appreciate that coffee. Love a cup or two if you'd just take a minute?"

"No problem." Though his body leaned toward the closed door where the action was. Last thing he wanted, kitchen chores. "Maybe J.T.'ll want some coffee," he said, "Dawn too." He filled the water tank and put a filter in, opened the Maxwell House and counted the scoops. He flipped the *on* switch, then opened the cabinet doors and then the dishwasher. "Mugs are all dirty," he said. "Wait, we have Styrofoam cups, let's see." More flipped cabinet doors.

Seconds passing. Kate said, "Mugs—do singers bring their own? Like Dawn and her friend Beca? Do you know Beca Yowell?"

"The redhead, you bet, anybody'd remember her." He capped the coffee can. "High voice, soprano. Really *in* it." He leaned one hip against the counter, waited for the coffee to drip through. He dug a nail into a Styrofoam cup. "Styrofoam, it reminds me, something funny when they were recording the *Fool Moon* album." He grinned. "The redhead, Beca, she brought her uncle in from the farm. I remember his name, Arlen Burnett. You, you're not from around here, are you?"

"Boston."

"Yeah, I'm from Miami, but the suburbs. Coral Gables. Definitely not the farm. This uncle, he was strictly country. Someplace way out in the sticks, Dickson County I think. He was her family guest. Toured the studio, heard a recording session. Then everybody took a short break because J.T. was changing a tape reel. So Beca says, 'Eugene, fix my uncle a cup, will you? A Styrofoam cup with a paper towel.' "

"I thought, cup of coffee. She says it's for his Beech-Nut. I thought she wanted the coffee in the cup and a paper towel for his gum. But you know what?—it's a spittoon. A spittoon. You fold the towel into the cup so they can spit the tobacco juice. It's Beech-Nut chewing tobacco. He had this bulge in his cheek . . . I shouldn't make fun, I'm just . . ."

"Custom of the country."

"How'd I get off on that? What I meant to say was, I think it's better not to have friends and family in a studio." He put the cups out, ready to pour. Another moment, goodbye Eugene.

Kate said, "Why don't I wash a few cups from the dishwasher? Won't take a sec. The Styrofoam—after that story, I couldn't drink from it now no matter how much sugar or milk I put in." Quick, reach for the dishwasher door and grab the upturned mugs. "No time at all." She smiled at him. Three more minutes? Four? Eugene rubbed his hair, as if undressed without the earphones. Kate lathered a mug that said Martin Guitars. She said, "It must be great to work on actual recording."

"Sure is. You help figure what special sound the producer's looking for and help them get it. Sometimes less is more. Like this morning, a fiddle player's coming in later to re-record some fills. But if the fiddle still doesn't sound right, Dick will want to eliminate that track. At the board J.T. will ax it."

"Cut it out of the recording?" He nodded. "Even after the performers record their parts?"

"Sure. Happens. Producer tries it out, and the engineer works on the mix. But if it isn't what they want—" He drew a finger across his neck. Kate winced. "Hey, everybody gets paid. You can't let your ego get in the way. Ego's a big trouble maker. Mess you up."

Kate rinsed the mug. Lots of slow rinsing. She said, "But you've seen egos up close and personal?"

"A little, yes. Just an intern, but I've seen it."

She reached for a second mug, Jimmy Buffet and the Coral Reefer Band. Keep probing. She said, "Even backup singers—?"

"Oh yeah, harmony vocalists too. Beca, that redhead, she was supposed to have a duet on Brandi Burns's album. You probably know that story since you know the family. Virgo was pushing for it."

Virgo? Pushing? Kate said, "Seems like I might have heard it mentioned."

"Sure. A little bit of a showcase for Beca. It was something new one of the Virgo execs wanted to try. One of the new guys from L.A."

"You mean Roy Benniger?"

"Yeah, Mr. Benniger, his idea. To open a pipeline for potential new artists. Sort of ride the newest singer piggyback on one of the main artist's songs. In this case the liner notes would say, 'with special guest Beca Yowell.' Like that. Just open the door a little for the duet singer, give her a little exposure. Open the future."

"Interesting." Kate wet her lips. "And Brandi, she liked the idea?"

"So-so. She was okay about it. Went along. Mr. Benniger kept saying he'd personally make sure Virgo showed its appreciation for her generosity. Sharp dresser, Mr. Benniger. Anyway, it was a call-and-response arrangement; they both had solos. And you know, it wasn't a first-time innovation. Reba McEntire did that kind of a duet with Linda Davis on 'Does He Love You?'. They sang it on tour and on TV, and it got Davis signed to a record deal."

He put the Maxwell House can back on the shelf. "Anyway, the two women worked hard on it. Tried it over and over here in the studio. Good faith effort. Mr. Benniger stayed right with it. Big bucks on the studio clock. But nobody liked the sound. J.T. worked with it every which way, but the tape doesn't lie; that's what I think. If it doesn't sound good on playback, then cut it."

Kate paused. "So they cut it?" He nodded. She circled the sponge in the coffee mug. Sound interested but not involved. "That must be hard to take if you're the duet partner. You think you've got a guest spot, and you've got nothing."

"Got your check for the session."

"I'll bet the singer wants the recording. I bet Beca did."

He turned to her. "For sure. She got real upset. It was like bad weather in here. Then Mr. Benniger took her out for lunch, and they stayed out and didn't come back till late. Held everything up. J.T. called a few restaurants but they weren't there. Everybody was hanging.

"Anyway, Mr. Benniger finally brought her back and stayed right with her all afternoon here, talking real quiet to her. Soothing. Everything went on like nothing happened. Later I heard he promised her a feature spot in the video, some special scene when they shot the 'Fool Moon' video." He shook his head. "Before lunch, though, she was like a tornado. Same day as the uncle with the Beech-Nut. Embarrassing. That's why I say no relatives."

Kate pushed the faucet to the side. Beca Yowell the tornado? Brandi caught in a twister? "Sounds hard on the main artist too."

"Not Brandi. She was really cool. Amazing. One of the guys started playing old tapes, like Eddy Arnold's 'Jealous Heart.' Brandi had him play it two or three times straight. I believe she asked to take it home. Anyway, she sat in that orange chair and did her puzzles through the whole thing."

"Jigsaw puzzles?"

"No, crossword puzzles."

"Brandi Burns worked crosswords?"

"To relax. She'd sit and work them out. I've seen musicians whittle, female vocalists knit. Anything to keep calm and relaxed. Brandi just stayed out of any negative stuff. And boy, was there negative air that day."

"But it blew over?" Suds. Third mug.

"Sure. Couple days later, Beca worked real sweet on another track. Helped chart a song. Good song."

"Not 'Fool Moon.' "

"Guess again."

Her pulse thudded. "Not 'Envy Green.' "

"Yeah. It was the last one they cut. I think Brandi wrote it at the very end after the storm. They were down to the wire. Uh . . . I think you could rinse that now; I think it's clean."

Kate splashed the mug obediently. "Then 'Envy Green' was a last-minute song?"

"Wrote it overnight and needed help to chart it. She had a notebook, and J.T. offered to help her, but the redhead did it. Beca. She made such a fuss about the duet; she wanted to smooth things over. She really studied the song in the notebook. Concentrated. She worked along with Brandi. Very nice. No hard feelings. Sweet as honey. See, there were no visitors that day. You just do better without the distraction."

Kate nodded. "I'm sure you're right." Lather the fourth mug one more time. Slow sponge. "So they sat down and worked from the green notebook?"

"Green? I don't remember. It was an ordinary notebook." He crumpled the last Fig Newton wrapper. "I do remember something about the melody line. Couple of notes. Brandi wanted her original way, but Beca worked out the chord charts, and there was some back-and-forth and then a change. Everybody in the studio thought the change worked better, J.T., Dick Hayes. Time was really tight. A studio clock's so expensive. There's pressure, and Brandi was real eager to record it. She said it was a big one. Said it came to her like a gift of knowledge. Songwriters say that sometimes, that a song's a gift.

"Brandi said something kind of poetic too. Bitter-something-or-other. Bitter knowing? Bitter-cold knowledge?" He shook his head.

"Can't remember exactly, it was unusual."

"But Beca changed some notes?"

"Maybe one note. I don't remember exactly. Mr. Benniger was co-producer, and he liked the new way too. He thought Beca should get co-write credit on it, but Brandi wasn't too crazy about giving her a co-write on that particular song, and nothing came of it. Hey, don't bother drying those. Let's just pour it out. I need to get back inside." He took the mugs and began pouring. "J.T. likes it black. I'll just take his. You make yourself comfortable. Dawn'll be out."

He took two mugs and disappeared.

She sat in one corduroy chair, stood and walked in circles. Going in circles. Whirlwinds? Tornadoes? She imagined Brandi in one of these chairs at work on puzzles while Beca Yowell's tantrum raged and Roy Benniger escorted her to a very long time-out lunch. Slick and sleazy Roy, the album co-producer, the label executive.

And, briefly, Brandi Burns's own recent lover.

What did Brandi think, witness to the tantrum and virtually shelved during the very long lunch? And seeing Roy act like Beca Yowell's mentor right before her eyes? What did she think when he tried to move Beca into her album, then into co-writer status on "Envy Green"?

Kate paused, at work on her own puzzle. Take it further from Brandi's viewpoint. Imagine the young country singer-songwriter getting certain vibes from the employee backup singer, the off-hours pal, fitting-room chum, tour bus buddy. Imagine months of these negative vibes—but months also discounting them, shrugging off intuition for the sake of smooth day-to-day work in rehearsal, travel, performance.

Yet that day in the studio could not be forgotten. The day Beca boiled over and apparently nominated herself to become Roy Benniger's next fling. Imagine the vibes when the sex-and-power theatrics played out in the studio on Brandi's album timeclock, literally in her own face.

Wouldn't it be second nature to dip her pen in the well of music and register her protest in a song?

Her anger. And her fears too?

And what about Beca herself, so angry that she lost control in front of the others—then got a certain reward for it. Momentarily placated by the promise of a video spot, but cut out of a prime spotlight track on the *Fool Moon* album. Making Brandi jealous, but consumed with jealousy herself? Kate recalled the two women onstage singing with a cardboard cutout. The blonde and the redhead. The color coordinated backup singers. Blonde with blue eyes, redhead with eyes of—weren't they green? Right now it felt unmistakable. It felt so much like envy green.

Chapter Twelve

Thompson Lane is a commercial strip with appliance discounters, furniture centers, custom security grills. From a railroad underpass Kate took a left, a short detour, then left again at the entrance to Cascade Gardens Apartments which featured a sign in foot-high rustic lettering.

The units were named after woods. 237-Oak was on the second floor around back to the left. The apartments were white stucco with cedar shingles and little balconies. A late-model dark blue Escort was parked in the 237-Oak slot, its trunk lid up and two vodka cartons on the concrete walk beside it.

In the gathering dusk, Kate looked into the cartons and saw women's shoes—size six?—most of them five-inch spikes in every color from ruby to royal. They were tumbled and jumbled in the stage of moving when you gave up order and system and threw everything in. The vodka cartons signaled that a moving company was not involved. The spike heels said a woman either wanted to feature her legs and/or she wanted the height.

Kate climbed the stairs. A bamboo wind chime clinked in the light breeze. The door was ajar.

"Beca? That you?"

"No, it's Kate. Kate Banning."

She opened the door with a frown. It was the blonde. Dawn. She wore tight cutoffs and a neatly tucked T-shirt with a silhouette of the Marlboro man. Her bare toes were separated by cotton wads, the nails a wet scarlet. Her deep frown said she was not expecting a visitor, and not pleased by the interruption of her pedicure. "Kate, you say? Oh, you're *that* Kate, Bobbie's . . . friend. Beca said she met you too. And hey, you were at the studio this morning. How come you didn't wait? Eugene said it was important."

"It is. But I ran out of time. Sorry. Thought I could just stop by. I got your address from the phone book. It's the 'Fool Moon' video; I'd like to borrow it. These days I'm trying to give Bobbie and her mother a little help."

"I know. They talk about you." She opened the door a little wider as if obliged. Up close, without makeup, her face was not so pert and not so young. A web of lines spread under dull but wary eyes. Kate said, "I really should have phoned first. I was on Thompson Lane looking at washing machines. I just wanted to borrow the 'Fool Moon' video for a day or so. Hope you don't mind. I felt sure you'd have a copy or two, you and Beca. She here?"

"Down at the storage area with her Uncle Arlen. Every apartment gets storage, and he's here to help her load up and move." Dawn walked gingerly on her heels, toes angled up. "Have a seat if you can find one. Here, let me give these a shove." A pile of magazines splashed to the floor. *Country*, *Country Weekly*, *Music City News*. Faces of young hunk stars in big hats, of Reba McEntire and Vince Gill and Shania Twain.

Dawn let them lie. She gestured to the cleared cushion of a blue sofa. Kate sank into lumpy foam and broken springs. "Beca'll be up in a minute." She sounded listless. Kate gazed at the cramped, cluttered, half-dismantled apartment. It looked all too recent and familiar, the boxes, hangers, plastic bags stuffed and twist-tied.

But the disorder here went further. On a smeary glass coffee table a dozen dead roses stood in water the color of pond scum. A breakfast bar was crammed with eggy plates, hair rollers, a toy xylophone, spilled nail polish, an open and half-empty bottle of red wine and a nail clipper. "I just moved a couple months ago myself."

"Well, I'm not the one moving. Beca is. Everything from old prom gowns to her xylophone. Been moving for days now."

"But she's here?"

"Oh, yeah. Her uncle came over from Dickson County about an hour ago to help. He brings his truck. He's a bachelor. He farms and tinkers. Must be nice to have an uncle that thinks the sun rises and sets in you. Me, I'm from D.C. and divorced twice. I got a red Jeep with a hundred twenty thousand miles on it. Nobody hauls my stuff around but me. Hey, you want some wine?"

Kate glanced over at the bottle on the breakfast bar. "No thanks."

"Well, I'm having some." Dawn reached toward the cluttered coffee table, and then Kate saw the jelly glass half-full of red wine.

Maybe she was tipsy. Maybe the listlessness was really drowsiness from the half bottle she'd downed. "California vineyards," Dawn said. "Beca's boyfriend brought it over. He's from L.A. It's called Merlot. There's a 't' but you don't say it. That gourmet stuff's wasted on me. If it's not vinegar, I'll drink it. Cheers."

At that moment, the front door opened, and a silhouetted figure appeared backlighted against the sun. "—you see that, I'm driving this girl to drink." The voice from the doorway blazed with a corona of red hair. The very petite redhead moved into the maze of a living room as if to stage center.

Today she wore skin-tight jeans, black cowboy boots, and a crisp white V-neck T-shirt that looked starched. Her turquoise drop earrings matched the turquoise insets of her narrow western belt. In the light, Kate noticed green hazel eyes glowing hot beneath the mascara. Her smile was dazzling. "Kate, how you doing? Glad to see you again, but I have to say, one of these days I hope we'll meet up in a room that's not an unholy mess. Don't want you to get the wrong idea about us."

Kate smiled. "Sorry to barge in. I came to borrow the 'Fool Moon' video. I live about fifteen minutes from here, and Joelton's so far."

"Tell me about it." She raked a hand through her hair and pulled a stick of Doublemint from her jeans pocket. "When we worked with Brandi—God rest her soul—we were on I-65 all the time going up there to rehearse. Or to keep her company when Wade Rucker showed up—who was nothing but trouble, even burned Dawn with a cigarette once, can you believe it?" She shrugged. "Joelton, I could drive it in my sleep. Put a thousand miles on my Escort. Of course Brandi was getting a place in town. She looked at condos and atrium apartments. You probably know all that." Kate nodded.

Beca pushed on. "Hey, with all due respect, let's not go down that road; we'll all be cryin' and feeling just terrible. I have to stay on track enough to get the last of this moving done. Got to keep some feelings bottled up. Thank heaven for Uncle Arlen's Sierra. That's how much stuff I've got, and he's ready to drive off with a load, and my car's about packed for another trip."

She winked at Kate. "And I'm driving Dawn crazy, speaking of driving. Believe me, you don't want to make your duet partner crazy. Anybody want half of this last stick?" Beca folded the Doublemint and bit it in two before Kate or Dawn could shake reply. She looked at Kate again. "You're after the 'Fool Moon' video, is that it?"

Kate nodded. "Grady Stamps probably has copies, but I can't get past his receptionist."

"That's Marvene. She's tough. We joke about it. We call her his police."

Kate smiled pleasantly. "Don't you have his private number?"

"Grady's? Honey, nobody has Grady Stamps's direct line except Brandi, God rest her soul, and now Jon Hartly Owens and his top people. That's the music business. When we talk to Grady, we go through Marvene. Now let's see about that video. Any ideas where those cassettes are at, Dawn?"

"With your shelf knickknacks? How about down at the car with the shoes?"

Beca shook her head. "Why don't I just see if it's in with the towels? Give it a quick look." She disappeared into a back bedroom.

Dawn sank to the carpet, drew up her knees, reached for her bottle of nail polish, angled one foot. "Second coat." She glanced at Kate. "Raspberry Ice. Second time I'm using it. I put it in the medicine chest behind the Advil so I wouldn't even see it. Actually got it the last day we saw Brandi alive."

"At Dillard's, Beca told me."

Dawn nodded. "The very day she died. The very afternoon. I remember we took time getting our right skin tones. Brandi and I are more fair, but Beca needed a shade darker. She took forever."

"Brandi?"

"No, Beca. Beca took forever." Her tone carried a weary scorn. "Taking forever right now."

"You spreading stories about me?" Beca stepped back into the room. The twinkle in her eye was colder. She was empty-handed. "No sign of that video. Vanished in thin air." She laughed. "You came in at one of our flashpoints, Kate. Moving gets on everybody's nerves. I dumped my shoes in boxes, and Dawn and me almost came to blows over it."

She looked at Kate. "See, Dawn's neat as a pin, and I drive her nuts. Why use a hanger when you can drape it across the bed? Why bother with the toothpaste cap? Bras and pantyhose just hook themselves over my bedpost. That's how I am. Living with me has been torment and torture for this neat gal. Sometimes I think it's just as well we didn't do the *Fool Moon* tour. We'd've fought like two cats on that cramped bus."

"You mean the Silver Eagle? Bobbie said it's wonderful."

"If you're the headliner." Now Beca's voice had an edge. Her green eyes seemed at once wider and narrower. "The star's stateroom is pure luxury, no question. Rare wood panels and a private dressing table and wet bar and indirect lighting. And big closets. Mirror walls. State of the art everything. Brandi'd get the custom queen-size 'cause she's *it*. We're backup; we'd get overheads and bunks. You get the picture. Leave it at that."

Her eyes flashed. Kate wanted to get around to the studio duet—to the tornado. "I won't stay a minute longer," she said.

"I just thought you'd have plenty of copies. I understand you're both featured."

"Featured? You said featured?" Her voice cracked. She stood back, hands on hips. Her irises glittered. "Hey, lady, when you see the video, don't hold your breath looking for Dawn Mulligan or Beca Yowell. Dawn and me come on 'Fool Moon' for about four seconds—wouldn't you say, Dawn, four seconds? Like a snapshot in somebody else's album."

The moment crackled. Kate looked from one to the other. They both looked away. Resentment for sure. Brandi? Grady?

"Grady tried getting us better exposure. He did his best." Dawn dipped the nailbrush and painted the big toe of her left foot. She blew toward her toes. "They shot enough footage for it, I tell you that. Froze our buns. It was last April—"

"March." Beca bit the word as if in frost and chill.

"A cold day, anyway." Dawn's shoulders shuddered. "And that warehouse was freezing. The lighting crew took forever getting the little colored moons just right, and we both caught cold in those skimpy tops. Fredericks of Nashville, the guys in the band said. Beca and I kept sipping hot tea and lemon and honey because I had a studio session the next day, and so did Beca."

"Which is the daily bread, you know, if you're not a star," Beca said. "Sessions and demos." Contempt.

"You can't get sick. You just can't." Dawn's voice was plaintive.

"Speaking of which, I'm just stepping over to cork this." Beca moved to the breakfast bar and picked up the wine bottle. She pushed the cork, guarding her nails. And guarding her designated duet partner and soon-to-be ex-roommate? It seemed clear who was under whose thumb. "Producers to meet with next week," Beca said to Dawn. "Wouldn't want any achy breaky headaches. Listen to Mommy Beca. Think future. Think beyond overdubs."

"Overdubs—" said Kate. Get a clearer notion of the working relationship between these two. "Aren't overdubs the harmony back-up voices?"

"Not exactly. Hey, Dawn, tell Kate about overdubs while I wreck my nails on this cork."

Dawn painted another toe and wiped. She spoke as if ordered to recite a lesson. "They're laid down about last on a recording, after the basic instrumental tracks, the special instrumentals, the main vocalist. Then it's overdubs, harmony vocals and background vocals, and then on to mixing and mastering. We both did overdubs this week. It was a little spooky being back at Noah's Ark. Not since the *Fool Moon* sessions— 'Fool Moon' to 'Envy Green.' " Dawn said it quietly, "envy green."

Freeze-frame moment. Kate looked closely at both. Dawn seemed hushed, as if cowed by the memory. Beca rolled her shoulders as if shedding dandruff.

Dawn hunkered down and screwed the cap on the nail polish. She worked that cap, Kate saw, long after it was on tight. She repeatedly blew at her toes. "To tell you the truth," Dawn said, "the *Fool Moon* album's a sad memory. Maybe someday it'll be a keepsake, but not now. It reminds you Brandi's gone."

"And it reminds us we're just a singing snapshot in the album *and* the video. We're not going to let that happen again, are we, Dawn?"

The blonde seemed reluctant. "What Beca means is, we were supposed to get some exposure on that video and on the album too—I mean, Beca was. And we got cut down to practically nothing. It's just one of those things. Work in Nashville, you get used to it. Get your hopes up, and the disappointments come thick and fast."

Her smile was rueful. A career veteran of bad news. In the fading light, Kate saw the lines in her face and guessed Dawn had a full ten years over Brandi and Beca too. Dawn Mulligan looked on the weary downside of her dreams. Maybe she pinned her last hope on the new duet act with Beca. "Beca's new at this," Dawn said. "She'll learn."

"I will not learn to eat dirt."

Kate tried to bring her focus back. "You mean Grady couldn't really help you?"

"Not behind the cameras."

"And not at the studio mike either." Beca's eyes flashed. "He'd love to. But his hands are tied. It's mostly the producers and executives. You want to take their word, but you get this run-around. You're cut down here, there, and everywhere."

She began to fold the Doublemint wrapper into smaller and smaller squares, her nails like pincers. "Fact is, if you're not a signed artist, you're just backwash." She pitched the wrapper toward the trash. Missed. "Dawn, hon, if your toes are dry, would you see if you can't find one of those videos?"

Dawn bent to touch her nails. "Not too tacky now." She stood, reached for the jelly glass, sipped. "Never mind," she said, "this girl right here's going to get hers." She pointed toward Beca. "She figured things out. Picked herself a real power boyfriend this time. Got the prince and the castle and gonna be on her way. Boy, were we fooled."

"Dawn, hon—"

"Thought she was leasing a little one-bedroom out by the airport. Everybody worried she wouldn't be able to sleep with the planes and all." She looked at Kate. "Not to worry, babe. This girl's not gonna have her beauty sleep wrecked by airplanes. This girl's off to live with the man of the moment and have maid service too." She sipped again and looked at Kate. "Number six Ballantine Lane, Belle Meade. Doesn't that sound rich? Doesn't that sound like an L.A. label exec. Even the name, Roy, doesn't that mean king? Oh, the stars are coming out." She hiccuped. "Just hope some duet stardust will sprinkle on me."

"Plenty to go around, hon. Every good girl will get her share."

In the banter, Kate heard a certain edge. Drunk talk with a warning? A threat? Beca said, "Look, I got to get going. Roy's waiting; I got to take him to the airport later on, and Arlen'll wonder what happened to me. Dawn'll look around for the video, won't you, hon? What was it you wanted with it, anyway?"

Kate shrugged and tried to seem pleasantly bland. "Just to check it out. So I can tell Bobbie and her mom I'm doing everything I can to help."

Beca looked at Kate, this time with a narrow-gauged look, a look that gave some quick test for instant results. "Awful what somebody did to that little dog," she said. "And that crazy person burning their house in the night."

She cracked her gum. "Bobbie, though, she's so upset she's making some kind of a conspiracy out of it. You hear how she talks about Brandi's notebook and the car wreck like they're connected."

"And you think Brandi's death was an accident?"

"Don't you?"

Kate shrugged. "I don't know."

Beca cracked her gum again. "Unrelated events, if you ask me. Bless her heart, we listen, we're there for her. Don't get me wrong, we sympathize. But if this was anything like she thinks, the police would be in it. The TBI would too."

"Tennessee Bureau of Investigation."

"You got it," Beca's gaze held. "Well okay," she said. "Okay, good luck. See you." She picked up two ferns and an armload of framed pictures from the rug and told Dawn she'd call her later. She stepped toward the door, paused and walked back into the kitchen as if in an afterthought. From the back Kate saw her arms move and then heard a gurgling at the sink and smelled an unmistakable aroma. Beca was pouring the wine down the drain. Then she was gone.

It felt like a vacuum, as if Beca Yowell sucked volumes of air out with her. Dawn had a defeated look. "I'll go find that video." She disappeared into a back bedroom. Kate heard the car and truck engines start up below and drive off. From the bedroom, rummaging sounds.

And her own mental rummaging.

Dawn—and what dawned on Kate, a glimmer of a glimmer. And a kind of countdown, a process of elimination. Grady

Stamps was off this particular chart. Ditto Wade Rucker. Judy Swan, same.

Beca Yowell, though— In a class all by herself? From the tantrum in the recording studio to the move to the castle. Resentment, jealousy, desire—capital-E, envy.

Murderous envy.

Beca Yowell charted the song. And changed it too, so said Eugene Gilster, apprentice sound engineer. And the pros in the studio liked it better the new way. Instrumentalists, producers, technical people—everyone liked it better. Roy Benniger liked it better too. So far, so good.

But not good enough for Beca? Did the redhead have to settle every one of her old scores as she got ready to hopscotch her way up? Did she think Brandi was involved in her every slight, wound, disappointment as her rage built onstage, in the studio, at every photo shoot? Did Brandi symbolize the Nashville that Beca was driven to win for herself alone, winner take all?

How could Brandi not feel all this? She worked with Beca Yowell daily and weekly for months, probably sensed over time the lengths to which bile-green ambition would go.

So she sent Beca a message in the "Envy Green" lyrics. A message about values.

Yet it was the music that Beca altered, not the lyrics. Not the words that Kate had scoured and sifted and screened on the *Fool Moon* tape and CD. Beca made a change, yes, but the words stayed the same. It was notes that shifted.

Shifted from the notebook to the album. Eugene said so. Kelly said so. One stepped-down note from a C to a B. It was C in the notebook, B on the album. Kelly called it a mistake.

But what if it was a calculation? Kate imagined Brandi in the orange corduroy studio chairs working the puzzles and listening to that song, "Jealous Heart." And feeling angry at Roy Benniger and Beca Yowell. Anger at the ex-lover flaunting his position as record executive and his drawing power as a man. Anger at a woman hired to help her and yet driven to upstage her.

Letters across, letters down. Egyptian sun god, first president of United States, king of dinosaurs. Letters in little boxes.

Letters spelling words. What if Brandi put a certain damaging word in "Envy Green"? What if Beca saw it—and set out to conceal it? Conceal it by changing the music.

Suppose Beca Yowell's improvement was erasure?

Kate stood and reached for a piece of scrap paper and pencil in her purse.

Then she spotted the toy xylophone on the countertop. Fisher-Price xylophone with wheels and a bright pull cord. The kind Kelly had years ago. Many years now. Colored metal bars, a little wood mallet. Kate went to it and reached for the mallet, immediately put it down. No noises. Not with Dawn Mulligan so close. Spoon, maybe? No, too loud.

But try fingernails. She stood over the xylophone and flicked a nail on the red-colored bar. Very light ding. Okay. So key of E, "Envy Green." She positioned her nails to sound the chords as Kelly had. And lightly dinged. "Oh, envy green . . ." Beca Yowell's version: B-E-B-A.

But the green notebook had the original. Reverse Beca's charting. Kate flicked her nails, tapped the whole phrase once, twice. A third time to make sure. The chords in place, plain as day. Elementary education. Tapped again and again. Her heart rate up, pulse pounding. Crossword letters, crosswords to murder. The tones spelled out B-E-C-A.

Chapter Thirteen

Seven-thirty P.M. Saturday. Five hours since Dawn Mulligan lent her the "Fool Moon" video. Five hours thinking while it rained. Five hours waiting for the cover of darkness. And planning to hit Interstate 40 west toward Memphis. Toward Dickson County when the drab, rainy skies faded from gray to black. Wipers on low. One hand on the wheel and a flashlight at her side, fresh batteries, latex gloves, and a mission. Check out one farm. Snoop. Trespass. Verify a hunch, get evidence. And get out alive.

In the left lane, Kate pushed her speed to sixty and checked the flashlight. Twist to high, twist to low for a pencil-thin beam of light. She shone it on her map, on her handwritten directions. She was alone in the car. Sam was due in tomorrow. Kelly and schoolmates were at a football game and school party. Midnight curfew. Kate was in a game too. Mortal stakes.

Was it conspiracy when one party to crime was the brain, the other the brawn? Envy green and its willing servant, was that a partnership of equals?

Arlen Burnett, Uncle Arlen, was a telephone listing in Dickson County. Eugene Gilster's memory was correct—assuming it was the same Arlen Burnett in the Dickson County Bell-South directory on the reference shelf at the Green Hills branch of the Nashville Public Library. Kate and Kelly's local branch. There was just one listing for a Burnett spelled with two t's, first name Arlen. Not that Triple-A offered route maps to number 27 Suggs Hollow Road.

But at mid-afternoon, at Tower Books on West End, she paid $8.95 for a *Tennessee Atlas and Gazetteer.* "Back Roads and

Outdoor Recreation," read the back cover. Fishing, camping, hunting. Did tracking a possible killer on a rainy night count as outdoor recreation? The atlas featured a big map of every county in the state. Kate planned her route and paperclipped it to the cover. U.S. 40 West into Dickson County, exit at Tennessee 46, then go north to Old Highway 47 and a right off Lime Kiln Road to Butler Creek Road. Make a left onto Suggs Hollow Road and hope Arlen Burnett's name was on the mailbox. Have yourself some recreation. Visit the farm. Beware Old McDonald.

As for dress? She chose her darkest jeans and a black cotton long-sleeved mock turtle pullover. And dark socks and her dark green urban trekkers that used to pound the Boston pavement. From Beacon Hill to the Tennessee hills. Kate also clipped back her hair on both sides with Kelly's barrettes. No jewelry, though she had a pick-like rod that could be mistaken for a pin or hair device by anyone but a cop or locksmith.

No rain gear either. Too noisy. Her new Tennessee license with the smiling face and shaggy hair was in her left back pocket. The bump in the front right pocket was a cartridge of pepper spray. In the backseat in a fanny pack, certain supplies in plastic wrap.

Figure travel time of forty to fifty minutes one way. It was 8:03 when she crossed the county line, 8:17 when she reached Tennessee 46, a two-lane asphalt with light traffic mostly going in the opposite direction. She tried to spot a Sierra pickup among them. If only Uncle Arlen were among the mall moviegoers and not sitting with a shotgun across his knee waiting for his niece's summons.

Or waiting for a trespasser.

Kate changed radio stations. WSM *Cryin', Lovin', Leavin', and Lookin',* a country radio call-in. Gloria T. out in Gallatin requests Mark Chesnutt's "Old Country," going out to her very own country boy, Jeff R. Mark Chesnutt sang his song. Deep Texas voice and steel guitars. Kate turned it low. She was passing Dickson proper, eyes open for old Highway 47.

It was another, narrower, two-lane blacktop. A couple miles on this if the map were drawn to scale. The rain nearly stopped, and she turned off her wipers. This was farm country, the barns outlined against the gray-black sky, lights on in the houses. One car ahead of her turned off and disappeared. Two pickups passed in the opposite direction, both Fords, not Chevy Sierras. Kate turned the radio down again and almost missed Lime Kiln Road, then overlooked Butler Creek Road and had to backtrack.

At Suggs Hollow, however, the pavement stopped. Nothing on the map about road surfaces. She was on gravel now, rumbly, bumpy. The rain hadn't softened it. She slowed to twenty-five, then twenty. She turned the radio off and cut her headlights. Parking lights would do.

There were fences and open fields. But the patches of grays and blacks meant it was much hillier here. The mailboxes marked steep-pitched driveways that fell away on either side. The boxes stood on posts, some in clusters, some singly. Arlen Burnett's number 27 should come up on the left.

She found it, a single black box with crude white numerals on a post tilted about thirty degrees. No name.

And what did she hope to find down in the hollow of the hollow? A farmhouse, at least a cabin, and a barn, perhaps a shed or two. Livestock. Cows, pigs, chickens. Maybe a tractor.

But the farm itself wasn't on her mind. Tools of destruction were. Inside one of those buildings in the hollow she imagined a crowbar flecked with rust-red paint from the file cabinet at Trystar Music. Or stuck with dried bits of canine tissue. Or a rag with gas cans. Arsonist's still-life, rag with gas cans.

To make the best approach, she deliberately drove past number 27, proceeded another quarter mile, then turned around and headed back. Her car was now pointing back toward Nashville. Kate drove on for another three hundred yards past Arlen Burnett's property so he would not hear her engine die. At the roadside, she let her Buick idle a moment before pulling the key. Hope Arlen mistook it for a distant sound. Doubt he did. Hoped he was hard of hearing. Doubt that too.

She detached the ignition key from her ring and stuck it in her jeans' watch pocket, then slipped the ring of keys under her seat. She reached around to the backseat and buckled on the fannypack. Then she opened the door as quietly as possible and stuck the flashlight in her right back pocket. With the car unlocked, she walked quickly back toward number 27. She kept to the left side of the road. The air was rain-soft and cool. The luminous dials of her watch read 8:37.

Which meant she was on time and yet late, very late. Delayed and sidetracked by the obvious, starting when Bobbie described Brandi's terror of a snake in her new career Eden. The violent boyfriend, the mercenary manager—two obvious pit vipers. Every rock Kate turned up, one of them was there. And farther out, a few figures like Judy Swan slithered.

Beca and Dawn, meanwhile, played bit parts as though they, too, were cardboard standups. As though they were only the girls, Bobbie's buddies. Chicks on the fringe.

Instead, the center. Or vortex. A driven redhead bound and determined to be a solo artist no matter what it took, including sex, slaughter, arson, homicide.

And what would push Beca Yowell over the edge?—maybe a combination of things. A bunk instead of a stateroom on the tour bus, a cowgirl outfit instead of the feathers and fur and beaded doeskin of the female headliner. A career door slammed in her face with the xxxx'd-out album duet—which meant that the *Fool Moon* CD would not feature "special guest Beca Yowell," and Beca would not have her tour highlights when Brandi invited her to come forward onstage to sing the duet number. Add it all up to rage that Beca would stay where she was, in the background, in the small print. And eaten alive with envy, a green-eyed monster so poisonous she made a play for a record executive right in front of Brandi and moved the singer-songwriter to plant an indictment deep in her song, in the very melody. B-E-C-A in the refrain. Inscribed in the notebook, it was a time capsule. If anything happened to Brandi, it was to be dug up and opened. And decoded.

Once more, Beca's best wasn't good enough. Maybe next time.

Next time? Kate paused. Maybe "next time" itself was a big part of Beca's motive, to make herself a "next time" by shoving Brandi offstage so she could make her own bid for the center spotlight. The center mike. And immediately. At the Hermitage Hotel, didn't Bobbie describe her friends, the backup singers, as ambitious enough to fight down to the gristle given half a chance? So get rid of Brandi and make it a one-woman feeding frenzy. Seize the moment.

Seize this moment.

Kate passed one mailbox, then another on the tilted post. Number 27. Uncle Arlen's. A steep gravel drive led down to the left. She could just make it out in the deep gray night. She took a breath and took a step down, then another.

She skidded on the third. Stones rolled under her shoe soles like ballbearings. When her legs flew out, Kate sat down hard, ankle wrenched, stunned and winded too. Pratfall like a circus clown.

Stones rattled down the driveway. She felt wet mud against her backside. Somewhere down the road a dog barked, then another. She expected dogs, the rural alarm systems. She held her breath against the predictable shotguns and .357 Magnums that would come next. Private property and firearms, the rural yin-yang.

It took a minute to get her breath, and her resolve. Gingerly Kate stood. And listened. Dripping rainwater from the trees. And a keening sound, the last insects of summer. Her ankle hurt but moved. Rotate it, stand on it. Listen to the silence. Proceed.

She moved to the knee-high weeds at the side of the drive and worked her way down. The ground was soft from the rain, her jeans wet to the knee. Beside her the driveway was rutted, passable for a truck, though a car would scrape its axles. She followed along to a break in the trees.

And came suddenly to the truck. Water beaded on the hood and cab. A glistening rock.

Chevy Sierra.

Her stomach clenched. So Arlen Burnett was home. She took cover by the cab, concealing herself on the driver's side. Slowly she peered through the window. *Déja-vu* to Wade Rucker. She looked around. No Chuck Munde, no surprise.

Try for a blessing in disguise, Arlen being here at home. How convenient if the cab or truck bed held a toolbox with a crowbar and/or gas can with incendiary rags. She could spot them and get out fast, get on the phone, get the police out here immediately.

Fantasy. The windows were misted, and on the seat and floor she saw triangle shapes—clothes hangers only, doubtless Beca's. Uncle Arlen as Mayflower man. The truck bed was empty.

Over the sides, then, she peered at the house. A dim outdoor light glowed from what looked like a kitchen door on the left side. Ordinary house, shingled siding with a tin roof. Chimney, no satellite dish. No shrubs or flowers. Or grass. The space in front looked like mud. Planks were laid to the door.

Inside, no lights were visible, no flickering of a TV. Arlen Burnett in bed asleep? Early to bed, early to rise? The windows looked shut. At least that. Kate looked up. Gray sky. No moon in sight but the atmosphere bordered on luminous. Not good. She had counted on total darkness.

She looked to the left and right of the house. In the gray the shapes arose, a hilly field to the right. Also two buildings, one small, the other clearly a barn. To get to them, she must cross an open space, about a hundred yards.

But there was a fence, the pedestrian's guide to the shed and the barn. And a cover of sorts. The zigzag fence rails would help to conceal her. She could hunch low and run along. She listened. No human sounds. No animal sounds either. No whinny, no moo, no oink. Beasts of the field all asleep? It was starting to drizzle. Count to three, take a deep breath and get on with it. Run.

Did seconds pass before she heard the growl? Was it time-lapse as she felt earth vibrate? There was no bark, only the guttural. Wild and mad. She turned. Teeth and two glass eyes. Kate froze in place. Barrel chest, splayed legs. Braced to lunge. Fangs out from the dark-as-night gums. Hologram from hell.

Kate in slow motion. Do not look in the eyes, make no sudden movements. Implore the gods no barking, as slowly, ever-so-slowly, you reach back to the fanny pack, unzip, bring out your bribe, your offering, your devil's food.

Cheapest fatty beef on the market.

And with your other hand, the pepper spray.

Slowly, drop the patty and step back. And watch the primal
force. Carnivore at feeding time. Wrapper and all, one bite. Kate
began to coo, the low soothing sound for herself and for it. It
seemed all teeth, ears, mange, tail, and ribs. Especially ribs.
Some kind of hound. Underfed. Slowly she moved her arm back
again. Same reach, back step, more meat. More biting, wolfing.
Less growling. Then no growling. Beast in dog. Kate had six of
these patties. By the third she dropped the meat and held her
ground. Another step back, and she'd be exposed to view from
the house, caught between Arlen Burnett and his ravenous guard
dog, which chewed at the plastic wrap as much as the meat.
Shook it as though to subdue it. Better the wrap than her leg. But
the dog showed how stupid Arlen Burnett was even in country
terms. This animal was too bony, too starved to stay faithful to its
training. Too hungry to attack the stranger that fed it.

Fourth, then fifth. It ate slower now, nosing the beef from
the wrap. She dropped the last patty. It ate half, looked up at
her, Kate shunning eye contact. No challenge, no provocation.
Her hands folded across her chest. No dangling limb. It looked
down, up, down, then whined. Then took the remaining meat
in its mouth.

And trotted off.

She waited, heard the paws on gravel, in weeds. A rustling.
Gone. Gone for now. She felt her knees knock together. She
could let go and shake and tremble. Could run away. Get back to
the car and go. Call it a night. Call the Burnsides. Take back
Brandi's notebook, sit them down, explain "Envy Green." De-
code the refrain, spell out the melody line, B-E-C-A. Emphasize
Beca's eye color, too. Show and tell. Let them take it from there.

Precisely what she worried about, Dukie and Bobbie trying to
handle this. Both of them in way over their heads, no match for
envy-green Beca and her uncle. Not even with the Joelton police
working on the fire and the bludgeoned beagle. Lambs v. wolves.

So do what she came for. Take her turn. Get on with it. Run
for that fence.

Burrs and thistles grabbed her sleeves when she vaulted the

split rails to the north side away from the house. Vines grew around the fence rails, and weeds too. Arlen, it seemed, was a sloppy farmer. All the better for Kate. She crouched and watched the bungalow windows. Coal black. She moved ape-like, the wet weeds and drizzle soaking her jeans and shirt. Almost at the shed, she stopped to look and listen.

And froze again. Perfume. It caught her nostrils. Somebody here, a woman. Then her sleeve got snagged. From thorns. Rosebush. A crimson rambler along the fence, blooming its last for the year. Couldn't she tell a rose bush from a perfume bottle? City woman, what was she doing in the Tennessee outback? Her heart fluttered. Then she took a deep breath and approached the shed.

It was big as a one-car garage. With an eye on the bungalow windows, Kate felt for the door. She found it easily by the hasp and padlock. The lock was not pushed up into position. Arlen not wanting to fool with a key?—fine with Kate Banning. She didn't need proof she could still pick a lock. She removed and set it on the ground, then opened the door.

It creaked loudly, and she spun inside, closed it fast, stood with her back against it. Excited and scared. Adrenaline pumped. She turned around and faced the house, searching for a peephole crack in the wallboards of this shed. A small knothole let her see the house. Its windows were still black, Arlen still asleep. Hope and pray.

Twenty minutes, maybe thirty counting the barn. Get in and get out. Try to find what she came for. Hope that Arlen Burnett did not sleep with his crowbar under the mattress and gas cans by his side. If he did, rest in peace. The house was off-limits. She wasn't totally crazy.

Kate slipped the flashlight from her back pocket, hooded it with her hand and turned it on the lowest beam. Minimal diffused light. If Arlen should wake and see gleams from his shed— She checked her watch. 8:48. Smell of kerosene and oil. Get to work.

First, the latex gloves from the fannypack. They crackled and snapped, not quite big enough but okay. Her hand moved

like a scanner, wall by wall, bench and table. The usual tools
were here, Mason jars of assorted screws and nails, bags of
fungicides and one of rodent poison. Aggie products too, Bag-
Balm and Ivorex, a pour-on for cattle. Whatever. It meant
Arlen owned some cows. Or did. The shed was orderly in a
crude way. Screwdrivers and chisels dumped in a wood box,
saws hung on nails driven into the shed wall in no particular
order. On a workbench stood a pint of Wild Turkey with
maybe two swallows left, and a carpenter's apron that hung
from the same nail as one of the woodsaws. Three clawham-
mers and a chain saw lay on a side table, the saw blade showing rust.

Oddly, there was a turkey baster beside it. Eyedropper for
cows? She picked it up, squeezed the bulb. Empty. She held it
to her nose and smelled some chemical odor. Familiar, but
strange too. She put it back down carefully beside the saw. At
her feet there was a gallon can marked Coal Oil. She thought
of Bobbie because its spout was stoppered with a potato.

But what about a crowbar? None in sight, not on the bench
or side table. Not on the dirt floor. No gas cans either. Cob-
webs hit her face. Something scratched in the corner. Mouse?
Rat? Snake? One last pass with the light. Nothing. She sucked
in, ready to exit the shed.

But then on a whim, Kate reached across to the carpenter
apron. Something about it was peculiar. The apron pockets
bulged, but not from nails. Too smooth. She felt in the pockets.
Softness. Cloth. She reached, pulled out a handful. Chamois?
No, more like flannel. She brought up her dim flashlight and
inspected the contents of her palm. It held rags, one dingy
white and the other checkered. Checkered orange and cream.
She tried to swallow. Then couldn't. Her mouth suddenly was
too dry. Her head felt light, and the dim flashlight flickered because her hand was shaking.

Shaking with the rag in it. The scavenged trash, the treasure.
The gold she came for. Between her twitching and muddy fingers lay the proof she was right. Right at the eleventh hour.

The cloth in her hand matched the strip she stooped to pick up in Dukie Burnside's yard the morning after the fire.

Time stopped, then started. Get away right now. Retrace steps, get out, call the police or sheriff or Tennessee Bureau of Investigation. Or the fire department if it came to that.

Yet if . . . Yet if . . . Another voice in her head. The turkey baster—that chemical odor, to suction steering fluid? Panic and possibility in debate. If the crowbar that killed Chop was lying in the barn, how could she retreat now? A few more minutes, taking all precautions. Just a few. Utmost care.

From the knothole she looked to the house. Black windows. Arlen deep in slumber. Who knew, maybe he kept other bourbon bottles around. In the shed, by the bedside. Maybe nightly he drank himself into a stupor to blur the memory of what he did for his niece.

She turned off her flashlight and stuck it back in her pocket. Take nothing for granted. Step outside, close the shed door and hunker down fast. Replace the lock. A steady rain fell now, and the sky was even more luminous. Her scalp felt wet, almost cold. Her jeans and shirt clung. She looked out toward the south. The barn was about seventy-five feet away. She listened closely. Same sounds as before, minus the bugs. Maybe the rain silenced them. In the distance she thought she heard a whinny. Arlen's fields seemed to stretch farther back, the farm property narrow but long. Maybe horses were out there. Or cows or sheep.

Forget the livestock, head along the weedy fence toward the barn.

One side of the barn was open, a door on a side away from the house. Kate stood at the open door. No sounds of animals. Not even their breathing. No moo, no baah. Just hay, the sweet old smell of a hayride. The smell of the elementary school fieldtrips she chaperoned when Kelly and her schoolmates sat on the bales and heard about butter and milking and filed past cows and touched their warm flanks.

Count on fear to snuff out nostalgia. She took one step in, stopped, took another. No sign of the dog. But suddenly, a meow, and Kate's gut clenched before she registered *cat*. Barn cat, maybe the only animal in residence at the moment. She braced for the feel of it. Sure enough, the arched back and tail took a pass across her legs, then moved off in wet loathing.

To turn on her flashlight? She hesitated. Too risky in this big space. She felt her nostrils tingle from the hay and stifled a sneeze. The barn itself felt full. She reached out and felt the hay, from the floor on up, high walls of hay in squared, stacked bales. Maybe the winter supply. She could make her way around the perimeter. In any cleared work space, she'd look quickly for the crowbar.

For the needle in this haystack.

But just a few feet along, Kate stopped. The center of the barn floor was piled, mounded with hay. But not in bales. It looked loose, as though you could jump down on it, a big soft pile. She stepped forward and pushed her hand into the mound.

And felt something hard. Then took another step, pushed again. And again. She put her hand into the hay a third time, slowly, tentatively, fingers working through the straw. It prickled through the latex on her fingers.

Then she hit a surface. It was smooth, it was hard. There was a ridge, a scoop. Like . . . a car door.

A car door you could open. Because she did. Right now. Through the hay. The latch gave. Immediately she took the flashlight and leaned against the mounded hay and pushed the light as far in as she could and twisted it clockwise.

And saw the metallic blue. The paint. And felt her heart race as she pulled back and stepped a few feet down and around the huge mound. And did the same thing again. And felt a smooth shape, then moved in with the light. And saw the red of a tail-light.

And around to the other end, lower this time, feeling for a rough place, a driver's side area where the metal and fiberglass would be crumpled and jagged and rough.

And found it too. Blind man's bluff, or like a Halloween haunted house with peeled-grape eyeballs and cold spaghetti brains. Except here it was wrecker yard salvage, fender and bumper and the real life death car that was Brandi Burns's Taurus.

Kate did not hesitate, did not linger. Flashlight in pocket, pepper spray in hand, she moved swiftly to the barn door and back along the fence. Twice, three times she stopped to listen and look at the bungalow windows. Black. No Arlen. No dog. All the way back, no nothing.

Except her footprints across the front of the property, the plastic wrap the dog might throw off or throw up. The disturbed hay mound. The intruder's calling cards.

And more to come. A swarm of cops by morning. First, to her car, then a phone. She was panting at the top of Suggs Hollow Road, gloves peeled and jammed in the fannypack, the ignition key ready as she slid behind the wheel, wet, muddy, shaky.

The car locks snapped as she dropped it in gear and rumbled off. In her headlights by the road she saw the weeds move, a gaunt form with marble eyes and a rib cage and teeth. Stockstill. Arlen's hound.

Vibration tattled her teeth all the way to Butler Creek Road, Lime Kiln Road, Old State 47. At each turn she checked the rearview for that dog. At a Mapco convenience store off Tennessee 46, she pulled in, unfastened the fannypack and went to the phone. 9:38 P.M. First the Burnsides, then the police. Put Dukie and Bobbie on alert, then summon help.

Dukie picked up on the third ring. "—why, just thinking about you, Kate. We're so excited. Tried to get you for the last couple hours."

"Dukie—"

"Course, bein' Saturday night . . . But I left a message. We got the best news."

"I have news—"

"From the Virgo people. Saturday and all. They've been talking, and they want to help Bobbie."

"Dukie, I want to help. Listen to me—"

"With music. To work on her voice and image and put together a spring tour. Recordin' too. To take up where Brandi left off, if you know what I mean. A dream come true . . . and electronic duets with Brandi on the big video screens. Technology does wonders. And even keep the band—"

"The band? You mean the backup singers?"

"Like a family. Dawn and Beca. Fact, Bobbie's over at Belle Meade right now with Beca. That Roy's out in Los Angeles till next week, so Beca's all alone. And Bobbie's so worked-up she couldn't wait to talk about it."

"Dukie, let me talk about something—"

"Dawn's going out on a date, so Bobbie just took off down to Belle Meade. Beca's thrilled. Virgo wants to work up some of Brandi's music—bring in the song doctors that can fix up Brandi's lines so good you'll think it's Christmas and your birthday both. Believe me, that notebook can be a treasure box. We need to have it back right away. I told Bobbie I gave it to you for safekeeping."

"Safekeeping, that's the idea."

"Beca's dying to help out with the notebook herself. Couldn't wait to get with Bobbie on it. That little redhead is a fireball, and she's thrilled, thrilled to death. You home right now, Kate? Most likely Bobbie and Beca'll want to come get that notebook from you tonight."

At the phone like ice. Congealed, frozen. Dukie Burnside, babble and bubble. On and on. Deaf.

Kate cupped her hand around the receiver and forced her voice to a flat dead calm. "Dukie, listen to me."

"Kate, honey, you all right? You sick—?"

"Just listen to me. Listen close. Look at your watch . . . okay, then, your wall clock. I want you to sit by your phone. In exactly one hour—one hour—if I do not phone you back, you are to call the Belle Meade police and send them to Roy Benniger's house on Ballantine Lane. Number six. You hear me? Dial the Belle Meade police and tell them it's an emergency."

The receiver buzzed with tiny whoops and cries as she cradled it and ran for the plateglass door.

Chapter Fourteen

At 10:13 Kate left Harding Road and crossed into Belle Meade on Lynwood Boulevard. Wet asphalt glistened in the head-lights, and the moon was a silver blur. On either side, the lawns swept a hundred yards back from the winding roadway. Speed limit 35, strictly enforced, everybody said so. Question was, should she deliberately speed and hope to get chased, bring the cops with her to Roy Benniger's?

Or should she go home and wait for Bobbie and her good friend Beca to show up for the notebook?

Bobbie and her bosom serpent.

Neither of whom knew about the Xeroxes. Nor Dukie. But once Beca Yowell got hold of that notebook, count on her to summon Uncle Arlen for yet one more errand. Perhaps this very night.

Or would Beca act on her own without his help? Controlled substance dropped in an icy coke might do it. Bobbie could fall asleep and veer off I-65 while driving back to Joelton. Envy's pecking order, Brandi to Bobbie. Equal opportunity fury, equal opportunity sabotage.

Equal opportunity 911. It seemed simplest to hit the emer-gency phone number. That was the problem. Too simple no matter how you figured it. From the Mapco store to Belle Meade, Kate spun it around three different ways. Scenario Number One—911 sends patrol car at Suggs Hollow Road to awaken peaceful citizen Arlen Burnett. Wrecked Taurus in his barn? Reckon so. Legal bill of sale from Hillgate Wreck and Tow in his possession. Within his rights to protect private

property from theft or weather by concealing it under barn
straw if he so chooses. No search warrant. No unreasonable
searches and seizures. Good evening, officers.

Scenario Two—Patrol car at number six Ballantine Lane,
Belle Meade. Owner out of town on business. Current occu-
pant and friend spending social Saturday evening. Nothing out
of the ordinary. Identification gladly shown. Everybody mind-
ing their own business. Have a nice evening, ladies, officers.

Or Three—Lawler Road in Joelton. Poor Miz Burnside.
Lost her daughter in that wreck. Grudge feud, somebody killed
the dog and tried burning the house. Currently under investigation. Stepped-up patrols. Skittish lady. Itchy finger for 911.
Evening, Miz B.

Not to mention Kate Banning as caller. Kate who? Involved
how? Since when? On what basis?

Fumble, bumble, crumble.

Except those calls would not go to waste. They'd be wake-
up signals to Beca and her uncle. By morning, the Taurus engine compartment would be rearranged. Hoses stripped, all
clamps gone. Maybe a partial engine tear-down to make it
look like a shade-tree mechanic pursued his hobby. A barn-
floor mechanic.

And of course certain remnants of checkered fabric would
be disposed of. Arlen and Beca would work the night shift to
guarantee it all. As a tip, 911 would be dazzlingly efficient and
ruinous.

Bottom line—Kate needed a couple hours with a smart
Nashville police detective. But her job now was getting Bobbie Burnside out of harm's way within the next hour.

So take a right off Lynwood onto Parkhurst. The lovely
homes and estates of Belle Meade. Baby Buckingham Palaces,
mini-Versailles, versions of Tara with columns. Trust funds
and portfolios and heirlooms. Much floodlighting after dark.
Crime deterrent.

But not at number six Ballantine. Kate shined her flashlight
on the brass *six* in one of two stone cairns that flanked the entrance to the drive. The cobbled paving curved some two hun-

dred yards to a very large house profiled against a gray sky.
Stands of tall trees rose on the grounds, oaks and magnolias.
But no welcome mats. No welcome lights. Kate eased in,
speed at five mph.

She made a lazy S-curve to a turnaround circle in front with
three parked cars—a Jaguar coupe, an Escort, a Malibu. Beca
and Bobbie were accounted for, the Jag probably Roy Benniger's, safer here than at airport long-term parking. Kate circled
and pulled over to the side, again to maximize opportunities for
a swift exit. She unfastened Kelly's barrettes and raked a hand
through her damp hair. A little lipstick to freshen up.

The fannypack was on the floor in the back. She felt
clammy and knew she looked a mess. Plead no umbrella in the
rain. She wiped her muddy shoes with Kleenexes and dropped
them, too, on the floor in back. Then she got out and closed the
door as softly as possible. Through the cloud cover, the moon
cast an aluminum sheen, and she could see the house, a Nor-
mandy stone chateau with a turret at the east end. All around
were boxwood hedges clipped to look rounded and soft. Diamond lead panes in casement windows showed darkened
rooms.

One exception, a lighted window toward the front entrance
drew her closer. Kate leaned against a boxwood, felt new cold
wet against her thighs, peered in. Inside it was timbered and
dark, a reading room lighted by two ginger jar lamps. Easy
chairs in leather, campaign chests and glossy magazines in
studied casualness. *Architectural Digest*, *California Living*,
Details. As far as she could see no one in there, reading or otherwise.

She backed away and moved toward the front entrance,
which had a medieval look, smooth paving stones and a shell
light fixture made to look centuries old. Reaching for the doorbell, Kate changed her mind and decided instead to go around
back. A music executive might have a music room. At least a
bigscreen TV. Or the two women could be in the kitchen, a
good place for Bobbie and Beca in a *tête-à-tête* over a glass of

wine or diet soft drinks. Bobbie would looked animated—in
Dukie's words, "worked up." Excited, flattered, tempted.

Oblivious to danger.

Kate was on the grass now. Hoping no guard dog. Meat
market closed. Her feet were wet, the temperature dropping,
and she felt cold. She left the flashlight back in the car on a
close decision. She walked upright. No prowler-type body language in case she was seen. No snooping look. She walked
around the west side of the house to the back.

In the back there was a patio big enough for a cocktail party
of, say, two hundred guests. The patio was slab concrete, nothing special. Outdoor furniture from Sears. The showplace
house ended here in the back, even with the pool. She stepped
toward it. Kidney shaped, big enough for laps, and gurgling
from a pump in need of adjustment. Autumn leaves swirled in
a circular current, and vapors off the surface suggested heated
water. Swimming all year round. Sharp tang of chlorine.

But the pump noise covered her as she stepped past the dark
windows. She approached the backdoor entrance. Screen and
all-weather doors both shut. A doorbell here too, but instead of
ringing, she continued on, walked down to the east end and
back around the house to the front.

She turned the corner, peered once again into a window
where a wall sconce glowed dimly. Inside, an expanse of
green—a pool table. Billiard room. Cue sticks in a rack, balls
on the green felt in their triangle formation. Let the game
begin. She turned and looked at the outdoor grounds to her immediate right. Trees, more shrubs, a flower bed. Tire tracks in
the loam.

And a truck. In the flowers. No garage or carport, just the
truck. A light pickup parked in the bed of mums between two
oaks, like a magazine layout except for the ugly ruts. In the
moonlight it was pale. She approached it. Ford Ranger. Kate
walked around to the passenger side. Vapors rose off the hood,
meaning it was hot, meaning parked here for a very short time.
Scratches and dents. A gunrack across the back window. And a

gun too—a shotgun? Rifle? She put her hand on the passenger door. It felt bumpy. No, it felt dimpled.

It was dimpled.

And beige. Unmistakably beige.

She stared. The wheels looked big. She touched the surface to feel the . . . dimples. The pool pump gurgled.

Kate did not hear footsteps with her in the grass.

"You lookin' for something?"

The voice not six feet away. Hard as mineral. Quick follow-up. "I said, lookin' for something, girlie?"

She did not turn. Nor flinch. Nor run. The pump and its guttural noise. She managed to nod.

"That there's a truck door. The folks you're looking for, you won't find them by knocking on a truck." His arm and hand extended like a rail. "Front door's around that way."

He marched her to the front. To the cars, to her Buick. He walked just behind her, so close she felt his body heat. "It's open," he said when she stood at the entrance. Was he the groundskeeper? Security guard?

The beige truck.

He wore khakis and a dark work shirt. He pushed the bell in three bursts. Ta-Ta-*Taaa*.

The beige truck. *The* beige truck.

He stood behind and beside her. Now Kate saw his face. About sixty, stubble on his cheeks, pale amber eyes. His jawline was irregular, swollen on the right side. Slightly bulged. And now she saw what he held in his left hand.

A Styrofoam cup.

The front door opened. "Arlen, everything okay? . . . why, looky here, if it isn't Kate Banning too."

"Found her out by my truck. Touching my truck."

Beca Yowell stood in the open doorway. Ribbed sweater, suede miniskirt. Gold hoops at her ears. Her smile glittered. She seemed unsurprised to see Kate. "I don't know what we're coming to, Arlen," she said. "I send you outside for a chaw and look what you bring back." She shifted her gaze. "Guess you don't stick to the paths, Kate. Guess you got a little problem that way. Bobbie, come look who's here."

Inside, they stood on the red oriental runner. Prints of Arlen's workshoes, Kate's mud-smeared trekkers, Beca's gold suede mules. And Bobbie in cowboy boots. Worst possible footwear to make a run for it.

"—gracious, Kate Banning," she was saying, "wet enough to sprout watercress. Why, you're wetter than Beca's Uncle Arlen, and he's workin' out back on the pool." She smiled. "Fancy mansion like this, and a person can't sleep for that pool garglin' like it's got a sore throat. Imagine, plumbing work on a Saturday night." Another bright smile.

Kate managed one too. So that was the lie, that Arlen came to fix the pool pump. Satisfied Bobbie.

She hadn't a clue.

"So where you been, Kate?" Three sets of eyes. One luminous blue, the others emerald and amber ice. "Hey, you must've talked to Mama, right? That's how you know I'm here. So you heard the news."

Innocent. Endangered species.

Kate's shirt felt like an icy compress.

Beca smiled bright as crystal. "Not being rude, Kate, but we need Brandi's notebook."

Kate wet her lips. She looked at Bobbie. "Dukie gave it to me for safekeeping after the fire."

"Well, Bobbie's got a big break now, and we need it. Time for you to turn it over, Kate. Isn't that right, Bobbie?"

"I s'pose."

"Just s'pose? Why, hon, Virgo comes callin', and *s'pose* is the best you got to show?"

Bobbie flushed. "I mean yes."

Flicker of doubt. Just a flicker. Nanosecond. If Kate could feed it long enough to get Bobbie Burnside out of here. "I was just thinking, Bobbie," she said, "you might want a little time to sort this out. Maybe take the weekend. Why don't you come over to my condo with me? You can pick up the notebook."

Bobbie looked at Beca. "Maybe Kate's right." Her face

asked for the time-out. "You're a big help, Beca, but it's all just so quick."

"Hold on here. Now just hold on. A deal's a deal." Beca's voice rose. Her earrings flared coppery against her hair. Green eyes flashed. "First off—Arlen, you get back outside and see about that wrench. Find it. You always have the right tools. So get the wrench."

Niece and uncle, their gaze locked. Green eyes, amber eyes. Code of some sort?

Arlen nodded, turned slightly sideways and squirted a brown stream into the white cup. Kate looked at him again. Taller than she thought at first. Six-two or three. Wiry, tensile strength. A dribble of tobacco juice at a corner of his lip. Grizzled. Amber eyes in a squint. Dumb. Brute machine.

Then he moved toward the front door, stepped out, shut it behind him, to prowl the dark.

Beca stepped quickly to block the door with her back. No exit. "Now Bobbie, let's think positive. We need to get that notebook. You got a showcase to think about." She put her hand on Bobbie's shoulder. "Remember your mama's counting on this." Her grip tightened.

Kate blinked. Count on Beca to play the "mama" card. "Bobbie," she said, "you don't have to—"

But she drew herself up in the cowboy boots, sighed, stood tall. "You're wrong, Kate. I do have to." She bit her lip. "My mama made big sacrifices moving us to Nashville. Sewing our costumes—you ever sewed sequins? Tiny little things. Middle of the night she'd just fall asleep over the sewing table. With Brandi gone, it's like I owe them both."

"But what about you? You owe yourself."

She sighed. "It's a big chance for my own good. Like Mama says, do I want to spend my life at the motel desk or do I want to go for it?" It sounded forced.

"—so Bobbie and I'll follow you to your place for the notebook," Beca said. "Let you get on with your weekend, Kate." Another cut-glass smile.

Except there could be no weekend. Kate saw the beige truck, and Beca Yowell knew it. Schedule a mishap for Kate too. Arlen Burnett to work overtime.

"Get my car keys so we can get going, Bobbie. Be a sweetie and fetch my purse from the master bedroom, would you? On the bed. You can't miss it." She stood guard at the door.

And watched two targets, one clueless, glad to retrieve keys. For the moment, Bobbie's safety depended on that. A signal, a whispered warning and her jeopardy would spike like a fever.

But play the notebook game Beca's way, and Dukie Burnside's surviving daughter would get at best a short reprieve. Meanwhile, Arlen would be dispatched to Kate's condo. Lurking in the magnolias with Kelly due home. A football game, a teen party, a stalker.

And Beca ready to exact her bile-green vengeance on Bobbie as soon as she "fixed" the original "Envy Green" in the notebook. Or tore it out. Beca stood by the front door. More guard duty. Kate under surveillance every second. The deadbolt key stuck out of the lock, the bolt drawn back to the open position. Beca did not throw the bolt when Arlen went outside. The exit was clear.

Clear to Arlen. Kate turned her wrist to check her watch. 10:35. Six minutes before Dukie Burnside called the Belle Meade police. So keep this going. Stall. She heard Bobbie's cowboy boots approaching on the floorboards. Scramble for a delay tactic.

Here came the boot sound—Kate looked up. Footstep rhythms, but they were off. Offbeat, more like stumbling. Staggering. She saw Bobbie in the doorway. The boots were toed in. Her face was pale, fluttering fingers. No purse.

As though she'd seen a ghost.

Against the doorframe she leaned, clutching the molding. Pop-eyed. Staring without seeing.

"Bobbie, hon, you get lost? You look like you seen a werewolf."

She opened her mouth, tried to speak. Nothing.

Kate reached, took her hand. Dead fish. "Bobbie, what is it?"

The pop eyes stared at Kate's own. "—tried to find the bedroom. As God is my witness, I didn't mean to—" She broke off.

"What, Bobbie? What didn't you mean to do?" Kate kept her hand.

"To turn on the lights, the pool—"

Beca said, "You went out to the pool?"

"No. I didn't. I went—" She stopped again.

Kate said, "Do you mean the pool table, Bobbie? The billiards room?"

Barest nod, yes.

"You went to find the bedroom but lost your way—so you ended up in the billiards room?"

Another nod.

"And you saw something?"

"I only wanted a light. God is my witness."

"And you couldn't find one?"

"—lots. Many lights."

Beca frowned, stood her ground at the door. "Bobbie, where's my purse?"

"I didn't mean to turn . . . the outside lights." She said, "The floodlights, they just came on." Voice so soft Kate barely could hear. "Lights in the trees and flowers. The truck in the trees. It's beige." She looked into Kate's eyes, focused. "It's beige, Kate, and with bumps on the door. It's the one. It's the one that ran us off the highway." She squeezed Kate's hand, hard. The life was back in the fingers. "Kate, what's it doing here?" She looked at Beca. "What's that truck doing here?"

Beca Yowell stood silent.

Kate squeezed her hand back. "Bobbie," she said, "it's Beca's Uncle Arlen's truck."

The moment felt like forever.

The denial but a second. "—his truck's black. He has a black truck."

"He has two."

The breath escaped her. Bobbie looked at Beca.

"You know that time Kate and I nearly got killed, it was that truck. Is it your uncle's—?"

Beca shook her head no.

Very quietly Kate said, "Beca knows it's her uncle's, Bobbie. Beca knows all about it, because she planned it." She held the hand tight in her own. "She knows about Brandi's Taurus too—because she planned the wreck."

A gasp. The eyes wide open, verging on that mindless stare. "Beca, that's not true, is it? Kate's just dealin' in dirt. Isn't she?"

"Up to her eyeballs. Don't listen to her."

Kate turned her wrist again. 10:46. The Belle Meade police on their way by now. "Bobbie, I'm talking straight to you. Look at me—no, look me in the eye. Now listen. Brandi was right on target. She knew about Beca. Beca's eyes—that's what Brandi meant in the song. Envy-green eyes. Brandi spelled the name, B-E-C-A, in the refrain. It's in the original version in the notebook. That's why Brandi told you to look in the notebook. Now look at Beca's eyes."

The glance was quick, furtive. Beca stared like a cat. "Crazy," she said. "She's crazy, Bobbie. She's making up evil stories."

"Brandi knew how jealous Beca was," Kate said. "Deep down, she knew. She was watching out for Beca, and she was afraid. She fooled herself into thinking nothing bad would happen. After all, if she could handle Wade Rucker, she could handle this too. But she made a tragic mistake. She didn't know about Arlen Burnett. That was her mistake."

" 'Course she knew him. He's my uncle. Like one of the family. You're defaming my family."

Kate kept her wrist turned. Any second now the cruisers, blue lights, red. She needed Bobbie with her, beginning to believe the unbelievable. Needed to count on her behavior when the police showed up. Tell her more. "The day Brandi died, before her car crash—she spent the afternoon with Dawn and Beca at the makeup counter."

"At Dillard's. Green Hills Mall. We all knew that, Kate."

Kate moved closer to keep Bobbie's hand in hers. "But the timing was crucial—because Beca took much longer than Dawn or Brandi. 'Beca took forever,' that's what Dawn said."

The green eyes flickered, annoyance over rage. "Some girls choose makeup with care, Kate. We don't all of us favor that northern scrubbed look."

"Look at me, Bobbie. Look at me when I tell you this. The fact is, Beca held Brandi for a long time at that makeup counter to give Arlen time to get into the engine compartment and drain the steering fluid. He sucked most of it out with a turkey baster. The steering would get stiff when she drove. Beca kept Brandi and Dawn busy with cosmetics while he sabotaged the car right in the parking lot. Any passerby would think he was fixing his own car."

"Kate, you watch too much TV."

"—and Beca might not have meant to actually kill Brandi. Maybe injure her, paralyze her. Or disfigure her. Get her out of the picture. Make room for herself. But Arlen did his work too well."

"We don't need this . . . raving."

"Then why is Brandi's car buried under a pile of straw in Arlen Burnett's barn in Dickson County?"

Beca's turn to gasp. The gold hoops jangled. Beca Yowell bit her lip.

"That can't be, Kate." Bobbie's tone protested. "The wrecker yard fella, he told me and Floyd the buyer's name's Clyde Bunrat in Cheatham County. I wrote it down."

"You wrote the version Beca made up for Arlen," Kate said, "the falsified version. I'd bet cash the uncle's middle name is Clyde. And say it or spell it, but 'Bunrat' isn't that far from Burnett. Flip some letters, and it's a variation but not a substitute, especially not for a country singer like Beca. She knows all about song lyrics. She knows wordplay. Substitute Cheatham for Dickson County, and it's a nasty false lead. A pun. It's one of Beca Yowell's private cheatin' songs. To cheat your sister out of her life."

"Now that's enough." Beca hissed. Her voice was tight. "Crazy lies."

Yet Beca seemed poised. The expression on her face, wasn't it a smirk? "You are trouble, Kate, but I'm ready. Dukie warned me about you."

"Warned?"

"Not an hour ago, Dukie called to give me a warning. Trouble with you Yankees, you're cocky."

"Mama called?"

"You were in the powder room, Bobbie. Kate made this lunatic call to your mama and it worried her. Something about phoning the police. She called over here to make sure we're doing fine. I comforted her on that point. I told her none of us had to go calling the Belle Meade police. Let 'em go after the real criminals; that's what I said." She looked at Kate. "Dukie's saving herself a call. She's probably in bed for the night."

Fear. Blood stopped. Whiteout. Beside her, Bobbie was nodding. A schoolgirl nod. Wanting to believe.

Believe in the cops, the 911 call. Nothing. Zero. Kate felt the room go white, go black. The floor heaved, and she put a hand against the wall. Steady herself. Think. Bobbie nodding. Two poles, negative poles. The truck and the truth. Bewildered. Kate frozen. Think.

"Cocky Yankee. Meddling where you don't belong," Beca's mouth was close to the door. "Arlen, you there?"

A muffled "yeah."

She opened the door to let him in.

Kate noticed how gruff his voice. Phone spook, Uncle Arlen.

Shotgun in one hand, wrench in the other. Pipe wrench. A plumber's wrench. Caveman's club.

Beca turned the deadbolt, pulled the key, dropped it in her uncle's shirt pocket. Fairy-tale monster.

"Now what, Beca?"

Arlen Burnett awaited orders.

He turned his head. Another greenbrown dribble. He wiped his mouth on his sleeve.

Beca pointed down a hall. "We got out back, like I said we might need to." He nodded.

And he raised the rifle.

"Beca, I want to go on home. And Kate—"

"Shut up, Bobbie. You shut right up."

It was angry and clear. "Now walk. Walk down the hall." Their feet clumped along. It was dark. To grab Bobbie and plunge into the darkened rooms? No—the diamond-pane windows too hard to break through. No terrace doors. They moved front to back of the house, Beca leading, Arlen in the rear. The shotgun.

And wrench. Long heavy jaws.

The file cabinet at Trystar. She remembered the imprint like a half-moon or cloven hoof—the jaws of a pipe wrench could make that mark.

The skull of a little dog.

Skull of Bobbie Burnside?

And Kate?

Backdoor, now. Wood, glass, screen. Beca opened the locks with practiced movements. Behind them a metal sound. The wrench? Shotgun cocked? "You two listen real good." Beca's voice was all business, efficient and low. "We're going outside now. One of you screams, Arlen shoots the other one. You both scream, he'll shoot you both. Got it?"

Kate took Bobbie's hand again. Cold, wet. She said, "Beca, this whole thing won't work. You're going too far—"

"You shut up too."

They stood in the night air. Kate and Bobbie together, Arlen behind them, Beca to the left out of the line of fire. The moon broke through. Big disk. Big ceiling light in the sky. Trees, acreage. Not a house in calling range.

In screaming range.

The pool gurgled.

"Bobbie, strip down to your boots."

Kate squeezed her hand, felt the protest rise.

"Jeans and shirt off. I said, strip."

Kate turned. Arlen. Simple man with simple tools. Farmer, a plumber. Artisan of death. His left cuff was open, and she saw a white patch, like gauze. Bandage. Poison ivy? A cut.

Or maybe a dogbite?

From his half-starved hound?

Or from a doomed beagle? A dogbite if he drove up to Joelton with his pipe wrench and had trouble bludgeoning a pet.

The western shirt was off, jeans unzipped, pulled down over her hips. "Get a move on. Get those jeans off. Arlen, where're you going?"

To the edge of the patio, with shotgun pointed every second at Bobbie and Kate. He turned his head to spit.

Tobacco juice. Spatter in the boxwoods. Then Kate remembered the two-toned spots on the plywood ramp at the Burnside house—the red and the brown the day Chop was killed. Now she knew. Blood and tobacco juice. Arlen's blood and his spit. His DNA fingerprints.

The pieces coming together.

And falling to pieces.

Bobbie in her underwear. "Take off the bra and panties and put your boots back on."

"Beca, why—?"

"Shut up and do it." No hesitation, no wavering. No desperation either. As if this were a plan.

Kate looked left, looked right. More than desperate. To grab Bobbie and run?—suicide.

"Nice night for a swim. So Bobbie, you're gonna take a dip in the pool. It's heated, don't worry."

The voice print was engraved on the very brain: "Beca, you know I can't swim."

"I said take off your goddamn panties."

White flesh. Her breasts, buttocks. Arlen cocked, uncocked the shotgun. Nervous tic. Twelve-gauge tic.

Time stopped. If she could get close to Arlen, knock him off balance. The rifle in his left meant left-handed. Wrench and gun would slow him down. Could she get in sideways?

"Get in the pool. Boots on, I said get in the pool."

A spectacle. Naked in cowboy boots on a pool ladder. Thighs, shimmy, breasts. Shuddering flesh. Beca, Arlen watching. Kate inched sideways toward Arlen's left. Toe-heel-toe. She closed the gap from eight to six feet.

To four.

Then Bobbie yipped.

"Shut up, girlie."

Up to her breasts and yipped again.

"You shut up."

"Arlen, watch the other one—" And he moved away. Back to eight feet. It felt like a mile. The gun barrel pointed at Kate.

"You yell again, Kate dies. That's it." Beca crouched at the tiles, hissed as Bobbie shook her head. Wrenched it side to side. Hair dipped in, water flew. Blubbering. "No, please no, Beca."

But Beca reached down at the patio edge and picked up a skimmer pole. She stood back. Held it like a rod. A pole vault.

No, a prod. Prodded Bobbie to the deep end.

To sink her. Drown her. She grabbed the pole. Which pushed her down. A grab, a push under. Grab, push. Lifeline as deathtrap.

Beca Yowell manned it like a charter fisherman in a fighting chair.

But not one scream. Not one shriek for life. For Kate's death. Bubbles and gasping. Bobbie's head, self down under. Long, longer—longest?

The pole arched, pulled her up for a breath as the pool rippled. Underwater, Bobbie's flesh showed milky green. She coughed, sputtered, looked like a little child in a swimming lesson, faltering.

Pluck her out, bundle her in terry and calm her down. Soothe her, give comfort—

Or tease her. Beca raised the pole, which Bobbie grasped, clutching like a bird on a highwire as Beca pulled her up for an instant. Beca let her gasp once, twice, then pushed her down again. Her hair under water looked like seaweed.

And this, Kate saw, was deliberate. A strategy. Beca pushed her down, held her, then let her up for a breath or two. Each breath was a lungful of hope.

But hope dashed with each new push under. Tease her, tire her out until she sucked water and died.

Torture her to death.

Another breath, and Bobbie's eyes rolled in panic, sought Kate's face. Those blue eyes fixed there. Blind and beseeching, Bobbie who spoke no evil, tried to be her mama's good girl, her sister's sister. To live by the code of friends and kin and die for it.

She had tried to back away from this whirlpool, to call Kate off. Cancel it all. Decent. Helpless.

Bobbie dying right in front of her.

No.

The water was a cold slam. Kate did a racing dive. Then an underwater somersault to reach her feet and get the trekkers off.

To push Bobbie up, get her off the pole. Pry those fingers loose. She grasped Bobbie's arm, hands. Get her in a rescue headlock.

Scissor kicking to tread water, shoes off, came the mental flash. The image—two women, one clothed, one naked in cowboy boots. Something kinky.

Kinky, Nashville style.

Was this just what Beca wanted? Counted on? That Kate would not stand by. Would leap to Bobbie's side.

To a lost cause.

Bobbie fought her, clutched the pole with her left hand, Kate's neck with her right. They both sank down.

Kate could see it, double accidental drownings.

Not one load of buckshot to be fired from Arlen's gun. Not one skull smashed by the wrench. Quite simply, a pool party gone sour. Playgirl fun turned deadly.

No public sympathy for two women getting it on in a borrowed Belle Meade pool. Kate and Bobbie clutched in terminal embrace. Cause of death: a kinky lady from Boston. Another tragedy in the Burnside family. Plan A.

And Kate fell for it.

Dived into it.

Choked in it. Chlorine in her head, throat, windpipe. All her strength went to pry Bobby's arm from her neck. She stroked away, Bobbie thrashed.

Kate had surfaced, gasped for air. Get Bobbie to the pool edge.

But no, impossible. Stupid, that was the fallback plan. If they got close to getting out, escaping Beca's skimmer pole, then the wrench was waiting.

—hit their head on the edge tiles.

Obituary.

And Kelly.

Kate took a deep breath, dived and grabbed Bobbie. Pushed at flesh, thigh and armpit. Up to breathe. Elbow in her jaw, knee, groin. Her own lungs bursting.

Breath for Bobbie, breath for Kate. Open eyes.

And the pole, the wrench.

And gasping, sucking air, the moon over the pool. Full. White. Double drowning trick. She saw it in a time-lapse instant. Fool moon in Nashville. Bobbie thrashed, choked. Grabbed Kate, again her neck. And pulled. Not a sound but deep water, deeper. Kate's chest seared, sight patched and ripped. She swallowed. Chlorine and death and Kelly. Death and Kelly and stupid failure. She pried at Bobbie's fingers. Her rings. Aquamarine. Aqua. And the blue lights and siren. Mermaid, dolphin, whale screams were the last sounds she heard.

Chapter Fifteen

Kate stood by the sink and heard Kelly ask Sam, "What if you took the rubber bands off now?"

"They'd kill each other."

Claws tapped against the stainless. Faucet water hissed. Kelly stared into the stoppered sink, Kate peering in beside her. Underwater beasts in miniature. Breathing, banded, programmed for attack. Kate stepped back. Tanks of water, pools of water. Too recent, too scary.

Too inland, this dinner. At the stove with his sleeves rolled back, Sam Powers sprinkled flour into melted butter and stirred with a wood spoon. He looked at a scribbled recipe. "Kate, I need a cup and a half of hot water or fish stock." His voice was tight. "Kelly, how about it, squeeze me a teaspoon of lemon juice?"

"Orders from Chef Powers? Sam, let's just melt a stick of butter."

"Nope." His jaw was set. "This is by-the-book drawn butter, you're both gonna love it. Including you, Miss Kelly."

"From Wichita? I never heard of lobsters in Kansas."

He stirred in small circles. "Don't be provincial, ladies; life's where you find it. Recipe from a restaurant in Wichita, and Maine lobsters from your local grocery. Kelly, I thought you were going to read me your science hypothesis on plant growth."

"I am. Should I get my notebook?" He nodded. "Even while you're cooking?"

"—While we wait for the water to boil. Never mind the lemon, just get the notebook."

She started upstairs, and Sam reached for the lemon.

Kate shuddered. He looked at her. "Did I say something wrong?"

" 'Notebook,' Sam. It's a word I can do without. For the next month or so, anyway."

He put his arm around her, held her against him at the stove. "But it's over," he said. "Call it a bad dream."

She sighed. She looked around her new kitchen. Table, place-mats, forks, lobster cracker. Things of the living. She said, "It's like a dream only because Dukie Burnside couldn't sleep. Otherwise, you'd be clipping my obituary from the *Tennessean*."

"But she followed your orders. She did call the cops."

"Only at the very last instant, Sam. If she just waited a minute more—literally one more minute, both of us, Bobbie and I—" She shivered.

"Shhh." He held her close and stirred the pot. "Dukie Burnside did it her own way, that's all. She had to check in with Fawn first."

"Dawn. Her name's Dawn."

"Right. Dawn." He nodded. "Good thing Dawn had a car phone."

But Kate shivered again. Another near miss. A near-fatal time-out because Dukie Burnside took a Saturday night opinion poll. Over and over Kate mentally clocked the sequence as if to replay a bad movie she could not escape. She and Bobbie were being marched to the pool to be drowned at the very moment Dukie got on the phone to Dawn Mulligan to ask, should she obey Kate Banning's orders? Really? Surprise when Dawn answered yes. Surprise when Dawn's own voice carried a certain tone of alarm.

Kate turned to Sam at the stove. She said, "You know, I think Dukie called Dawn Mulligan because she was worried about bad publicity. Danger's not in her game plan. She dreaded some nasty scene with police and her country starlet daughter on the six o'clock news. Stage mother to the core."

He nodded, hand on her shoulder. "But finally, Kate, she also behaved like a mother. She heard your voice too. She heard the urgency. Besides, that call to Fawn—"

"Dawn."

"Dawn, Dawn. Anyway, it moved Dukie to action. Didn't Lieutenant Cahill say so?"

Kate nodded. Nice Southern-speaking Belle Meade Police officer. Rapid response patrol cars. Resuscitation and arrest. Arlen Burnett and niece Beca Yowell in handcuffs. Kate's ribs banged up on the pool edge as cops pulled her out. The least of it, a few bruises. Coughing up gobs of water, nose and throat and lungs. And the ambulance to Saint Thomas Hospital, in and out. Kelly home, okay. Bobbie in blankets. Kept overnight and released, Bobbie who would drown in silence lest Kate be shot dead. Keeping quiet to help Kate stay alive.

Both of them at Belle Meade Police Headquarters answering questions forever. Plus, Dickson County law enforcement impounding one Taurus, one carpenter apron with fabric pieces, one turkey baster. Eighteen charges pending, including homicide, theft, aggravated assault, arson, conspiracy to commit all of the above. Gun, wrench, pool skimmer pole confiscated.

Sam stirred. He squeezed the lemon to soften it. "The important thing is, Dawn came forward."

Kate paused. "Let's just say she finally acted on her suspicions at a timely moment." Kate took the lemon from his hand, reached for a paring knife, sliced and flicked seeds into the sink. Then she squeezed a thin stream of juice into a measuring spoon and set it down. "Let's say that after living with Beca, Dawn felt suspicious enough to send out her one-and-only warning."

" 'Check the fluids.' "

" 'Check the fluids.' " Kate wrapped the lemon. "It was her one-time-only distress signal. No wonder she's drinking, the bind she's been in."

"Rock and a hard place."

Kate nodded. "Duet work with envy-green Beca was Dawn's last best hope of staying alive in country music, so she tried to bury her suspicions. And she might have managed to forget all about it, except for Bobbie's obsession. Once we went to the wrecker yard and found the steering fluid actually drained, Bobbie talked about nothing else. At least twice a week, she'd be at the Cascade Gardens telling her good friends, the backup singers, about the fluid drained from Brandi's Taurus.

"I think Dawn got scared. Scared for herself. If Beca would sabotage Brandi, why not Dawn too? A duet partner can be expendable."

"So Dawn was primed to tell Dukie to go ahead and call the police."

"Yes. And probably relieved deep down. She couldn't bring herself to come forward, but others were doing it for her." Kate took out the round loaf of sourdough and began slicing.

Sam stirred his roux. He said, "You're really sure that creep of a manager had nothing to do with any of it?"

"Grady. No, he's clear. I was skeptical too, but the police really checked him out. Questioned him all morning, and he finally did admit to scaring me with his threat at Dukie's that night we had dinner. No, take that back. His lawyer was at his elbow, and he did not actually admit he threatened me, only that he used language that could be construed as a threat."

She put four thick bread slices in foil and slid them into the oven to warm. "It seems Grady was worried I'd stir up bad publicity about him and affect his career in management with Jon Hartly Owens. After all, the ink on the new deal was barely dry."

"So he tried to scare you off?"

She nodded. "Remember, he helped Brandi select that Taurus, and he did refuse the brake job, and if that got into the country music tabloids, he'd look bad. Irresponsible, poor judgment."

"But why—?"

"Refuse the brake pads? To save a few dollars, he says, because he was about to trade the car for a convertible to surprise Brandi." Sam turned, skeptical. "I know, but it checks out. Papers were in process at Jim Reed Chevrolet as of the first of August. A Camaro custom ordered from the factory. The Taurus trade-in was all arranged. Grady had a surprise party planned. The car was to be delivered with a big bow around it."

"Meanwhile, he just thought he'd save his client a few bucks in brake pads?" They both shook their heads. "So he's not a perpetrator or a conspirator."

"Just a creep with a stupid idea about economy. And a velvet-tongued bully too. Doubtless he'll go very far in life." Kate peered across at the stove. "Hey, that roux looks done. You ready for the hot water?"

"Or fish stock."

"Cup and a half. I remember." She dipped hot water from the big pot on the stove. "Your water, sir. Unless you want me to boil up a mess of catfish for stock. By the way, stir that to get the lumps out. Like this." She rolled the spoon against the sides of the pan and handed it back to him and watched. "Atta boy."

"Atta girl" They bumped hips. They kissed.

At that moment they heard Kelly's footsteps. With hair clipped back with the silver barrettes, she came into the kitchen with a red notebook that said SCIENCE in marker pen. "Sam, you ready? You, Mom?"

Kate nodded. Sam said, "You are cleared for takeoff, Kelly."

"Okay. Here it is. I am growing begonias under controlled conditions. I will read my working hypothesis." She held the notebook at a scientifically dignified distance.

"The aim of this experiment is to test the highest water retention of five different types of soil. The assumption is that the potting soil will absorb the most water. This is believed because this is the type of soil that is used to grow plants in; therefore, the plants would need a lot of water to grow well."

She stopped. "All this for two pots of begonias." Kate stifled a smile. Where had her daughter learned irony?

"Sounds good to me, Kelly."

"I'm growing begonias on a shelf at school, and Mom's out catching a killer."

"You're both doing what needs to be done." He winked.

"Mom, tell Sam your working hypothesis."

"About Trystar?"

Kate nodded and slid the Reynolds Wrap into the drawer. "Beca'd been to Trystar many times with Brandi. She'd watched Judy Swan punch out—literally watched her fingers on the security system keypad. Memorized the combination and gave it to Arlen. He took it from there."

But Kelly shook her head. "Not that hypothesis, Mom. I mean when the guy with the wrench . . ." She looked at Kate and now, suddenly, Kelly's voice dropped. She looked sad. "I mean the day he . . . killed little Chop."

Kate took her daughter's hand. "—it's not all that much of a hypothesis, sweetie. It's just that nobody was home at the Burnsides'. Dukie was at the mall, and the kitchen workmen were through for the day. Bobbie was at work at the motel. It was easy for Beca to make a phone call to dispatch the . . . the guy with the wrench. And to write down a phone threat for him to read to Bobbie over the phone—just as he followed her orders to phone me at work and home several times a day and hang up.

"But you see, Bobbie remembered spitting sounds and the man on the phone stumbled over his words. That's because he was chewing tobacco and reading a message somebody else wrote. Beca wrote."

"And like he could hardly read. Did you tell Sam that part?"

"She did, Kelly."

"But Chop bit him, didn't he, Mom? Bit him hard?" Kelly's chin trembled. Trying not to cry.

Kate squeezed her daughter's hand. "We think Chop fought as hard as he could."

A silent moment passed.

"Sam the pot's boiling," Kelly lifted the lid.

"Okay, Kelly Banning, rubber band time. Get your knife."

Kate stood back. A Boston ritual here in Nashville, half like continuity, half like betrayal in an alien land. Sam held the lobsters by their backs, and with knifepoint Kelly shot the rubber bands flying off the claws. They hung down, the fighting claw, the holding claw. Nature's wrenches. Splash.

Sam said, "Six minutes to dinner. How about some music? We could play that ocean tape, the surf tape. Pretend it's Cape Cod."

Kate started to say yes, then hesitated. Boston, Nashville. Reality, virtual reality. Close the shades and pretend for an hour? She took a deep breath. "Or we could play the *Country Classics* album."

"Dolly Parton?"

"And George Jones. Maybe some Emmylou Harris and Merle Haggard. Sure, Kelly, why not?"

Sam grinned. Kelly shrugged. "Well, I'm pretty sick of 'Whoever's in New England' over and over. But lobster and Dolly Parton? Weird. And hey, Mom, no more borrowing my barrettes without asking. Anyway, aren't you getting a haircut?"

"This week. Haircut for me, flute teacher for you. Sacred promise. Right now let's ask Sam to deejay the dinner. Lobster and country music together, let's give it a try."

Kate Banning returns in

Cryin' Time

by Cecelia Tishy

Coming soon to Signet Mystery

Turn the page for a preview. . . .

CHAPTER ONE

Why are restaurants with cute names so hard to find? "Catered events and banquets too. The Mad Platter. Convenient location. Minutes from downtown Nashville."

"Minutes from downtown" sounded suspiciously like "one size fits all." With her index finger, Kate Banning traced the route across railroad tracks that curved like a scar through grids, cuts, dead ends. This was a dumb shortcut. She had not planned to navigate a bizarre part of town with an atlas spread across her lap. She nudged the accelerator of the Buick wagon and headed straight out Fifth, watching for the left at Monroe. The Mad Platter. Cute name. By all accounts, nice place.

But why would the out-of-state, newly arrived friend of a friend insist on lunch in north Nashville, a.k.a. Germantown, across a stretch of warehouses, stockyards, railroad tracks? Why go out of the way when there were plenty of restaurants closer to downtown and Music Row?

And what was the "little matter" he wanted to discuss? Something fun, she hoped, eager for a friendly hour with the baritone voice who introduced himself over the phone in New York warmth and wisecracks. She imagined their Nashville lunch seasoned with hometown "herbs" like La Guardia and Logan, Madison Avenue and Storrow Drive, the *Times* and the *Globe*. Plus lots of Northeast Corridor rhythms and repartee. She was glad this newcomer to Nashville's music scene wanted a time-out lunch with a geographic soulmate. Was the "little matter" he wanted to discuss some informal welcome-wagon-type advice? Or a try for a blind date?

Any of the above. She would just settle in and enjoy the

ride, so to speak, starting with this route through a part of the
city as yet unexplored in the six months she had spent in
Nashville. Amazing that it was already six months from blaz-
ing summer to this facsimile of winter. The branches were
bare, but the wind chill factors sounded downright balmy.
Token flurries and flakes fell weekly, and weakly too. The
warehouses to the left and right in the gray daylight reminded
her of certain industrial areas around her hometown, Boston.
Dicey areas ripe for warehouse heists and hijackings in the
dead of night. At least the scene was familiar. Boston and
Nashville. Appreciate the similarity. Get in the spirit.

Just one word of caution to herself—a note not to let nostalgia slip into yearning and homesickness. And not to over-
commit when he asked whatever "little" favor. She had plenty
on her plate at the office, at home. She needed no extras.

It was 11:32 when Kate eased her Century toward the curb
along Sixth. The Mad Platter, she saw, was a redbrick con-
verted Victorian in a quaint block with wide brick sidewalks
and a stark view of the city skyline, including the BellSouth
Building, nicknamed the Bat Building for the towers that made
it look like an architectural Batman.

She parked down the block and checked her hair in the
rearview. Dark blonde hair of medium length, she had told
him. Five-six and in her later thirties. The mirror verified the
good new earth-tone lipstick and the okay hair day. Though
she still had not found the right stylist in town, this was a decent cut, easy blow dry. She neglected to mention the few stray
hairs of silver—no, face it, gray—from motherhood. So be it.
She got out, locked up, and walked toward the restaurant entrance. It was Thursday, mid-January in the upper forties. On
the Monroe Street side, directly in front of the entrance, a
black Lexus coupe gleamed like modern sculpture. She
reached for the restaurant door.

Kate found herself in an open dining room with maybe
twenty tables, a long room with a waxed pine floor and a high
ceiling painted a dark blue-green. There were hardwood tables
and chairs, snowy tablecloths and napkins. Bookcases to the

left held random titles, and three walls displayed oil paintings of the city by a local Monet-come-lately. No private booths, no hiding places. Twosomes dined with work portfolios open on a table, men in corduroy suits and sportcoats, businesswomen at a table for four. Nice conversational buzz. She began looking for a single man who fit the image of a country music executive. He would probably wear something like a suede bomber jacket, cowboy boots, a ponytail.

"Kate Banning?"

She recognized the baritone and turned.

"Phil? Are you Phil Armstead?"

"I am." His grip was firm but a bit moist. Despite the deep baritone, he was slender and wiry, about five seven in a camel cashmere sportcoat, blue broadcloth shirt and a silk tie figured with Tabasco labels. His hair was curly but thinning, close cropped. The mustache and goatee were impeccably trimmed, the single gold earring a bid for hip authority. Intensity glowed in the dark, darting eyes, though he smiled broadly and guided her efficiently to the table for two against the right wall.

The half-empty coffee cup meant he'd arrived early, though at first sight Phil Armstead seemed an unlikely candidate for leisured moments. Edgy anticipation was more likely his style. He stood behind her chair while she took off her tan trench coat and scarf and sat down. "It's wonderful to meet you, Kate. East Coast . . . any friend of Henry Kidd is someone I want to take to lunch. Henry's circle should be unbroken."

Kate blinked. Unbroken circle—was that a music reference? She decided not to ask. She straightened the lapels of her black-and-white houndstooth jacket over a black sweater with a silver chain necklace. Her skirt was red, her new pumps black cherry. She had paid too much for the whole ensemble in the after-Christmas sales, and the left shoe now hurt across the instep. As always.

She said, "Really good to meet you too, Phil. Let's promise to drink a toast to Henry and let him know we've met. If only he could be here too. Imagine a colony of us in Nashville." She stopped. "Colony" felt like exile, and "us" just a bit too cozy with a new acquaintance. They were about the same age, but she felt no special vibes, except a kind of hum, as though his inner engine idled on high. New York rhythms. She scanned the dining room and said, "I know Henry would be surprised to see all this iced tea in January, and I bet you find it strange too."

He said, "Weird."

"In Nashville," she said, "they call iced tea the house wine of the South. And the lunch hour comes early here. Six months in town, and I'm finally getting used to salad before noon."

He nodded. "Bagel time. Danish." The waitress approached to take their orders, and Phil asked Kate, would she like a glass of wine?

Sad to say, not with that pile of work on her desk in the office. She said, "Coffee."

"And a refill." They studied their menus. The waitress returned, poured, opened her book, and it was spinach salad with grilled chicken for Kate, a Mad Platter burger well done for Phil Armstead. Then he raised his coffee mug, looked Kate in the eye and said, "To Henry. And to his friends, Kate and Phil."

Kate raised her own mug, clinked, sipped. She said, "So here we are, both of us, the friends."

"So we gotta swap Henry stories. You first?"

She paused. It was the natural path of acquaintances, but it somehow felt more like an exercise from a handbook. She took a deep breath. Out of respect for Henry, avoid adjectives sounding like the Hallmark rack. Phil Armstead was East Coast brusque, so cut to the specifics. Kate said, "I'll tell you this—Henry Kidd helped me at one desperate point in Boston when I had a toddler to feed, rent due, nothing coming in from my almost ex-husband, and about seven dollars to my name."

"He floated you a loan?"

"Better. Henry helped me get a job. I'd just quit my police reporter job, and he was the only friend who understood why."

"Why'd you quit?"

She nodded. "I couldn't handle it." She saw his eyes narrow.

"Not the work itself, but the content." She raised her coffee mug and sipped. Did she owe him an explanation?—No, but the story should be straight. "You know, police reporters talk to suspects and victims, and they cover the gore at the crime scenes. That's the daily fare. At home, though, I had this gorgeous baby. My marriage was collapsing, and it felt schizoid, like I was a middleman between the nursery and hell. It was affecting my mental health. I didn't want my baby to be my rehab from those workdays, so I quit." He nodded, probably more from politeness than understanding. "Anyway, Henry understood. He had a contact at *New Era* and he helped get me a staff writer job."

"*New Era*? Like New Age? Crystals and stuff?"

Kate smiled ruefully. "*New Era* ran investigative stories on consumer fraud, political corruption, business criminality. It never made it to the rack with *Time* and *Newsweek* but it was a great little magazine."

"It folded?"

She nodded. "It's tough to woo advertisers when you're exposing fraud and corruption in their backyards and back pockets. It's a minor miracle the magazine didn't go under sooner."

"So that's why you moved to Nashville?"

"You might say that. How about you?"

Phil Armstead drained his coffee and said, "Here's my Henry story. I was just out of school, in Minneapolis managing a rock band called Satan and the Jolly Ranchers. Bar gigs, clubs, warehouse lofts, anything we could get. Really strung out. Flat broke most of the time. Any given night it was a toss-up whether the band would get paid. I was too stubborn to ask my old man for plane fare back home for my sister's wedding. I was gonna hitch. Henry sent me a plane ticket."

"Great."

"Of course I paid him back."

"Of course." A silence fell. Kindness turned into economics. Their lunches came. He asked, was her salad good? Did she want anything else? He asked these things as if memorized from Miss Manners. Then he asked the waitress for another basket of warm rolls. Kate speared a bite of chicken. What now, old hometown sports banter, Celtics and Knicks, Yankees and Red Sox?

He ate a french fry, then leaned across and said, "Henry tells me you're a hotshot investigative reporter."

Kate laughed a little uneasily. "Exaggeration in the line of friendship—pure Henry."

He smiled with the edges of his mouth, and she noticed a certain focus in the back of his gaze. "He says you uncovered a big baby food scandal."

"Adulterated infant apple juice." She nodded. "I worked with some other people on that. That was a *New Era* project."

"And also, you did some private investigation work on the side. Off the books because you're not a private detective. That's what Henry told me."

Kate put her fork down, reached into her purse and slid her business card across the table. The card was the best corrective.

"Fleetwood Publications," he read. "Kate Banning, Chief Coordinating Editor." He smiled tightly and pocketed the card. "So what's a chief coordinating editor do?"

If his tone held a trace of grilling mockery, she decided to ignore it. Keep things pleasant for the sake of the old friend and the quasi-social hour. She said, "Fleetwood prepares trade magazines for businesses and industry groups that no longer want the expense of in-house editors and writers. No more care and feeding of employees. We do their magazines on contract. Content, format, layout—we do it all. I probably got the job because I have a lot of contacts with writers around the country, and I can offer them freelance assignments tailored to the specific magazines. I get to authorize the checks that keep writers alive. That's the fun part."

She paused, chewing a forkful of spinach. "You could say I got my job because a lot of staff writers and editors lost theirs in the leaner-and-meaner movement, the layoffs and downsizing. I dispense a little backwash money. And I have health care and benefits. That's why I moved to Nashville."

"Henry says you missed your calling."

She managed a laugh. "Henry's a romantic." She wiped her mouth and reached for a roll and broke off a piece. All the while she watched Phil Armstead's gaze. Intense. Unrelenting. Something told her she couldn't brush it off. Crumbs were falling into her napkin. For a moment they chewed in silence.

He said, "So is Henry all wrong about you? Or lying? Self-deluding?"

"Whoa, hold on." Kate's turn to smile, if a little tightly. A luncheon game of Gotcha!, and she was caught. She said, "Look, police reporting, investigative reporting—they're in my bio. And I helped out informally in a few odd cases in Boston, I admit that. A missing child case and a bomb case. And a few others. Let's say I felt personally responsible to try to do something because they involved people I knew. It was personal." She looked him in the eye. "But not anymore."